OF JADE AND DRAGONS

OF JADE AND DRAGONS

AMBER CHEN

VIKING
An imprint of Penguin Random House LLC, New York

First published in the United States of America by Viking,
an imprint of Penguin Random House LLC, 2024

Visit us online at PenguinRandomHouse.com.

Library of Congress Cataloging-in-Publication Data is available.

ISBN 9780593622759 (hardcover)

ISBN 9780593692905 (international edition)

1st Printing

Printed in the United States of America

LSCC

Edited by Kelsey Murphy
Design by Lily Qian
Text set in Adobe Caslon Pro

To my 老爸 and 老妈—

for always being there for me

CHAPTER 1

PERCHED AT THE EDGE OF A CLIFF, a tiny figure watched as a dark cloud floated toward her, accompanied by the thunderous whir of rotating engine blades.

A furrow appeared on Aihui Ying's smooth forehead.

The High Commander's airships were far noisier than they should be. It was a low-level problem that could have been easily fixed with mufflers fashioned out of bison leather. Her father's hypothesis was that the guild masters had let this flaw slip through on purpose, because noise was apparently an effective show of intimidation.

"Why stop there? Might as well make lightning bolts shoot out of the keel," she muttered.

The airships passed overhead. Two smaller ones in front and two behind, guarding the behemoth in the middle. Each of them was a black monstrosity emblazoned with the silver emblem of the cobra, bamboo-battened sails extending out from both sides of the hull and flapping majestically against the cold winds.

In her childhood, Ying had once disturbed a sleeping lizard lounging on a rock to find out if it was dead. It awoke in a fury, brightly colored frills flaring from its neck in a spectacular display. That was where the Engineers Guild must have gotten their inspiration from, she reckoned, when they added those sails to the airships. Again, for intimidation more than functionality.

"By decree of the High Commander," a monotonous voice issued from above, "the Cobra's Order is transporting a traitorous prisoner from the capital city to the mines of Juwan, where he is to serve his sentence till death. All civilian airships, keep away—I repeat—keep away."

Ying snorted, covering her ears with her gloved hands to shield them from the racket. Trust the High Commander to make an exhibition of his own son's exile.

Nevertheless, she had little sympathy for the former beile and High Commander–designate. He had dug his grave by trying to incite conflict between his brothers and then having the gall to declare that he would execute everyone he deemed a threat once he assumed command. The story of his downfall had spread far and wide across the nine isles, no doubt with silent approbation by the authorities, as a warning to all who might threaten the stability of the Aogiya High Command.

Once the airships had gone by, Ying focused her attention back on the task at hand. She was losing daylight, and while the night views of the Huarin isle were magical, landing was far more challenging in the dark. She tucked loose strands of hair behind her ears, adjusting the cloth band at the back of her head to make sure her bun was secured. Inhaling the frigid summer air, she stretched her hands out to the sides.

"In Abka Han we trust."

She leaned forward, tipping her center of gravity over the edge of the cliff. Her body hurtled downward, the distance between her and the perilous rocks rapidly shrinking.

A sprinkling of ocean spray kissed her cheeks—and she sprang to action.

Ying yanked at one of the colorful silk cords dangling off the bulky contraption strapped to her back. An enormous pair of wings unfolded, bamboo bones clicking as each segment snapped into place, stretching the thin silk fabric that lined the frame.

The wings caught a gust of wind, sending their wearer flying upward and out.

"Thank you!" she yelled to the sky, eyes glimmering with excitement as she soared above the waves. Abka Han, the god of the skies who watched over the Antaran territories, was probably sneering at her foolishness, but the proper respect still needed to be paid.

Respectfulness she had learned from her mother; the foolhardy part was all from her father.

Ying closed her eyes and basked in the serenity of her surroundings. The occasional cooing of gulls punctuated the soft humming of the waves. By the time she opened her eyes again, the circular white roofs of her village's gers came into view, looking like tiny mushrooms sprouting amid the grass and snow. Farther in the distance, small specks of white and brown dotted the grasslands, the village's many flocks of sheep, yak, and horse herds grazing peacefully. Tugging at the blue cord on her left, she adjusted her course so that she was now homebound.

Before setting off, she had identified a clear patch of grass off the western edge of her village as her landing spot. She had even stuck a large red flag into the ground. But landing was more difficult than she'd imagined.

Instead of sailing comfortably toward her flag, Ying lost the updraft midway over the cluster of gers. She was cutting it so close to the sloping roofs that she could see her bewildered clansmen pointing at her and hear their exclamations of incredulity.

"Hi," she yelled, waving stiffly, "just passing through—"

Then suddenly a wooden wind vane caught her right wing, mercilessly ripping through its sheer fabric. That marked the end of Ying's little experiment. She smashed straight into the felt-lined roof of the ger before tumbling down the side and landing on the ground with a loud crash. The intricately carved wooden door of the circular tent swung open, revealing the perplexed faces of its occupants.

A small crowd gathered around her, clucking with disapproval.

"Look at you. Such a disgrace! How is it that the chieftain allows his daughter to run amok like a wild boar? To think you're the oldest girl too. You're supposed to be looking after your younger siblings in your mother's stead, but instead you're always creating trouble." The voice, harsh and scratchy, belonged to a walking contradiction called Roya. Despite her jolly appearance, the owner of the village tavern was one of the most obnoxious and disagreeable personalities in the clan.

Ying fumbled to get herself off the ground, dusting away the flecks of dirt and snow that clung to her azure woolen robes and fur-lined boots. Picking up her broken wings, she smiled at her spectators as sweetly as a silver fox might.

"How kind of you to show concern for my a-ma's parenting methods. I'll be sure to convey the message," she said, turning to walk away. As the second child in a line of six and the eldest girl, there were certain expectations that the villagers would force upon her shoulders—expectations she chose to willfully ignore.

"Insolent brat," Roya muttered loudly. "It's no wonder no decent young man will take her for a wife."

Ying rolled her eyes. It was not the first time she'd heard things like that, whispered behind her back as if she could not hear them. She was infamous within the Aihui clan. Blessed by Abka Han with the beauty of a winter snowdrop, yet she received no love from the matchmakers. She was too odd—they said—and would not make a good wife. Were she not the daughter of the clan's chieftain, she would have been expelled long ago.

The superficial opinions of her clansmen meant little to Ying. Marriage had never been on her list of priorities anyway. She wanted a different future: one day, she would join the ranks of the masters in the hallowed halls of the Engineers Guild, where her father—Aihui Shan-jin—had once been.

She weaved her way between the white tents to her father's workshop at the western fringe of the village. It stood on its own, a lone sentry some distance away from the other dwellings. Some years back, an experiment gone awry had burned down the Aihui chieftain's ger and two others beside it. After that, the clan folk unanimously voted to shift their leader's den to where it wouldn't cause collateral damage to anyone else.

"A-ma!" she called loudly as she approached. It would thrill him to hear of her success. Her beloved father had always been her biggest supporter. She pushed open the door with a flourish. "I did it. I managed to—"

Her words dropped as she stepped into her father's workshop. The place was in shambles, as if a violent sea storm had raged through and torn it asunder. His tools, usually neatly hung on their wooden rack, were scattered beside the toppled table; the glass receptacles he used to store various herbs were shattered, their contents strewn haphazardly amid broken shards;

and his treasured books and scrolls, once meticulously arranged by topic on the many shelves, had been thrown onto the floor in disarray.

And the person responsible for the catastrophe was *still here.*

A figure clad in black, his face masked, revealing only a pair of narrow, menacing eyes, was digging through her father's belongings. Across the man's left eye was a reddened scar, twisted and gnarled, remnants of an old wound healed poorly.

"What do you think you're doing?" Ying shouted.

The intruder dropped the book he had been flipping through and flicked his wrist in her direction. A flash of silver caught the light.

A dart?

Instinctively, Ying whipped out the fan that she always kept hidden in her sleeve and held it up in front of her face, its metallic silver leaf unfolding smoothly. A sharp *clink* and a dent appeared, followed by a metal dart landing on the floor amid the clutter.

Flipping her fan horizontal, she tapped the rivet, and a flurry of small bamboo arrows shot out of the slim barrels built into the ribs.

The trespasser leapt up into the air, using the shelves as footholds to propel himself sideways. Most of Ying's arrows missed their mark, but one drove itself into the man's left thigh. His pupils darted back and forth, surveying his options: there was only one exit to the ger, a red latticed door faded with age, and Ying was standing in front of it.

Should have been more diligent with the upgrades, Ying thought as the man charged toward her. She had been meaning to improve the arrow-firing mechanism so it could hold more than one round, but procrastination and a slew of newer projects had rendered it forgotten. But she couldn't think about that now. Slapping her fan shut, she jabbed it at the rogue's eyes.

Other than a few basic strokes of self-defense, Ying had not much in the way of combat skills, and it showed. She barely touched the fabric of the intruder's sleeve before he struck her on the right shoulder with a forceful blow, sending her flying against a shelf.

Gritting her teeth, Ying lunged after the man, who was already halfway out the door. Her fingers brushed his cloak, closing around something smooth and hard, like a pebble. But then she lost her balance, landing on the hard floor in a painful heap. The intruder disappeared into the dusk.

She slammed her fist against the ground in frustration. How could she have let him escape like that? But when she opened her clenched fist, an oval jade pendant lay on her palm. Black like obsidian, there was an intricate carving of a dragon etched on one side, surrounded by the waves of the clouds up in the heavens.

She hadn't come away empty-handed after all.

“Ying,” a soft voice called out.

“A-ma?” Ying quickly clambered to her feet, looking around for her father.

The chieftain of the Aihui clan was lying on the ground, his body crushed under the weight of one of the toppled shelves. A puddle of garish red pooled beneath him, seeping from the wound through which a gleaming blade remained stabbed.

“A-ma,” Ying whispered, her voice trembling with fear as she stared at the blood. “What happened? We need to get you out of here.” She struggled to lift the fallen bookcase, but the weight of the wood was too much for her to bear. Despair and helplessness gripped her heart. “I’ll get help, I’ll—”

“Ying, don’t.” Her father mustered a sad smile, then pointed a finger across his workshop toward an octagonal lamp carved from sandalwood. It had been knocked onto the floor, partially obscured beneath large sheets of parchment. “Will you fetch that for me, please?” he asked shakily.

Ying nodded, quickly running over to pick up the lamp.

Her father had made it many years back as a gift for her mother. Every surface had been painstakingly carved to tell the story of how they had met, when Aihui Shan-jin was just a headstrong, self-assured young lad, and his wife-to-be a shy daughter of the village horse rancher. Since her mother’s death ten years ago, that lamp had sat on her father’s worktable, its subtle fragrance keeping him company while he toiled.

"Let me get help," Ying begged.

The chieftain shook his head. "I haven't got much time." Reaching into the lamp, he lifted its wooden top and withdrew a leather-bound book and placed it carefully in Ying's hand. Ying blinked, surprised that something had been hidden inside.

"Tell no one you have this and do not look inside, do you understand?" he said with urgency impressed upon every word. "When you are alone—burn it."

"What is this?"

"Something that will bring about the downfall of our clan, and possibly the rest of the nine isles. I should never have agreed to be a part of this, but my mind—and heart—were not strong enough. This is the price of Abka Han's displeasure. Do as I say, my most precious lamb, and promise me you will not hunt for the man who was here before. There are forces behind this that are far beyond our control. I would not rest in peace knowing that you are in danger."

Ying nodded, her eyes brimming with tears as she watched the life slowly seep away from her father's warm brown eyes. "Tell E-niye I miss her," she said, clutching on to her father's callused hand.

"You are so much like her, my child. But I pray that you will not walk down the same path that we have . . ."

Aihui Shan-jin smiled, and then he closed his eyes for the eternal slumber.

CHAPTER 2

A WEEK LATER, YING STOOD BEFORE HER parents' graves, at the edge of a soaring cliff that overlooked the rise and fall of the tides. Her long dark hair drifted with the wind, and the turquoise beads of her headdress rustled like the sound of rain.

She stared at the miniature ger that carefully marked out their final resting spot. An Antaran tradition, to ensure the dead would have a comfortable dwelling in the afterlife. Her father had crafted it himself when her mother passed on. Ying had been only eight then. Now the tiny tent had become his home too.

Sighing, Ying walked over to the cliff's edge. The ocean seemed to go on forever. She couldn't even see the tip of the nearest isle, Kamar.

"You still owe me so many stories," she whispered to the wind, hoping it would carry her words to her father.

In his youth, her father had journeyed across the seas to the fabled capital city of Fei, with its skyscraping pagodas and shimmering tiled roofs, and been granted a place among its greatest engineers. But he never said anything about it. Instead, there was always a flash of sorrow that appeared in his eyes whenever anyone mentioned the capital, and Ying knew that there were shadows in her father's memory that pained him to touch.

Now she had her own shadow to bear.

"*These seas can never trap those who are meant to fly*," her father used to tell her. And so she did take to the skies, but he would no longer have the chance to see it.

Ying clambered onto a large boulder and took her folding fan from beneath her sleeve, running her fingers along the edge that had been accidentally stained with her father's blood. It had already faded from red to rust brown.

The day she'd invented it, she'd run into her father's workshop, excitedly waving her sketch for the fan in his face. It was her very first design, entirely out of her own imagination. She had showed it to her older brother, Wen, but he had only scoffed, treating it like a child's drawing. She showed it to her younger sister, Nian, but she'd merely smiled and carried on twirling around the bonfire, too enchanted by the rhythm of the drums. But not her a-ma. When she showed it to him, he ruffled her hair affectionately and praised her for a job well done, then they hunkered down to create it together, heads bowed as they carefully whittled tunnels into the fan's bamboo ribs so that the darts could fit within.

The villagers often criticized her father for indulging her eccentricity, but Ying would be eternally grateful for it. She didn't expect them to understand her. Now the only people who did were no longer around.

Tucking away the fan, Ying pulled out two items from her leather pouch—the black jade pendant and the leather-bound book, the last thing her father had given her. She had meant to speak to Wen and Nian about these, but they had been so busy with funeral proceedings that she didn't have the chance.

"*Burn it*," her father had said. But why? What could it possibly contain that would be so damning to their clan? And what of those mysterious forces that he had warned her about?

Her fingertips traced the worn and frayed edges of the leather, telltale signs of the days and nights that her father had kept this book in close company. A smile tugged at her lips. All the books in her father's workshop were in the same state—overly thumbed pages, faded ink, and the occasional drool stains from when he had fallen asleep while reading. "*Knowledge is what keeps our people alive*," he had once said, "*and it is what makes a person truly* feel *alive.*"

Ying's hand hovered hesitantly over the cover. Her father's parting words echoed in her mind, warning her against what she was about to do.

"I'm sorry," she whispered. If he had wanted to destroy it, then perhaps he should have done it himself. It was too much to ask of her, not to even try investigating what exactly it was that had cost her father his life.

What harm could there be in reading a book?

She flipped open the cover gingerly, holding her breath.

Her father's neat handwriting appeared on the page. It looked like one of his regular record books, those that he conscientiously kept for every single idea, experiment, and wild flight of fancy that had ever crossed his mind.

Ying quickly skimmed through the pages, frowning as she read. Much of it was too complex for her to comprehend. And then she found something odd, sandwiched between pages—a carefully folded piece of parchment. It looked innocuous enough, but when she held it out in front of her eyes, digesting the neat, angular lines of her father's elaborate sketches and the tiny labels and equations that explained each part, she finally realized the true weight of his last words.

This, she recognized.

Cannons and gunpowder.

Weapons.

Harbingers of death and destruction.

"'Charcoal mixed with powder ground from shar rocks and a combination of the following dried herbs—'" she read. The ingredients for gunpowder. Yet it didn't look like the standard formula she was familiar with. Her father had made modifications and added new elements, some of which she had never even heard of before.

"Why would you add this into gunpowder?" she murmured, her fingers resting upon the characters that spelled "ming-roen ore."

The infamous ming-roen ore, or devil's ore, was the stuff of legend across the nine isles, first discovered almost fifty years back by a group of prisoners serving their sentence at the Juwan mines. They had been digging for a source of kaen gas, the extremely valuable lift gas that helped keep the airships of the Cobra's Order afloat. Instead, one poor soul hit upon a mysterious silver fluid oozing from the cracks in the underground caverns. He reached out to touch it, mesmerized by its otherworldly shimmer. Then his companions heard him scream—a tortured, anguished cry that echoed through the tunnels—and when they found him, grotesque, bleeding pustules completely covered his arm. If the foreman hadn't had the good sense to chop off the man's arm right there and then, death would have claimed his soul.

The highly corrosive liquid that was ming-roen ore had the potential to become a lethal weapon, but the problem was that it was rare, and its destructive nature made it difficult for any vessel to contain it for extended periods of time. The masters at the Engineers Guild had been trying to find a solution for years, to no avail.

Ying couldn't understand. Devil's ore could destroy anything within a matter of minutes, so it had no obvious uses. Why would her father mix it with gunpowder? Perhaps the other puzzling sketches and equations in this book held the key to this mystery.

Even though she could decipher little of what her father had drawn, Ying knew the implications of this work. The little novelties and gadgets that sat in his workshop paled in comparison to what this book contained. This was a book of weaponry—and even in their unfinished form, she could see the devastating potential that they had.

Weapons of war were keys to power.

Is this why you had to die? Because of someone else's hunger for power?

A single teardrop slid down her cheek and landed on her father's sketch, smudging the lines.

"No!"

She quickly rubbed at the spot, not wanting to leave the slightest blemish on what could have been her father's final work. Then she noticed something strange peering through the small wet patch that had left the parchment translucent.

Ying flipped the sheet around. There was a message written on the other side, but it wasn't in her father's handwriting. Four lines in some unintelligible code and a few equations in small, even print with elegant curves.

Someone else had seen this. Someone else had been working with her father on all of this—but who? No one else on Huarin did any engineering except her.

Ying carefully folded the parchment once again and slipped it back between the journal pages. She then held up the jade pendant to study the intricate pattern that was carved into the smooth obsidian surface.

This was no ordinary jade. Hetian jade—comfortingly warm to the touch, unlike the cool nature of other jade types. There were no characters whittled into the stone, unlike the family pendants of the Antaran noble clans. Just an image of a dragon baring its razor-sharp fangs, talons raised to strike. A symbol of aggression and superiority—but it was a long way from home. The mythical dragon was a symbol of the Qirin royal family, the emblem representing the sovereign of the Great Jade Empire, the greatest enemy of the Antaran isles.

A fraught relationship had always existed between the nine isles and their far wealthier neighbor. Blessed with fertile grasslands and mild weather, the Qirins of the Great Jade Empire were able to live far more comfortably than the Antarans, who often struggled with poor harvests and scant resources. In exchange for the import of various necessities, the Antarans found themselves at the mercy of Qirin hands. Were it not for the vast stretch of treacherous ocean lying between the isles and the closest Qirin border city of Fu-li, perhaps they would have been conquered by the Empire a long time ago.

But it was preposterous!

Even if her father's work was immensely valuable, how could the Empire have learned about it when they were so far away? The only outsiders who traveled to Huarin were trade merchants from the other isles, and even then, it was mostly limited to their closest neighbors, Kamar and Noyanju.

If Fei was a distant dream, then the Empire was a place that she couldn't even begin to fathom. She had read hazy passages in books that alluded to its riches and decadence, but that was all it was—a fantasy as surreal as the heavens.

Ying continued staring at the pendant, as if the dragon would speak and answer all her doubts if she persevered for long enough. The creature remained silent. Her shoulders sagged in despair. She knew too little to be able to unravel this mystery. Would she have to leave everything here with her final goodbye and never be able to avenge her father's death?

Then she remembered the dying embers in his eyes, the dagger mercilessly stabbed into his chest. Her father's life had been snuffed out so callously, all for the sake of an incomplete manual and a glimpse of its potential.

She got back onto her feet, her gaze hardening with determination as she regarded the snow-dusted plains of Huarin, the white domes of her tiny village, and the mysterious shimmer of the sea beyond.

These seas can never trap those who are meant to fly.

That was what her father had taught her, and that mantra had long taken root inside her heart.

Ying rode atop her horse, a fierce white mare she had named Ayanga—lightning—and galloped down the winding path that led her back to her village. She didn't stop until she reached her family ger, the biggest in the village, as befitting the status of clan chieftain.

Aihui Wen, her older brother, sat in conversation with a few of their clansmen, issuing instructions about his upcoming chieftain anointment ceremony. He had gathered his braids at the back of his head today, fastened neatly with a bronze circlet, instead of letting them hang loosely like he preferred. Swathed in fleece-lined gray pelt, the somber tones cut a solemn figure, making him look far more mature than his twenty-four years.

Like A-ma, she thought. Her brother had always borne the greatest resemblance to their father, with their squarish jawlines and dense brows, even though their personalities were miles apart.

A flash of displeasure appeared in Wen's deep-set eyes when Ying burst in. He quickly dismissed the men.

"How many times do I need to remind you of the proper decorum expected of a young lady?" Wen reprimanded. "After you become someone's wife, you will need to change that careless and impulsive attitude of yours. Your new family will not indulge you the way we have."

"A-ge, I'm not here to listen to that," she said, marching up to him. She took out the jade pendant, slamming it down on the table. "Look at this carving. The dragon is the symbol of the Empire, isn't that right?"

Wen picked up the pendant and studied the carvings in the stone. "Where did you get this?" he asked.

"I took it from the man who murdered A-ma."

Her brother's dark pupils constricted, his long fingers curling themselves around the pendant until it was obscured completely in his palm.

"Why didn't you show me this earlier?"

"It's the Empire, isn't it? They were the ones who killed him!" Ying cried. "We have to do something."

"Do what?" Wen replied, his tone harsh and curt. The muscles of his jaw tensed visibly beneath his tan skin. "You can't conclude that based on this pendant alone." He tossed the black jade back down onto the table as if it were a worthless piece of rock.

"We can't just let A-ma die without doing anything! Whoever was behind it needs to pay. We deserve justice." Her pitch rose with every word, along with the burgeoning anger inside her. Anger at the culprit. Anger at herself—for not having done enough.

Her brother's expression darkened, and he got up from his chair, towering almost two heads above her. When they were younger, their father used to call Wen his "little ox," much to his chagrin. He had taken offense to both parts of the nickname—he was hardly little, neither did he like being compared to cattle.

"We sent out a search party on the day of the incident. They found no sign of the man. Whoever it was, he's probably already left Huarin, and we don't have the means to search further. Maybe he was only an opportunistic thief, or one of those refugee seafarers seeking shelter from pirates. This pendant means nothing. What's done is done. A-ma and E-niye would want us to move on with our lives as soon as we can."

"No they wouldn't. Not in this way," Ying hissed. If their parents had wanted them to "move on" and live carefree, ordinary lives, then they shouldn't have left the way they did, when they did.

"There's nothing more that I can do," Wen answered, averting his gaze. He picked up the jade pendant again and walked over to one of the wooden cupboards that sat next to the family altar, fresh incense sticks burning before their father's newly installed tablet. He locked the stone inside, then waved his hand to dismiss her, turning his attention back toward the numerous parchments laid out on the table. "Go back to your ger, Ying. The chieftain of the Ula clan is coming to our village for a diplomatic visit next week, and there is much to be done. I don't want to hear any more of this absurdity. Don't make A-ma and E-niye worry about you up in the heavens."

Fists clenched tightly by her sides, Ying took another glance at the cupboard where Wen had locked the jade pendant, then she turned and stormed out of the tent.

Later that night, Ying tossed and turned in her bed. Her fur blanket, usually warm and snug, felt uncomfortably prickly against her skin. She threw it off altogether, and it landed on the floor in a heap.

"Is something bothering you, A-jie?" Her younger sister's gentle voice came drifting from the other side of their shared ger.

Ying sat up, turning to look at Nian in the darkness. She could only see a hazy silhouette. "Nian, have you wondered about A-ma's death?" she asked.

"What about it?" Nian replied, a tinge of melancholy lacing her words.

"Don't you want to find out who was behind it? To take revenge for what he did to A-ma, to our family?" The agitation inside her burst forth once again as she recalled her futile conversation with Wen. Talking to him was like ramming against the side of a cliff.

There was a brief pause, then the shadow moved, accompanied by the creaking of the wooden bed frame. The hearth that sat in the middle of their ger was lit, casting a warm glow across the interior. Nian poured some goat's milk into a small bronze pot and hung it from the trestle above the fire, then she sat and drew her knees up against her chest.

"Of course I do," the younger girl answered quietly. "But A-ge already tried his best, didn't he? They couldn't find the culprit anywhere. He's long escaped." Her brows knitted tightly together, tiny creases appearing in the space between them, and in that moment Ying could see her father's shadow in her sister's face.

Even though they were sisters by blood, there was little resemblance between them. While Ying had inherited the delicate beauty of their mother, Nian had the harsher, more angular features of their father—like Wen. Personality-wise, they were also as different as the sun and the moon. The colorful tapestries hanging from the walls of their ger? That was all Nian, whose deft fingers wove the most beautiful embroideries and produced melodies on the sihu that even the heavens would weep for.

Sometimes Ying wished she shared her sister's calm and docile nature so she could fit in better, but mostly she preferred being the "reckless mare" that the villagers labeled her. Just because she was a girl didn't mean that she had to accept the limits and restraints that everyone insisted on shackling upon her.

"And you believe him?" Ying scoffed.

She knew what was going through their brother's mind. What mattered most to him was not seeking justice for their father's wrongful death—what mattered was his impending ascension to the position of clan chieftain. She despised him for that.

"Why shouldn't I? A-ge is as saddened by A-ma's death as we are."

"I don't doubt his sadness, what I doubt is his resolve. He will mourn, but he will not go out of his way to demand justice, especially not if it compromises his anointment as clan chief." Ying swung herself out of bed and sat down on the floor beside her sister. Her gaze hardened as she stared at the flickering flames, as if she could see the assassin reflected in the embers.

"What would you have him do? The trail has gone cold."

"No it hasn't. I have a clue, one that could potentially lead us to the culprit. Shouldn't we pursue it?" Ying's fingers balled up into fists, the regret and guilt from allowing the assassin to slip between her fingers once again invading her mind. "Shouldn't we try to unearth this bastard and see to it that he gets his retribution? We can't just let A-ma die for nothing!"

"What clue?" Nian asked.

Ying quickly explained about the pendant.

"A . . . dragon?"

Ying nodded. "A symbol of the Qirin empire," she added. "The trail *hasn't* gone cold, Nian. Wen just refuses to acknowledge it. He doesn't want any unnecessary trouble. He's a coward!"

"Shh!" Nian whispered, pressing a finger over her lips. "You know that A-ge won't like to hear things like that."

Ying honestly couldn't care less if he heard her. Her father's journal was pressed against her skin, hidden beneath her sleeping robes. She was grateful that she hadn't revealed it to Wen earlier in the day. The last thing she wanted was for him to confiscate this as well.

Nian poured the warmed milk into two earthenware cups, handing one to Ying. "Even if we know that the person came from the Great Jade Empire, what could we do?" she asked with a soft sigh. "This is Huarin, A-jie. We haven't even seen the shores of Fei."

"I know, I know," Ying replied irritably. As usual, Nian was the voice of reason, but Ying's mind automatically rejected the path most reasonable. "But I can't sit here and continue living my life knowing that I did *nothing*. If not the Empire, then what about Fei? A-ma was at the Engineers Guild for years. I might be able to find something there."

Her thoughts drifted to the cryptic message and equations that had been left by someone else's hand—someone who could very well be hiding within the guild. If only she could locate that person, she might get a step closer to the truth.

"You're thinking of going to Fei? Alone?" Nian stared at her older sister, aghast. "That's impossible! A-ge would never let you."

"He can't stop me if he doesn't know."

Nian sat her cup down. She intertwined her fingers and began chewing on the nails of her thumbs, like she always did when she was nervous. "But it's not safe. The first beile has just been exiled—the High Command is unstable. Who knows what will happen when you're there? What if there's a coup?"

"Nian, you're being paranoid. The High Commander's still in power. Nothing will happen."

Ying sucked in a breath and held it there, then she slowly released it. Even as she tried to brush aside Nian's fears, she could not do it so easily for herself.

But if Wen won't help me seek out the culprit, then I'll have to do it myself.

When she had gathered enough evidence, her brother would have no excuse to not take action.

"Are you sure you're not just doing this because you want an excuse to enroll in the guild?" her sister asked, giving her a pointed stare.

It was an open secret that Ying yearned to join the prestigious Engineers Guild the way her father once had. She harped about trying for the guild's apprenticeship trial every year, and each time their father would stiffly remind her why it was impossible. The guild only accepted male apprentices, and she did not meet that criteria. Wen would then snidely add, "Even if they did, you would *never* pass the trial."

Ying pursed her lips. The thought had crossed her mind, but she didn't need reminding that she could never enter those halls. Some traditions, no matter how archaic and illogical, were here to stay.

"The trial has probably already begun anyway," she grumbled. "I'll just go to Fei and find some of A-ma's old acquaintances from the guild. Someone must know something, some reason why he might have been killed." Her voice strained as she recalled the memory of the dying light in their father's eyes. The pain of it cut like a knife. "What if he offended a powerful emissary from the Empire during his time in Fei? Or some

Qirin mercenary got wind of A-ma's engineering discoveries and wanted to sell them for profit? Do you think that's why he left so suddenly and never wants to talk about his time there?" She knew that she sounded nonsensical, that she made impossible leaps of logic, but it was difficult to rein in her emotions.

"If any of that were true, should you really be wandering into Fei looking for whoever it is?" Worry clouded Nian's eyes, her slender fingers clutching tightly to her cup. "You've never been there before, A-jie, and there won't be anyone to protect you if you get into harm's way."

Ying tried to smile, to comfort her sister and lighten the mood, but she barely managed a twitch of her lips. "I'll be fine. I'll be as discreet as I can, and I'll disguise myself as a boy—a traveling merchant, like how I used to when I accompanied A-ma on trips to Kamar. I know I'm not much good with throwing punches or wielding swords, but I have my fan, don't I? I'm not completely defenseless."

Nian opened her mouth to say something, then she shut it again, a look of resignation appearing in her hazel eyes. "When are you leaving?" she asked.

Ying blinked in surprise. "You're not going to try and stop me?"

Her younger sister shook her head. "We both know that it's already a foregone conclusion, right?" she said. Ying was notorious for being stubborn.

Ying smiled sadly, leaning to rest her head on her sister's shoulder. The warmth was comforting, reminding her that she was not alone in all this. She raised her cup to her lips and drank. The milk tasted exactly like the kind their mother would prepare for them when they couldn't get to sleep at night. If only their mother were still here to pat her back and tell her that this was all a nightmare that would fade away once morning came.

"The Ula clan is coming next week. Wen will be too busy trying to impress the Ula chieftain to care about anything else," Ying said. "I'll leave then, when everyone's distracted. If Wen asks, pretend you know nothing. He'll assume I've gone gallivanting to Kamar because I'm throwing a tantrum."

"Do you need me to help with anything?" Nian offered, her large eyes staring earnestly at her older sister.

Ying was about to say no, but then she caught her tongue. "Wen confiscated the jade pendant that I snatched from the assassin. He locked it in the cupboard beside the altar. Could you help me get the key?"

Nian helped with the washing of their family's clothes, which meant she had regular access to Wen's ger and belongings.

Without hesitation, her sister nodded. "Promise me you won't put yourself in any danger," she warned. "The moment you discover anything, send word home so that we can help, all right? I'll help you convince Wen, I promise."

Ying reached over to ruffle Nian's hair. "Who's the older sibling here?" she quipped.

"Haven't we already established that Abka Han made a mistake when blessing our family's birth order?" Nian joked. "When you're away, don't worry about things over here. I'll look after the younger ones—although I'm sure Min will be asking for you nonstop. You know how much he adores you. Wen keeps trying to teach him martial arts, but all he wants to do is leap off cliffs like his reckless big sister. I'm not sure this clan can survive a second Aihui Ying, to be honest."

The sisters laughed, just like they had done on many a cold, wintry night growing up, neither of them knowing when they would be able to do so again.

The Ula contingent arrived at the Huarin harbor on a cloudless day with great pomp, sailing in on a sizable vessel with four majestic battened sails and steam-powered propellers that kicked up huge waves of sea-foam, hulking above the smaller merchant ships like a proud peacock. At dusk, wood fires were lit, and the musicians began to drum, signaling the start of the banquet to welcome their honored guests. The plains bordering the village quickly transformed into a scene of revelry as dancers circled the fires with their swirling skirts and tinkling bells, while raucous voices echoed in the air as the villagers feasted on food and drink.

As everyone in the village had abandoned their gers for the plains, no one saw the lithe figure darting through the darkness toward the chieftain's tent.

Ying had traded her usual robes for a set of boy's clothes that she used to wear on trips out of Huarin with her father, so that she would appear less conspicuous among a crowd of men. Her hair was tied back in numerous plain braids, the way Wen liked to do his, without the colorful beaded headdresses that girls typically wore, and she had done away with any rouge on her cheeks and lips.

There was a cargo ship leaving Huarin tonight, and these ships usually accepted a few passengers for a fee. The disguise would hopefully allow her to make the journey from Huarin to Fei with as little unwanted attention as possible, since lone female travelers were significantly rarer across the Antaran isles.

A bundle was tied securely around her back, packed with a few sets of clothes and silver taels that she had been stashing away for a moment like this. Her fan was slipped comfortably up one sleeve and her father's book wrapped tightly beneath her clothes, pressed against her pounding heart. In her hand was a set of bronze keys, stolen by Nian from their brother earlier this morning.

When she was certain that there was no one in the vicinity, Ying slipped into Wen's ger, quickly making her way to the cupboard. She tried a few keys in the heavy padlock before the fourth one made a click. The black jade pendant was just where she had seen him leave it. Ying scoffed. As expected, Wen had not spared a further thought about it after their conversation.

But there was something else besides it that caught her eye. The pendant sat upon an ivory envelope, like a dense paperweight suppressing the secrets beneath.

Ying slipped the pendant between the cross-folds of her robes and then picked up the envelope. There was no recipient named, only a blank box.

Curious.

Ying's eyes darted around. When she was convinced that the surroundings were still, she opened the envelope and gingerly withdrew the letter. Confident yet nonchalant brushstrokes flew across the rice paper.

Do not probe further into the circumstances surrounding Aihui Shan-jin's death, else the Aihui clan will not be able to sail out of this storm intact. You do not want the blood of your fellow clansmen on your hands.

Just a few simple characters, yet they were worth their weight in lead.

So this is why Wen refuses to investigate. He's afraid.

Ying's fingers trembled, clutching tightly on to one corner of the flimsy sheet. She read the lines over and over, before her gaze finally settled upon the seal stamped at the bottom-left corner. There was no indication of the sender beyond that squarish, blood-red imprint, reminiscent of a family seal belonging to one of the noble clans. She lifted it up, squinting at the venation crawling within the seal's boundaries. It looked like a stylized depiction of some sort of animal, with a singular character, "sha," fitted within its gaping jaw. Beneath was a tiny, almost illegible line of text: *These seas can never trap those who are meant to fly.*

Her throat went dry. There was no way she would have failed to recognize it, because she used this exact same phrase to practice her own calligraphy.

It was the motto of the Engineers Guild. The motto that her own father had lived by.

Someone with links to the guild, warning—threatening—her brother against seeking justice for their father's murder, and then signing off with the mantra that her father had treasured so dearly. The irony.

Anger and resentment ran cold in Ying's veins, solidifying her determination. She would find the one responsible for her family's tragedy. She shoved the letter back into the envelope and slipped it beneath her robes, together with the jade pendant. There was a ship waiting for her, a ship that was bound for the capital of Fei—and the Engineers Guild.

CHAPTER 3

YING STEPPED IN THROUGH THE OPEN DOORWAY of the Maiden's Well, one of the larger taverns on the isle of Muci, as a torrent of rainwater rolled down her oiled cloak to form a large puddle on the wooden floor. She had been out in the pouring rain trying to solicit shelter from the heartless Muci residents, only to finally have one of them direct her to this tavern instead.

If the signs from the heavens were anything to go by, then perhaps Ying should have decided to turn around and sail back to Huarin, but she wasn't intending to. She had never been the superstitious sort. Besides, she was already so close. Muci was the final stop before she arrived at the capital.

The interior of the tavern, warm and toasty, was a stark contrast to the bleak situation outside. Ying looked gratefully toward the roaring hearth in the center of the main hall and quickly surveyed the many tables filled with jolly patrons, some more drunk than others. Unlike Roya's tavern back on Huarin, which was merely a larger-sized ger, this one was a more permanent construction that echoed the architecture of Fei, rectangular in shape with a tiled roof held up by sturdy, cylindrical pillars.

As the isle closest to the capital, Muci reflected Fei's influences much more than the other isles. It also received the largest volume of trade flowing to and from its shores, accounting for the wealth and snootiness of its populace.

Ying stood by the entrance for a long while, awed by the colorful sights and sounds. Music was playing from a mechanical ensemble sitting at the far end of the hall, the steam-powered fingers of the wooden musicians strumming the strings of the zither and pipa to a somewhat stiff but nonetheless pleasing rhythm.

"Are you here for a drink?" a curt, high-pitched voice interrupted, slicing through the tavern's noise like a sleek blade. It belonged to a portly matron, hands stuck on her hips and head tilted sideways as she studied Ying like one would a cricket. "If you are, then get in, if not, then get out. You're blocking my entrance."

"Yes, I am," Ying answered, shifting inward a couple of steps. "I'm sorry. I'm from out of town."

"Figures." The matron pointed to an empty seat at a table that was already occupied by two men. "That's the only one left, take it or leave it. Order chits are on the table. When you're ready, just send it to the kitchen." She waved at the intricate network of wooden tracks that crisscrossed overhead, sending small bamboo tubes carrying orders from patrons zipping toward the kitchen.

Ying slipped the hood off her head and hung her cloak on one of the many hooks by the entrance. She squeezed her way through the crowded space, siddling into the empty seat she had been assigned. The men at the table didn't bat an eyelid when she sat down, which meant that her disguise was still holding. Her disheveled appearance probably helped. Besides, it was not uncommon for boys to have softer features, since not all of them had to go through long hours of martial arts training or farmwork that would harden the lines on their faces and turn their skin a rougher, sun-kissed shade of brown.

She scribbled an order for warm fermented milk and a bowl of steamed mutton dumplings before stuffing her chit into a bamboo tube and placing it gingerly on the rails above. She stared in amazement as the tube was shuttled precisely along a predetermined path by a series of rotating gears and cogs, until it finally disappeared through a small window leading to the kitchen.

The dreamer inside her stirred into being. If such inventions were employed in a tavern on Muci, then the reality in the capital could only be better. Beyond the interior of her father's workshop, the use of any such technology on Huarin and the other outer isles was few and far between. It was an extravagance that most could not afford, and engineering talent was selfishly hoarded by the capital city, so there were hardly any engineers stationed on the peripheral isles who were able to maintain such intricate technological systems.

"I told you we should have done a prayer ritual before we left Kamar," one of the men at her table said to his companion, his thin mustache twitching in displeasure. "This rainy weather is going to set us back by at least a couple of days. Our produce will be rotten by the time we reach Fei!"

"We can try to ply it here. The prices won't be as good, but at least we won't make a loss."

"That's assuming we can find someone to off-load it on. And you're right about the prices. I was hoping to sell our stock to the Engineers Guild. They'll be wanting to increase their supplies, what with the influx of trial candidates and all. They would've given us such a good price!"

The Engineers Guild?

Ying peered across the table, ears perking up.

"Excuse me," she interrupted, "but did you say the Engineers Guild? The one in Fei?"

The two men turned, only just realizing that there was a third wheel at their table. The mustached fellow frowned. "Of course the one in Fei. Is there any other?" he replied.

"What about the trial candidates? Isn't the guild's annual apprenticeship trial already over?" Ying probed.

The man let out a loud harrumph, then he said, "Have you been living under a rock? The trial hasn't even begun! It's only starting in two weeks."

"Really?" Ying's eyes lit up. News from the capital came to

Huarin across a broken chain of gossipy mouths, so it wasn't always accurate.

"Were you not listening to what I was saying?" the man snapped, shaking his head. "If you're thinking of competing, then I suggest you forget about it. They close registrations tomorrow. You wouldn't make it even if you hop on the fastest boat from here." He clucked his tongue impatiently, then turned away to continue his conversation with his companion.

Ying became an invisible figure in the noisy tavern once more, but her mind was too preoccupied to care.

The apprenticeship trial.

The only way that someone from the outside could be granted entry into the Engineers Guild. She had dreamed of this so many times, of joining the prestigious ranks of the engineers and becoming a guild master just like her father had been. A ludicrous thought popped into her mind. Maybe, just maybe, if she had been successful in disguising herself as a boy thus far, she might be able to squirrel her way into the guild trial as well?

The light in her eyes dimmed when she recalled what the man had said. Registrations for the trial would be closed by the time she arrived in Fei. That door was shut to her—as it had always been.

Perhaps this was Abka Han's way of telling her to accept her lot in life, instead of constantly dreaming of what wasn't meant to be hers.

Just then, her order arrived, piping hot and comforting for a dreary evening, but the rich, spiced flavors were not enough to distract Ying from the thoughts circling inside her head. She chewed absentmindedly, eyes flitting around the tavern hall.

Then she saw him.

A man stepped in, shaking droplets of rainwater off his dark hair and somber black robes. He had a rectangular face, with thick, heavy brows and a nose that tilted slightly left. He could have been any other patron, now being directed toward a newly vacated table by the tavern owner, were it not for a singular scar running across his left eye.

Beside him walked a creature whose menacing head almost came up to the man's shoulder. A nine-tailed fox with rust-brown fur, its bronze mechanical tails fanning out proudly behind it. Only one of its eyes remained, the other having been replaced with a shiny metal socket that likely had its own insidious function.

A chimera.

Chimeras were curious engineering projects, often viewed with apprehension and distaste—fusions of beast and machine to form hybrids that were neither. They were extremely difficult to engineer and extremely expensive to maintain.

But what caught Ying's attention was the scar on the man's face. A scar that she would never be able to forget as long as she lived.

A strangled cry escaped from her lips. Her chopsticks fell from her fingers and onto the table.

It can't be. She turned to hide her face behind her left hand. *What would he be doing on Muci? Maybe it's just a coincidence and it's not him—?*

In her mind, the assassin who had murdered her father was a man of the shadows, someone who had stolen across the seas from the lands of the Empire. He wasn't supposed to be walking around a tavern in plain sight like an ordinary Antaran citizen.

She widened the cracks between her fingers to take another look.

Their eyes met.

Ying's elbow slipped on the table surface, crashing into her bowl of dumplings and sending its contents spilling all over the table. The two men she was sitting with yelped and leapt out of their seats, as the sudden commotion drew everyone's attention toward them.

She made a beeline for the door.

The tavern owner squeezed her way over to Ying and grabbed her by the arm. "Hey, you haven't paid yet!"

"I'm sorry." Ying fumbled for her pouch and took out a few bronze coins, pressing them into the matron's fleshy palm. Out of the corner of her eye, she saw the scarred man stand from his seat. Did he know it was her? Or was it just the noise that drew his attention? Ying angled her face away and tried to relax. She had to get out before things got worse.

All the while the fox was staring at her, studying her suspiciously with its one real eye.

"Don't think you can get away with a free meal. No one tries to—" The matron looked up from counting her coins, but there was no longer anyone standing beside her, just the tavern doors swinging on their hinges.

~

The rain pelted down relentlessly from the murky skies, soaking through Ying's wool robes. In her haste, she had left her oiled cloak back at the tavern, but it was a small sacrifice. If she wanted to seek revenge, she needed to stay alive, and that meant not confronting her father's killer until she had a proper plan, until she had time to figure out why things had happened and whether there were larger forces behind all this.

Hugging her bundle of belongings close to her, she wound her way down the unfamiliar streets of Muci. The cobbled streets reminded her of how far she was from home. There were no streets on Huarin, only grassy pathways running between the patchwork of white tents.

I'll be fine. He can't have recognized me like this. He wouldn't have.

She was dressed like any other male traveler, without any of the beads and other adornments she had been wearing in their last encounter, and the rain had given her a damp curtain of hair that obscured half her face. He couldn't know it was her.

But still the fear coursed through her veins, making her heart beat erratically inside her chest. Ying turned her head to check that she wasn't being followed—and her blood ran cold.

There through the hazy curtain of rain stood a dark silhouette, its unmistakable set of tails glinting as they reflected fragments of light coming from the flickering street lanterns.

The chimera!

Did that mean his master was not far behind?

Ying slowly turned away, trying her best to hide the tremble in her step as she carried on walking. Behind her, the clipped sounds of the creature's mechanical feet against the stone grew louder as the gap between them closed.

She broke into a run. It might be foolish, but it had to be better than waiting for the creature to catch up with her.

The fox let out a high-pitched howl, giving chase.

Ying made a sharp turn down a long, narrow alley, pushing aside rattan baskets and bamboo poles to slow down her pursuer. She leapt over clay jars and slipped under washing lines, praying that the practice she had in running away from Roya and other irate villagers as a delinquent child would come into use now.

But how could she outrun a creature—a machine—that was not truly flesh and blood?

Just as she turned a corner, the fox leapt into the air, front paws landing heavily upon Ying's back. She crashed face-first to the ground. Pain shot through her body as the chimera's metal claws dug into her flesh.

She struggled to free herself, turn over, but it was impossible to do anything with the weight of the beast bearing down on her. Lifting her head from the rainwater and grime, she saw the hulking shadow of a man approaching. Its master had caught up with them.

Ying said a silent prayer to Abka Han and to her parents up in the heavens, for them to protect her and not let this foreign town be her final resting place, so soon in her journey. But the faith in her own chances of survival was quickly fading. Nian had been right—she had underestimated the dangers that she would face, and her quest was to end before she even stepped foot on Fei.

She clenched her fists in defiance, tasting the bitter, metallic sensation of blood against her lips as she waited for the inevitable—but then—

Thump!

The pressure pushing down on her suddenly lifted. The fox's body went flying into the air, kicked away from her. It landed hard against a wagon parked by the side. The creature yowled in anguish. Picking itself up, it ran back to its master, whimpering pitifully. The assassin took another glance at Ying on the ground, then up at her unseen rescuer.

Ying's gaze remained fixed upon the assassin, bracing herself for another attack. But it didn't come. Instead, the man simply retreated into the curtain of rain with his injured companion, disappearing from view.

"Are you all right?" a mellow voice called out to her, and suddenly the raindrops vanished.

She looked up at the yellowed paper umbrella that was sheltering her from above.

A young man peered down at her, the cold and distant look in his gray eyes drawing a stark contrast to the words of concern. His dark, braided hair was pulled to the back of his head with a silver circlet, highlighting his well-defined, angular cheekbones and two gold cuffs hooked to his earlobes. A black fur cloak hung off his shoulders, pinned in place with a silver brooch. It looked like bear, and bear fur cost an arm and a leg in the nine isles.

He was the one who had kicked the chimera away. *Kicked* a beast that was half solid metal—and sent it flying.

Perhaps that had made the assassin feel threatened enough to back off.

"Yes, yes, thank you," Ying replied, looking around anxiously to verify her assailant had truly gone.

The streets were empty. There was no one there—as if it had all been a hallucination. She heaved a sigh of relief.

"This . . ." The young man bent down and picked up a

small jade pendant carved with the characters "Aihui" from the ground.

Her anxiety spiked again. "That's mine!" Ying exclaimed, hastily grabbing her clan pendant back from him and clambering back to her feet. It must have slipped off her broad belt when the chimera had pounced on her. She stole suspicious glances at her rescuer, wary that this stranger could also be dangerous.

"Did you offend someone?"

"Excuse me?"

"The chimera. It might have bitten off your head if I had showed up a second later," the man said. He studied her from head to toe, as if to assess what value she might have, to warrant such an attack. He did not seem impressed with what he saw. "A chimera of that size and quality can only be owned by nobility. I don't suppose you stole from a traveling noble, did you?"

"Of course not!" Ying retorted, her face twisting with annoyance. How could he think her a thief? Then she saw the dirt stains covering her robes, and her indignance deflated somewhat. She didn't even have to worry about her disguise, because no one would be able to tell what manner of human lay beneath the grime. Even Nian might not recognize her in this pathetic state. "Thank you, again, for saving my life. I owe you a debt of gratitude," she mumbled, giving the man a respectful bow before turning to leave. Best get out of here as soon as she could, instead of continuing to embarrass herself.

"Wait."

She stopped, wondering what else he had to say. If he wanted her to pay him in coin, then she would be in trouble. She didn't have that much in traveling expenses that could afford to be whittled away.

"Do you want to get that looked at? If you leave it unattended, it could fester quite quickly," the man said, gesturing toward her back.

Ying threw a quick glance over her right shoulder, only then remembering the bloody scratch marks left behind by the fox's sharp claws. Fear did wonders for numbing pain.

"I have a physician with me on my ship. If you don't mind, he could help treat the wounds."

She hesitated, eyeing him apprehensively. Why would a stranger be so kind? Did he have a hidden agenda? She quickly shoved the thought aside. The encounter with the assassin had left her on edge.

Buying medicine in Muci would cost her far more than she was willing to spare, but leaving her injuries untreated could derail her quest. If someone was offering help, then it was to her advantage to accept—with precautions, of course.

"I know how to treat my own injuries," she said, "but I could use some help getting the necessary herbs. I'm not native to Muci, so I'm not sure where the herbalists are located."

She couldn't risk exposing her identity by having a physician examine her, but if she could get the medicinal herbs for free, then why not? Judging from this fellow's getup, he could certainly afford to give her some.

"Of course." The man pointed toward the north. "My ship's parked that way. It's not far from here." He turned and headed down the street, and Ying hurriedly followed along.

As she walked, her eyes kept darting to and fro, praying that the assassin and his dreadful chimera wouldn't be lurking around the next bend. She didn't know what new dangers might be waiting ahead, but right now, it was reassuring to know that she had a companion. Whether or not this companion could be trusted was a question for another time.

Ying's jaw nearly fell to the ground when she saw her rescuer's "ship."

This wasn't any ordinary ship—it was an *airship*.

She had only ever seen airships from afar, black orbs floating high up amid the clouds, their engines whirring noisily. They had drifted past the cliffs of Huarin every now and then, oblivious to her village's existence as they went about their important business. Airships were a luxury that only Fei and the wealthier Antaran clans could afford, along with the intricate chimeras like the one that she had almost been mauled to death by.

Ying stared in awe at the ship's black hull looming before her. Deckhands were busy rushing about, shouting out instructions to one another as they filled the airbags with kaen gas to prepare for the journey ahead. The massive envelope inflated until it was suspended entirely above the ship's body, straining to be free of the ropes that kept it tied down to the ground.

The rain had stopped, and the clouds parted to allow the sun's rays through. The silver insignia of the cobra on the black silk surface of the ballonet gleamed, reflecting the light as the wind made its surface ripple. A wooden figurehead extended from the prow of the ship—the image of the same spitting black cobra arching its back in a graceful curve.

"The Cobra's Order," Ying whispered. The military arm of the Antaran High Command. "You're a bannerman?" she turned to the young man and asked.

Her companion opened his mouth to answer, but a shout interrupted him.

"Sir, there you are!" a skinny attendant with a long plait trailing from the back of his head cried, running over to them. "Where have you been? We were so worried! You should have let me come with you."

"What could possibly happen to me? Although I did have a rather *curious* encounter," the man replied, glancing sideways at Ying. "Nergui, where's the physician? Bring him over and let him take a look at my"—he paused, as if considering the right word to use—"*friend* over here. He has some scratches on his back that need tending to."

"Friend?" the attendant called Nergui spluttered, shooting Ying an imperious look that made her feel like she was a mere ant. "But if we delay departure any further, we won't be able to get the shipment to Fei before the next full moon!"

"Fei?" Ying's ear perked up. "Are you going to Fei?"

The young man nodded, the corners of his eyes twitching imperceptibly. "Is something the matter?" he asked.

"I'm headed to Fei too, but they told me that the ships wouldn't be able to sail for a few days because of the storm," Ying explained. "If you're leaving today, could I hitch a ride with you? I can pay for passage, I promise." She dug in her bundle and pulled out a string of coins. "Here's twenty copper coins. That should be enough—"

A commotion near the ship's stern distracted Ying, and she turned to see several panicked deckhands rushing toward the cargo hold.

The young man started marching toward the site of the chaos, and Ying quickly jogged along with his crabby attendant. They walked up the gangway and into the hold, which was already crowded with jostling men.

When the shiphands saw the young man approach, they immediately parted to the sides, leaving a clear path.

A man was squirming on the floorboards, his face flushed red with agony as he clutched his right forearm. To Ying's horror, huge bleeding pustules lined his hand. The festering wound seemed to be spreading up his arm, as if something was eating away at his skin. Beside him stood a bamboo barrel wrapped in a thick layer of cow's hide, with a trickle of silver fluid leaking from a small hole in its side. A large oil-lined sheet of leather had been laid beneath the barrel.

Her rescuer walked over to the writhing man, and a brief frown appeared between his dark brows, then he reached for his waist.

A wink of silver reflected sunlight into Ying's eyes, blinding her momentarily. There was a loud scream, and when her vision cleared, she stared aghast at the pus-ridden hand that lay on the ground—detached from its owner. A thin sliver of blood slid down the blade that the bannerman was holding in his hand.

He gestured for two men to come forward. They lifted their injured comrade, hauling him away. A trail of blood remained in his wake. The bannerman wiped the surface of his sword with a cloth, then slid it back into its scabbard without so much as a twitch of a muscle on his cleanly sculpted face.

Ying continued to stare at the detached hand, appalled.

"Beile-ye," the other men bowed and greeted in unison.

Beile-ye?

Ying turned to her companion in shock, momentarily forgetting about the severed limb. She didn't know whether she had struck a gold mine or a hornet's nest, to have had her life saved and to scrounge a ride to the capital off the back of one of the High Commander's sons.

The young man waved his hand to dispense with the formalities. "What happened?" he asked, his voice so calm that it made Ying doubt whether or not she had indeed witnessed him slicing off a man's arm.

"This is terrible!" Nergui shrieked, flailing his arms about the leaking barrel. "The High Commander will not be pleased *at all.* Who did this?" He looked around at the gathered crowd, searching their faces for any signs of guilt. "Was it that bumbling fool? Should have just let him die for his crime."

The callousness of his words struck Ying like a sledgehammer. A person's life mattered less than a barrel of—

She glanced down at the leaking silver liquid that was slowly puddling on the tan leather. The hole it was dripping from seemed to have grown a little bigger already.

The fabled ming-roen ore.

The innocuous shimmer drew her closer, like the devil whispering to the foolish passerby. The descriptions in her father's journal appeared in her mind, the ideas he'd outlined for containing and transporting the capricious resource. She walked toward the barrel and peered down at its gaping mouth, gazing down at the silver pool inside.

They had lined the inside of the barrel with a layer of well-oiled leather—one of the materials that was more resistant to the ore's corrosive properties. The same could not be said of bamboo, which the barrel's frame was made of. Without the hole, the leather would have kept the liquid ore from directly contacting the bamboo frame, but the cavity in its side had ruined that careful construction. It wouldn't be long before that slow trickle grew into a rushing stream.

"Have we got any spare barrels?" Nergui demanded.

"No, sir," one of the men replied. "We've used the very last one."

"It's fine," the beile said, his voice remaining a calm monotone. "Get the men to bury the entire barrel. Make sure it's deep enough so no one digs it up by accident."

Ying took a quick look around the cargo hold.

"Wait," she called out.

Everyone turned to look at her, regarding this scrawny newcomer with suspicion.

"I might be able to salvage it," she said.

Nergui snorted. "Even the masters at the Engineers Guild wouldn't have a solution to this. What could a beggar boy like you know? Once a barrel is compromised, it's worthless. If we don't get it off the ship, then it'll burn a hole right through the hull! We don't have time to deal with another half-wit who wants to die from bleeding pustules."

Ying ignored him and ran over to a toolbox that she had spotted nearby, fishing out a wooden bolt. Grabbing a handful of straw that was used as packing material in some of the cargo crates, she wound it around the cylindrical bolt. Next, she ripped off a strip of cotton fabric from her sleeve and made that the outermost layer. She held out the little stump at eye level, assessing the cross section carefully.

In a few minutes, when the ore had burned through a little more of the barrel, it would probably fit.

"Is there any horse oil or lard around here?" she asked.

The men turned toward the beile for instructions, and he gave a slight nod. Someone immediately scurried off and returned moments later with a bottle of lard oil from the ship's kitchen.

Ying grabbed the bottle from the man and carefully poured a healthy amount of oil over the stub. Squatting in front of the barrel, she waited until the hole looked about the right size.

The plug went in.

Everyone stared at the barrel with bated breath. Almost all of them were expecting the makeshift bung to dissolve and the silver liquid to ooze out again—but it didn't happen.

"How did you do that?" the beile asked.

Ying startled, not having realized that he had walked alongside and was now kneeling beside her.

"The oil plays a big part in slowing down the corrosion process—that's why the leather lining in the barrel works," she explained. "Wood is porous, so it helps to absorb a larger volume of oil that can hopefully keep the ore away from the bamboo for a longer time. It's not a permanent solution, though—you'll have to replace that after a few hours."

"A lucky guess," Nergui muttered. Still, he immediately gave instructions to prepare a few bungs on standby using the method that Ying had devised.

The faulty barrel remained in the cargo hold along with the rest of the shipment, and everyone returned to the preparations for takeoff as if the interlude had never happened. The beile turned and headed back out, and Ying followed behind.

"Nergui, arrange for a cabin on board for him," the beile said.

"Excuse me? But, Beile-ye—"

"You're giving me a ride to Fei?" Ying interrupted.

"Take it as payment for helping me to solve the problem with the leaking barrel. Devil's ore does not come cheap, so you've more than earned your fare."

A tiny squeal escaped her lips, but she quickly clamped her hands over her mouth, hoping that no one detected anything amiss about that high-pitched exclamation. Still, she couldn't control the broad smile spreading across her face.

They made their way toward the main gangway of the ship, leading up to the passenger cabins. Before she stepped onto the sturdy plank, Ying paused.

"Quit gawking and hurry up. We're losing time," Nergui snarled, giving her a rough nudge from behind before he pushed past her and scampered up the gangway.

The silver cobra loomed menacingly from above, reminding Ying that she was about to board a ship belonging to one of the Eight Banners. The engines of the airship roared to life as the crew cranked the giant propellers attached to the ship's stern.

She ran up the plank, but right when she was about to step into the ship's interior, her foot slipped on a wet patch. She braced herself for another fall, but before she knew it an arm circled her waist, steadying her, and her gaze met a pair of still gray pools, the shade of the sky before a storm.

"Are you all right?"

Ying nodded, eyes widening in panic. She instinctively wriggled out of his grasp and took two steps back.

The beile arched an eyebrow. "I would like to have a word with you. Come to my cabin once you've changed out of those wet clothes," he said. "The physician . . . I'll have him bring some fresh bandages to your cabin. You can tell him what medicinal herbs you require later."

"Yes, Beile-ye."

A tiny tremble ran up her spine. What could he possibly want to speak to her about? Had she done something wrong? Something that raised suspicion?

She recalled the sensation of his arm around her and silently cursed herself for being so careless. She had bound her chest tightly, not that she was especially well-endowed to begin with, but an observant person might still have sensed the distinct curve of her waist beneath her baggy robes. It was already risky enough for her to be on board an airship of the Cobra's Order—the last thing she needed was for her identity to be exposed.

She heard the rattling of metal chains from behind her, and the door to the ship's hold shut with a loud slam, sealing them in. The gas lamps fixed to the sides of the narrow corridor flickered, casting ominous shadows across the walls.

No turning back now, Ying.

The only way left for her was forward.

CHAPTER 4

"You don't sound like a native of Muci."

"I'm not. I'm from the Aihui clan of the Huarin isle, Beile-ye," Ying answered respectfully.

After she had dried herself off and changed into a spare set of clothes, she was led to the beile's cabin, as he had ordered.

The cabin was located at the bow of the ship and was vastly more spacious and luxurious than the one she had been assigned. It had translucent windows constructed from yun-mu glass, a sturdy material born out of the Engineers Guild and far more insulating than the flimsy rice paper that the Antarans had used for window coverings prior to its invention.

As the airship pierced its way through the low-hanging, wispy clouds, the loud whir of the propellers reduced to a dull hum. At least the engineers had the common sense to soundproof the inner cabins.

"The Aihui clan," the beile murmured, peering thoughtfully at the mulberry leaves at the bottom of his cup. He was seated by a mahogany table at the center of the room, wearing a fresh set of plum-colored silk robes that made him appear more refined and less like the intimidating character who had not even blinked after taking off someone's arm. "You're related to Aihui Shan-jin?"

Ying's back shot upright. "You knew my father?"

Nergui, who had been standing rigidly in one corner of the room, immediately pounced into action. "You will address the fourth beile as Beile-ye," he chided.

So he's the fourth beile, Ying mused.

Being a beile was a position of lordship awarded only to the eldest of the High Commander's surviving sons and nephews in recognition of their contributions to the nine isles, and came with command of one of the Eight Banners of the Cobra's Order. There were only four beiles in the High Command, and Ye-yang—the eighth prince—was the fourth and youngest of them.

"It's all right, Nergui," the young man said. "Why don't you leave us for a moment. There are some things I wish to discuss with Aihui . . ."

"Aihui Min."

The name rolled uncomfortably off her tongue. She frequently impersonated her younger brother when traveling outside of Huarin, but to lie in front of a beile was a dangerous first.

She heard Nergui mumble something unintelligible under his breath, probably curse words, but he obediently retreated out of the cabin anyhow. When the door had closed behind him, the beile set his cup back down on the table.

"Don't mind him. Nergui is very strict on protocol. It's part of his job description. You can just call me Ye-yang," he said mildly. "I don't think I'm much older than you, and that address adds ten years to my age."

Ying stifled a smile.

"So," he said, studying her carefully with his unusual gray eyes, "is Aihui Min *really* your name?"

The blood drained from her face as she stared at the bemused young lord, who might well be more terrifying than the chimeric fox at this moment. Was it her voice? A slip in her disguise? Or had the earlier incident while boarding the airship exposed her identity? She had been extremely careful in readjusting her outfit when tidying up, yet it hadn't been enough.

"I can see why you might need to disguise yourself as a boy while traveling, particularly when you're alone, but if you are truly from the Aihui clan as you claim, then you're a very long way from home. Why's that?"

Ying sucked in her breath, trying to calm her pounding heart. Lying to a beile was punishable by death, and she was a thousand feet too far above ground to escape, so her only chance was to come clean and hope for the best.

She dropped to her knees.

"I am Aihui Ying, Beile-ye, eldest daughter of the Aihui clan. I'm here because . . . because . . ." She struggled to find a plausible reason to explain her presence here and what she wanted to do in Fei. "I heard that the apprenticeship trial for the Engineers Guild was about to start, and I thought that maybe . . ." Her voice dwindled to a whisper. Perhaps a half-truth would be more convincing than a complete lie.

"Maybe you could follow in your father's footsteps?" Ye-yang completed the sentence for her. "No need to look so terrified. I know what it feels like to have big shoes to fill, and the extents to which one might be willing to go to do so." He reached over and took her by the arm, gently helping her back up to her feet. "I never had the good fortune of meeting your father, although I've heard many stories about his talents. Is he well?"

Ying heaved a sigh of relief. The beile did not sound angry, so it appeared that she had crossed this hurdle. But the light in Ying's eyes faded a little at the reminder of her father. "My father passed on a few weeks back," she said.

"I'm sorry to hear that." Ye-yang ran his index finger along the rim of his cup, letting a moment of silence pass between them.

With her eyes, Ying traced a line down his sharp nose bridge to his lightly parted lips. He looked pensive, thoughtful, and at that moment she wished she knew what was running through his mind.

"Surely you are needed back at home. Does your family know that you are headed to Fei?"

Ying gave a noncommittal nod, looking away so she

wouldn't continue to be distracted by his every move. Technically *someone* in her family knew where she was going. Thankfully, he didn't probe further. Her father's death was not something that she was ready to discuss with someone she had barely met—and did not yet trust.

"My older brother, Wen, has taken over as chieftain. He doesn't need my help," she replied. *Or at least not the type of help I'm willing to give.* "My father used to tell me stories about his time in Fei. I was hoping to walk in his footsteps and experience things for myself. Huarin is a tiny place. There is only so much one can do there."

She stared out the windows at the wafting clouds, reminiscing on some of the enigmatic tales she had heard about Fei and the guild.

The guild.

The Engineers Guild was exalted across the Antaran isles and its masters revered by noblemen and commoners alike. Compared to the other guilds that handled issues like protocol, agriculture, and trade, the engineers were by far the most lauded. The responsibilities and trust placed upon them by the High Commander and the critical importance of their work on all aspects of Antaran life had elevated them into prominence.

Two weeks from now, a fresh group of bright-eyed young men would enter its heavily guarded walls and vie for the chance to learn from the best minds in the Antaran isles—but she would not have that opportunity. She would be so close, yet so far.

Ye-yang traced the rim of his cup again. "You want to enter the guild," he remarked, as if he had read her mind. "Judging from your skill with the ore barrel, it seems like you've inherited much of your father's gift. It would be a waste if you didn't have the chance to hone it."

"That's not possible, Beile-ye," Ying said sullenly.

"If you're willing," he continued, "I might be of some help. The four beiles may nominate one candidate each for the Engineers Guild trial, and it so happens that I haven't nominated anyone this year because I've been away at the Juwan mines. Our nominees aren't required to register along with the rest of the candidature."

"Really?" The spark in Ying's heart ignited once more, only to be immediately extinguished. "But the guild doesn't accept girls."

"True. The guild is traditional—stuck in their ways. But then again, you don't necessarily need to enter the trial as a girl," the prince replied, gesturing at her outfit with a mysterious twinkle in his eye. "We can keep your identity a secret between us. For now. Until you can prove to the guild masters that you deserve a place. Prove that you can be an exception."

Ying nodded eagerly. She'd had plenty of practice keeping up a disguise successfully before—although it bothered her that the fourth beile had seen through it so easily. If she was to enter the guild's trial, she would have to make sure her cover was foolproof.

"Although, I should warn you that going in on my card could make things a lot harder for you within the guild," Yeyang mused. "You'll have to do a lot more to prove your mettle, as I do."

"But why would you help me?" Ying asked, trying to read the beile's intentions. "We barely know each other. I could be a good-for-nothing who might drag your name through the mud."

"Maybe that's for the better," the beile replied cryptically. "Getting past the front door of the Engineers Guild is only the first step for you, though. If you hope to do as your father did, you must pass the apprenticeship trial to be formally inducted into the guild. After that, it's another arduous battle to climb the rungs to become a guild master."

The Engineers Guild was mostly a mystery to Ying, her patchwork understanding built from sparse bits of information and exaggerated tales she had gathered over the years. Her father rarely spoke of his time in the capital, so most of what she knew came from the mouths of traveling merchants. Still, its allure was great.

Excitement and anticipation brewed inside her, but then the soft echoes of her father's last words whispered at the back of her mind once more. The jade pendant and journal bound beneath the folds of her robes weighed heavily on her, reminding her of her purpose in going to Fei.

A-ma wouldn't want me to do this.

He had told her to burn the book. He had told her to stay out of danger. He had told her not to go searching for the assassin. Accepting Ye-yang's offer and entering the guild would be going against everything she had promised her father.

But I have to.

"I'm not afraid," she declared. She wasn't afraid of leaping off cliffs, so what else should she be afraid of? She *needed* to do this. If she became a recognized engineer in her own right along the way, would that be so bad?

She wanted to be the exception Ye-yang spoke of, to show everyone that she was capable of holding her own within the guild. Perhaps this had always been part of her destiny, and she could finally acknowledge it now that the goal was actually within reach.

"Good." Ye-yang stood up and walked over to the windows, turning his back to her as he gazed out at the gray skies ahead. There was an air of solemnity to his silhouette that contrasted sharply with his youth. "You can go. When we land in Fei, you can stay in my manor until the guild's apprenticeship trial begins."

"Thank you, Beile-ye," Ying said with a bow.

"It's sad when you have a name that no one will use," he replied wryly. Waving his hand, he dismissed her from his room.

Ying spent most of the journey to Fei holed up in the little cabin that she had been shoved into—a cupboard, quite literally. The rest of the crew proved to be well-trained, highly regimental members of the Order who preferred to treat her like she didn't exist. Thankfully, there was a small porthole in her cabin to watch the clouds float by.

Leaning her head against the glass, she stared at the gulls flying past.

If only she had found a way to pack her glider with her. Flying was a sensation that she would never get enough of, and flying in an airship just wasn't the same as flying with the icy wind against your cheeks.

Her breath hitched as the clouds parted dramatically to reveal the view down below.

The island of Fei was at least ten times larger than Huarin. The city itself was concentrated at the western side of the diamond-shaped land mass.

Fei—the capital city of the Antaran territories and seat of the Aogiya High Command.

Multistory pagodas pierced toward the sky, scattered among a complicated maze of emerald-tiled roofs. Her eyes traced the network of canals that crisscrossed the isle, with stone bridges arching gracefully across the waters. Wooden poles with brightly colored banners and auspicious red lanterns lined the streets.

As the airship began its descent, Ying spied the hundreds of people pounding the pavement. Merchants and traders, street performers and musicians, scholars and schoolchildren—like crawling ants going about their day.

"Hurry up," Ying murmured, willing the ship to move a little faster. She wanted to get a closer look at every single detail of the city she had only ever dreamed of.

Unlike most of the other isles, whose people retained the traditional Antaran nomadic way of life, Fei's infrastructure was modeled after the Great Jade Empire. Some claimed it was a hint toward the ambitions of the High Commander, but no one dared openly speculate about his intentions.

Outside, she could hear the men shouting out instructions for landing. Anticipation bubbled in her chest.

A loud, methodical clicking drifted in through the wooden walls as the large sails that stretched out sideways like wings of a bird started retracting back toward the hull. The ship was now gliding toward a vast, grassy plain to the north of the city, where a collection of black sentries sat in neat arrangement. More airships belonging to the Order.

The sounds of the propellers waned. The airship bobbed up and down a few times, then came to a complete stop.

With her face plastered to the window, Ying watched as

men dressed in the black uniform of the Order jogged toward the vessel, deftly fastening it to the ground with thick ropes.

"They're setting up the gangway," a crabby voice said. Nergui had flung open the door to her cabin without knocking. "Beile-ye said you are to come with." His wide nostrils flared as he regarded her with condescension, then he snorted and left.

Ying scrambled to collect her things, fastening her bundle as securely around her as she could. She pressed her palm against her chest, feeling her father's journal sitting safely beneath the down-lined cotton of her clothes.

"Watch over me, A-ma," she whispered.

Ying sat quietly in a corner of the carriage, her knees glued tightly together and back as stiff as a board. The carriage was trundling through the busy streets of Fei, its steam-powered wheels taking them from the airship port to the beile's manor. From time to time she would glance over at Ye-yang, who was leaning casually against the backrest with his eyes lightly shut.

He looked even younger than Wen, she thought, and hardly like what she imagined a beile to be. But Ye-yang, with his mild, unassuming manner and youthful countenance, was in fact one of the most powerful individuals in the Antaran territories.

This realization both intimidated and puzzled Ying.

"What do you think?" Ye-yang lifted his eyelids and looked at Ying.

"What do I think of what?" Ying quickly averted her gaze, lifting up the curtain to peer outside instead. A blush crept up her neck and cheeks. She hoped he hadn't caught her staring.

"Fei. It's very different from Huarin, or all the other isles, for that matter, even Muci."

They were passing through one of the capital's principal streets of commerce, and it was bustling with activity outside. Ying gaped in awe at the never-ending row of shops, taverns, and the occasional brothel, all built from brick and mortar, many several stories high. Music filled the air—not coarse, cacophonous drumming but melodious, graceful melodies of zithers and pipas. On the streets, elegant palanquins bearing their wealthy owners trotted along on their spiderlike legs, powered entirely by steam-driven motors fixed to their bases, much like the carriage she was now sitting in. Horses were too humdrum for the fancy Fei residents.

Everything just seemed to move faster over here. It was a completely different world from the calming grasslands and felt-lined gers that she knew.

A trader selling colorful dough figurines stuck his face in front of her carriage window, trying to convince her to buy his wares in his crisp, impatient Fei accent. She dropped the curtain and plastered herself against her seat, startled.

The corners of Ye-yang's thin lips tilted upward in an imperceptible smile. "I expect things will change in the nine isles eventually. It's about time we moved on from our ancestors' nomadic ways. The climate of the Antaran territories is cold and harsh all year round. We will soon find sustenance a challenge if we insist on holding on to traditions," he said.

"There are those who feel that progress is a novelty we don't need."

"When survival necessitates progress, they *will* change their minds." Ye-yang drew circles absentmindedly on the wooden surface of the seat with his finger. "That time might arrive sooner than some may like. Our granaries are dwindling and each harvest is poorer than the one before. The responsibility placed upon the shoulders of the Engineers Guild is heavier than it has ever been. We must be prepared when change comes knocking—and we place our trust in the guild masters to ensure that we are. Perhaps one day I will have to place that trust in you." He smiled.

Ying listened quietly, lifting the curtain once again when she was certain the persistent figurine maker was no longer clinging to her window. The sights were slowly changing as they moved into a visibly richer and more exclusive part of the city. The carriage rolled past several manor doors with imposing plaques hoisted overhead, gold brush lettering spelling out family names in the cursive strokes of Antaran script.

She stuck her head a little farther out, squinting to focus on the glint above the rooftops that had caught her attention.

Something was reflecting the sun's rays directly into her eyes, preventing her from figuring out what lay beyond.

"What's that over there?" She pointed a finger toward the painful glare.

Ye-yang lifted the curtain on his side of the carriage and took a quick glance. "That's the new palace that's still being constructed. It's almost complete," he replied.

"A palace? For the High Commander?" Ying strained her neck to get a better look, but the carriage turned a corner and the gleaming roofs vanished from view.

Ye-yang nodded. "He feels it is overdue. It's been years since the nine isles were united, yet the High Commander still resides in a small manor that is befitting only a lowly governor in the Great Jade Empire. Others will not look up to us if we do not accord due respect to ourselves."

So the rumors are *true—the High Commander has lofty ambitions*, Ying thought.

There were rumors that the High Commander wished to invade—and eventually conquer—the rich lands of the distant Empire, to avenge the years of suffering and humiliation that the Antarans had endured thanks to their supposedly more refined neighbors. After the last poor harvest, the High Command had issued an edict listing out the Seven Grievances—seven injustices that the Antaran Isles had suffered at the hands of the Empire—and many considered it a prelude to the war that was to come.

The wheels of the carriage ground to a halt, and Nergui's voice rang out from outside.

"Beile-ye, we have arrived."

Ye-yang got up to his feet and lifted the curtains to the exit, stepping out of the carriage. Ying clambered down after him.

She looked up at the plaque hanging above the manor doors, bold strokes carved into the dark wood identifying this as the manor of the fourth beile. Two stone lions stood guard by the sides, baring their menacing teeth to ward off wandering spirits. A tradition borrowed from the Empire.

When she took a step forward, the glassy, marble-like eyes of the stone lions rotated to trace her motion, accompanied by a soft whir. Ying yelped, startled by the bizarre movement.

"Don't worry, that's only a deterrent feature that doesn't actually do anything." Ye-yang chuckled. "Their defensive mechanisms need to be manually triggered."

Ying didn't dare to imagine what those defensive mechanisms were. Arrows shooting out from their claws? A flamethrower hidden within their mouths? She pitied any thief who dared try to break into the beile's manor.

"Beile-ye," a stout man who had been waiting by the main door greeted with a bow.

"This is Aihui Min, my guest for the time being until the start of the Engineers Guild's apprenticeship trial," Ye-yang said.

"Arrange for his lodging. He can stay in the Chrysanthemum Pavilion."

"But, Beile-ye, the Chrysanthemum Pavilion is the best guest room we have in the manor. It's reserved for *important* guests," the man replied.

Ying scuffed at the dirt beneath her feet, ignoring his supercilious glare. Her coarse clothes seemed to fall under the category of "peasant" in the minds of these Fei residents. Even a housekeeper dared look down upon her.

"And I believe it's up to me to decide who qualifies as important and who doesn't," Ye-yang replied calmly. He lifted the hem of his robe and stepped over the raised threshold of the front doors, striding into the manor before his steward could get another word in.

Ying looked up and gave the miffed steward a shrug, then walked confidently through the open doors.

Ying's nonchalant façade began to unravel the moment she crossed the threshold. By the time she reached the Chrysanthemum Pavilion, her home for the next few days, it had fallen apart completely. It was unbelievable that this was where she would be staying for the next week or two, until she needed to report to the Engineers Guild for the start of the trial.

The manor was far bigger than she had expected, with

numerous interlinked courtyards and carefully cultivated gardens separating the many living quarters. As she walked down the passageways, she marveled at the intricate carvings that lined the stone pillars and beams, depicting legendary beasts and heroic murals from Antaran tradition and history. The maidservants and attendants she passed along the way walked briskly and with perfect posture, reminding her of the regimental order she had witnessed on board the airship.

Ding!

The ringing of a loud bell made her jump like a startled cat.

"What was that?" she exclaimed.

"Need you make such a fuss? It's only the tea brewing in the kitchens," the chief steward, Hitara Qorchi, said. In contrast with the scrawny Nergui, Qorchi was a plump man with a bulbous nose and well-filled belly. He clucked his tongue in disapproval and turned to Nergui. "Where did the beile pick up such a ragamuffin?"

"Off the streets of Muci. Apparently, he's the son of Aihui Shan-jin, the late chieftain of the Aihui clan in Huarin."

"*The* Aihui Shan-jin?" Qorchi sounded impressed.

Nergui nodded. "Could be a lie," he said. "But the beile's sending him into the guild's apprenticeship trial. Those wolves will eat him alive. Maybe then he'll learn his rightful place in the world."

Ying was too busy gawking in awe through the open

kitchen windows to register their conversation. The tea brewing that Qorchi spoke of was not being made by hand, but by an elaborate machine made of several glass cylinders filled with different assortments of fragrant tea leaves, suspended above little zisha boilers that were cheerily bubbling over gentle flames. The bell dangled from one side of the machine's wooden frame, triggered by a set of cogwheels that alerted the kitchen staff to a perfectly brewed pot of tea. A timer, of sorts. A young maidservant hurriedly removed the pots from their holders and popped them onto trays, ready to be served.

There was so much to see along the way that it took the two stewards much reluctant cajoling to herd Ying to her allocated quarters—the Chrysanthemum Pavilion. It was a quaint, stand-alone building with elegantly sloping eaves and auspicious maroon-colored roof tiles and latticed doors.

"Here we are," Nergui announced snootily. "Stay within this perimeter, and don't go wandering to other parts of the manor. If you need anything, let the servants know." He clapped his hands, and a maidservant came rushing out, bowing respectfully to them. After issuing some instructions, Nergui and Qorchi promptly left the compound.

"Welcome to the Chrysanthemum Pavilion, my lord," the girl said to Ying. She was tall and gangly, almost an entire head taller than Ying. Poised and well-trained, like all the others.

"There's no need for all the formality," Ying said, purposefully lowering her tone a notch. She had promised Ye-yang to guard her identity carefully, and she didn't want to be caught out once again.

"Yes, my lord."

Well, that was useless.

Her skin crawled with discomfort to be addressed so subserviently. There was never a need for such pretense on the Huarin grasslands, but this was not Huarin.

Ying marched into her new living quarters, noting the many porcelain vases and trinkets arranged on the shelves. Everything looked expensive. There was even a set of nine glass snuff bottles painted with the iconic sceneries of each of the nine isles.

"Can you tell me about the fourth beile?" she asked, fiddling with a vase. Perhaps she would have more luck with this maidservant than she had with the airship crew.

"What would you like to know, my lord?"

"What's he like?"

"It would be improper for me to discuss such things." The girl's expression remained inscrutable, her back still painfully straight and her hands layered neatly in front of her.

Ying wrinkled her nose. Ye-yang obviously ran his household the same way he ran his army. She would have no news from the maid.

She dismissed the girl, sinking down onto the silklined

cushions of a bamboo chair. In her hand was a snuff bottle that had Huarin's palm-shaped mountainscape drawn onto it. She traced the inky outline with her index finger.

What was happening back home? Had Nian kept her secret? What if her brother found out her whereabouts? Wen would be furious. When she returned, he would surely have her flogged. Maybe even throw her out of the clan.

Clutching the snuff bottle in her hand, she closed her eyes and leaned back against the chair. Now that the exhilaration of arriving in Fei had dimmed, the reality of her situation began to sink in, weighing heavily upon her shoulders. In a matter of days, she could be walking into the Engineers Guild. Was she ready? She'd always believed she was, but all of a sudden she wasn't so sure. Self-doubt cast a grim shadow in her mind. She could almost hear Wen's sneering voice inside her head, chiding her for being foolhardy and naive.

If the road from the airship port to the beile's manor was anything to go by, Fei was far more different from Huarin than she had expected, with its strict protocols, elaborate infrastructure, and haughty citizenry—and home felt like a long way away.

CHAPTER 5

YING DIDN'T SEE YE-YANG AGAIN AFTER THE day she arrived at the manor. Whenever she asked the attendants, they would tell her that the beile had left at dawn to settle official matters, and he wouldn't return until after sundown. She spent a week fretting, wondering if he had forgotten about her. Perhaps he had offered her the guild nomination in jest and Nergui was about to kick her onto the streets.

But Ye-yang hadn't forgotten.

"Why does he want to see me?" she asked Qorchi as she followed the steward down the confusing passageways. She had just finished dinner when he showed up at her door, announcing that the beile had requested her presence in his study.

"It is not my place to question our lord's intentions," Qorchi replied, though he gave her an apologetic smile.

He led her through the circular archway of a moon gate, emerging in a quiet courtyard with a small bamboo grove. They walked toward the two-story loft that sat at the far end.

Qorchi knocked on the door.

"Beile-ye, Master Aihui is here."

"Send him upstairs." Ye-yang's mellow voice echoed from within.

The door creaked as Qorchi pushed it open. He jerked a thumb toward the stairs. "I'll be waiting down here to take you back to your quarters after you're done," he said.

Ying stepped in, carefully making her way up to the second floor.

Unlike the Chrysanthemum Pavilion, which had been furnished extravagantly to impress guests, the interior of Ye-yang's private study was far simpler. A few ink paintings hung on the walls. Books and scrolls were stacked neatly on rosewood shelves. In the center of the room sat a square mahogany table upon which a map of the Antaran territories and the neighboring Empire lay unfurled.

Ye-yang was seated by an open circular window, one leg casually draped across the other as he studied the weiqi board in front of him. In his robes of midnight blue with silver embroidery unfurling into patterns of swirling clouds, he cut a subdued figure that, coupled with his thoughtful posture, reminded Ying of a graceful snow leopard she had once glimpsed on Huarin. His long braids had not been pulled back with a circlet today, and instead cascaded freely down his back. He didn't look up when she entered.

"Come and look at this," he said.

Ying walked over to his side, peering at the arrangement

of weiqi pieces. Ye-yang was holding a white seed between his fingers, hovering thoughtfully over the board.

"If I put it here"—he tapped the piece on a square—"I'll be safe for at least the next five moves, with a chance of winning the game in ten." He moved his fingers and tapped on a second square—one that was frightfully surrounded by black seeds. "But if I make this move, I could win in only two. Problem is, if my opponent doesn't move as I expect, I could lose it all in the next one."

"Even if you take the first option, there's no guarantee you'll win by the tenth move. All you're doing is giving the opponent many more chances to turn the game around," Ying answered.

"So you think I should take the gamble?"

"It looks dire," she said, running her fingers over the row of black seeds, "but you've already seen past that, haven't you? 'To yearn for great opportunity without the courage to accept great risk is naive.' My father used to say that."

Ye-yang smiled. "Your father was a wise man," he said.

He set the white seed in the middle of the black. Ying picked up a spare black seed lying in its bamboo receptacle and placed it on an empty point next to his white. The game was over.

"You didn't have to humor me like that," Ye-yang said.

Ying wasn't listening. She had reached for a second black piece and was gripping it tightly in her clenched fist. A familiar aura of warmth flowed from the little seed to her fingers.

"This is hetian jade," she murmured.

"Yes," the beile replied. "I like the warmth it gives off when you least expect it."

He gestured at the empty seat on the other side of the weiqi board. "Sit," he said, then walked over to a side table and poured two cups of tea, setting one down in front of her.

The subtle floral fragrance of tie guan yin wafted in the air.

"Is hetian jade common over here?" Ying asked, wondering if the jade in this weiqi set was somehow linked to the assassin's pendant.

"I wouldn't call it 'common,' but it's not unusual to have one or two pieces in the homes of high-ranking nobles. Our supply comes from Rongcheng, one of the Empire's main trading ports. This weiqi set was a gift from the Emperor to the High Commander during last year's Solstice Banquet." Ye-yang picked up a white seed and held it up to the light, studying it thoughtfully.

"How did it end up here?"

"I asked for it, as my reward for settling the pirate threat off the south coast." He began sorting the seeds into their respective receptacles. Black and white, black and white, in a neat, methodical manner.

Ying arched an eyebrow. "The High Commander wanted to reward you and you asked for . . . a weiqi set."

She had heard stories about the escalating pirate problem.

Living conditions in some border counties of the Empire had become extremely trying under the watch of corrupt and incompetent officials, forcing many out to the seas to adopt a life of piracy. It was ironic, that a land so fertile and rich could have people so downtrodden and poor.

The pirates didn't fascinate her, but their vessels did. She had seen sketches of their frightening yet magnificent vehicles in her father's journals—narrow, slender ships with massive propellers at the stern, slicing through the water like the blade of a butcher's knife. They would rise from the depths when you least expected it, like a deep-sea monster stirring from slumber.

The corners of Ye-yang's lips tilted upward a little more. "Nothing wrong with a weiqi set. He was happy to give it and I was happy to accept," he said. "Why are you so interested in the jade? Have you seen it before?"

Ying shook her head, quickly dropping the seed back onto the board. The black jade pendant pressed against her chest felt like it was searing through her skin. She had been too eager, forgetting that it could be dangerous to reveal so much.

"I'm just curious. I've never felt a warm piece of jade before," she lied.

Ye-yang took a sip of tea. "Tomorrow is the start of the guild's apprenticeship trial."

"Tomorrow?" she squeaked.

Since she was entering the trial via Ye-yang's nomination

and didn't have to register in person along with everyone else, she never had the chance to find out more about the trial—including when exactly it was due to start.

"Nervous?" Ye-yang asked, his lips quirking upward. "I realize I might have been a bit hasty when I asked you to enter on my card. I only meant to help, seeing as I didn't have a better candidate to nominate anyway. And it seemed a waste to let your talent remain undiscovered. But there's significant risk involved, especially given your disguise. Are you sure this is what you want?"

He was watching her intently. It took Ying a great deal of resolve to maintain eye contact. She couldn't recall knowing anyone else with eyes the shade of overcast skies, with the occasional spark that reminded her of lightning—dangerous, but captivating.

She nodded, tearing her gaze away. "I want to enter the guild," she said.

She didn't just want to—she *needed* to. She shuddered at the memory of the scarred assassin and the nine-tailed fox that had almost ripped her to shreds on Muci. Her father's killer—and whoever was behind him—were still out there somewhere. It could even be safer for her inside the guild walls.

"Good," Ye-yang said, clasping his hands. "I'm not sure how much you know about the guild and its entrance test, but I can assure you it will be far harder than whatever you've heard. The guild did not build its illustrious reputation off the backs of straw men."

"I can do it. I'm not afraid," Ying answered. "My father taught me everything he knew." Her father was the best there was, and he had trained her well. She had no reason to doubt her own skill.

Ye-yang ran his finger along the rim of his cup. "I'm sure he did," he said, "but talent and confidence may not be enough. The guild has its dark side, and the heat of competition can sometimes drive good men to do bad things. Exercising a little caution won't hurt."

Ying could sense the genuine concern in his voice. The young beile had a quiet charm that she rarely saw in boys. Those from her village were either hypermasculine types like her brother Wen, or self-absorbed fools. The beile reminded her of her father, when she watched him comb through her mother's long tresses as a child.

She quickly shook the association out of her head.

"There are three stages to the apprenticeship trial—" Ye-yang explained, "mind, heart, and soul. Throughout the six months, you will take lessons with the masters in Materials, Design, Construction, History, and Strategy, and use what you know to complete three tests, one at the end of every two months. Candidates who fail to meet the requirements for any stage will be axed immediately."

"How many people actually make it till the end?"

"No more than three, out of a starting pool of around a hundred. Last year the guild only accepted one."

"One!" Ying squeaked. Her confidence faltered a little.

"It's too early to worry about that," Ye-yang said. His smile was reassuring. "When you enter the guild tomorrow, you'll have a better idea about what things are like and who your competition is. Trust me when I say they will try to intimidate you with all they have, and they will want to beat you down. But since you've made the choice to take this step, then don't give in." He picked up the final white seed that still remained on the weiqi board—the winning seed—flipping it back and forth between his fingers. "As you said, opportunity comes with risk, and we must have the courage to face it."

The next morning, the fourth beile's carriage trundled through a colossal archway, entering a vast stone courtyard that led to a long flight of steps. An imposing, somber compound in dull gray tones sat at the top of the stairs, resembling a military fortress more than an institution of research and learning. This was the revered Engineers Guild, and once they passed through its gates, the vibrant, flamboyant cityscape of Fei was left in the dust.

A small booth had been set up at the foot of the stairs, where two scribes were checking identity documents of the long line of candidates who came in all shapes and sizes. Ying peeked at her competition from behind the carriage's curtains.

"Should I go down?" she asked, tugging nervously at her robes. She had checked her reflection in the mirror several times before leaving the manor to ensure she would be able to blend in with the other apprentice hopefuls—braiding her hair in a masculine style, hiding her slender build below swathes of tightly wrapped cloth—but still the butterflies were running amok in her stomach.

"Nergui will settle it," Ye-yang replied, rotating the jade ring he was wearing on his index finger. "You can wait here for the time being."

Ying didn't know what they were waiting for, but she continued sitting obediently anyway. She watched as Nergui cut the line and went straight to the scribes. They didn't look too pleased at the outset but immediately exchanged their scowls for obsequious smiles once Nergui flashed a white jade pendant in front of them. Presumably identifying him as a member of the fourth beile's household.

"Aihui Min of the Huarin Aihui clan," the skinnier of the two scribes bellowed loudly, as he had done for each of the other candidates. The duo exchanged curious glances, then the rounder one hurriedly scribbled down the name and clan details into his little record book.

A rectangular wooden pendant was handed to Nergui and

he quickly brought it back to the carriage, shoving it into Ying's hand through the window.

"Congratulations," Ye-yang said with a faint smile. "You're officially an apprentice-designate of the Engineers Guild."

Ying stared down at the pendant in her palm, using her index finger to trace the grooves that carved out the characters "Engineers Guild" in the sandalwood. The pendant gave off a subtle fragrance that reminded her of the incense that her father used to light in his workshop.

A bell tolled in the distance. Thrice.

"Come, it's time," Ye-yang said, lifting the curtain to step out of the carriage. Ying tied the wooden pendant securely at her waist and followed suit.

When she emerged, Ying noticed that theirs wasn't the only steam carriage in the courtyard. There were three others that were parked, each of them equally luxurious and stately, well-polished roofs gleaming under the sunlight. Their occupants had also just alighted and were proceeding toward the foot of the steps.

"Ye-yang," a riotous voice hollered. It belonged to a bulky man decked in a maroon, down-lined silk garb topped with a black fur collar and cuffs. Much of his head was shaven—a popular trend Ying had noticed in the capital—leaving only a circular patch of hair that was tied around the back of his head in a single queue. He walked up to Ye-yang from behind and gave him a patronizing clap on the back. "I heard you'd only just got back from Juwan. Didn't think you were going to poke your nose into the guild's trial this year."

He was smiling and his tone was friendly—perhaps a little too friendly.

"Erden," Ye-yang greeted.

"Always such a serious kid," Erden said, loud enough for everyone to hear. "Doesn't hurt to loosen up from time to time. No one's expecting you to bear the burdens of the nine isles, cousin."

Ye-yang smiled wryly, but said nothing in response.

Standing some distance behind, Ying fumed as she watched the exchange take place. "Who's that?" she asked Nergui.

The attendant regarded her with scorn. "That's Erden, the second beile. The High Commander's eldest nephew," he said begrudgingly. He gestured at the other two men walking over from the carriages. "That one," referring to the man with a hawklike nose and a mean gaze, "is the first beile, Ye-lu, and the other," pointing at the man with a rounder frame and sleepy, hooded eyes, "is the third beile, Ye-han." They were the High Commander's older sons.

The four beiles of the Aogiya High Command, Ying marveled. Collectively, these four men controlled the most formidable forces of the Cobra's Order, their authority second only to the High Commander himself.

Funnily enough, the four of them couldn't have looked more different. If she hadn't been told, she might not have guessed that they were related at all.

She turned her gaze toward Ye-yang. His aura had changed completely since he stepped out of the carriage. The mild-natured, subdued boy she had grown accustomed to had been replaced by a stern, austere man. With his defined shoulders and the clean, chiseled angles of his jawline, Ye-yang was by far the most striking of the four, even though he was much younger than the other beiles and slightly smaller in stature. When they stood shoulder to shoulder, he didn't seem the slightest bit inferior. Erden had tried to thumb him down with his jokey words, but those attempts slid off Ye-yang in vain.

"Ye-lu, Ye-han," she heard Ye-yang greet the two other beiles as they approached. They nodded in acknowledgment, neither engaging in the same contrived banter as their cousin.

The other three beiles had also brought with them their nominees for guild apprenticeship—three young men who looked like they came from well-to-do families, judging from their expensive embroidered silk robes. They came to stand beside Ying, each of them sizing up the competition with impudence. Behind them, the other candidates had also gathered to await the arrival of the guild masters, although they kept a clear berth from the beiles and their representatives.

Ying instinctively took two steps sideways to put more

distance between her and the nearest boy. She clutched on to the sides of her robes with clammy fingers, praying that no one could tell that this scrawny kid swimming in his clothes was actually a girl.

"I'm Chang-en, from the Tongiya clan," the boy closest to her said, bringing his fist up to his chest in greeting. He was tall and lanky, towering almost a whole head above her, and when he smiled his eyes creased into cheery crescents that somehow made her feel less antsy. He was entering under the banner of the first beile, a second cousin from Ye-lu's maternal clan.

The other two were Fucha Arban and Niohuru An-xi, representing the second and third beiles, respectively. Standing side by side, they struck an amusing contrast, with the former being bulky as a bull and the latter a flimsy reed. An-xi was even shorter than Ying was, and his feline-like eyes made him look possibly more feminine than her. Both came from illustrious families that resided within the capital city. Arban made it a point to emphasize that his father was overall commander of the Bordered Blue Banner and his sister was one of the High Commander's most favored concubines.

"Aihui Min," Ying said when they all looked toward her for her introduction. She cautiously lowered her tone and roughened her voice, hoping that it wasn't too unnatural.

"Aihui? Are you related to Aihui Shan-jin?" Chang-en asked with a frown.

Her father was *very* well known, it seemed.

"He was my father," she said. "But he's passed on. How is it you know of him?" As far as she was aware, her father had not returned to Fei since she was born, and Chang-en looked like he was about her age.

"Your father is quite the legend," An-xi interjected. "He was the star pupil of the guild's founding grand master, the venerable Aogiya Rusha. A prodigy! Everyone thought he would inherit the position of grand master after Rusha's retirement."

Chang-en nodded enthusiastically. "He was supposed to have been the greatest grand master in the guild's history. But then he left." He pulled a face. "He could have ushered in the golden age of Antaran engineering."

Ying lapped up every word that they were saying, letting each line weave a new dimension to her father that she had never known. "Why didn't he stay?" she asked.

The boys stared at her strangely. "Shouldn't you know the reason better than us? You're his son," An-xi said.

The words hurt, because they were true. She *should* know the reason, yet she didn't.

"My father never talked about his time in Fei or the guild," Ying replied. "I was hoping to learn more about him by coming here, and maybe finish what he hadn't managed to do."

Arban howled with laughter. "Finish what he hadn't done? You mean to say you're dreaming of becoming the guild's next grand master?" he said, wiping tears from his eyes. "Look, you might be his flesh and blood, but that means nothing except a common surname. Besides, I reckon the stories about him are exaggerated. If he was that good, he wouldn't have gone running back to that little hidey-hole of Huarin with his tail between his legs."

Anger flashed in Ying's eyes. Her fingers curled into tight fists by her sides, blood pulsing furiously through her veins. She itched to punch the smile off Arban's face.

"Min," Ye-yang's voice suddenly cut through the tension that was building in her mind. Ying snapped back to reality, looking past Arban's shoulder at the pair of cool gray eyes laced with concern. Ye-yang shook his head lightly, and she understood. Her fingers slowly unfurled.

Arban's tone and choice of words had been rude, but he did have a point. Why had her father abruptly left the guild and not spoken a word about it all these years? She looked up the long flight of steps toward the staggering building at the top. There were secrets hidden behind those stone walls, she was certain of it, but were those secrets related to her father's death?

The bell tolled once more. Thrice again.

The crowd of over a hundred candidates fell silent.

Five figures slowly descended from the top of the stone steps, all of them wearing identical maroon robes the shade of fresh blood, pinned at the right shoulder with a silver brooch.

As they got closer, Ying could make out the cobra insignia on their brooches, reminders of who the guild answered to.

When they reached the base, they bowed to the four beiles, and to Ying's surprise, the beiles bowed in return. No words passed between them.

"Congratulations on making it this far," the wizened elder standing in the middle with thick, snow-white braids said to the youthful faces that had gathered. His voice was deep but scratchy, grating on the ears in a manner that forced attention. "Only these steps stand between you and the halls of the Engineers Guild, home to the brightest and most valued minds of the Antaran territories, where simple ideas have flourished into extraordinary feats."

"That's Grand Master Quorin." Chang-en leaned over and whispered into Ying's ear. "They say his hair turned white overnight because Abka Han spoke to him in his dreams and showed him the enlightened truth of existence."

Ying snorted. Enlightened truth of existence? Trust the tavern storytellers to spin such tall tales. People would believe anything nowadays.

"Unfortunately for most of you," Quorin continued, "your time here will be brief, so I advise you to make the best of it. There are strict rules and high expectations behind these walls, and we will not hesitate to remove anyone who fails to meet our bar. The trial will last for six months, two months for each stage—mind, heart, and soul. This year, however, the stakes are a little different."

Over a hundred pairs of eyes were glued to the grand master. The candidates stuck near the back were balancing on tiptoes to get a better view. An-xi stuck his little fingers into his ears, giving them a good shake.

"To show the respect and importance that he accords to the guild, the High Commander will personally preside over the final test for this year's trial. Even we, the masters, do not know what that test will be. He has also sent the four beiles"—Quorin gestured at the four men standing up front—"to observe the trial proceedings, and they shall be residing in the guild. I expect all of you to show them the highest respect if you cross paths in our hallways, is that clear?"

"Yes, Grand Master," the apprentice hopefuls chorused.

Ying stared at the back of Ye-yang's head, tracing the twists of his braids from the intricate silver circlet that held them together. *He'll be staying for the entire trial? Why didn't he say so earlier?* She clucked her tongue against the roof of her mouth in mild irritation. They had shared a carriage for the entire journey from the manor to the guild, and he never thought to let her know he was going to be sticking around.

The grand master said more generic words that spoke of encouragement but didn't quite feel like it, then he gave the apprentice hopefuls the go-ahead to proceed up toward the guild compound. The beiles walked ahead with the masters, occasionally engaging in an exchange of empty pleasantries.

Ying stood at the base of the stone stairs, trying to assess exactly how many steps there were before she would reach the top. A thousand? The other candidates swarmed past her, buzzing with excitement as they began their ascent, eager to reach those hallowed halls that towered at the other end.

But those innocuous steps proved to be a torture. Despite the chilly temperatures, Ying started panting halfway up and still didn't feel any closer to the top. The group thinned out as the disparity in stamina began to show. Chang-en offered to slow down his pace to keep her company, but she waved him along. No reason to prolong the pain for anyone else.

She was bringing up the rear, but she gritted her teeth and pressed on. The forefathers of the guild had probably built this torturous flight of stairs to test the resolve of those who wished to join their ranks. If she couldn't even overcome a few steps, then she didn't deserve to stand in her father's place. She wouldn't disgrace the Aihui family name that way.

Someone collided with her left shoulder, sending her tripping over the next step. She landed on her knees, breaking her fall with outstretched hands.

"Don't you know how to get out of the way?"

Ying looked up. The voice belonged to a strange fellow who was wearing a straw hat with a black veil covering his face.

Although she couldn't make out his expression behind the layer of gauze, she could imagine his sneer from the conceited tone of his voice.

"You're the one who collided into me!" she retorted. "Shouldn't you at least apologize?"

He scoffed. "You're asking *me* for an apology? Do you know who I am?"

Ying picked herself off the ground and dusted down her clothes. Blood oozed from both her palms. "I don't care who you are, but this"—she held out her bleeding hands—"is your doing. Apologize."

"It's not my fault you're so clumsy. Why are they letting all sorts of riffraff into the guild?" he muttered. Pushing past Ying, he continued rushing up the stairs.

"I'd like to know the same thing," Ying mumbled.

CHAPTER 6

THE STENCH OF MEN WAS UNBEARABLE. SOUR and rancid, like Wen's socks when he went for days wearing the same pair. Or Roya's infamous cabbage stew that was bound to give you the runs.

Ying stood at the doorway of her assigned dormitory, her feet reluctant to take a step farther. There was one long, raised platform inside, flush against the wall, meant to serve as a bed for the six people sharing the room. Four of them were already inside, lounging on the platform with their shoes kicked off. Chang-en caught sight of her and waved, beckoning for her to come in. She tightened her grip on her bundle.

This was where she had to stay for the next few months, surrounded by these boys. It hadn't struck her how uncomfortable it might be, considering she had only ever shared a room with Nian before.

What if someone saw through her?

Before she could make up her mind about entering, someone else's shadow appeared beside her.

"You can't be serious. I'm supposed to sleep with these peasants?"

Ying turned. "You again?" She scowled. It was the same oddball with the veiled hat who had pushed her over on the steps. Her palms were still stinging from the fall. "If you don't want to live here, then go somewhere else," she said. She steeled her heart and walked over to where Chang-en was, setting her bundle down on the platform.

Be calm. Be confident. Become Aihui Min.

"Who's that?" Chang-en pointed at the fellow by the door.

"Some rude kid."

"Hey, take off that stupid hat," Chang-en hollered. "Have you got hives on your face or something?"

The boy hesitated at the entrance for a moment before finally stepping in. He studied his surroundings, then pointed at the best sleeping spot by the window, which was already occupied by a behemoth who reminded Ying of the bulls they reared on the grasslands. "I want to sleep over here," he announced. "Move over."

The burly boy he was trying to displace ignored him, continuing to banter with the others.

"I said," the kid repeated loudly, "*move over.*"

The beast rose slowly from his perch. At full extension, he towered almost two whole heads above the insolent child. "I'm sorry, I don't think I heard you properly," he said. He lifted his arms above his head in a slow stretch, and his thick biceps strained against his sleeves.

"Move! You should be thankful I'm even allowing you to have floor space and not chasing you out of the room altogether," the boy snapped, unperturbed by the show of strength.

"He must be out of his mind," Chang-en whispered to Ying. The two of them sat quietly by the side, watching the drama unfold with voyeuristic pleasure. "The fellow he's up against comes from a long line of generals from the Plain Red Banner. To fight barefisted against him is asking to be crushed like an ant."

"What's he doing here if he's from a military clan?" Ying asked.

Chang-en shrugged. "I heard he wasn't doing well in his clan's succession tussle. Maybe he's thinking of putting his eggs in more baskets. If he makes it into the guild, he'll be guaranteed a stable footing in the clan hierarchy."

A shriek interrupted their conversation.

"What do you think you're doing? Let go of me!"

The impertinent little squirt was dangling in midair, suspended by a viselike grip around the scruff of his neck. He was kicking and shouting relentlessly, though none of what he said sounded like an apology.

"What's this? Hiding your face like a girl," the giant scoffed. His voice was thunderous, booming across the room.

A girl?

Ying stiffened, hackles rising.

The hulking beast had ripped the boy's straw hat off his head and tossed it onto the floor.

A flushed, indignant face appeared, filled with rage. He looked no more than fourteen, on the brink of transitioning between boy and man, and the angles of his face still held a soft, childlike quality. "I will cut you down, you boor!" he spat. "I'll have you hung upside down outside the guild walls." His dark irises flashed dangerously, but his flailing arms and legs made for a comical sight.

"Is that so?" His tormentor chuckled. He flicked the boy on the forehead, then dropped him onto the ground. "Go on, then." He sat himself down on the platform, turning to continue his conversation.

The boy scrambled off the ground, nostrils flaring. He reached for his broad belt.

Ying saw a glint of silver catch the light. She quickly stepped forward and grabbed hold of the boy's wrist.

"Don't be foolish," she hissed. "Do you really think you can hurt him? He'll break your arm before you even get close." She didn't like the kid's arrogance, but she didn't want to see him ruined either.

He reminded her of herself. Hotheaded and rash—the "reckless mare," as her brother liked to call her.

The boy pressed his lips together in a hard line, then he swung his arm away. The dagger that he had whipped out went back into its scabbard. "Give me your spot, then," he demanded, walking over to where Ying had placed her things.

He marched over without waiting for her response, pushing her bundle to one side and climbing onto the bed.

"Hey, Min was here first. How could you—"

Ying placed her hand on Chang-en's shoulder, shaking her head. "What's your name?" she asked the kid. Since they were going to be bunkmates, it was best to keep things cordial. She didn't need any drama interfering with her progress in the trial, or in the search for her father's killer.

"Ye-kan," the boy replied. "Don't think I'll be grateful to you for giving up your spot. It's what you should do."

Chang-en flipped the whites of his eyes. "Don't know where you get that confidence from," he muttered.

A senior apprentice appeared at the doorway, wearing a uniform that was the same shade of maroon as the masters' robes. Until they were formally accepted into the guild, Ying and the other apprentice hopefuls were not allowed to wear that uniform. They were issued drab gray outfits fashioned out of cheap, scratchy fabric instead. A reminder of their value.

"Everyone report to the main hall in five minutes."

The main hall of the Engineers Guild was as sober as the rest of the compound. Ying entered alongside the other candidates, curiously studying the tall pillars of polished stone that lined its two sides, its dull, slate-gray walls adorned only with long scrolls that carried the guild's teachings.

A model airship was suspended from the ceiling, constructed entirely out of yellowed rice paper and slender reeds. Unlike the one that she had ridden in from Muci to Fei, or those patrolling the skies over Huarin, this model looked a lot simpler. Just an oblong ballonet attached to a small hull that looked like a fisherman's sampan. No propellers, no battened sails, no portholes.

"The first airship," Chang-en whispered, his voice laced with awe. "Designed and built right here. Can you believe it?"

Ying continued staring at the model overhead, the shadows in her mind reenacting the scenes she imagined had taken place all those years back. The masters hunched over long strips of bamboo as they bent the ballonet into shape, weaving the very first prototype of an airship hull under the dim illumination of the oil lamps lining these walls. Refinement after refinement had been layered upon this original frame, iterating the design over and over until it evolved into the impressive feats of engineering that soared above the nine isles.

Without this very model as a starting point, the Antaran people would never have known what it felt like to fly.

Ying felt her blood rushing through her veins, her heart beating fervently in her chest.

This is where dreams are made reality.

She couldn't imagine why her father would ever have chosen to leave.

"We lost the little squirt," Chang-en said, his voice bringing her back to the present. He was looking around, peering across the shoulders of the other candidates who were slowly streaming into the hall.

Ying turned and did a quick survey of the faces in the crowd. Sure enough, Ye-kan had vanished. They had brought him out of the dormitory with them, but somewhere along the way he had gone missing.

While there was no sign of Ye-kan, Ying spotted a familiar silhouette standing near the front of the hall with his back to her. She instinctively weaved her way through the sea of heads, gravitating toward him. Before she got close enough, someone grabbed her by the collar.

"Where do you think you're going, Aihui Min? Why don't you stand here with us?"

It was Arban, who appeared to have found some lackeys in his dormitory who were eager to follow his lead. They were looking at her contemptuously, as if she were a worm.

Better a worm than a girl, she thought. The fear of being exposed for who she really was kept teetering at the back of her mind, reminding her that her decision to come here could end up sending her to the guillotine.

"Put me down."

"Why so prickly? I'm just trying to be friendly," Arban said, his full lips twisting into a sneer. He raised her a little higher into the air. "Thought I'd help get you a better view, so you know what the air up here smells like." He laughed, and his cronies followed suit.

Ying's wrist moved imperceptibly, and the rivet of her fan slid into her palm. The small but lethal bamboo darts hidden within their barrels were poised and ready.

"Fucha Arban," a stern voice rang out.

Ying pushed her fan back up her sleeve.

Arban immediately set Ying back down, bending stiffly at the waist in a reluctant bow. "Beile-ye," he greeted, though there was no hint of respect in his tone whatsoever. Even when he had straightened himself up again, there was no ounce of humility in his eyes.

If Ye-yang noticed the insubordination in the man's attitude, he showed no signs of it. He walked closer and stood beside Ying.

"Aihui Min is here on my account," Ye-yang said coolly, "and I don't quite appreciate you manhandling him in that manner."

"Manhandling?" Arban snorted. "Surely a bit of banter and roughhousing is normal. We're just getting acquainted, that's all. When the second beile arrives, you can ask him what he thinks—I'm sure he'll agree that this is all in the name of good fun."

"I'm sure he will."

Ying caught a momentary flash of irritation in Ye-yang's eyes, but it was gone in a blink. The gray pools regained their usual stillness, as if a pebble had never struck the surface. Her fan slid down once again, but a gentle tap on her wrist by Ye-yang stopped her from sending a flurry of arrows into Arban's annoying face.

"Don't," he said at a volume that only she could hear. "Come with me." He turned and walked back toward the front of the hall.

Ying shot Arban a defiant glare, then pushed past him and followed behind Ye-yang. They stopped when they were out of earshot from the other candidates.

"There are far worse than Arban out there. Are you going to school them all?" Ye-yang warned. He reached for her sleeve and pulled out her modified fan, and Ying startled at his fingertips brushing against her skin. "I'm taking this for safekeeping. You can get it back when you can control your own emotions better."

"Give it back to me! You have no right," Ying retorted.

Ye-yang swiftly slotted it up his own sleeve and moved his hands behind his back. "I think you'll find that I have the right to do many things," he said. "I had the right to order Arban beheaded back there."

Ying searched the beile's composed expression for any sign

that he was joking, but there was none. "Why didn't you, then?" she said weakly.

"Because one move can win you the battle but lose you the war," he replied. His gaze softened. "Go back to your position, and don't do anything else that could draw unnecessary attention to yourself. You don't want to be the first candidate to be kicked out before the trial has even started."

Ying opened her mouth to argue, but on second thought clamped it shut when she saw the other three beiles and a few guild masters enter the hall. She swiveled on the balls of her feet and stormed back to Chang-en, taking a detour to avoid Arban and his motley crew.

"What happened? You okay?" Chang-en asked when she rejoined the line.

"Nothing. I'm fine," Ying replied stiffly. She stared at Yeyang's left sleeve, where her precious fan lay confiscated. *I'll get it back soon*, she swore. Then she turned toward Arban, eyes narrowing dangerously. *And* then *I'll put a few holes in that face.*

One of the guild masters walked toward a raised platform at the front of the hall. He was a skinny man with a pallid complexion and shallow eyes framed by a pair of downward-pointing brows that made it seem like he wore a perpetual frown. As he reached the platform, a short flight of wooden steps unfolded from behind a hidden panel with a series of sharp, rhythmic clicks, which he swiftly stepped up. The other masters were seated on the left, on stately chairs carved from zitan wood, all with solemn expressions on their faces. The beiles were seated to the right—and had just been served tea.

"Candidates," the master started, "I trust you have all settled in well. I am Master Gerel and I oversee the administration of the entire trial. As Grand Master Quorin said in his address earlier, we have strict rules and high expectations within the guild, and mediocrity is not tolerated here." He unfurled a scroll he had been holding and started reciting a long list of rules and regulations, his monotonous voice echoing across the expanse of the hall like a dull gong.

"Why are there two empty chairs?" Ying whispered to Chang-en. She assumed that one of the empty chairs belonged to Master Gerel, but the other one?

Chang-en shrugged his gangly shoulders. "Shh, Master Gerel is staring at us."

The master was indeed staring—glaring—their way. He reminded her of the proud eagles back on Huarin. Maybe it was the way the bridge of his large nose curved on his narrow face.

"You will take lessons in Design, Materials, Construction, History, and Strategy. Each of these areas will be taught by one guild master. I teach History." Gerel recited the names of the other guild masters, who nodded their heads in acknowledgment when mentioned. ". . . and last of all is Master

Lianshu"—he paused, glancing toward the empty chair with a tinge of exasperation appearing in his eyes—"who teaches Strategy. You will not begin Strategy lessons until after the first test, *if* you pass. Mastery of all five areas is a prerequisite to becoming a good engineer, so I expect all of you to put in your fullest effort in every lesson. As I said before—"

"Mediocrity is not tolerated," Ying and Chang-en whispered the rest of his sentence in unison. Gerel had repeated that phrase at least five times during his monologue. Ying pressed her palm against her mouth to stifle a laugh, while Chang-en tipped the right corner of his lips in a lopsided grin. A loud harrumph from the guild master wiped the smiles off their faces.

She looked toward the empty chairs again. One belonged to Master Gerel, and apparently the other belonged to Lianshu, Master of Strategy, but where was he? His absence weighed uneasily on Ying's mind, the first sign of something amiss in this stern and foreboding place.

Guild trial aside, she needed to start searching for answers within these shadowy guild walls. There were clues that led to her father's killer hiding somewhere. Looming large in her mind was the letter from her brother's cupboard, stamped with the guild motto, and the parchment in her father's journal, with the notes from his collaborator. She would start there. Their handwriting would give them away—as long as Ying had the opportunity to observe the guild members.

"The first test of the apprenticeship trial will be in two months' time—the trial of the mind," Gerel continued. "It will be a written examination. There will be only one question, and you will have a day to put together your responses. This is a test of patience and diligence."

"An entire day to answer one question?" Ying arched an eyebrow.

"You!" Master Gerel pointed one knobbly finger straight at her. "What is your name? Were you not listening when I went through the rules of the guild? When a master is speaking, you are to listen *quietly*."

Ying took a step forward and bowed. "Aihui Min," she answered. "I'm sorry. I didn't mean to disrupt anything."

A string of whispers went around the hall the moment she reported her name. Master Gerel stiffened visibly, and disconcerted frowns appeared on the faces of the other guild masters.

"Ye-yang, isn't that your boy?" the second beile's voice boomed across the hall, interrupting the awkward pause. Erden was leaning forward in his seat, studying her the way a predator would its prey. "You never said he came from the Aihui clan. Trying to pull a fast one on us?"

Ying was starting to regret using her clan name. She hadn't expected her father to be as prominent a figure in Fei as he evidently was. It was drawing far more attention to her than she liked.

"Nobody asked," Ye-yang replied, his face expressionless as always, "and I didn't think it worth mentioning. I met him by chance when we stopped on Muci to refuel."

"You're expecting us to believe that?" Erden laughed. "This is why you volunteered to go to the Juwan mines! You had this up your sleeve all along. You knew that the High Commander would preside over the final test, so you went out of your way to plant this fellow here."

Ying couldn't understand how her clan—the unremarkable Aihuis of Huarin—would be of concern to the High Commander in any way. Why was the second beile making it sound as if Ye-yang had nominated her for some hidden agenda?

Erden was still smiling, but she saw only animosity in his eyes. She rubbed her fingers against her clammy palms as she waited for Ye-yang to reply.

"Erden, that's enough," the first beile said. He raised his cup to his lips and took a sip of tea. "You're making a scene in front of everyone. If your candidate is good enough, then it doesn't matter who the competition is, and if he's not, then the both of you might as well go home instead of wasting everyone else's time." He shifted his gaze toward Ying, eyes narrowing. "I heard that Aihui Shan-jin had one grown son who recently took over as clan chief. Never knew he had another . . ."

Ying stiffened. She had assumed that no one in Fei would

know much about her family situation, but if she was proven wrong, the first beile could execute her for lying to enter the guild. No one would bat an eyelid.

The moment seemed to drag as she waited for the guillotine to fall. She didn't even dare look toward Ye-yang for help, in fear that the slightest movement would expose her.

Fortunately, Ye-lu did not probe. He returned his attentions to his tea. "Master Gerel, please continue," he said, waving the guild master along and ending the debate.

Erden leaned back in his seat and crossed his arms over his chest, face reddened with the embarrassment of having been told to shut up so publicly. He glanced sideways at Ye-yang, but the fourth beile's head was bowed as he nonchalantly turned the jade ring on his index finger.

Since she had arrived in Fei, Ying had come to learn of some of the political undercurrents that simmered within the Antaran High Command from the matrons who worked in Ye-yang's kitchen. Since the High Commander had yet to name an heir, a tug-of-war had begun between the most likely candidates. The guild's apprenticeship trial was one such battleground—and the beiles were warring behind their feigned pleasantries. In this battle, she was seen as Ye-yang's sword.

What would the other beiles say if they knew that this "sword" was in fact a girl?

Gerel cleared his throat, his frosty gaze resting upon Ying

for a moment. Then he looked back down at his scroll and continued reciting his speech.

Ying kept her eyes glued to her fur-lined leather boots for the rest of the spiel, trying to meld with the stone floor. She could still hear murmurs passing between the other candidates—probably about her. She had barely begun to discover her father's legacy and already she had a target plastered to her back.

The words that Ye-yang had said to her suddenly floated to the forefront of her mind.

"Trust me when I say they will try to intimidate you with all they have, and they will want to beat you down."

His words had come from personal experience.

Her gaze drifted toward him, blinking back when their eyes met. It was barely noticeable—but he smiled.

CHAPTER 7

THERE WERE COMMON BATHS IN THE GUILD. And the new recruits were assigned one fixed hour to bathe.

Ying lay curled up on her corner of the raised wooden platform, her face buried against her bundle of clothes. It was the only way she could stay in the dormitory without having to witness the varying states of undress around her. She felt a piece of clothing land across her legs and prayed that it was outerwear and not Chang-en's undergarments.

"Aren't you coming to the baths?" Chang-en asked.

"No," she answered. "I'm not feeling too well. Head hurts."

"Oh. Best get an early night, then. You don't want to be nursing a headache when our lessons start tomorrow. You sure you don't want a bath, though? A good warm soak could help." Chang-en sniffed in the air. "I can't tell whether that smell of sweat is coming from you or me," he joked.

"I'll pass," Ying mumbled, raising her hand and waving him along.

"Suit yourself."

Ying heard the voices of her roommates rumble past and their footsteps slowly recede down the corridor. There was finally peace and quiet. She waited for a while, then tilted her head to briefly open one eye. They were all gone.

She flipped herself upright so she was cross-legged on the platform, taking a deep breath to calm her nerves. After Master Gerel's address, some of the senior apprentices had taken the fledglings on a quick tour of the dark, twisty corridors of the guild compound, and by the time they had dinner and returned to the dormitory, it was bath time. One of her roommates had whipped off his waistband in a flourish the moment he stepped into the room, declaring that there was nothing better at the end of a tiring day than a warm scrub of the grime. He had moved with such agility that she had no choice but to catch a good glimpse of his chest of fur.

The thought of it made her feel like retching up her chicken-and-cabbage stew.

Ying lifted her arm and took a whiff, immediately wrinkling her nose in disgust. After spending a whole day with these boys, she smelled as stale as them. The sweat from the morning's arduous stair climb had dried, leaving the fabric on her back stiff and grungy. She needed to find a way to solve the bath problem—but how could she do it without being found out?

Picking herself up off the platform, she poked her head cautiously out into the corridor, emerging only when she was certain there weren't any half-naked stragglers prancing around.

The sprawling compound of the Engineers Guild was structured into four wings—north, south, east, and west—surrounding the main hall situated in the middle. Each wing comprised a series of interconnected courtyards and buildings, linked by narrow corridors and covered walkways, all fashioned out of the same grim stone. Even the gabled roofs of the buildings used dark tiles that were almost obsidian in shade, unlike the emerald green or crimson red favored in other parts of the city. No carvings, no embellishments, no frivolity, as if any fanciful ornamentation would sully the eminence of the guild.

Ying and the other apprentice candidates had been housed in the north wing, along with all the other guild apprentices. The masters had more luxurious and exclusive accommodation in the south wing. Classrooms and workshops were located in the east wing, and the west wing was reserved for guests. The four beiles were occupying rooms in that wing.

Ying took care to take a route that would veer far from the common baths. She did not need to see another man in partial—or worse, complete—undress. Her mother would have been horrified that she was even here, sharing a room with so many boys. Her father would probably have laughed.

A pang struck her heart as the thought floated into her mind. She would never hear her father's laughter again.

Her footsteps slowed out in the open courtyard past the north wing. She lifted her head and looked up at the night sky, clear and shimmering. The northern star blinked back at her, and she imagined it was her father winking from above.

You should still be here, she thought, *showing me all this yourself.*

In the courtyard, there was a single evergreen Antaran pine planted in the center, its branches and needlelike leaves twisting gracefully toward the heavens. A gust of wind blew past, forcing her to wrap her arms tightly around herself.

There was no cozy fire waiting for her outside her family's ger. No tall tales from her a-ma, no rude interjections from her a-ge, and no whining from her younger siblings clamoring for bed. She wouldn't be falling asleep cuddled beside Nian after coaxing the latter to sleep with the gentle, repetitive stroking of her hair.

She looked at the stars and sighed.

A rattling sound suddenly disrupted the quiet of the night. Ying looked upward.

There was a familiar figure perched on the tiled roof with a jar of wine beside him, the silver embroidery on his black outfit glinting under the moonlight. He was peering down at her, unapologetic about the disturbance.

"What are you doing up there?" Ying exclaimed. Then she quickly brought her fist to her chest and bowed. "I'm sorry, Beile-ye. I didn't mean for it to come out like that."

The corners of Ye-yang's lips twitched. "Do you want to

join me?" he asked. "The view from up here is quite spectacular. One of the best in Fei."

Ying hesitated. It was one thing for a beile to be disregarding decorum and drinking on rooftops. It was another for her to join him.

"How did you even get up there?"

The distance between the roof and the ground was at least twice Wen's height from head to toe. If Ye-yang slipped and fell, he would have a few broken bones.

"My qing-gong is quite good," Ye-yang replied.

"What?" Ying yelped. *Qing-gong is real?* In her mind's eye she imagined Ye-yang leaping across rooftops and flying through forests, lifting high into the air with a delicate tap of his toes against brittle branches.

The village storyteller back in Huarin liked to regale the children with stories from the older dynasties of the Great Jade Empire, where noble swordsmen and elusive assassins would partake in epic battles—mostly while suspended in midair. The term coined to explain the magic behind their gravity-defying acts was "qing-gong," the art of being light as a feather. It had inspired her flying contraptions.

Ye-yang chuckled, and for the first time Ying realized that he had a dimple on his left cheek. "I'm joking," he said. "You don't have to look so scandalized." He gestured to the left, where a bamboo ladder stood leaning against the roof's edge, partially concealed by shadows. "Come up, unless you're scared."

Scared? She leapt off cliffs. A measly roof was nothing compared to that.

Ying never backed down from a challenge. She shoved her fleeting concern about propriety aside and checked the surroundings to make sure there was no one around, then she clambered up the rungs of the ladder. When she came up to his side, she sat herself down and tilted her nose upward with a haughty air.

Ye-yang held out his jar of wine. "Want some?"

Ying grabbed the jar out of his hand and took a quick glug. The pungent fumes of the wine shot right up her nose. She erupted in coughs and splutters.

The young beile threw his head back and laughed, his dimple deepening. When he laughed, he felt less like a beile and more like any regular boy. "Aihui Ying," he said, "I'm beginning to wonder how you were brought up back on Huarin. I thought the women of the grasslands were far less delicate than those from Fei." He took one look at her skinny frame and shook his head. "I guess not."

"I'm not delicate. Even if I was, why does that matter? An engineer uses brain, not brawn," Ying huffed.

"Very true. That explains why the guild masters are mostly shriveled prunes who could be blown away by a strong gust of wind."

"Are you drunk?" Ying asked, eyeing the beile suspiciously. A slight blush was creeping across his tanned cheeks. She squinted into the wine jar. It was almost three-quarters empty.

"Maybe."

"Give me back my fan."

"I'm not *that* drunk," Ye-yang replied, giving her a sideways glare. He leaned back so he was lying against the tiles of the roof, his head propped by his hands. "It's been a while since I've had someone to drink with. Thank you," he said.

"You're . . . welcome?" Ying turned and studied Ye-yang curiously. His eyes were lightly shut. The broad smile he had been wearing earlier was gone, and his expression returned to the calmness she was more accustomed to.

Ye-yang was an enigma. A puzzle she hadn't quite figured out. There seemed to be two sides to him, and she couldn't be sure which one was the real one. He was a convergence of youth and authority—a combination that her brother Wen had always yearned for, and one that Ye-yang pulled off effortlessly.

"Do you drink alone often?" she asked.

He shook his head. "Having time to drink is a luxury," he said. "I'm using the guild's trial as an excuse to skive."

Ying followed his lead and lay back against the cold tiles, turning her gaze toward the heavens. The guild compound was situated on high ground, far from the city lights, so from this vantage point the stars seemed innumerable, like fireflies blinking in the darkness.

A-ma, did you once lie here counting the stars too?

"How do you find the guild so far?" Ye-yang asked. "Is it what you imagined?"

The recollection of the first airship hanging in the main hall appeared in Ying's mind, and her eyes glowed with rapture. "It's even better," she said. "This is where it all happened. The greatest feats of engineering in Antaran history. This is where dreams are built."

"Dreams and nightmares are but two sides of the same coin," Ye-yang murmured.

Ying frowned. His words struck a chord inside her, reminding her of the terrible memories of her father's death.

"Beile-ye, what do you know about my father?" she asked. "You said you heard many stories about him."

"It's Ye-yang," he reminded, shooting her a wry glance. "I was only a child when he left Fei, so everything I know comes from my teachers. Your father, Aihui Shan-jin, was a prodigy on a level that had never been seen before in this guild. He was under the tutelage of the then–grand master, Aogiya Rusha. My grandfather." There was a reverence in his voice that she had never heard before, speaking volumes of how much he respected the man.

"The previous grand master was your *grandfather*?"

"Yes. That was a time from before the nine isles were united, and the Aogiya High Command was just the Aogiya clan of Fei—much like your clan. My grandfather was obsessed with the art of engineering, more so than with running the clan. He was a perfectionist, so I can only imagine how talented your father must have been for my grandfather to have taken him under his wing."

Ying imagined her father in his younger days, walking across these very courtyards, bent over at his workstation, toiling through his intricate sketches and designs. She had never doubted her father's skill—to her, he had always been the sky—but to hear such high praise coming from the lips of so many people still made her swell with pride.

"I remember this one specific story," Ye-yang continued softly, "because it was so incredulous and incredible at the same time. Every year the guild holds a competition for all its apprentices—much like a sparring session of sorts where you get to pit your skills against everyone else. The guild masters set a question, and the apprentices are given a week to construct a solution. That year, the masters' challenge was deceptively simple. To light up the dark. There were many extravagant, complex pieces of work that came out of that—gas lamps that lit up with the crank of a handle, self-kindling flames, even fireflies trapped in orbs of yun-mu. Gerel thought he had the winner. He had created a miniature model of lightning in a jar using a precise combination of kaen gas and powder, and it shone so bright that it blinded everyone present for a good couple of minutes."

"Master Gerel? You mean he was in the guild at the same time as my father?"

Ye-yang nodded. "Gerel and your father were from the same batch of apprentices, but Gerel was taught by Quorin." He returned to the story. "Back then, Gerel thought he had this competition in the bag, but then your father showed up. Late. To add insult to injury, the piece of work he brought along was so simple that it felt like a joke. A throwaway. It was—"

"The octagonal lamp," Ying answered with certainty. "It was the octagonal lamp."

She had grown up with those lamps. To make them, her father would hunch over his workstation for days on end, carefully chiseling sandalwood to carve out images that would adorn each of the eight panels. Each lamp he made told a story—folktales from the village storyteller. He would fix the lamps on stands with a rotating axle, so that when they turned, they cast shadow images onto the white walls of the gers. When Ying was a child, she would be mesmerized by the revolving pictures, listening to her father's mellow voice as he told their stories, then she would slowly fall asleep accompanied by the comforting glow.

"You're right," Ye-yang said with a tinge of surprise. "It *was* the lamp. An ordinary lamp that any street carpenter could have made, not a masterpiece of engineering. But your father was unanimously declared the winner that day, because—"

"'A lamp can light up the darkness around you, but a story lights up the darkness within.'" Those had been her father's own words. "It wasn't just an ordinary lamp," Ying said quietly.

Those were the most special lamps in the entire world. Especially the one that her a-ma had made for her e-niye. She remembered badgering him to tell her about their story time and time again. She never got tired of listening to how her father and mother met and fell in love.

"I'm sorry. I didn't mean to remind you of sad memories," Ye-yang said when he noticed the glistening in her eyes.

"No." Ying rubbed her eyes vigorously. "It's all right. Thank you for telling me that story." Another new leaf in her father's book that she hadn't known.

She let the story steep, but as she did she recalled Gerel's expression earlier in the day, when her identity as an Aihui had been revealed in front of everyone. A flame of suspicion flickered through her mind.

"Master Gerel—were he and my father on bad terms?" The question spilled out of her before she could stop herself.

The beile shook his head. "I'm afraid I don't know. Gerel had high hopes of becoming my grandfather's apprentice. He must have been bitter when he lost out to your father." He pursed his lips as he stared up at the skies, as if he could see the complex web of Antaran clan politics mapped in the stars. "Gerel comes from the Niohuru clan. I'm sure you know what that means."

The Niohurus were an old and well-established noble lineage in the Antaran territories, comparable to the Ula clan. Niohuru men had occupied high official positions for generations, while Niohuru women often married into power, becoming principal wives of other clan chieftains. Her fellow apprentice An-xi was from this clan, a nephew to the High Commander's fifth concubine.

In comparison, the Aihuis were dirt on someone's shoe. Ying's ancestors were born and bred on Huarin, the least consequential of the nine isles, and had no illustrious achievements to their name. It was no wonder Gerel was peeved when someone like her father pipped him to the position of Aogiya Rusha's apprentice.

But was it enough to push him to murder? Or even be an accomplice in it?

The suspicion inside Ying started to grow, sinking roots in the crevices of her mind.

"You know, you could visit the guild archives to discover more. Every single member of the guild has to keep detailed records of the work that they do. I expect your father's journals would also be there." Ye-yang took a swig of wine from the jar, and Ying flushed as she watched him lick the remnants off his glistening lips.

Her breath caught in her throat, and she quickly turned away.

Stop being embarrassing, Aihui Ying!

It wasn't as if she hadn't drunk wine with a boy before. Communal drinking was a common feature of celebrations on the grasslands. The alcohol must be messing with her mind. It tasted far more potent than what she had drunk back home.

"Try to stay away from Arban." Ye-yang changed the topic. "His kind are not difficult to figure out, but he'll keep trying to provoke you if you get close. As for the others . . ." He paused. "It's best to be cautious when interacting with them. Those who appear friendly are often the ones you should be most wary of."

Ying turned back and studied Ye-yang's side profile closely, her eyes tracing the elegant angle of his sharp nose bridge. "We must be about the same age, right?" she asked.

"I was born in the year of the Dragon."

"You're only one year older!" Ying exclaimed. "So why is it that you always speak as if you're a doddering old man who's experienced all the hardships of life?" It was definitely the wine doing the talking now.

Ye-yang turned toward her, and the closeness of those smiling gray eyes abruptly shook her out of her daze. His warm breath tickled her cheek, contrasting sharply against the cold night air. Her throat clenched. What had she just said? Had she called the fourth beile a doddering old man? And since when was he so *close*?

Ying shot right up, back stiff as a washboard.

"I'm sorry, Beile-ye, I don't know what came over me," she rattled.

To her relief, Ye-yang didn't explode in fury and order her beheaded. Instead, he picked up his wine jar and finished the rest of it in a series of gulps.

"Be glad that you haven't experienced enough to become like me, then," he replied.

Ye-yang didn't nag any further, and Ying didn't dare say anything, in case her loose tongue got her into real trouble. He lay there while she sat beside him, both of them quietly admiring the serenity of the night view. It almost felt like being back on Huarin again, with the grass beneath her back and the sky as her blanket.

A chilly breeze blew past and Ying sneezed loudly.

"I find nights in Fei tend to be the coldest, even when I am surrounded by many," Ye-yang remarked. "We should head back down."

Ying nodded. She rubbed the tip of her nose with her index finger, a habit that she had developed as a child. Picking herself up off the tiles, she followed behind Ye-yang as he headed back toward the ladder.

"What are you doing wandering about the guild at this hour anyway?" Ye-yang asked.

"It's bathing hour. The others have gone to the common baths— Ah! Can I ask you for a favor, Beile-ye?" It was a brazen request, but it was the only solution she could think of. Since he knew that she was a girl—and was obliged to help her protect that identity—Ye-yang might be more amenable to her suggestion.

"You want to borrow my private bathing quarters," Ye-yang answered on her behalf.

"How did you know?!"

Could he read her mind? That would be terribly dangerous.

She watched as a furrow appeared between the beile's brows and the regret immediately set in. She had to stop forgetting that Ye-yang was a beile—someone who could crush her like a fly with the snap of his fingers.

Run away, Ying, just run away. Then feign ignorance tomorrow.

She rushed for the ladder, but in her haste, the tip of her left boot caught itself between the roof tiles. Her center of gravity shifted, and her entire body lurched sideways, threatening to send her hurtling off the rooftop.

"Ying!"

Ye-yang was in front of her in a flash, his arm catching her around the waist. Still, it wasn't in time to pull her back onto the roof. Instead, the momentum swept both of them off, and Ying shut her eyes tightly to brace for the impact. To her surprise, it never came. Instead, her body experienced a brief sensation of weightlessness—of flight—and then they landed gently on the ground below, feetfirst.

Her eyes flew open.

Qing-gong? Maybe what he said earlier hadn't been a joke.

Then she realized that her arms were circled around his neck, and her cheek was pressed tightly against his sturdy chest. Flustered, she released him and backed away. She bowed her head, hoping that the shadows would hide the furious blush spreading across her cheeks.

It was the second time now. She had to stop letting him catch her when she fell, else it might become a habit.

Ye-yang cleared his throat. "About the bathing quarters," he started, continuing their earlier conversation as if the interlude hadn't happened, "make sure you scrub it well. I don't want to see a layer of grime anywhere."

Wait, what?

Did that mean yes? Ying could hardly believe her luck.

She looked up to say thank you, but somehow Ye-yang had already vanished, his shadow disappearing a little too quickly through the nearby archway. A tiny smile curved upon her face.

Maybe she wasn't the only embarrassed one after all.

CHAPTER 8

When lessons began in full force, the apprentice hopefuls were thrown straight into the deep end. The masters had no intentions of going easy on them, with each lesson packed to the brim with theories and equations, design and practical work. For someone like Ying, who had never undergone formal training before, keeping up with the pace was a struggle.

Back in Huarin, her father had never imposed such a rigid curriculum on her, allowing her to experiment with anything and everything she fancied. Whenever she had a question, he would patiently explain the background theories and concepts to her; whenever she had an idea, he would work on it together with her to make it even better.

Over here, no one cared.

If she got an answer wrong, her classmates would laugh and mock her incompetence. If she asked a question, the masters would cluck their tongues and brush her off with their brusque replies. Gerel was especially impatient with her. Chang-en or An-xi could ask a question and he would sometimes bother to provide semidecent explanations, but when she was the one who opened her mouth, all she received was a sharp rebuke.

"Aihui Min, are you telling me that you still haven't memorized the chapter on yun-mu discovery in *The Annals of the Nine Isles*?" Gerel rapped her tabletop with his wooden staff.

The Annals of the Nine Isles was a massive tome that was considered the most critical and influential text in an engineer's training, a consolidation of knowledge from the wisest minds that ever lived. Her father had used the book as a footstool. Perfect thickness, he said.

"Master Gerel, it's not that I haven't memorized the text. What I'm trying to say is that the properties and composition of yun-mu recorded in the book aren't entirely accurate—"

"So you think you know better than the great masters?" Gerel interrupted, his pitch rising a notch.

"No, that is *not* what I'm saying. I have the fullest respect for the great masters, but—"

"If you knew what 'respect' meant, then you would be treating their books the way they should be instead of using them"—Gerel jabbed his wooden staff and knocked over the thick tome that Ying had been sitting on—"as a seat for your useless posterior."

Ying tumbled onto the floor. The other apprentices hid their laughter.

Gerel stared down at her with the same amount of disgust one would accord a worm. "Exactly like your father. Cocky and arrogant. Always thinking he knew better than everyone else, too busy showing everyone else up just to boost his own ego. Did you know that he told the masters that the *Annals* were wrong too? But look where we are now. The *Annals*"—Gerel tapped the thick volume lying on the floor with the tip of his shoe—"are still here, and Aihui Shan-jin is not." His lips curled in a cruel sneer. "You'd do well to learn your place, Aihui Min, if you don't want to end up like him."

Ying's facial muscles tightened, the color draining from her cheeks. Her fingers clenched into fists. The man Gerel described was not her father. It was Gerel's jealousy rearing its ugly head. She couldn't let him smear her father's name this way.

"My father was not—"

The gong cut off her words, ringing out to signal the transition between classes. Gerel promptly turned his attention away from her.

"We will be learning about the development of irrigation mechanisms during the next lesson. I expect *everyone*"—he gave Ying a pointed glare—"to have read and memorized chapter four of the *Annals*. There will be a short test at the start of the next lesson to make sure there are no skivers about."

After Master Gerel left the room, there was a rumble of activity as everyone rushed to pack their belongings and hurry to their next class.

"You all right?" Chang-en asked, reaching out his hand to help her back to her feet.

Ying took it gratefully, moving to sweep the dust from her robes once she had straightened herself up. "I'm fine," she mumbled, fingers reaching for the space within her sleeve where her folding fan should have been. Perhaps Ye-yang had been wise to confiscate it, because she would have lost control when Gerel insulted her father.

"Come on, let's head for the airship yard, then. The carts will already be waiting up front," Chang-en said, heading toward the door.

For Ying, the next item on her timetable was repairs and maintenance duty at the airship yards. Everyone was assigned shipyard duty twice a week. It was positioned as "valuable practice to help hone your practical skills," but they all knew it was just an excuse to exploit them for hard labor.

Ying actually found shipyard duty the most enjoyable out of all the classes she had to sit through. At least there wouldn't be an uptight master breathing down her neck, trying to find fault so they could get her expelled. If she hadn't entered the trials on Ye-yang's account, they would already have kicked her out just for being an Aihui. There was no shortage of people waiting to see her fail—including the masters.

"Why does Gerel keep picking on you?" Chang-en asked while simultaneously digging his nose. For one of the more refined-looking candidates, with his narrow nose and silky hair, Chang-en had some nasty habits. Nose digging was one, farting in his sleep was the other. "I mean, he picks on *everyone*, but with you it's like he has a very specific axe to grind. For the record, I completely agree with what you were saying about the inaccuracies in the *Annals*."

"Didn't hear you stick up for me in front of Gerel, though," Ying replied drily.

They were all squeezed in the back of a horse-drawn cart, en route to the Order's airship yard, a half-hour journey from the guild. Horses had been her main mode of transportation on Huarin, so Ying had never felt they were slow. Compared to the fancy steam-powered carriages and palanquins that zipped through the streets of Fei, though, the trot of the horse slowed to the pace of a snail.

"Why would he? Speaking up for you means getting into Gerel's bad books. Not a very smart trade," An-xi said matter-of-factly. "And Gerel doesn't hate Min—he hates Min's father. I heard my father talk about this before. The rivalry between Gerel and Aihui Shan-jin was intense back then. My clan elders were not pleased *at all* when Min's father beat Gerel to becoming the grand master's sole disciple."

Ying pursed her lips together and remained silent. An-xi's words reinforced what she had learned from Ye-yang about the animosity between Gerel and her father. She had to investigate, to determine whether Gerel could have played a role in her father's death. Still, it was difficult to believe that the cranky guild master would resort to murder. But what about someone else in the clan? Those elders that An-xi spoke of? The Niohurus were powerful, and it was entirely possible that someone had ties with the Empire and had tried to sell her father's work there. That would be tantamount to treason.

She carefully shelved those thoughts in the recesses of her mind, holding out her hand to catch the flecks of snow drifting down from the overcast skies. There would probably be a heavier snowfall later, hopefully after they were done with shipyard duty.

"It's been *years* since Min's father left the guild. You're saying the masters have been holding a grudge against him for so long?" Chang-en snorted. "Either they're really petty or Aihui Shan-jin ran off with their women."

"It's called jealousy," An-xi replied. "All the incumbent guild masters crossed paths with Aihui Shan-jin at some point. Out of all the apprentices in the guild, Grand Master Aogiya chose only Aihui Shan-jin to tutor personally. If you were in their shoes, how would you feel?"

Chang-en shrugged. "If I'm not good enough, then I'm not good enough," he said. "But that'll never happen to me, because I'm the best." A cocky smile stretched across his face, and he broke into a laugh when he saw the disdain written all over An-xi's.

"Well, I'm not afraid of any of you. I'm going to get into

the guild, by hook or by crook, so all of you can step aside." An-xi turned and stared at Ying with such intensity and determination in his beady eyes that Ying thought they would start spitting fire.

Sighing, she stared up at the sky, letting the small flakes of snow land on her cheeks and eyelashes.

The Order's airship maintenance and repair yard was a sprawling compound that could fit as many as ten large airships, kept away from the prying eyes of commoners by a surrounding stone wall and an imposing wooden gate. Guards from the Order, clothed in their stern black uniforms, patrolled the perimeter of the compound. Two ran checks on the apprentices at the gate before letting their cart through. The heavy doors groaned loudly, heaving shut behind them.

Once they were inside, Ying and the others hopped off the cart and proceeded across the sandy terrain to the rallying point where the shipyard's chief engineer, Kyzo—affectionately known as Master Potato for his potato-like girth—was waiting to hand them instructions for the day's repair and rescue works. Unlike most Antaran men, who wore their hair in braids, Master Kyzo had shaved all his off, purportedly to hide a bald patch. It only made him look more like a root vegetable. He also had a mechanical left arm fashioned from metal—the first person that Ying had ever seen using an actual mechanical limb, one of the more sophisticated inventions of the Engineers Guild. He had apparently lost his arm in a cannon blast when he was accompanying the banners on a guerrilla attack against pirates.

"Tongiya and Jalai are on Berth One, regular maintenance; Kaldasu and Narai on Berth Three, also maintenance; Mardan and Tanggur on Berth Six, got a stuck propeller there; Niohuru and Aihui on Berth Seven, that baby's got an engine issue, might need a bit more work," Kyzo rattled off the scrap piece of parchment he was holding in his hand that looked as if he tore it off the corner of an illicit book he had been reading. Ying thought she could make out the svelte lines of a woman's body on the back of the scrap.

She liked Kyzo, though. He was the only guild master who didn't flinch at her clan name. He also didn't worship the texts like they came from the mouths of gods. "No point in memorizing a whole pile of horseshit if you can't build a decent engine or fix the cannons," he had said to them on their first day of reporting. It sounded like something her father would have said. She made a mental note to ask Kyzo if they had known each other back in the day.

Ying and An-xi headed to the assigned berth where their airship sat waiting, its ballonet deflated and lying limply across the hull. A few engineers had already opened the access panel on the starboard side and were crouched inside the compact space, fiddling with the wooden bolts and axles that were responsible for keeping the airship's propellers spinning.

The Antaran airships ran on engines that burned kaen gas, unlike the more common vehicles seen on the streets of Fei that ran on steam. Kaen gas was lighter and more efficient, the large quantities of energy generated from its combustion powering the rotation of the massive airship propellers, but it was also far rarer. The only source of kaen gas for the nine isles was the Juwan mines—and it was rapidly depleting.

The engine was the energy-generating heart of the ship.

The young apprentices weren't allowed to touch actual engines—there was far too much risk involved—so their role was only to serve as errand boys for the senior engineers.

"Bring me some water."

"Fetch the chisel."

"It's getting hot inside here. Fan harder."

Ying did everything without a single word of complaint. She executed her duties as if there were wings on her shoes. All she wanted to do was to rush back to the engine hold as quickly as she could so she could observe what the senior engineers were doing. There were no airships in Huarin, so she relished every moment of witnessing an actual engine being taken apart before her eyes. Every single word that passed from the lips of the engineers was diligently recorded into her notebook.

"Stop behaving like such a frog in the well," An-xi hissed, pushing past her to deliver a sack of charcoal. When he came back, he shoved a different sack into her arms. The stinging smell of sulfur made her eyes water. "Take this back to the stores," he said. "I have to get more water for them." He wiped the sweat off his brow and plodded off, dragging his leaden feet behind him.

Hugging the hefty bag of sulfur to her chest, Ying made the trip to the store, located within large hangars on the west side of the shipyard, and hurried back toward the ship. As she walked, a merry smile stretched across her face as she looked around the sandy compound, breathing in the chilly but refreshing air. The expansive grounds of the airship yard, with the vast blue skies and billowing clouds stretching overhead, were a welcome contrast to the claustrophobic corridors and stuffy classrooms of the Engineers Guild.

Arriving at her berth, she hummed a tune as she headed to the engine hold. Then she stopped in her tracks. A separate panel on the airship's port side had fallen open, revealing two ominous barrels hidden within.

The ship's air cannons.

Ying slowly walked forward, eyes fixated upon those dark, circular hollows. She took a quick look around—there was no one in the vicinity. She sucked in a breath and grabbed on to a rung of the wooden ladder that was built into the side of the ship's hull, scaling upward to the open panel. Stretching across, she deftly slipped herself into the cabin where the cannons were housed.

Ying ran her fingers across the icy cold surface of the innocuous iron barrel, her breath hitching in her throat. Reaching beneath her clothes, she pulled out her father's journal and withdrew the loose sheet of parchment from between the pages. She unfolded it carefully, staring at the complex construction of lines and curves that her father had drawn.

It was an incomplete set of instructions for building a cannon—she was certain of it now.

When she had first discovered the drawings and equations, the only thing she had recognized was the bizarre recipe for gunpowder. Even after staring at the parchment night after night, she had not been able to figure out what everything else on the page meant. But that was because she had never seen actual airships up close, nor the destructive weapons they carried.

The moment she laid eyes on those cannons, the connection formed.

"But it's not the same," she murmured, her gaze flitting between the airship's cannons and her father's drawings. She walked around the cannon, peering left and right, up and down. There were parts of the cannon that she could identify, but upon closer look, there were many things that looked different. Then there were the parts that were missing altogether. Unfinished.

"Who's up there?" a gruff voice barked.

Ying jumped, and she hurriedly shoved her father's journal and parchment back beneath her clothes. Adjusting the fabric to make sure everything was secure, she popped her head out of the cabin. It was Master Kyzo, looking unsurprised to see her. He raised his mechanical hand and beckoned for her to come down.

"The catch of the panel came loose, so I went up to shut it," Ying blabbered, praying that he wouldn't call her bluff.

"You do know that apprentices aren't supposed to touch the cannons, eh?" Kyzo replied. It sounded like a reprimand, yet at the same time it didn't because of the twinkle in the guild master's smiling eyes. He slapped her across the back, so hard that it sent her flying a step forward. "I was wondering whether I would get one of you Aihuis in my shipyard. Shan-jin was so determined to cut off ties with the guild I imagined I'd have to travel all the way to Huarin to see any of you."

"You knew my father?" Ying asked, jumping at the chance to probe further.

Kyzo nodded, then shook his head. "He was a few years older than me, so we moved in different circles." A slight crease crossed between his brows, then disappeared. "He did mentor me on a few occasions though. Such an excellent mind, particularly when it came to airship design," he said, gesturing toward the looming vehicles. "I expect no less from you, young Aihui. Now hurry up and get back to where you're supposed to be. Don't let me catch you wandering again."

Ying opened her mouth to ask more questions, about what

Kyzo used to work with her father on, about who else in the guild her father might have been close to, or might have offended, but the master had already walked off to examine the other ships. What if Kyzo was the one that her father had been communicating with?

Taking one more glance at the ship's smooth hull, the cannons now concealed, she sighed, then quickly headed back toward the engine hold.

Later that night, Ying lay tossing and turning on the bed, her mind plagued by thoughts of the air cannons and her father's work. She could feel the journal pressing against her chest, constantly reminding her of its presence.

"*Burn it,*" her father had said.

She sat up, eyes wide open as she stared into the darkness. On one side of her, Chang-en released a loud fart that punctuated the snoring coming from the fellows on the other end of the long platform. On her other side, Ye-kan was curled up in a ball, plastered tightly against the wall so that there would be as large a berth between him and the rest of them as physically possible.

Ying slid off the platform and adjusted her robes, making sure that the bindings across her chest had not come loose. Then, she headed outside. She made her way quietly to the workshops in the north wing that the apprentices were allowed to use for their own work. Clearing some space on a table, she lit a lamp and smoothed out the parchment containing her father's half-finished cannon design.

She picked up a stray bamboo brush and dipped its pointed tip into some leftover ink. In her mind, she imagined the lines slowly forming on the sheet, extending out in myriad directions from where her father had left off. She lowered the tip of the brush to the parchment.

Then she lifted it again, slamming it down on the table.

Focus, she reminded herself. *I shouldn't be wasting time like this. I need to find the person who sent that letter to Wen, and the one who's been working with A-ma on all this.*

She wasn't just here to become an apprentice, or to build things like cannons. She was here, first and foremost, to uncover the truth behind her father's death.

But what would she do once she found out who the mastermind was?

Ying stared at the warm amber glow of the candle's flame, and then back down at her father's drawings, the twisting lines extending like tendrils on the page, suffocating her. She wanted to avenge her father's death, but she wasn't sure she was capable of getting anywhere close. Time was already running short as they inched closer to the first test of the guild's apprenticeship trial.

Burn it, Ying. Do it.

She picked up the sheet of parchment and slowly raised it up to the flame. Her father had wanted her to get rid of it, to destroy these vile inventions that had taken him away from her before his time. The flame licked at the corner of the rice paper, a wisp of black smoke rising as the edges began to singe.

"What're you doing?"

Ying's hand went back down to the table, and she quickly stamped out the glowing embers with her other palm. A sense of relief washed over her when she saw only a slight charring at the parchment's corner. She folded the sheet back up and slipped it under a stack of books lying on one side of the table.

"Nothing," she answered, turning to face Ye-kan.

The boy was eyeing her suspiciously from the doorway. When he heard her reply, he marched in and peered down at the empty table space in front of her. "I saw you looking at something," he said. "Where did it go?"

"I wasn't looking at anything," Ying fibbed. "I couldn't sleep, so I thought I'd come out and do some reading. Memorize those chapters that Master Gerel assigned." She did have to find time to swallow those dry books eventually, since the first trial was almost guaranteed to be a test of how much knowledge one could squeeze inside their brain.

The first test was the easiest for most candidates, but for Ying, who had always been more of the trial-and-error sort of engineer, a theory test was equivalent to pointing a knife at her throat.

"You must think I'm awfully gullible," Ye-kan replied, narrowing his eyes. "If you're really here to memorize books, then why haven't you got a copy of the *Annals* with you? You're hiding something."

"I was looking for it and then you interrupted me." Ying reached out, pretending to riffle through a stack of books. "What are *you* doing here?"

"Needed to relieve myself." Ye-kan flipped through some books on the top of the pile.

Ying swallowed, her gaze flicking to where her father's parchment lay hidden. Thankfully, Ye-kan stopped and circled to the other end of the table instead. He ran his fingers back and forth across the candle flame, looking amused by how he was disrupting its steady glow.

"How did you get nominated by the fourth beile?" he suddenly asked.

"What do you mean?"

A touch of irritation flashed across Ye-kan's eyes. "Do I have to repeat myself? I'm asking how you managed to get into the guild? Did you know Ye-yang beforehand? How?"

Ying studied the boy curiously. Other than the older beiles, she had never met anyone who dared openly address Ye-yang by name, and in such a rude tone, no less. Ye-kan had always been a bit of an oddball, but surely this level of arrogance and audacity was not normal. The more she stared at his features, the more she started seeing the possibility. It was barely there, but there was something about the angular jawline that seemed to match.

Ye-yang. Ye-lu. Ye-han . . .

"You're brothers?"

Ye-kan's fingers froze in midair, his index finger in the middle of the orange flame, and he immediately leapt backward with a loud yelp. He quickly shoved his seared finger into his mouth, sucking at it gingerly.

"You're *brothers*," Ying repeated, more confidently this time. "How could I not have realized this!" In hindsight, it was so obvious.

Ye-kan was a prince of the nine isles, one of the High Commander's many sons. That explained his high-and-mighty attitude and disdain for practically everyone in the guild. To him, they were all commoners, unworthy of being in his presence. But there were so many other things about Ye-kan that didn't make sense.

"But if you're a prince, then why are you skulking around and sharing a dormitory with the rest of us? Why are you even taking part in the trial?"

"Shut up!" Ye-kan exclaimed, lurching forward to clap a palm over her mouth. He looked around in alarm, as if there would be people bursting into the workshop at any minute. "You're not to tell anyone about this, not even Ye-yang—clear? This is an order."

Ying couldn't get a single word out beyond a muffled grunt, so she nodded her head instead.

When he was convinced that she had understood his intentions, Ye-kan finally let go. "If you dare breathe a word of this to anyone else, I'll have you hanged," he said.

"You don't have to threaten to kill people all the time," Ying muttered. This kid really wasn't cute *at all.* She watched as his eyes kept darting back and forth, like a rabbit expecting an eagle to swoop down from the skies. "Nobody knows you're here," she said. "Your brothers don't know that you entered the trial."

Ye-kan pursed his lips together in a stiff line.

"But how did you manage to get past the guild masters? We were all supposed to register on the first day and—"

She saw his hand slide subconsciously to his waistband, where a luminous white jade pendant was hanging from its matching silk cord.

"You used someone else's clan name." Reaching out, she yanked the pendant off the cord and flipped it around. The characters carved in the jade read "Bayara" instead of the High Commander's clan name of "Aogiya."

"Give that back! You already know who I am. I'm the fourteenth prince. When I become High Commander, I'll have your entire clan exterminated," Ye-kan yelped. He launched himself at her, fists raised.

Ying ducked, sliding deftly to the side. The boy went

hurtling into empty air, collapsing onto the ground in a pathetic heap. He groaned.

Laughing, Ying squatted down beside him, patting him on the head like she did with all her younger siblings. "Bayara Yekan, maybe when you decide that you're ready to be an Aogiya again, then you can come at me with those threats," she said patronizingly. "Until then, I think it's probably wiser if you're nice to me, unless you want me telling the beiles that you're hiding here, so they can send you back to where you belong."

CHAPTER 9

YING WAS INCLINED TO THINK THAT HER threat backfired. In a way, it worked—Ye-kan was notably less antagonistic toward her—but on the other hand, he was now sticking to her like a little leech, claiming that he didn't trust her to keep his secret.

There were times when she had to resort to hiding in the latrine to get him off her tail—like now.

She kept her ear up against the latrine door. It had gone quiet outside. She opened it a crack and peered out, heaving a sigh of relief when she didn't see Ye-kan there. She dashed out of the foul-smelling wooden cubicle and toward the west wing. Besides the latrine, this was the one place that Ye-kan wouldn't dare trail her to. Not if he wanted to keep his presence a secret from his older brothers.

She lifted her right arm and took a sniff, retching when she caught a whiff of latrine odor. *Probably time for a bath anyway*, she thought.

Ye-yang had kept his word about letting her borrow his private bathing quarters. Whenever she went over, she would find the door unlocked with a tub full of piping hot spring water waiting for her. There was never any sign of the fourth beile, though, and thankfully no sign of Nergui either. She would take a quick soak and let the warm water wash away the day's exhaustion, then give the tub a good scrub before sneaking back to the apprentice quarters.

Today was no different.

Ying used a generous handful of bath beans to rid herself of the stink, rubbing her skin so hard with the coarse towel that there were tender, reddened patches all over after she was done. Once she was done and dried, she redid the cloth bindings around her chest and slipped on some clean robes before heading back out with her bundle of dirty clothes. Just as she was shutting the door, a familiar voice called out to her.

"Done with the bath?"

Her eyes lit up. How many days had it been since she last saw him? Forty-five days exactly. She hadn't even realized she'd been keeping count.

Ye-yang had come through the passageway leading to the small courtyard adjoining his rooms. The black fur cloak she had seen him wearing the first time they met was hanging over his shoulders and there were a few strands of windswept hair framing the harsh angles of his face. He gave her a small smile, enough to make her heart skip a beat.

Something had changed since the last time they met, back on the rooftop. Like the distance between them had shrunk, a barrier fallen, bringing them closer together.

"Did you just return to the guild?" Ying asked. He must have been busy, given his absence for such a long period of time. She had occasionally spotted the other three beiles around the guild compound over the past weeks, but not Ye-yang.

The beile nodded. "There was some business to settle," he answered vaguely. He walked over to his room and pushed open the door, gesturing to Ying. "Come inside. The other beiles will return soon. Although there isn't any rule forbidding us from speaking, I'd prefer they not find out that you're here. They could make things more difficult for you in the trial than they already are."

Alarmed by the potential appearance of the other beiles, Ying quickly followed him. Although she was dressed in her guild uniform, her long hair hung damp over her shoulders, making her feminine features more pronounced. She typically hid on the roof—the same rooftop that Ye-yang had introduced her to—after baths until her hair was dried and braided back up.

She peered around curiously the moment she stepped in. Even though the room looked more sparse and plainly decorated than the rooms in the fourth beile's manor, these guest quarters were still far cozier than the apprentice dormitories. She glanced wistfully at the soft layers of silk blankets laid over the bed.

Must be more comfortable than my wooden platform, she thought.

Ye-yang caught her staring at the bed, and he coughed lightly. "I hope you're not thinking of borrowing my sleeping quarters too," he remarked in a teasing tone. He moved to sit by the window and beckoned for Ying to come over.

"No, of course not, Beile-ye," she replied frantically, her face reddening at the thought of what could possibly be running through Ye-yang's mind. Hopefully he only thought her a country bumpkin, drooling over the sight of silk blankets, instead of—

She shooed the mortifying image out of her head. Of Ye-yang lying on that bed, and the incredulous possibility of her sleeping beside him. That was crossing a very forbidden line. Her thoughts about Ye-yang seemed to be getting more brazen with each passing day—and it was dangerous, albeit enticing.

"How have your lessons been coming along?"

Ying sat down stiffly on the wooden chair across from the beile, resting her hands awkwardly on her knees. "Fine," she lied.

Just this morning she had received ten strokes of the cane at the back of her legs from Gerel for questioning the legitimacy of some of the statements about the invention of flame-resistant materials in the *Annals*. And then she'd been punished with the backbreaking task of cleaning the fiddly bamboo irrigation systems in the guild masters' gardens because she'd failed to correctly recall the steps to put together said irrigation system one time too many.

Facing punishments meted out by the guild masters for failing to meet expectations was a common occurrence for all the apprentice hopefuls, but Ying seemed to be suffering the worst of the lot. Perhaps it was because her maverick ways made her a poor fit for the rigid structures of the guild, like a square peg in a circular hole, or maybe being an Aihui meant that the bar had been set higher for her from the get-go. Either way, she was increasingly anxious—and discouraged—about her chances in these trials.

Ye-yang arched an eyebrow. "That's not what I heard," he said. "According to Nergui, you anger at least one master every day, and Gerel has even floated the idea of petitioning Quorin to have you removed."

Ying's face fell, her shoulders sagging despondently. "Since Nergui's already been reporting everything, then why bother asking?" she mumbled. To say she was unaffected by the discrimination toward her by the masters would be a lie, but she hadn't felt this ashamed until Ye-yang called her out. She wanted to sink into the ground and disappear.

She didn't want him to see her like this. It was as if she had let him down, after he had handed her this golden opportunity.

Ye-yang's expression softened. "Perhaps it might have been easier if you weren't an Aihui," he mused.

"No," Ying said immediately. "I am my father's daughter. I will not hide who I am because I'm afraid of having a hard time." The moment the words left her lips, she realized how hypocritical she sounded. Here she was, masquerading as her younger brother, precisely because she knew that her true identity would set up barriers that she would never be able to cross. She withered a little more inside.

"You are indeed," Ye-yang murmured, "and that may be both a blessing and a curse. In any case, you are already here and the first test is tomorrow. Gerel can't expel you from the trial officially, because you entered on my nomination, but he can if you don't meet the test requirements. Are you ready for it?"

Ying bit down hard on her lower lip. She had barely gotten her footing in this place and accustomed herself to life in the guild, and already two months had flown by. Tomorrow was the day of the first test of the apprenticeship trial—the trial of the mind—and if she failed to meet the mark, she would be sent packing. All the other candidates had been burning the midnight oil to cram as much knowledge into their heads as possible in preparation for the essay they would need to write—but her own mind felt like a sieve despite all her best efforts. She could already see the gloating face of Master Gerel when her name failed to make the list.

She clenched her fists, letting her nails dig into the flesh so that the pain could help harden her resolve. Ye-yang reached over and gently patted the back of her right hand. Ying startled at his touch, but when she looked up and her gaze met his clear, gray eyes, the anxiety quickly faded away.

Ye-yang had a calming effect on her, she realized. Maybe it

was because he always seemed so composed and self-assured. Like there was no storm he couldn't weather.

"Everyone expects you to live up to your father's name," Ye-yang said, "and maybe you expect that of yourself. Don't—it's not worth it." He pulled his hand away, shifting his fingers toward his jade ring. "You have to be your own person. Living in the shadows of someone else means you'll never realize your own potential."

But what was her potential? What did *she* want to be? Ying's brows knitted tightly together as she pondered upon the meaning of Ye-yang's words.

Loud footsteps approaching the room interrupted her train of thought.

"Ye-yang!" The door rattled as someone tried to open it from outside, to no avail. "Open up!"

Ying looked up at Ye-yang in dread. It was Erden, the second beile.

"Stay behind that." Ye-yang pointed toward a sandalwood partition screen carved with plum blossoms that was standing next to the bed.

Ying nodded, scurrying toward it. Squatting down, she held her breath when she heard the door creak open.

"Erden," she heard Ye-yang greet.

The second beile's plodding footsteps entered the room. "Why the locked door? Afraid that someone will barge in on your secrets?" Erden said, bursting out in a guffaw of laughter. He set something down on the table—probably a ceramic wine jar—that landed with a loud clang.

"Just a habit," Ye-yang replied. "What brings you here?"

"Can't I drink with my cousin without a reason? Might be a long while till we get to do this again. That was some impressive plan you presented to the High Commander earlier. Uncle's been eyeing Fu-li for ages, and you're handing it to him on a silver platter."

So that was the "business" that Ye-yang had alluded to earlier. Ying couldn't help but feel like she was listening to something she wasn't supposed to. There was danger in knowing too much, but there was nowhere for her to run even if she wanted to.

"Nothing impressive about it. We're all serving the nine isles, that's all. And we don't know what the outcome will be yet."

Wine bowls clinked loudly.

"True, you might not make it back alive! Or maybe the guild masters will need to build you some mechanical limbs." Erden chortled. He made it sound like a joke, but Ying could tell that it was anything but. "Where did you even get an idea like that from? You're not that sort of a risk-taker."

Ye-yang chuckled wryly. "I have my advisors, as you have yours."

Was he intentionally skirting the subject? Because he knew she was here?

"You should have them hanged! That was a tightrope you were walking, Ye-yang. The High Commander could have you shipped to the Juwan mines like Ye-lin if you tread wrong. Fool lost his chance of inheriting the High Command for nothing."

The memory of the flock of airships sailing across Huarin returned to Ying's mind, and the thunderous voice announcing the exile of Ye-lin, the High Commander's eldest son—once heralded as the heir to the Antaran seat of power, now just a forgotten prisoner. Ye-lin had been the first beile, but with his removal, the remaining three lords received promotions in rank. Ye-yang was newly appointed as the fourth. Judging from Erden's tone, he still viewed Ye-yang as an inferior, a child who could be bossed around and told what to do.

Ying silently seethed at the disrespectful manner in which Ye-yang was being treated.

"I only suggested what I thought would be best for the High Commander's larger plans," Ye-yang said. His response was muted, as she noticed it always was in the presence of the other beiles.

Erden was right about one thing—Ye-yang was walking on a tightrope, and it wasn't only around the High Commander. Maybe that was why he seemed to let his guard down when he was with her, because he didn't have to put on this act, the way she didn't have to pretend in front of him.

"This is why they say you're his new favorite."

There was tension in Erden's laugh. Ying didn't like the

second beile a single bit. His jovial, affable nature was clearly a façade. There were often daggers concealed behind his seemingly harmless words.

When he received no reply, Erden continued, "The banners will probably be deployed before the month is up. If you think you're not up to it, you should let everyone know early. Can't speak for the others, but I'd be more than happy to help. I have more battlefield experience, after all. Just say the word!"

"It's not for me to decide who gets to go, Erden," Ye-yang said. "I suggest you not try to predict the High Commander's intentions either. He will send whoever he thinks is best suited."

"Of course, but you could turn it down," Erden pressed. "This isn't child's play, Ye-yang. Fu-li is the gateway to the Empire. It's not the same as those little border skirmishes you're used to. You will be facing Qirin's elite."

Qirin?

This was a war Erden was speaking of, a war against the Empire. Ying reached for the jade pendant buried beneath her robes, wondering if it was this exact war that had implicated her father. She pressed her ear against the wooden partition, willing them to say more.

"It's not my decision to make."

Erden slammed his palm down onto the table. The sudden, resounding bang almost made Ying lose her balance. She held her arms out, palms pushing against the ground to stabilize herself. Despite her efforts, her head poked out briefly from behind the wooden screen. She caught a slight frown on Ye-yang when he spotted her. Thankfully, Erden didn't.

She quickly retreated behind the screen, exhaling softly in relief. It was bad enough if Erden discovered her here. It would be much worse—for both her and Ye-yang—if he realized she was a girl.

"Can't you see that I'm trying to help you? You are young and inexperienced, Ye-yang, so maybe you don't quite understand the situation. In order to be High Commander, you need strong backing from the noble clans—backing that you don't have. So don't let praise get to your head and make you think you stand a chance in this contest. You don't want to end up like Ye-lin."

"Thank you for your . . . *concern*, Erden," Ye-yang replied calmly.

Threat, more like it, Ying thought with disgust.

Ye-yang continued, "You came to drink, didn't you?"

The fourth beile expertly steered the conversation toward more mundane topics, like the training regimens of bannermen and the new songstress at the capital's most renowned pleasure house, dragging on for much longer than Ying had hoped. She had gone from squatting to sitting on the floor, and still her legs were beginning to cramp up. What time was it? She usually made it back to the dormitory before lights out after her baths, using the excuse of working late in the workshops. But no one would notice her missing today, because they would be too busy stressing about tomorrow morning's test.

By the time Erden's footsteps finally headed for the door, she was almost asleep, with her face pressed against the frame.

As the door shut, Ye-yang's face appeared on her side of the screen, peering down at her. His cheeks were flushed and the whites of his eyes were streaked with red, the inebriation far more obvious under lamplight than it had been when they were up on the roof.

The boy did not hold his liquor well.

Ying waited for him to say something, but it never came. Instead, Ye-yang stumbled past her and headed for his bed, almost tripping over her feet.

"Are you okay?" Ying asked, clambering back up.

Ye-yang sat down on the bed, staring blankly ahead for a moment. Then he waved his hand in the direction of the door. "I'm fine," he murmured. "You can go."

Ying immediately pushed the partition aside and made a beeline for the door, but then she hesitated. She turned and took one more look at the young man, who was still seated upright, his eyes glazed and weary. In her mind, Ye-yang had always been a formidable presence, aloof and imperturbable. He had to be, in order to be the overall commander of an entire banner and withstand the pressure from the likes of Erden.

Sometimes it was easy to forget that he was barely older than she was.

She turned and walked over to the table, pouring out a bowl of water. Then, she brought it over and held it out in front of him. "Drink some," she said. "Helps get rid of the alcohol."

Ye-yang's eyes flickered upward and rested upon her face. He took the bowl out of her hands. "Thank you," he said, gurgling everything down in one gulp.

"I didn't mean to eavesdrop, but I kind of couldn't help it. Are you heading somewhere? Are we going to war?" If the Qirins did have something to do with her father's death, she needed to understand why, what was at stake.

"We've been at war for a long time, Ying," Ye-yang replied quietly. He handed the bowl back to her. "The nine isles, the High Command, the Cobra's Order—everything we know was built from years of war. This time, we'll finally be fighting someone else, instead of among ourselves." He shook his head, wearing a bitter smile on his face. "Huarin must be a nice place. Far away from all the conflict and bloodshed."

An-xi was right when he called her a frog in the well, Ying thought. Huarin was a safe haven, a small patch of land where the biggest dispute ever witnessed was between Roya and Khatan, the village butcher, over the increase in the price of beef. Under her father and mother's protection, she had grown up with the luxury of not having to care about anything but herself and the things that made her happy.

Ye-yang was different. Being a prince and a beile meant that he had to bear burdens that she would never be able to comprehend. She suddenly felt the urge to pat him on the head and smooth away his worries, the way she did for Nian.

"There's no need to feel sorry for me," Ye-yang said. "I lied to Erden when I said it wasn't my decision to make. I chose this path. This has nothing to do with what my father wants, or what anybody else wants. This is what *I* want."

Ying was surprised by his openness. It was effectively an admission of his personal ambition, something that he had been cautiously trying to hide from Erden—yet was trusting her with.

"But you could lose your life out there," Ying burst out. It was one matter to be ordered to fight a war, and another to volunteer for it. "What are you trying to prove? That you're better than the second beile or your other brothers? That you belong in this position?"

A flash of anger appeared in Ye-yang's eyes. He got up and took her by the shoulders, pinning her down to the bed in one swift motion.

"Who do you think you are, talking to me like that?" he said. "You're just like them. You don't think I can do it. All of you think I'm just here to make up the numbers. I wouldn't even be a beile if Ye-lin had toed the line the way he should have. Is that what you think?"

"I never said that," Ying cried, alarmed by his sudden aggression. "Let go of me!" Fear shot through her spine as she struggled against his viselike grip.

Right now, with his fingers digging painfully into her flesh, she was acutely reminded of her rightful place in the hierarchy, and that she might have misinterpreted the relationship they had. She had grown too comfortable in his presence, forgetting that it was still a beile she was speaking to. Or maybe she believed that she was different to him. That they were different.

Tears stung her eyes, then trickled down the sides of her cheeks.

The intensity in Ye-yang's stare suddenly extinguished. He loosened his grip on her shoulders, raising one hand to her left cheek. With the soft pad of his thumb, he gently wiped away her tears. "I'm sorry," he whispered. "I didn't mean to scare you."

He was leaning closer, so close that she could see each slip of an eyelash framing his clear gray eyes. His lips were almost brushing her own, the touch barely there, featherlight.

She turned her head aside.

"Ye-yang, you can't . . . I mean, we can't . . ." Her tongue was tied up in knots and her thoughts were equally tangled. Her heart was beating so loudly that she swore he would be able to hear it in the silence of this room.

What was he doing? Why was he being this *confusing*? One moment he looked like he could shred her to pieces, the next he was holding her so tenderly, as if he was afraid that she would run away. Which one was the real him?

The world seemed to go still. Then, Ye-yang abruptly flipped himself over, slipping one arm behind her neck and pulling her closer so her head rested upon his shoulder. Ying remained stiff as a washboard, unable to reconcile the intimacy of their current state.

"Finally," he said, with the hint of a laugh.

"Finally what?"

"You're finally using my name."

Had she? She hadn't even realized, because she had been too astonished by the turn of events. This wouldn't do. She took a deep breath to calm her nerves, then tried to wriggle out of this entirely inappropriate position.

"Don't move." Ye-yang clamped his fingers around her shoulder, holding her firm.

She turned to protest, but when she looked up and saw his face, his dense eyebrows and eyelashes in such close proximity, the words remained trapped down her throat. His eyelids were partially lifted, stormy irises gazing down at her.

"Do you really think I should give in to Erden? Or to any one of my brothers?" he said softly. There was a sincerity in his voice that dissolved her indignance, that made her feel like her opinion mattered.

Was that why he had been angry? Because he cared about what she thought about him?

She let herself relax, sinking against the warmth of his embrace. After a moment's pause, she said, "No. I think you'd do a far better job than any of them, whatever it is you're supposed to do."

That was her honest answer, even though she didn't want him to go. Whatever they were planning at Fu-li sounded like a suicide mission. She glanced at the fingers wrapped around her shoulder, felt the curve of his arm fitting snug against her back. Even if she still wasn't certain what this was—what *they* were—and even as the rational side of her knew that the gulf between them was too wide for anything to ever come out of this, she didn't want to see him in harm's way.

The right corner of his lips tipped upward in a self-deprecating smile. "Thank you," he said, "for being willing to lie to me."

"I'm not lying."

"Mmm."

Ying pried herself free and sat up. "I mean it, I'm not—" The rest of her objection faded into a sigh.

Ye-yang had already fallen asleep, but there was a furrow across his forehead, as if his mind was plagued by unpleasant dreams.

Instead of leaving, as she knew she should, Ying couldn't help but sit quietly for a while longer. Her mind recollected all the things she had seen and heard since coming to Fei. There was so much complexity here that she had never imagined when living in her little bubble on Huarin. There were undercurrents that threatened to pull you under if you weren't careful, and for once she thought she had a glimpse of the reasons behind her father's decision to leave.

But not everyone had the luxury of choice. Ye-yang didn't.

This was where he was born. This was his family and kinsmen. This was the place he supposedly had to call home.

She reached out her hand and gently stroked his hair. Ye-yang's breathing slowed into a deeper, more steady rhythm, the tightness in his muscles relaxing.

But even when it seemed the nightmares had left him, a frown was still etched upon his forehead, adding an air of gravity to his otherwise youthful features. Ying gently touched the space between his brows, letting the warmth of his skin linger against her fingertips. The creases disappeared and the tension dissipated.

"Much better," she said.

Then, without a thought, she bent over and touched her lips lightly to his forehead. A stolen kiss. Yet another transgression she probably should not have committed. The realization of what she had done sent a rush of blood to her head, and she quickly stepped away from the bed and hurried toward the door.

At the soft click of the doors shutting behind her, a pair of pensive gray eyes fluttered open.

CHAPTER 10

Ying sat cross-legged on the hard platform, rubbing her bleary eyes. Her head was protesting against the shortage of restful sleep, a result of tossing and turning for most of the night with a confusing mosaic of her father, Ye-yang, and cannons cycling through her mind. The frenzy taking place in front of her didn't help.

"What's going on?" she mumbled. "It's not even daybreak yet."

The other apprentice hopefuls were scrambling around the room as if they were imbued with the energy of a dozen suns. A couple of socks and shoes flew overhead. Undergarments too.

"Wake up!" Chang-en grabbed her by the shoulders and gave her a hard shake. "We have to report for the first test."

"The first test?"

Of course, the guild's first apprenticeship test was today. By tomorrow, perhaps half—or maybe all—of the candidates she was sharing a dormitory with would be sent packing on a one-way ticket home. If Gerel had anything to say about it, she would be one of those tragic failures.

Ying immediately leapt up as reality struck her like a

sledgehammer. Most of their roommates were already awake (some might not have even slept), clutching books and scrolls in their hands. One of them was staring at his copy of the *Annals* so hard he would probably start ripping pages off and gobbling them soon. Ying herself had contemplated burning all her books into ash and then swallowing it together with her tea—an old wives' tale that was supposed to help one ace any examination.

"Why would he need to do that?" Ye-kan's voice appeared on her other side. He had put on his straw hat and was calmly adjusting its veil. "He's not going to make the cut anyway."

"Neither are you, if I rip this ridiculous hat off later." Ying reached out and yanked the offensive hat off Ye-kan's head. She was too anxious to be in a mood to entertain the kid's snide remarks.

Everyone gaped.

"What in Abka Han's name happened to you?" Chang-en exclaimed.

Bulging blisters littered Ye-kan's baby-smooth skin, and a few were even oozing a grotesque mix of blood and yellowish pus. It reminded Ying of the victim of ming-roen ore that she had seen on Muci, and her stomach did a backflip.

"Allergic reaction," Ye-kan answered. "Now, if you don't mind." He snatched his hat back from Ying and replaced it on his head, much to everyone else's relief.

"That is some allergy you've got," Chang-en said. "Keep that on." He rubbed his own chest ruefully. "Good thing I haven't had breakfast yet." A large plate of steamed buns sat on the table by the doorway, but no one had any appetite this morning.

Ying leaned over and hissed into Ye-kan's ear, "Allergic reaction? Really?"

"I had to take precautions."

The four beiles would be attending today's test, but with Ye-kan's face looking like a festering minefield, no one would focus their attentions on him long enough to recognize the fourteenth prince under that carnage. Ying twisted her lips together and shook her head. The kid was determined to stay in the guild, that much she was convinced of. She couldn't confess to understanding why.

Ye-kan was the only son of Lady Odval, the High Commander's principal wife, and had been brought up in the lap of absolute luxury. For someone like him, who could get anything he wanted at the snap of his fingers, it was perplexing to imagine why he would put himself through the suffering of the guild's apprenticeship trial when he could probably order them to take him in. Maybe it was pride, maybe it was sheer folly.

The shock from Ye-kan's horrific reveal quickly passed. When the first rays of dawn streamed in, the nervous candidates filed out of the room and headed for the main hall, where the guild masters would be waiting.

"What do you think the question for today's test will be?" Chang-en asked as they wound their way down the corridors.

"Don't know." Ying shrugged.

"Last year, the test question was about the history of the wheel. That's at least three thousand years' worth!"

That definitely qualified as a test of patience and diligence, Ying thought. Also, a test question that she would have no means of completing. Gerel's history lessons were the dreariest of the bunch, and his obvious dislike for her made his classes even more torturous.

The hopefuls spilled into the main hall, where rows of small, low tables had been set up, each carrying sheets of blank parchment, an ink slab, and a few brushes. Everyone slid into their assigned seats wordlessly. At the front of the hall, four of the five chairs were filled, the masters all wearing stern, dour expressions on their faces. Master Lianshu was still missing in action, as he had been from day one.

Ying stared at the empty chair. One incentive of surviving the first test was being able to start on Strategy lessons, and the thought of that made her heart clench. Her father had been obsessed with governance and strategy. He once told her, "*Without a proper understanding of the big picture, you'll never be able to fulfill your true potential. We shouldn't build for ourselves—build for the people. Build to make a difference.*"

She'd never taken his words to heart before. For her,

engineering had always been about creating for herself. Her flight devices, her dart-shooting fan, all of them were petty vanity projects that served no purpose but to curb her own boredom.

The model airship hanging above was different. *That* was engineering at its finest. *That* was the kind of invention that had far-reaching impact, that changed the face of society and ushered in a new era. Everything that she had learned since coming to the guild—of transportation systems, irrigation tools, household and commercial mechanical constructs, even the design of artificial limbs and the intricate chimeras—all of it felt so big and important. So *meaningful.*

Her father had worked on glorious things like that.

She stared at the airship model for a long while, until Grand Master Quorin's grating voice cut through the air. The snowy-haired master had stepped up onto the platform.

"Good morning, candidates, it has been a while since I last addressed you," he said. "The masters have been giving me regular updates about your progress."

Ying caught Gerel's eye and swore that she saw his lips twitch into a barely noticeable smirk.

"Most of you seem to be coping well, but we will only know what that means after reviewing the outcome of your test. There is no fixed number of candidates who will be allowed to progress to the next stage of the trial. Out of the hundred-odd candidates here, we will cull as many as required to maintain guild standards."

There was an audible sucking in of breath from the candidates. Ying took a quick look around the hall. Chang-en had his eyes closed, his lips making small, rapid movements—probably reciting lines from the *Annals* that he had been cramming in the morning. An-xi was pretending to be calm, but his left cheek was twitching every now and then, betraying his nerves. Arban had his head bowed, looking more subdued than usual. There were others who had gone white in the face, and a rare few who looked on the verge of retching.

Ying repeatedly clenched her fists, her palms getting clammy. She had tried her best to prepare herself for this day, but she wasn't sure it would be enough. After all, she never had the orthodox training that the other boys had. When she turned back toward the front of the hall, her gaze suddenly met a pair of cool gray eyes.

Ye-yang had just entered the hall together with the other beiles, and they were moving toward the seats that had been arranged for them.

Ying felt her cheeks warming. Did he remember what happened last night? Did he know what she had done?

Probably not, she thought, trying to convince herself of that fact. He had been drunk, and asleep.

"Without further ado, we will reveal the question for the

first test," Quorin announced. He walked over to the wooden frame that was standing on the platform, upon which a rolled-up scroll had been hung. Quorin reached for the string that was binding the scroll, undoing the knot with his wrinkled fingers.

All the candidates were staring at those hands, willing him to move a little faster.

The scroll dropped, unfurling with a flourish to reveal a simple line of characters from top to bottom.

Discuss the introduction and evolution of the airship within the nine isles.

It was not an easy topic.

The concept of an airship was born from beyond the borders of the nine isles and even the Great Jade Empire, brought to their shores by traveling green-eyed merchants from lands so far removed that Ying sometimes wondered if they really existed. Unlike the Empire, the Antarans didn't have the filled coffers needed to pay the mercenaries for their awe-inspiring vessels, so the masters of the Engineers Guild had had to design and build the airships from scratch, based on what little they had seen from the Empire's displays of military might.

One might go so far as to call them thieves, pilfering the ideas of others. But for the nine isles, the birth of the first Antaran airship was a turning point in history that they would never regret.

"You have until the sun sets to complete your essays," Quorin said. "You may begin." A senior apprentice struck a bronze gong, its loud toll echoing and reverberating across the hall.

There was a flurry of activity as the young hopefuls picked up their brushes and began frantically grinding their ink slabs. Some began writing immediately, as if ten hours wouldn't be enough for them to vomit everything they knew onto parchment. The masters got up from their chairs and began patrolling the aisles, peering down at the words that were quickly appearing on sheets of rice paper. When Gerel walked past Ying and her blank sheets, he let out one of his regular harrumphs and hurried on.

Ying sat there staring at her empty sheet for a long time. Her brushes lay untouched by the side, her fingers choosing to fold and unfold the edges of the rice paper repeatedly instead.

She knew what she should be putting down—each of the masters had spent several lessons discussing airship history and construction in extensive detail—but there was that niggling uncertainty at the back of her mind that she needed to untangle before she could pick up the brush.

She looked up at the dusty keel dangling overhead, the voice of her father echoing in her mind from a distant past.

"*The airship isn't just* any *ship, my precious lamb*," he used to say while they lay with their backs against the grassy plain, staring up at the black orbs floating across the azure skies. *"It represents the Antaran dream—and the Antaran future. No one thought we were capable of such wonder, but we showed them. We sent our people to the skies, on a craft built solely with Antaran hands, and now we can cross oceans in less than half the time. The world has shrunk because we can fly."*

"But, A-ma, we didn't come up with the idea," she had replied, rubbing her nose snootily. *"We copied it off someone else."*

Her father had laughed, and then he ruffled her hair affectionately, like always. *"No, we didn't. But no one has a monopoly on ideas, lamb, and that is the beauty of it. The same idea, in the heads of two different people"*—he tapped her lightly on the forehead—*"can take on wildly different forms, spinning vastly different magic. Antarans didn't invent the idea of an airship, but the airships that patrol our skies are not the same as the ones that hover over the Empire, or the ones owned by the green-eyed strangers from beyond."*

She remembered that exact moment when he had whipped out a miniature model of an airship, bent from reeds and bamboo strips, and placed it in her little hands. She pulled the string hanging from its rear, and her heart sang when she saw how the tiny wooden propellers rotated.

"This is only the beginning, not the end. Our airships will continue to evolve, to change into forms that we may no longer recognize. But they will only get better, won't they? Because that is what it means to progress, and progress will never cease."

She had nodded confidently then, the gears in her little mind rotating in unison with the propellers, imagining what magic she could infuse into her very own airship one day.

Only the beginning, not the end.

Something clicked in Ying's mind.

The introduction and evolution of the airship within the nine isles, she read, letting each character on the scroll slowly sink in. At first glance it sounded like a question about the past, but what value was the past if it couldn't inform the future?

She finally picked up her brush.

The hall was steeped in nervous silence for the rest of the day, disrupted only by the occasional rustling of paper and tapping of brush ends against tables. Midway, a minor commotion broke out a few rows behind Ying, when one of the masters tried to make Ye-kan remove his hat, only to retract his instruction when the boy briefly lifted his veil. The fourteenth prince's strategy worked beautifully—no such interruption happened again for the remainder of the test. Outside, the sun moved across the sky toward the end of its daily trajectory, until it began to set against the backdrop of Fei's ostentatious pagodas. As the light streaming in from the hall's open doors started to wane, there was a palpable increase in the tension and anxiety within the four walls.

Only a handful of candidates had finished. Everyone else

was writing with such ferocity that their wrists were in real danger of fracture.

Ying put down her last string of characters onto the sheet, then set down her brush with a flourish. She rotated her aching neck as she carefully skimmed through the stack of pages she had filled. There were only five sheets, far less than what she could see in the hands of her fellow candidates, but she had given it her all and that would have to be enough. Just when she had finished stacking her sheets in the correct order, the gong rang out once more, signaling the end of the first test.

"Time's up!" Quorin's voice boomed across the hall.

Some heads immediately went collapsing down onto their tables in sheer exhaustion, while others struggled to get another few characters in. Ying took a quick glance at her peers. Chang-en, An-xi, and Arban all looked composed and confident, as was expected of the beiles' nominated candidates and front-runners in the competition. Compared to them, Ying felt like a weed.

"Check that your candidate number has been written at the top right corner of every page. The masters will be coming around to collect your submissions now."

When Gerel stopped beside her table to pick up her script, he flicked through the stack and scoffed, "Only five pages? I wonder where you inherited that overconfidence from. Typical." He shoved it to the bottom of his pile and continued moving down the row.

Once all the scripts had been accounted for, Quorin turned his attention back to the candidates. "Your responses will be assessed by the guild masters, and the list of candidates who qualify for the next stage of the trial will be released tomorrow morning. Those who fail will have to pack your belongings and leave the guild immediately," he said. "If there's nothing else, you're dismissed."

The candidates leapt up from their seats and the hall descended into chaos. Chang-en came running up to Ying, gangly limbs flailing with excitement.

"Can you believe it? That was such an easy question!" he exclaimed, clapping Ying on the shoulder so hard that it hurt. "Classic Antaran engineering piece. I memorized the entire history of airship development when I was six." Pride exuded from his voice.

An-xi, who had been sitting just one row in front of Ying, overheard Chang-en's remark and said, "I finished that at five."

"Right." Ying scooped up her things and smiled stiffly, the little confidence she had in her own work slowly ebbing away.

"Min probably learned it all before he could even talk," Chang-en retorted, as if Ying's achievements could be used for his own bragging rights just because they were considered good friends. He tapped Ying's shoulder. "I wrote all about your father's creation of the air cannons, right down to every minute detail. If he were still alive, I'd be begging him to take me as his disciple."

Ying fought to avoid stopping short as the chatter continued.

"As if he'd want to take in a wreck like you," An-xi remarked. His delicate nose wrinkled up in his usual snooty manner, which, when framed by his considerably large ears, reminded Ying of a mouse sniffing for food. "It's not fair. I'm going to lodge an official complaint with the guild masters about the choice of test question. Aihui Min has an advantage over the rest of us because his father created the cannons. He'd have access to more information than we would."

"Stop being sour, Niohuru. You're just jealous that Min has a better engineering pedigree than the rest of us. Your complaint won't make any difference. The first beile told me that we're pretty much guaranteed a pass in at least the first round. The guild has to grant the beiles that much allowance, as a mark of respect for the High Command."

"I know. Not that I need that free pass. I would have qualified even if we were competing fair and square."

Ying had stopped registering the argument that was still taking place between Chang-en and An-xi, and the rest of their discussion in the background faded away.

Her father's *creation* of the air cannons? How did she not know something as important as that? She had been standing right next to those cannons; she had touched the cold metal surface of their barrels and shuddered at the thought of their destructive power, but she hadn't known that those weapons came out of her own father's hands. She recalled the pages in his secret journal, filled with intricate details about cannon design. He hadn't just been studying someone else's work and improving on it—he had been iterating his own creation.

What else did she not know about him?

Ying felt her chest clenching. She couldn't breathe. She needed to get out of here.

She turned and ran for the doors.

"Hey, Min, where're you going?" Chang-en was calling out to her.

She was going to find answers—now.

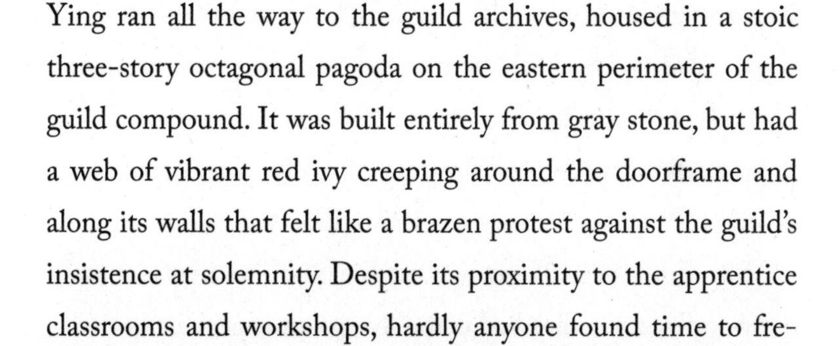

Ying ran all the way to the guild archives, housed in a stoic three-story octagonal pagoda on the eastern perimeter of the guild compound. It was built entirely from gray stone, but had a web of vibrant red ivy creeping around the doorframe and along its walls that felt like a brazen protest against the guild's insistence at solemnity. Despite its proximity to the apprentice classrooms and workshops, hardly anyone found time to frequent its many shelves. Everyone wanted to create guild history, not read about it.

She pushed open the heavy lacquered doors, and the first thing that struck her was the clean fragrance wafting through the air that smelled like freshly brewed jasmine tea. The interior of the archives was entirely different from what she had expected. Instead of musty hallways and dusty shelves left crumbling from disuse, everything was spick-and-span, and the books and scrolls were arranged even more neatly than those in the classrooms.

Soft humming came drifting from the upper floors.

An archive keeper? she wondered. It wouldn't be surprising, given how tidy the place was.

The humming stopped.

"Who's that!" a sharp voice called out.

A *woman's* voice.

Ying instinctively gravitated toward the stairs, eager to find out who it belonged to. Since entering the guild, she had not seen a single woman on the premises. Who was up there?

But the moment she lifted her foot and stepped forward, she knew that something was wrong. Her ankle caught on something—a fine string—and the loud whirring of cogs started up.

Hiss. Panels slid open from the walls.

She threw herself flat against the floor, narrowly missing the wooden darts that had come flying out from all sides. Her breath caught in her throat, heart thumping inside her chest. Had she been a moment slower, she would have been impaled by the sharp tips of those darts.

When she was certain that there were no more projectiles zipping overhead, Ying flipped herself onto her back, studying her surroundings warily. The thin, spider silk–like thread that she had tripped over glistened beside her. She reached out and plucked it.

More cogs whirred.

More hidden panels revealed themselves. This time, they exposed narrow bamboo tubes that began issuing ominous gray smoke.

Damn.

She had thought that triggering the mechanism once more might expel another round of darts, but this was far more insidious and difficult to escape. Ying quickly pressed her sleeve over her nose and mouth, hoping that she hadn't unwittingly released some poisonous gas that would leave her bleeding from all orifices. The front doors had already locked shut and there were no visible windows in this place. Even the way up to the second floor of the pagoda had been blocked by a sliding panel when the booby trap was activated.

Whoever designed this had covered all bases.

Think, Ying, think.

Her eyes swept across the octagonal room, searching for an alternative exit. When she found none, she picked herself up and followed the trail of the translucent thread to one of its ends attached to the wall. As expected, a panel lay camouflaged in the stone.

Ying frantically tapped all around the panel, then moved to search the nearby shelves for any sign of the lever that would open the hatch. Her lungs strained to cling on to that single breath she was holding. Then she found it—a heavy book sitting on a top shelf that couldn't be swept off. She grabbed the book by the spine and gave it a hard tug.

Something clicked, and the panel swung open to reveal a medley of wooden gears.

There was no time to figure out how the mechanism worked. Already the smoke filled half the room and a pungent, acrid smell stung her nose. Ying grabbed a stone paperweight off a shelf and smashed it into the entire set of cogs. She looked down to the pipe—the smoke was dissipating.

"Stop! What do you think you're doing!"

The door that had sealed the way to the upstairs levels opened once again, and a petite figure came pounding down the stairs, rushing over toward Ying. She wore similar robes to a guild master, but in a shade of flamboyant vermilion instead of somber maroon. Covering her face entirely was a copper gas mask with two circular eyeholes covered with frosted yun-mu glass that magnified her eyes in a frog-like manner. A mop of long, frizzy hair hung from the back of her head in a messy plait.

"Aieee!" The woman shoved Ying aside and picked up the broken pieces of splintered wood lying on the floor. "You've destroyed everything. How could you!"

"If I didn't, I'd have choked to death," Ying replied with a cough, though the air was clearing up through the now-open stairway.

"Nonsense. No one dies that easily," the woman snapped. She whirled around and glared angrily at Ying, making her bulging eyes look even more comical. In her hands she held a strange-looking contraption that looked like a small metal pitchfork, barely the length of one's forearm. Tiny sparks flitted from one prong to the next, threatening to burst out into a larger ball of flames. Ying did not want to imagine what would happen if any of it came into contact with her clothes or skin. "Who are you? Are you here to steal something?"

"No!" Ying pulled her wooden pendant off its cord and held it up. "I'm a member of the guild. Aren't all guild members supposed to be able to access the material in the archives?" She remembered Gerel mentioning this in passing during his first History class, though no one really paid any attention.

The woman took a glance at her pendant and scoffed, lowering her weapon. "You're only a trial candidate. Candidates aren't considered official members of the guild until you've passed the apprenticeship trial. Don't think I don't know that. Since you're new, I'll let this slide. Now shoo while I'm still talking to you nicely."

Ying hardly considered it a "nice" welcome, not when she had nearly died within these walls.

"Please," she pleaded, "there's something important I need to find out. I just need a short while. Half an hour—no, a quarter of that. My father was once a member of the guild. I want to take a look at his old record books. It would mean the world to me."

"Well, ask your father, then, you foolish child! Get out, get out."

"I can't," Ying cried. "If I could, then I would, but I can't. He's not around anymore." She wished so hard that she could get one more day with her father so that she could ask him all the questions she had, so that she could find out about the part of his life that he had kept such a closely guarded secret, even from his own family. She loved him so much, yet there was so much to him that was a mystery to her.

The woman folded her arms across her chest, pursing her lips together in a pout as she gave Ying's plea some thought. "What is your father's name?" she finally asked.

"Aihui Shan-jin."

The pause seemed to drag on forever as Ying waited for the archive keeper to respond. Her father's name always seemed to trigger *some* reaction in the guild members, for better or worse, so she hoped it would serve the intended effect here.

Unfortunately, it didn't.

"Do you think you can lie to me like that?" the woman suddenly shouted, her voice rising to a painfully shrill pitch that rattled Ying's eardrums. "Get out. I don't want to see you step foot in here ever again. Get out!"

She grabbed Ying by the collar and lifted her up with surprising strength for her small frame, hauling the younger girl over to the doors. With one forceful shove, Ying was thrown out onto the grass. The doors slammed shut with a resounding bang.

Ying scrambled back to her feet and pushed at the doors. They were locked.

"I'm not lying. Please let me take a look at my father's record books, I'm begging you!"

"Bullshit! I'm not gullible enough to fall for your tricks," the woman's voice came yelling from the other side. "You're one of those cunning liars trying to prey on my good nature to trick me into letting you steal Shan-jin's work. Let me teach you a lesson, kid—no amount of plagiarism will help you become a great engineer. Not everyone can be like Aihui Shan-jin."

The doors remained firmly shut.

CHAPTER 11

After her unceremonious expulsion from the guild archives, Ying trudged back to the apprentice quarters, a dozen questions swirling inside her head. She hadn't achieved what she set out to do, but she had come away with an interesting discovery—that there was another woman in the guild, the first and only she had seen since coming here. Even though she might only be an archive keeper, it did provide a glimmer of hope that someday, the guild would accept Ying the way it had accepted this woman.

Then her thoughts turned—the archive keeper seemed to have known her father personally, judging from the explosiveness of her reaction.

I have to find another chance to speak to her, she thought.

The dormitories were darkened. It was bath hour, and the other boys would likely spend a long time washing away the stress from today's test—and passing snide remarks about who was going to get the axe at daybreak.

It was just as well. She wasn't in the mood for small talk.

Before she even reached the door of her dormitory, she already spotted the hazy shadow standing inside. She frowned.

Was it one of her other roommates? If it was, then he had better not be half-naked, or else her bad day would hit rock bottom. The closer she got, the more defined the man's silhouette became.

He was rummaging through things—belongings that were kept in the small trunks given to each of them on the first day they arrived. He could be digging through *her* things.

"What do you think you're doing?" she yelled, rushing into the room.

Under the dim illumination from the gas lamps hanging along the corridor, she could just about make out the intruder's outfit. A plain dark suit covered him from head to toe, revealing only a pair of narrow eyes, and a frightening scar cutting across one of them.

Panic coursed through Ying's veins. It was him again, the same man who had killed her father and had nearly gotten to her on Muci.

The intruder flung his right arm out, and a flurry of darts came shooting out from his sleeve.

Ying quickly threw herself to the side, but she wasn't fast enough. A sharp pain struck her left shoulder and forearm. She instinctively reached for her fan and then cursed inwardly when she remembered that her only reasonable weapon wasn't there. She was completely unarmed.

"Help! There's an intruder!" Ying started shouting at the top of her lungs, clambering toward the open doors. "Somebody help!"

With nothing to fight with, calling for help was her best chance of survival. She had no means of winning in hand-to-hand combat, and she was already injured. If she didn't sound the alarm, her throat would be slit within the next minute. Her heart pounded frantically inside her chest.

As she looked back, the man swung his other arm and five more darts shot out, flying toward her head.

Ying dropped to the ground. The tiny silver needles flew overhead, piercing through the wooden ledge at the base of the doorway. Looking to the side, she spotted a string of rosary beads lying on the ground. It was Chang-en's. She remembered seeing him use it to meditate and pray for good luck in the trial. If only the gods could bless her with some of that luck now.

She lunged and grabbed the beads, then rolled left to hide behind one of her roommates' trunks. With one hard tug, she snapped the rosary string, then flung the entire chain in the direction of her attacker. In the darkness, the man stepped on a few loose beads and lost balance, stumbling in his approach.

Ying seized the chance to run. She scrambled out through the doorway and into the corridor.

Her mind spun. It felt like a million ants were gnawing at her injured arm. She took a quick glance down. The veins across the back of her hand had turned a ghoulish shade of purple, like someone had painted a spider's web on her skin.

Poison.

The darts were laced with poison.

Her vision blurred and her knees buckled. Turning back, she saw the man was walking toward her. A blade glinted in his hand.

No, I can't die now, she told herself. There were too many things that she still needed to do, too many questions unanswered in her mind. It would be a terrible irony if her life were to end tonight, under the exact same circumstances as her father's death, at the hands of the same man.

"Aihui Min!"

Urgent footsteps pounded in her direction. Help was arriving.

In her delirious state, Ying saw someone sprinting down the corridor toward her, the blurred outline of a straw hat bobbing up and down. She should have been elated, but the pain that was burning through her arm was too much to think.

Maybe I'm not going to die today. Maybe . . .

Her world went black.

When she opened her eyes, a flickering oil lamp was wobbling precariously overhead, courtesy of the light breeze. Ying was lying on a bed of prickly straw. She turned to her left and realized that she was not alone. The stall she was in already had an inhabitant, who was stomping his back hooves and flaring his nostrils as if to convey his displeasure at having to share accommodation.

"You're awake?"

She turned to the other side. Ye-kan was sitting there with his back against the wooden paneling of the horse's stall, his veiled hat lying on the straw beside him. He wore a stiff, uncomfortable expression, made slightly comical by the fake blisters on his face.

Ying struggled to sit up, but when she put weight on her left arm, the burning sensation flared up once again. She winced, collapsing back down on the hay. "How long have I been out?" she asked.

Her heart tremored at the thought of her near brush with death. Had Ye-kan not showed up when he did, she would already be reunited with her parents on the other side, having accomplished nothing since coming here. The sight of the assassin's scar flashed across her mind's eye—as did the memory of her father's blood staining her hands.

He knows that I'm here.

She wasn't certain if the assassin knew who she really was, but using the Aihui name in the guild trial had placed her in danger. She was no longer safe, not even within these heavily guarded walls.

"It's probably been less than one stick of incense worth of

time." Ye-kan could barely look at her. "You were attacked. I think it might have been a robbery. Everything in the dormitory was in a mess."

Ying waited for the rest of the story, but Ye-kan just sat there fiddling with his own fingers instead, looking like he had no intention of continuing.

"What happened to the . . . thief?"

"He escaped through the window when I ran over. Don't know why anyone would think of robbing the place though. All your bundles are filled with cheap clothes and useless books." Ye-kan paused, then he yelped, "Wait a minute, what if he was trying to steal *my* things? What if someone knows I'm here!"

Ying rolled her eyes. The kid was too dramatic. He needed to get over his princeling attitude. Their other roommates heralded from distinguished clans across the nine isles—hardly the poor riffraff that he always described them to be.

"What are we doing in the stables then?" Ying croaked. Propping herself up with her good arm this time, she sat up, taking another look at their surroundings.

"You got poisoned," Ye-kan replied, his eyes darting furtively from left to right, refusing to meet Ying's gaze head-on. He was wringing his fingers, then pulling at them one by one to make them pop.

Ying glanced down at her injured arm. The purple streaks she remembered seeing on the back of her hand had faded, and although her arm still hurt, it felt considerably better than when she had fainted at the dormitory doorway. She slid her sleeve up—no weblike venation there either.

"I pulled out the needles and gave you an antidote to help clear the poison," Ye-kan added when he saw her examining her arm. He tossed the two innocuous, shiny culprits onto her lap. "Do you know how valuable that was? Only our clan physicians know the formula. It treats almost all known poisons. I had just the one."

"Thanks," Ying murmured.

"That's all?" Ye-kan leapt up to his feet, bristling with irritation. "After everything I did for you, that's all I get? I should have just left you there to die—or let your secret be discovered first, and *then* die."

Her secret?

The realization dawned. Ying clapped one hand over her mouth, her other hand clutching on to the front of her top in alarm. She was passed out when Ye-kan had found her. If their roles were reversed and she had been the one to discover an injured man lying on the ground, the first thing she would have done would be to remove his robes to check the wound.

Ye-kan knew. He knew that she was a girl.

"Stop looking at me like that!" the prince yelled. "What do you take me for? Some kind of pervert? You're not even worth a second glance." Realizing his words could be misconstrued,

Ye-kan quickly shook his head and corrected himself. "What I meant is that you're not the least bit attractive—I mean, I didn't see anything except the, the, the—" He waved his hand about his chest, trying desperately to convey his meaning, to no avail. He sighed, sinking back down onto the straw in resignation. "I didn't see anything," he muttered.

Ying could guess what the prince was trying to drive at. She had bound her chest with white bandages so that she would look more convincing as a boy, so if Ye-kan had attempted to remove her clothes to check her injuries, that was likely the first and only thing he saw before he panicked.

Looking at his blushing cheeks and sour expression, she couldn't resist letting out a light laugh. Her anxiety dissipated.

"Thank you," she repeated herself, slowly and sincerely. "Not just for saving my life, but also for helping me keep my secret."

Ye-kan wasn't obliged to do either, but he had done both. Now she realized why they were sitting in the stables. If he had called for help or left her there for someone else to find her, then the guild physicians would have been summoned and her identity would be exposed. Instead, he had gone through the trouble of sacrificing his antidote and transporting her here, just so her secret would be safe. She owed him one.

The prince sniffled, looking somewhat appeased. "I didn't do it for you," he said. "I did it for myself. Now that I know your secret, you can't go blurting mine." He folded his arms across his chest, a smug smile appearing.

Ying shook her head. "You're really determined to stay in the guild, aren't you?" she asked.

"Of course!"

"But why? You're a prince. You could enjoy life in your manor with every material comfort a person could wish for. When you come of age, the High Commander will grant you a title and possibly even give you command over one of the Eight Banners. Isn't that good enough a life for you?"

"Who wants that?" Ye-kan scoffed. "I'm going to be the best engineer the nine isles have ever seen. One day I'll be the grand master of this guild, just like my grandfather." He puffed up his chest like a proud peacock. "As if *you* can talk, anyway. What's a girl like you doing in the guild? You can't be Aihui Min, so who are you really?"

"His sister, Aihui Ying," she admitted. After a moment's hesitation, she said, "My father used to be a guild master. I want to follow in his footsteps, but I can't because the guild doesn't accept female apprentices."

It wasn't the whole story, but it would have to do.

Two people now knew of her hidden identity—Ye-yang and Ye-kan. She hadn't yet told Ye-yang the whole truth about her being here, and she wasn't sure she trusted Ye-kan enough to reveal everything. If word of her investigation reached the ears of the mastermind, then she would come to regret her candor.

"You? A guild master?" Ye-kan threw his head back and laughed till the tears spilled from his eyes. "You're a *girl.* Why would you even think of becoming an engineer? The guild isn't for *girls.*"

"Oh, is that right?" Ying slowly picked herself off the hay, groaning as pain shot through her arm. She ambled toward Ye-kan, who instinctively leaned back and eyed her suspiciously.

"What are you doing?"

Scowling, Ying grabbed hold of his left ear and gave it a hard twist. "If a girl like me can't be in the guild, then neither can a kid like you," she scolded. "If I hear you spout such chauvinistic rubbish one more time, I'm going straight to the fourth beile to have you dragged back home. Have I made myself clear?"

"You wouldn't dare!"

"Try me."

Ying let go, proceeding to ruffle Ye-kan's hair the way she did to her younger siblings. Fire spouted from his eyes as he pushed her hand away. Smiling, Ying pushed open the door to the stall and headed for the stable doors. If they lingered for too long, the others would start getting suspicious.

A small crowd had gathered in their dormitory when Ying and Ye-kan returned, including Master Gerel. Raised voices spoke over one another, arguing about what had taken place. No one even noticed the duo entering the room, their attentions fixated upon the shambles around them.

Now that the lamps were lit, Ying could see the full extent of the disarray caused by the intruder. The mess was mostly restricted to her half of the room, although it wasn't only her trunk whose lock had been cracked and items ransacked. There were at least three other trunks that lay open, clothes, books, and personal trinkets strewn haphazardly around.

Ye-kan, who had since replaced his straw hat to avoid getting questioned by Gerel, pushed his way through the crowd, shoving past the others. He rushed to his own sleeping corner and flung aside the folded blanket that he had hidden his trunk under. When he saw that its lock was still intact, the young prince exhaled in relief.

"Where have you been?" one of their roommates asked. "You weren't with us at the baths earlier."

"Of course I wasn't. Why would I ever share a bath with all of *you*?"

The tall, hulking giant who shared their room—Muke—straightened out his back and seemed to grow a few inches, cracking his knuckles menacingly. He blew at his fist and swung it toward the oblivious Ye-kan. Ying could already see this ending in blood.

"Stop this nonsense!" Gerel bellowed.

Muke's arm froze in midair, his fist just a brush-width away from the veil that covered Ye-kan's face. The prince had backed himself into a corner, still hugging his trunk.

"This is the Engineers Guild, not some brawling pit. If you want to throw punches, then enroll in the military." Gerel jabbed at the foreheads of the gormless boys that were standing closest to him. "Clear up the mess and go to bed—all of you!"

"But, Master Gerel," Muke started, "aren't you going to question him?" He jerked his thumb in Ye-kan's direction. "He was nowhere to be seen during bath hour and his trunk's untouched."

Gerel rubbed his temple, eyelids fluttering in exasperation. "Fine," he said. "Bayara Ye-kan, where were you earlier?"

"Around," Ye-kan replied vaguely.

"Why weren't you with the rest of them?"

"He has a bad skin reaction, remember?" Ying voiced out from behind the horde, keeping her head down so that no one would notice that she was one shade paler than normal. "If he used the common baths, he could have spread it to everyone." It was a good thing that Ye-kan had drawn the attention away from her, but knowing the fourteenth prince, he was too stubborn and prideful to extricate himself from this hole, and the longer this dragged out, the more likely he was going to let something slip.

Everyone suddenly remembered the pus-infested face they

had witnessed in the morning. Someone made a retching noise.

"That's it then. It was probably a prank by one of the boys in the other dormitories," Gerel said dismissively. "None of you have anything worth stealing anyway. Now go to bed unless you want your name scratched off the list for the next stage of the trial."

"But why would they break the locks then? Isn't that a lot of effort to go through just for a prank?" Muke offered.

A storm started brewing on Gerel's face, his eyes narrowing dangerously as they swept across the crowd of young faces. "I already said, there is nothing to investigate here. It would be prudent if all of you stopped wasting time on conspiracy theories and spent more of it studying your books," he barked. "Pack up and go to sleep!"

The boys moved quickly. Those whose belongings had been ransacked scooped everything up and shoved them back into their trunks. The rest of them leapt onto the platform and pulled their covers up. The lamps were hurriedly extinguished.

Gerel stood by the doorway and surveyed the room. Once satisfied, he huffed and slammed the doors shut, footsteps retreating briskly down the corridor.

"It *wasn't* a prank," Muke's deep voice rang out in the darkness. "Those locks were broken by a professional. One stroke of the blade. I've seen my father's men slice through locks like that before."

"Shut up," Chang-en said. "Master Gerel already closed the case and no one lost anything. Go to sleep."

There was a little more grumbling, then loud snoring took over.

Ying lay there staring up at the ceiling, pondering the events that had transpired. Even the other boys could tell that it hadn't been a prank, not with the way the locks had been sliced like tofu. But why did Master Gerel brush it aside, eager to label it as a mere case of mischief? What if he had known about the intrusion from the start—and collaborated with the scarred assassin? The fact that the assassin had managed to breach the guild's tight security would suggest that there was an insider working with him. The rivalry between Gerel and her father drifted back to mind, and the seed of suspicion that had already been planted inside her sprouted ugly roots.

She sat up, lifting the blanket to reveal the messy pile of garments she had swept aside when they all jumped into bed. Opening up her trunk in the dark, she started folding her clothes one by one and placing each item neatly back in the wooden box. Picking up the broken lock, she ran her fingers along the smooth edge, shuddering at the thought of the man's sword plunged into her chest.

Ying glanced to her right. Ye-kan was curled against the wall with his hat over his face, still cuddling his small trunk to his chest as if afraid that someone would steal it in his sleep.

She lay back down, pulling the blanket up over her shoulders. The pain in her arm had subsided into a mild tingling sensation, yet it still provided a harrowing reminder of the poison that had flowed through her blood.

"You weren't with us at the baths either," Chang-en suddenly whispered from her left.

Ying startled. "I don't like the common baths. You know that." She angled herself away from Chang-en, afraid that he would see through her excuses.

"Where were you, then?"

"Are you accusing me of something?"

"No, you're so scrawny you probably can't even lift a sword, much less slice those locks in two. Just—where did you go after the test? You ran off all of a sudden."

"I went to the guild archives," Ying whispered.

"The archives? Whatever for?"

"I wanted to take a look at my father's old record books," Ying said quietly. "Wasn't allowed in." She had been so close. Her father's books were sitting somewhere on those shelves, locked in that pagoda. "Do you know anything about the guild's archive keeper?" she asked, recalling her run-in with the eccentric woman. It felt like such a far-off memory, even though it had only happened earlier in the day.

"No. There's an archive keeper?" her friend replied. When he got no reply, Chang-en sighed, saying, "Your father never told you about any of the things he did while he was in the guild, did he?"

Resentment flared inside her at the reminder of the secrets her father had kept. "He didn't like to talk about his time in Fei," she said.

"Must have been a nasty split with the guild then, looking at how Gerel and the other guild masters are always picking on you. I don't know much more than what I've already told you. You could try asking An-xi though, he might know more. Bookworm." Chang-en yawned. Moments later, Ying could hear his breathing settle into a steady rhythm as he drifted to sleep.

Closing her eyes, Ying tried to do the same.

In her dreams, faceless strangers clad in black chased her through the darkness, with insidious holes where their eyes should have been. She ran as fast as she could, but somehow the cold tips of their swords pricked against the skin of her back. A tiny spot of light appeared in the distance. It grew and grew, until she could make out a figure standing there, beckoning to her.

Her father.

"Ying," his familiar voice called out, like a ray of sunshine piercing through the endless night. He was holding out his hand to her.

She stretched.

Their fingertips touched.

But then, instead of the kindness and warmth that she remembered, her father's eyes flashed with anger. "I told you to burn it. Why didn't you burn it, Ying? Why didn't you listen?"

He was accusing her, berating her for not following instructions. He lowered his hand. He wasn't going to rescue her anymore—she didn't deserve it. She turned her head, only to find that the faceless monsters were still there, hot on her heels, their raised blades gleaming—hungry for blood.

"A-ma, please, I didn't mean to. I just wanted to know the truth. I wanted to know why that book, why those drawings were so important. I wanted to know why you had to die because of it," she cried, desperately clutching at her father's retreating figure. She ran forward, tripping over herself and falling to the ground.

She was kneeling in a puddle. Warm and sticky. Blood. She was kneeling in blood.

She opened her mouth to scream, but no matter how hard she tried, there was no sound coming from her lips. Behind, the distance between her and her pursuers continued to shrink.

The light in front of her was gone now. Her father was gone.

"Ying," another voice called to her. She felt someone's hand on her shoulder, gentle and comforting. She looked up.

It was Ye-yang. He held out his hand to her and she grabbed hold of it gratefully, clutching on to his fingers like a drowning person clinging to a piece of driftwood. He pulled her back up to her feet and lifted her into his arms. Then, he started running. Resting her cheek against his chest, she could hear the slow, rhythmic beating of his heart, like a soothing lullaby.

"You're safe now," he said. "You're safe."

CHAPTER 12

EARLY THE NEXT MORNING, THE EXCITED RUCKUS from the swarm of candidates could be heard long before anyone even got anywhere near the main hall. A wooden frame had been set up in front of the doors—frustratingly empty—intended for displaying the list of successful candidates. It was already past the hour when they had been expecting the results to be released, but still there was no sign of anyone bearing the coveted list.

"Do you think something's wrong?" Chang-en whispered to Ying.

"What could possibly be wrong! It's just a test," An-xi snapped, but the rapid twitching of his narrow brows said otherwise.

An-xi wasn't the only one who was on edge. Several of the other candidates were pacing nervously, a couple had beads of sweat lining their foreheads despite the freezing weather, and there was one doing squats in the middle of the courtyard. Even Arban was strangely withdrawn, looking like a giant bear twiddling thumbs.

"Don't know what you're so worried about," Chang-en said. "We already know we're guaranteed a pass."

"It's not *just* about passing. Passing won't get you top of the list. Passing won't get you into the guild." An-xi pursed his lips together in a thin, hard line, his cheek muscles so tense that they looked close to snapping.

"One step at a time. I'm happy enough to sail through one gate. What's the point of worrying so far ahead?" Chang-en nudged Ying and shrugged his bony shoulders, then he stuck out his tongue at An-xi when the latter turned away. "Always so uptight," he mumbled with a crooked smirk.

The anxiety from the others was like a dense, suffocating cloud that enveloped Ying and swallowed her whole. The longer the suspense dragged, the more jittery she became. Despite Chang-en's reassurance that they would get a free pass through the first test, she wasn't entirely convinced. Gerel and the other masters disliked her too much. Even Ye-yang had warned her that they were unlikely to give up on this opportunity to officially expel her from the guild.

She stared at the blank frame, rubbing both her temples in concentric circles. Her head was throbbing, a side effect of the string of nightmares that had plagued her mind the entire night. She couldn't remember any of them now, but she had woken up drenched in cold sweat, feeling like she had a fever coming on. The sense of dread from her close encounter last night still lingered on, and she couldn't help eyeing her surroundings warily time and again, worried that the scarred assassin might show up.

Even if the guild was no longer safe, she still had to stay on. She needed more time to investigate her father's death—and to prove that she deserved a place here, just like he used to.

She sneezed. And again. The headache got worse and all her efforts at massaging acupoints went to the dogs.

"You should stop by the guild physician's later," Chang-en offered. "Not the best idea to be falling ill in the middle of the trial."

"That's assuming I even make it past today." Ying rubbed her nose, sniffling as she tried to keep her mucus where it belonged. In any case, a trip to the guild physician was out of the question. She didn't go last night when she had been poisoned, so she certainly wasn't going because of a little cold. One tap at her wrist and her pulse would give her away.

The long-awaited list didn't arrive. Instead, the apprentice hopefuls were in for a bigger surprise.

A stream of soldiers dressed in the stiff black uniform of the Cobra's Order came striding through the covered passageway and into the courtyard. Marching like clockwork, they lined the entire square perimeter, with two especially menacing-looking fellows positioning themselves by the entrance of the main hall. Their hands rested purposefully upon the hilts of the swords hanging at their waists, polished black shafts curving at the ends into the fearsome heads of cobras.

Gerel appeared behind them, followed by the other guild

masters. All of them wore grim, stilted expressions on their faces, eyeballs constantly darting backward as if there was a monster lurking in the shadows.

"Master Gerel, what's going on? Where are the results of the test?"

The master's eyes spat fire as he stared down the unobservant fool. "Keep quiet," he said, his hands making impatient sweeping actions. "Clear a path. Clear a path."

The young men obediently stepped to the side, leaving a clear aisle leading toward the doors of the hall. They craned their necks, peering curiously toward the shadowy recesses of the passageway. Ying was too short to get a good look, so all she managed was a peek through the gaps between the other boys' shoulders.

Not long after, Grand Master Quorin emerged, together with the four beiles, but there was someone else with them. Someone unfamiliar.

He was a stern, imposing man with a pair of commanding eyes framed by thick, graying brows and high cheekbones, his head front-shaven in the recent favored style of Antarans, and the rest of his hair bound at the back of his head in a single queue. Thick gold hoops hung from his lobes, his black silk robes embroidered with shimmering gold thread in the pattern of fierce waves and finished with a matching black fur collar and leather gloves.

Ying knew who he was the moment she saw him. It was in the eyes. Gray—like Ye-yang's. Yet they were not identical. There was always a stillness and clarity in Ye-yang's gray irises, but this man had eyes like the storm, mercurial and volatile.

This was the High Commander of the Antaran people—Aogiya Lianzhe. The man who had single-handedly rallied an army and swept across the nine isles, conquering and cajoling, forming alliances and cutting down opponents until the fragmented Antaran clans were all united under one emblem. The mark of the cobra.

There was a sharp intake of breath from the few candidates who recognized the High Commander. The rest were curious and confused, itching to ask their neighbors who he was but not daring to breathe a word under Gerel and the other masters' hawklike stares.

Grand Master Quorin led the High Commander and the four beiles toward the hall's entrance. Once they had gone inside, the guild masters quickly herded the gaggle of young men in.

"I can't believe the High Commander is here," Chang-en murmured as they jostled with the crowd. "Do you think he's here because of the trial?" He shook his head. "Nah, can't be. No reason why he would be interested in us. He probably came to discuss more important business with Quorin and then decided to stick around out of respect."

Ying didn't think the High Commander needed to show anyone any ounce of respect. The deferential, subservient actions of the guild masters spoke volumes of who the master was and who the servants were.

She looked up at the man who had taken the central seat on the raised platform that was usually reserved for the grand master. He was handed a small bronze hand warmer by one of the senior apprentices, whose hands were visibly shaking. Removing his leather gloves, he wrapped his lean fingers calmly around the metal tripod as he listened to Quorin rattle on about something from his left. He tilted his head imperceptibly in a slight nod, and Quorin stood up to face the rows of curious young ones.

Clearing his throat emphatically, the grand master said, "His Excellency the High Commander has graced us with his presence today."

Everyone dropped to their knees and bowed their heads, right fist brought up across their chest in the traditional Antaran salute.

"You may all rise," the High Commander spoke, his voice mellow and resonant, like molten iron flowing through the mold of a sword. "I must apologize for disrupting the guild's plans. I understand the results for the first round of the apprenticeship trial were supposed to be released this morning."

Ying was surprised by how congenial the High Commander

seemed to be. His tone was measured and unhurried, his words courteous and thoughtful.

Back on Huarin, she had heard plenty of stories from the village storyteller about the High Commander—those were a favorite of the ladies, who swooned at every mention of Aogiya Lianzhe's valiant and intrepid conquests. Ying had never been impressed by those stories. To her, they were accounts of violence and gore. So much blood had been spilled—Antaran blood—in exchange for the High Commander's idea of progress and peace. She liked the outcome, but she didn't like the process, and from all those stories she had painted an image of the High Commander in her mind. Someone who was ferocious and bloodthirsty, selfish and arrogant.

Certainly not the same person she was looking at now.

"Not at all, Your Excellency," Quorin replied. "The guild is honored that you can be with us. The results are over here. We can announce it now." He snapped his fingers and a senior apprentice brought out a rolled-up scroll.

Backs straightened immediately and all eyes glued upon the all-important piece of paper that contained their fate.

The High Commander smiled. "Before we do that, I'd like to meet the candidates that the beiles nominated this year," he said. "I've heard much about them. Lady Xana tells me that it would be the guild's loss to not accept her brother, but what would a woman know."

Arban immediately stepped forward, chest puffed up with pride. He turned and gave Ying, Chang-en, and An-xi a smug smirk.

"Bet he thinks he's a shoo-in now," Chang-en muttered as he walked toward the front of the hall together with the other two.

"Arban's a fool. He didn't even catch the undertones in what the High Commander said," An-xi said quietly.

Although Lady Xana was the High Commander's current favorite, everyone knew that the only woman who had some degree of sway was Lady Odval—Ye-kan's mother. It was naive of Arban to believe that his connection to the concubine would bring him any favor. If anything, the High Commander would be less inclined to promote him, for fear that it might strengthen whichever faction Lady Xana's clan was part of.

On her way forward, Ying did a quick search for Ye-kan, but she couldn't spot him anywhere in the crowd. He had probably found some excuse to sneak away, she figured, in case his father caught him here.

The four of them stood in a neat line in front of the raised platform, and only Ying dared not raise her gaze to look at the High Commander. She was an impostor, a fraud, and she felt like the High Commander's piercing gaze would rip her disguise apart. She glanced to the left instead and found Ye-yang looking her way.

He nodded, and the corners of his lips tipped upward ever so slightly.

The dream that Ying had forgotten suddenly revealed itself. His steady heartbeat, the warmth of his chest, the sound of his voice—all of it flooded back into her mind and as she stood there staring at him, the boundaries between dream and reality blurred. Her cheeks burned. She looked away, her heart pounding in her chest.

Chang-en's elbow suddenly jabbed her in the side, jolting her back to the present.

"The High Commander asked you a question," he hissed.

Ying's neck snapped upward, looking toward the man seated on the platform. He was watching her—studying her—the way a snake would carefully size up every element in its surroundings.

In that moment, the High Commander reminded Ying of the cobra she had seen emblazoned on all the airships, banners, and uniforms that belonged to the Cobra's Order.

Back in her childhood when she had been running amok across the Huarin grasslands, she had come across a python circling around one of her rabbit traps. The trap had snared one fluffy victim that Ying had wanted to bring home for Nian as a pet. She squatted some distance away, observing the snake with fascination as it continued making its rounds. Snakes were rare in the nine isles. They didn't fare so well with the cold. The python continued to slither aimlessly, its forked tongue darting in and out of its mouth as it went along.

After a while, Ying tired of the snake's repetitive motion and decided to move on to check some of her other traps instead. She had only just turned away when a low hiss wafted into her ears. She swiveled back. The rabbit that had been whimpering in the trap was gone, with only a bleeding stump remaining—remnants of the foot that had been trapped by the jaws of Ying's bamboo contraption. The rest of that rabbit sat within the belly of the python, who was now staring at Ying with its frightful yellow eyes and slit-like pupils. It spat out its tongue in a victorious hiss, then quickly slithered away through the dense grass.

"Aihui Min," Gerel barked, "what are you doing? Answer the High Commander!"

"He asked why you wrote about airship modifications in your essay," Chang-en added, seeing the dazed look on Ying's face.

Airship modifications? Wait, the High Commander actually *read* her work?

"Oh, umm, the"—Ying stammered, trying to gather her senses—"the question asked us to discuss the introduction and evolution of the airship, so I took that to include the future possible iterations as well." She clenched and unfurled her clammy palms over and over. "I only made a few suggestions . . ."

"That was *not* part of the question requirements," Gerel said. "Your essay veered completely off topic."

"Let's not be too hasty, Master Gerel," the High Commander said.

The sneer on Gerel's face immediately gave way, and his face turned an ugly shade of ash gray. He gulped, taking a step back, as if that would help him fade into the background.

The High Commander was watching Ying with a glint in his eyes, a slight smile toying at the edges of his lips. "Aihui Min, am I right?" he said. "Grand Master Quorin graciously allowed me to take a look through all the scripts submitted by the candidates. Yours I found quite interesting.

"You're absolutely right," the High Commander continued. "The development of the Antaran airship is far from complete. On the contrary, we are still lagging far behind. The Empire"—he paused, his index finger tapping thoughtfully on the chair's handle—"has acquired some new *embellishments* to their airship fleet, bought from the emerald-eyed mercenaries beyond the eastern seas. Ideas like yours are what we need in the Engineers Guild right now. Tell me, how did you come up with those ideas? Was your work inspired by anyone in particular?"

"By my father, Your Excellency," Ying admitted. "He was an engineer too."

"Yes, yes." The High Commander lowered his gaze toward the bronze warmer on his lap, thoughtful. "Shan-jin was very talented, much more than most. His contributions toward Antaran engineering, toward the development of our airships, are no trifling matter. It is not surprising that you draw inspiration from him."

Ying carefully observed the wistful expression on the High Commander's face, listened to the solemn words leaving his lips, and pride welled up inside her like a burgeoning spring.

"Quorin," the High Commander said, turning toward the grand master, "it seems to me that Number Eight has sent someone with great potential to you. I'm quite looking forward to seeing how this trial proceeds."

The grand master subtly gestured at the apprentice who was holding the scroll, and the latter scurried off. "Indeed," he said, a self-effacing smile stretching across his wrinkled skin. "The guild is always happy to welcome new talent."

Out of the corner of her eye, Ying could see the colorful changes in the expressions of the beiles and their representatives. Chang-en immediately nudged her, a cheeky grin spreading across his face. Arban's lips were set in a hard line, his face reddened with the indignation of being completely overlooked. The second beile, Erden, kept his emotions more tightly guarded; only the twitching of his meaty jaw betrayed his resentment. An-xi's face had gone white as a sheet, nostrils flaring as he tried to keep his own ego in check. In contrast, the sleepy-eyed third beile simply wore a mild smile and reached out to pat

Ye-yang encouragingly on the shoulder. What that smile really meant, Ying didn't know. As for the first beile, he gave Ye-yang a curt nod of acknowledgment, but that was all. Throughout the entire exchange he had remained indifferent, his face like an unreadable slab of stone.

Ying suddenly remembered the eldest prince, who would be slaving for the rest of his pitiful life in the Juwan mines. She took another look at the four beiles, each with their own strengths and characters, standing proudly before the High Commander. One of these four men would be named the successor to the Aogiya High Command and be the next ruler of the nine Antaran isles. But who would it be?

A thought crept into her mind. Could any one of them have been involved in her father's death? All were powerful enough to command scores of trained assassins and vicious chimeras. Even Ye-yang.

While Ying pondered the succession of the Aogiya ruling family, the senior apprentice who had been sent off returned bearing the scroll.

Quorin cleared his throat. "Without further ado, we will release the results of yesterday's test. If your candidate number and clan name is not on the list, it means you have failed the test and must pack your things immediately. Lessons for the second stage of the trial begin tomorrow."

The apprentice promptly hung the scroll onto a wooden

frame and undid the string to unfurl the long stretch of parchment. There was a sudden forward surge as the apprentice hopefuls jostled to get a better look at the names on the list.

Already standing at the front, Ying skimmed through the list starting from the top. The masters had ranked the candidates based on performance. The name at the top of the pile was Niohuru An-xi. No surprise there. She heard An-xi exhale deeply beside her. The tension in his shoulders visibly lessened.

Arban was in second place, with Chang-en ranking within the top ten. As for her . . . Right at the bottom of the list, squeezed uncomfortably into the narrow sliver of white space between the fortieth name and the edge of the parchment, were the characters "Aihui Min." The brushstrokes used to fill in her name weren't even the same as that of the other forty qualifying candidates.

"I made it," she murmured. She reached out and grabbed Chang-en by the arm. "I made it," she repeated, a little louder this time.

It didn't matter that the characters of her name were half the height of everyone else's and barely legible, squeezed in because of the intervention of the High Commander, nor that Master Gerel was now glaring at her with poison oozing from his eyes. She—Aihui Ying—had made it through to the next round by the skin of her neck.

"The Engineers Guild has always been a vital pillar

supporting the High Command. I expect great things from all of you," the High Commander's resonant voice rang out across the hall. Then, he looked directly at Ying, a thoughtful twinkle in his slate-gray eyes. "I'm sure you won't disappoint me."

He had addressed his words to everyone present, yet Ying felt like he was speaking only to her. She was like the rabbit—being studied, observed, curiously contemplated by the python.

Everyone echoed a chorus of assent, and the High Commander threw his head back and laughed, seemingly pleased by the response. He got up from his seat and turned to Quorin. "There must be many important things in the guild that need looking into. I shall not impose any further." He walked briskly down the steps of the platform and paused in front of his sons and nephew. "The four of you, come with me. There are some things we have to discuss."

The High Commander and four beiles promptly left the hall, with Grand Master Quorin and the other guild masters trailing behind like the obedient servants they were. Once they were out of earshot, the entire hall erupted in a rowdy outburst.

The first person to say anything to Ying was Arban. "Aihui Min," he called out, walking up to her with a smile on his tanned face. He reached out to place one fleshy palm on her left shoulder, but Ying quickly stepped aside to avoid it, acutely wary of any sort of physical contact with the other candidates.

"Congratulations," Arban said. "Looks like you scraped through. You should thank your lucky stars that the High Commander showed up today, else you'd be like those pathetic losers over there." He jerked his thumb toward a group of dejected boys who were being comforted by their peers.

"But the first beile did say that the four of us would be guaranteed passage to the next stage," Chang-en said, scratching at his chin. "Surely the guild needs to give the beiles that bit of respect?"

"Respect has limits. The guild can't be accepting a complete rice bucket just because a beile sent him in," An-xi chimed in. He was looking more like his smug and superior self. Gone was the downtrodden expression from the earlier disappointment at having been overlooked by the High Commander.

"As long as the High Commander doesn't think you're a rice bucket, who cares what the guild masters think?" Chang-en said. "Especially this year, since the High Commander himself will be presiding over the final test. His is the only opinion that matters, eh?"

Ying shook her head. Chang-en was trying to prod An-xi. He was doing a marvelous job of it, judging from An-xi's look of loathing. Chang-en was entitled to his fun, but she wished he would leave her out of it.

The High Commander's sudden appearance had turned the tables for her. As Ye-yang had anticipated, the guild masters wanted to expel her from the trial—and they had almost succeeded, with help from her unconventional essay. She had taken a gamble. Luckily for her it had paid off, but things had not gotten any better for her in the guild.

Her journey ahead would be even harder than it already was—assuming the assassin didn't get to her first.

CHAPTER 13

When the adrenaline and anxiety from the morning had been forgotten, celebrations were in order. The afternoon was spent bidding goodbye to those who had failed to make the cut, while the night was reserved for unbridled revelry.

Ying tagged along with the rest of the group as they swarmed through the gates of the guild and traipsed down the streets toward the center of town. This was the first time any of them had left the guild compound on unofficial business since the start of the trial. There were strict rules that forbade them leaving without permission, and to ask for permission from the likes of Gerel would be foolhardy. Tonight, they had been given the rare opportunity to take time off and head out. The leashes were off.

"Where's he going?" Ying asked as An-xi separated from the group and turned a different corner. Some of the others had also started breaking away, heading in varied directions.

"Home. The Niohurus all have sticks up their asses. If you thought An-xi was bad, then you haven't seen his father and mother yet." Chang-en chortled. "He's probably expected to give them a full rundown of what's happened since day one of the trial. And any other insider information he's found out about the guild. I bet you'll be a big part of that report."

"And your clan is any better?" Arban snickered. He was walking some distance ahead, but that hadn't stopped him from eavesdropping. "You Tongiyas are better at being smiling tigers, that's all."

Chang-en threw his head back and laughed even louder. "I prefer to call it having *wit*, Arban," he shouted. "Unfortunately, Abka Han doesn't bless everyone with it."

Ying had hung around the boys long enough to know that politics within the Eight Banners was complicated and highly tense. In Fei, there was a precarious balance of power kept in check under the watchful eye of the High Commander, who was no less than a master in the art of human weiqi. He promoted and demoted members of various clans in a shrewd and calculated manner, wed concubines in droves as a means of consolidating power and securing loyalties, and spread out authority evenly among his many sons to ensure that no one could threaten his.

Still, there were strong, wicked currents hiding beneath the seemingly calm surface. No matter how powerful he was, the High Commander was getting on with the years, and factions had formed backing the different princes in the race to be named heir. The frequent gibes between the young men in the guild were only the tip of the iceberg.

The first stop that they made was to the Silver Spoon, one of the most famous restaurants in the capital. Ying let the others herd her along like a clueless duckling as she gaped in awe at the colorful lights and sights of Fei. Since arriving, she'd never had the chance to explore the city properly, having been holed up in the fourth beile's manor first and the Engineers Guild after that.

Fei—better known to the rest of the nine isles as the Cobra's Lair—was even more spectacular than the traveling merchants described. Wide cobbled streets were lined with elaborate brick buildings, their sloping emerald roofs like elegant hats sitting atop their proud heads. In the night, bright red lanterns lit the streets, adding a touch of mystery and enigma to the bustling city.

They crossed an arched bridge to reach the town center. As she climbed up the bridge's stone steps, Ying leaned out and peered curiously over the side, eyes greedily taking in the scenery below. The bridge stood almost ten stories above sea level, and from her vantage point she could see the intricate and unusual layering of the city. Streets and buildings crisscrossed to form a complex maze, different levels linked by a network of stairways, bridges, and the occasional mechanical lift. At the lowest level, waterways provided an alternate passage through the capital. Ying could see tiny boats sailing down the canals, like lanterns floating on the water's surface.

"Hurry up," Chang-en urged, dragging her along by the arm. "If we're late, they'll run out of goose and that'll be a tragedy!"

The Silver Spoon was a three-story building with strings of five pumpkin-shaped lanterns lining each side of the entrance, the characters of the restaurant's name emblazoned in bold gold strokes on its signboard overhead. Ying had already spotted it from afar, firstly because it stood out as the tallest building down the entire street, and secondly because of the long, snaking queue that had formed in front of its doors.

Arban led the pack, walking right past the queue and straight toward the entrance. He cut an imposing figure with his broad shoulders and stocky build, and was easily identified as nobility from his sapphire-blue silk robes and thick gold cuffs on his lobes. The young server who was guarding the entrance immediately bowed once he saw Arban approach.

"Master Fucha," he greeted, an obsequious smile plastered on his face.

Arban fished out a silver tael from his waist pouch and pressed it into the boy's hand, heading into the restaurant. "We're starving," he said. "Serve your signature dishes to our room. Quickly!"

"We don't have to queue?" Ying whispered to Chang-en.

She looked around, dazzled by the noise, colors, and smells that accosted her senses from the moment she stepped in.

Spices and perfumes mixed in a dizzying aroma. The first floor of the restaurant was an expansive space with plenty of square tables scattered around. Diners filled every table, chatting as they busied themselves with their chopsticks, snatching at the delectable morsels on plates. Looking up, she saw the same relay system of interlocking tracks and bamboo tubes that she had first seen at the Maiden's Well in Muci, sending orders zipping from the dining hall to the kitchen.

"Of course not. The first floor's for commoners. The Fucha clan has a private room that's reserved for their use. We have one too, but I'll let Arban do the showing off this time."

Ying reckoned her clan would be classified as "commoners" too. In the Antaran territories, there were only a select few clans considered nobility, those that historically produced streams of warriors, scholars, and engineers, and had consolidated much political power in their hands.

She followed them up to the third floor, where they were shown to a private room. A wooden plaque with the characters spelling "Ocean" carved into it hung by the side of the doorway. Unlike the busy first floor, the third was noticeably quieter and more exclusive. The moment she stepped into the room, a subtle jasmine fragrance wafted into her nostrils, coming from the bronze incense burner situated in a corner.

"Make yourselves comfortable," Arban said, settling himself into a chair by the window.

The six of them who had come along slid into empty seats. Ying immediately started looking around like a curious cat.

The Silver Spoon was so different from Roya's tavern, and even the Maiden's Well on Muci. Roya always had a fresh pot of her signature mutton dumplings simmering in her huge cast-iron pot that sat in the middle of the tavern, the meaty fragrance of her broth wafting out through the tavern's open doorway and tempting anyone who walked past.

All that seemed so crude and primitive compared to the Silver Spoon.

The room they were in was spacious and elegantly decorated with watercolor paintings hanging on the walls and porcelain vases sitting on curvaceous wooden stands. As befitting the room's name, the paintings were all of the sea, with ships bobbing up and down upon the gradient of blue, set against the backdrop of the rising sun. Ying leaned over and squinted at the name inked at the bottom of one painting. Borjigit Luyan—one of the most famous painters in Antaran history.

Ying gulped. One of those paintings would have cost a fortune. There were six hanging in this room.

"You like those?" Arban said when he saw her eyeing the paintings. "My e-niye collects Luyan's artwork. These are from our family's private collection. Plenty more where those came from. You probably haven't seen any of these before, eh? Huarin is so rural. Wonder why your father never did anything about that dump, especially since he's seen the magnificence of Fei before."

Ying stared sullenly at her cup of tea. She was used to Arban's not-so-subtle barbs, but hearing him belittle her father left a bitter taste in her mouth.

A knock at the door saved her from needing to engage further, as the servers entered bearing trays with over a dozen different plated dishes. Vibrant, tasty delights filled the entire table—roasted pork and yak, classic mutton dumplings in broth, millet cakes, a stir-fried assortment of vegetables, and even a hot pot with blood sausage and pickled cabbage.

"The Silver Spoon is famous for its blood sausage," Chang-en quipped, fishing some out from the pot and placing them in Ying's bowl. "Best thing ever. If I get kicked out of the guild and flayed by my father, this will be the one dish I'm ordering as my final meal."

Ying could see why. One bite into the sausage and a riot of flavors exploded in her mouth. It was exactly the right combination of salty and sweet, with a hint of spiciness from the chili. The more she chewed, the richer the taste became, and even after she had swallowed everything down her throat, there was a lingering fragrance of sesame.

Roya's tavern had much to learn.

"The second beile said he might leave Fei for a while," Arban said, chomping on a huge slab of roast meat.

"Why?" someone asked.

Arban leaned forward, and Ying recoiled at the thick layer of oil lining his lips. "Don't tell anyone I said this, but apparently the High Commander's sent the second beile on a big mission to Fu-li," he said, beady eyes glinting proudly at knowing something that everyone else didn't.

Ying's mind drifted back to what she had overheard between Ye-yang and Erden. Had the second beile convinced the High Commander to put him in charge of whatever mission it was that Ye-yang had proposed?

"You're just like them. You don't think I can do it. All of you think I'm just here to make up the numbers."

Ye-yang's frustrated and bitter words circled inside her head, and her heart clenched.

"What about the other beiles? Are they going too?" she asked, trying to sound casual.

Arban shrugged, then tossed a glance in Chang-en's direction. "Tongiya, did the first beile tell you anything? Your father's his right-hand man, surely you must know something."

"Nope." Chang-en lowered his chopsticks and dropped his voice. "But I hear that the winds of war are stirring on the horizon. If the Eight Banners make one wrong step, then we shall be ripped to shreds by the claws of the ferocious dragon that is the Empire!" He finished with a flourish, leaping to his feet and scratching at the air as if he were the beast itself.

The other boys stared at him for a moment, then the room erupted in peals of delighted laughter.

"Tongiya, I'll order you an extra goose for that!" Arban shouted, wiping a tear from his eye. "Winds of war and dragon claws . . . Wish I could go to Fu-li with the banners. Can you imagine actually wielding one of those air cannons? Firing a cannonball at those Qirin scum? Boom!" He dropped a dumpling back into its soup bowl with a little splash.

Hoots of agreement went around the room, but Ying remained silent. She shifted uncomfortably in her seat, eyes fixed upon the ripples left by Arban's cannonball of a dumpling. She didn't share the same glee and anticipation she could see in the faces of her peers, even Chang-en, although a part of her also wished to witness the prowess of an air cannon.

Would there not be the young and the old, the sick and the vulnerable, all going about their daily lives on Fu-li? To level a city for the sake of testing weapons felt horrifically cruel, as if all those Qirin lives weren't lives at all.

"*Abka Han gave us the ability to create things so that we can make the world a better place for others*," her father had said, "*so never treat it lightly, little lamb. It is, unfortunately, as much a gift as it is a burden.*"

Why then did you create such terrible things, A-ma?

None of this conversation would be taking place had her father not invented the air cannons, setting the stage for the war that the Cobra's Order was about to wage. There would be blood on her father's hands, even though he might not have fired a single one of those cannons himself.

For the first time in her entire life, Ying felt a hint of shame at the legacy that her father had left behind. She turned her gaze toward the open window and the crescent moon that hung low in the sky. In her mind's eye she saw the Order's airships gliding through the clouds—their undulating sails both beautiful and monstrous at the same time.

"Time for the real fun to start," Arban announced once every single plate on the table had been emptied. Getting up from his seat, he swung his arms across the shoulders of two of his cronies, heading for the door.

"What does he mean by that?" Ying asked, snapping out of her trance.

Chang-en wiped his mouth and stood up. "We're going to the Red Tower," he said with a wink. "Arban might be an asshole, but he sure knows how to have a good time."

The infamous Red Tower of Fei stood in the middle of the city's largest canal, a lofty seven-story pagoda that had its own private dock, allowing its rich and powerful clientele to be ferried to and fro. True to its name, the pagoda was constructed entirely out of red brick, with vermilion roof tiles to match.

Leaning against the rails of the ferry they had boarded,

Ying craned her neck to gaze at the imposing structure, wondering what mystery entertainment was contained within its walls. The alluring melodies of the zither floated through the air, and as they got closer, the overwhelming scent of floral perfumes tickled her nostrils.

She sneezed.

"Ah, the smell of women," Chang-en said, closing his eyes and taking a deep breath.

"What?" Ying yelped, shrinking away.

"Don't act like such a prude. I know Huarin isn't as liberal as Fei, but surely people everywhere have the same needs." Chang-en nudged her in the arm, his eyebrows bobbing up and down. "Let me tell you, the Red Tower doesn't let anyone and everyone through her doors. Madam Zaya is *very* strict on standards. Without this"—he held up his clan pendant—"we wouldn't even be on board this ferry, much less get a whiff of this heavenly fragrance."

"What do you mean?" Ying had a bad feeling about this.

"The number-one courtesan at the Red Tower is Sarnai," her friend continued, oblivious to her confusion, "and she doesn't receive just any client. Arban claims he's spent a night with her before, but I'm calling his bluff. My brother said it costs at least a thousand gold taels to get one night with Sarnai. There's no way General Fucha would let Arban spend that kind of money at a whorehouse."

"A w-w-what?"

"Oops." Chang-en covered his mouth with his hand. "My bad. Madam Zaya would ban me from ever coming back if she heard what I just said. The Red Tower is *not* a whorehouse, it's a pleasure palace."

The ferry docked at the base of the pagoda, and Ying felt a headache coming on. It was both the suffocating stench of perfume and the realization that she had just arrived at the doors of a brothel. Her e-niye would have been horrified if she knew.

"I'm not feeling so well. Maybe I'll just call it a night," she said weakly. The others had started stepping off the boat, but she remained rooted to her spot on deck.

"What are you? Twelve?" Arban suggested. His friends burst out in loud cackles, as did the random drunk customers milling around at the docks with their arms around the waists of waiflike women in barely there silks.

Chang-en ran back to the ferry and grabbed her by the arm, forcibly dragging her off. "Don't chicken out now," he said. "We earned this! It's not like we get to come here every day."

"I really don't think this is a good idea," Ying squeaked, feeling distinctly uncomfortable in her disguise. Waltzing into a brothel and partaking in the wanton merrymaking taking place required a whole other level of playacting that she was not confident of, and she did not want to risk her secret being exposed because of it.

"If you don't want to spend the night, you can just join us for drinks and enjoy the music! The courtesans in the Red Tower play the zither better than the musicians in the High Commander's manor. Nothing like those mechanical bands they use in the restaurants and taverns."

Chang-en wasn't taking no for an answer. Ying couldn't shake his firm grip off her arm, so she was dragged toward the entrance of the pagoda, where a middle-aged woman decked in a crimson fur-lined cloak stood waving off a group of inebriated clients.

"Master Fucha, I haven't seen you around for a while." The woman placed her well-manicured hand on Arban's arm, one lacquered finger coyly scratching at the fabric of his sleeve. "Xin-er has been pining for you. She thinks you've forgotten all about her, that silly girl."

"Is that so? Send her up to me. Can't have my little flower worrying her pretty head over things like that, can we?" Arban laughed, sounding pleased by the madam's words. He quickly stepped across the threshold and disappeared into the building with a few of the others.

As Chang-en and Ying approached, a hint of surprise appeared in Zaya's eyes, her smile widening even further. "Why, if it isn't Master Tongiya!" she exclaimed, waving her silk handkerchief at Chang-en. "It's been a long time. Does your father know you're here?"

"If I don't tell him and you don't tell him, then he won't have to know, will he?" Chang-en answered with a wink.

"And you've brought a friend! Who might this handsome young man be?"

"This is Master Aihui, a good friend of mine." Chang-en beamed, slinging his arm across Ying's shoulder. "He's quite timid and it's his first time at the Red Tower, so don't scare him away, eh?"

Ying found herself herded into the pagoda—Chang-en on one side and Madam Zaya's putrid perfume on the other.

Unlike the Silver Spoon, which had been decorated elegantly and tastefully, the Red Tower was the epitome of decadence and debauchery. On the ground floor, a stage had been set up in the center, where a graceful figure in fiery red silks was spinning and twirling to the music of the zither, reminding Ying of a vibrant peony in bloom. Men sat around drinking wine, bursting out in applause and whistles each time she dazzled them with the nimble twists and turns of her body. The dancer was incredibly beautiful and skilled, possibly even more refined at her craft than Nian. At the side, another courtesan accompanied the dance by singing to the tune of the strings—"Dance of a Thousand Flowers," a famous Antaran classical piece—and the depth of emotion in her dulcet, mellifluous voice left chills running down Ying's spine.

Her eyes continued to gaze in admiration at the artistry

happening onstage as they were led up the stairs—dimly lit, with just enough light to enhance the level of mystery and anticipation of clients that passed through these halls. They brushed shoulders with both male and female courtesans, some brazen and forthcoming, others wearing proud and aloof expressions on their intricately made-up faces.

When they reached one of the higher floors, Zaya showed them to the room where Arban and gang were already being served generous bowls of wine. Arban didn't even glance up when they entered, his attentions focused entirely on the little nymph who was perched on his lap, throwing her cute tantrum about his tardiness.

Ying stood by the door, not sure what to do with herself.

"What're you doing? Sit down!" Chang-en hollered, sliding into an empty seat. Another girl poured him a bowl of wine, which he immediately downed with a sigh of satisfaction.

"I—I think I need to relieve myself," Ying said. "Drank too much tea."

"Oh, you should have said so earlier, my dear," Madam Zaya said, a frown marring her heavily powdered face. She wrapped her bony fingers around Ying's arm. "The latrines are all the way back downstairs, by the back door. I'll show you the way—"

"There's no need," Ying interjected, wriggling her arm out of the woman's grip. "I can find my way." Zaya seemed to be studying her a lot more closely than she liked, and might become suspicious of her disguise if she stayed longer.

She turned and rushed out, eager to get away. As much as she appreciated the skill and effort that the courtesans placed into their trade, she would much rather spend her time with her tools and books instead—where it was both safer and more comfortable.

Ying hurried down the corridor toward the stairs, head bowed so that she wouldn't have to witness what was going on around her. Before she managed to get there, she spotted something—someone—that made her pause in her step. If only the corridors of the Red Tower weren't so dimly lit, tinted red by the lanterns hanging from the ceilings. She squinted her eyes to confirm whether her first instincts had been right.

It was Ye-yang.

He stepped out from one of the rooms farther down, deep in conversation with another man. They had their backs to her. Ying was almost surprised that she had recognized him anyway. When had his silhouette become so deeply ingrained in her mind that it only took one glance for her to spot him in the shadows?

And what was he doing here?

Two girls clad in sheer silks pushed past her, their seductive perfumes reminding her where she was. Indignation bubbled up inside her. She was too naive. What else would a man be doing at a place like this?

Ye-yang ended his conversation and the other man bowed respectfully before moving toward the stairs. The man turned his head for a brief sideways glance. In that instant, Ying glimpsed a familiar scar running across his eye.

The blood in her veins ran cold.

"Min?" Ye-yang called out, sounding surprised. He was careful as always, making sure he used her assumed name. He walked over. "What are you doing here?"

Ye-yang's tall frame blocked her view of the man momentarily, and when she stood on tiptoes to peer over his shoulder, the man was already gone. A phantom ache gripped her where those poisoned needles had pierced through her skin, where that nine-tailed chimera's claws had clamped upon her shoulders, reminding her of how the assassin had come so close to claiming her life the way he had her father's. Her fingernails dug into her palms.

"What's the matter?" the beile asked, frowning when he saw her anxious expression.

Ying ignored him and ran over to the stairs. She leaned over the balustrade, peering downward. All she managed to catch was a dark corner of the man's robe before he disappeared once more. She swiveled around to face Ye-yang,

"Who was that? The man that you were speaking with," she asked, doubt swirling inside her.

The furrows on Ye-yang's forehead deepened. "One of my guards," he answered. "Why do you ask?"

"I *know* that man—with the scar across his eye. I've seen him before."

And he's a murderer.

But if this murderer was indeed one of Ye-yang's guards, then what did that make Ye-yang? This *was* the second time that Ye-yang had been around when the scar-faced man had shown up. First on Muci, then now.

She shook the thought out of her head. It wasn't possible. Ye-yang could never have been involved in her father's murder.

Still, she could feel her own emotions—fear, anger, confusion—beginning to spiral out of control, fueled by the suspicion that was permeating through the crevices in her mind.

"That's not possible," Ye-yang replied after a brief pause. "He doesn't have such a scar." He was watching her with concern in his eyes, and his tone remained calm and collected. It didn't sound like he was lying.

"The lighting in this place must have played tricks on your eyes," he continued. "If you don't believe me, come downstairs. He'll be waiting at the docks with Nergui."

Ying was of two minds. A voice in her head was telling her that she was overthinking matters, that she should trust what Ye-yang was telling her, yet another voice was screaming for her to run away because she could be walking straight into danger.

When she didn't move, Ye-yang gently placed an arm around her shoulders, making the decision for her and guiding her down the stairs.

He led her out of the pagoda toward a boat that was parked at the brothel's docks. The boat was an elegant private craft that had a small, pavilion-like shelter built on its deck with soft gauze curtains protecting the privacy of its occupants. Nergui was waiting by the boat, like Ye-yang said he would be. Beside him stood a man decked in black, the familiar coal-black hilt of the Cobra's Order hanging at his waist. The man had his back toward them, revealing only a pair of hefty shoulders and a single plait running from the back of his head.

"Nergui, Fan-shun," Ye-yang called out, walking ahead.

Fan-shun.

Ying held her breath, trying to calm her fraying nerves.

She stopped.

Suddenly she didn't want to know the answer. What would she do if he did turn out to be the assassin? She wanted to go after him and put a blade through his heart, but she knew she couldn't. She didn't have the capability to—yet.

But it was too late for her to escape, because in the next moment the man turned around, forcing her to see his face under the illumination of the paper lanterns lining the docks.

There was no scar.

No scar.

There was a steely, aggressive aura to the man, but he was nowhere near as menacing as her father's killer.

"See?" Ye-yang turned and said. "I told you he doesn't have a scar. Do you believe me now?"

Ying exhaled. All the tension that had been slowly building up through her body was abruptly released. She turned to look at Ye-yang, her gaze falling directly into a pair of placid gray pools, tinted an alluring silver under the moonlight.

He wasn't lying.

Her relief at this conclusion surprised her. She hadn't realized how fearful she had been of the possibility that Ye-yang could have been associated with the assassin, that he could have played a part in her father's death. Thankfully, it wasn't true.

"Come," Ye-yang said, gesturing toward the waiting vessel. "The Red Tower is no place for someone like you."

"And it is for you?"

The beile arched an eyebrow, a mischievous twinkle appearing in his eyes. "It was once, but maybe not anymore," he said.

CHAPTER 14

YING FOLLOWED YE-YANG BEYOND THE TRANSLUCENT WHITE drapes of the canopy and found herself in a small private space where a bamboo table and a few chairs had been set up, with a fresh pot of tea brewing on top of its burner. Tie guan yin—with the fragrance of orchids that she had come to associate with the fourth beile.

"Sit," Ye-yang said. He lifted the teapot and poured two cups, pushing one to the empty seat across from him.

Ying sank down onto her prescribed chair. She could hear Nergui barking snappish instructions to the boatman, and the boat jerked into motion. Through the gaps in the curtains lifted by the occasional breeze, she saw them drifting away from the resplendent pagoda—and the last fragments of anxiety that had riddled her heart moments ago dissipated with the wind.

"Who is he? The man with the scar," Ye-yang asked.

Ying's fingers tensed around the porcelain teacup.

"You don't have to tell me if you don't want to. I just thought you looked . . . frightened, back there. If there's anything I can do to help, you only need to ask," the beile added.

She looked up, hesitating for a long moment. Then, she

said, "Nobody important. Just someone I knew from Huarin, that's all."

"Oh." A slight crease appeared across Ye-yang's forehead. "I see."

The subtle disappointment in his expression gave her the urge to retract her lie and tell him the truth, but eventually she chose to avert her gaze and hold her silence. She wasn't ready. The fact that she had even deigned to suspect that Ye-yang was in contact with her father's killer showed that she didn't yet trust him enough.

Ying glanced down at the tea swirling in her cup, a few curled leaves slowly unfurling in the amber pool. Tea—not warm goat's milk that her e-niye used to make for her, and then Nian after their mother's passing. If her mother were still around, perhaps she would not be so lost and confused about the way forward. Her mother had always been the calming, reassuring voice behind her and her father's more impetuous nature—the lighthouse that never failed to guide them home.

But she had to rely on herself now. Even Nian and her other siblings were too far away to help her.

If she had learned one thing from tonight's case of mistaken identity, it was that she was unprepared. That was the crux of the problem. If she wanted to make the culprit pay for what he had done, she needed to stop being the one on the defensive, sitting around waiting for him to catch her. She had to learn how to protect herself better. She had to expedite her investigation to find out who he was—and who he worked for—so that she could be one step ahead.

Reaching into his sleeve, Ye-yang retrieved the folded fan that had been hidden within. He put it on the table in front of Ying. She flinched, abruptly snatched away from her own thoughts.

"I'll be leaving Fei in two days' time, and I might not be back within a month or two. Try to stay out of trouble in the meantime," he said.

"What?" Ying stared up at him. "You're leaving?"

"The High Commander issued the orders today. I'm taking some men to Fu-li."

"But Chang-en said that the second beile was going. If he's going, then why do you still need to go?"

"Erden is leading the support. I've been appointed overall commander for this mission." Ye-yang pushed the curtains aside and stepped out, standing by the edge of the boat with his hands resting behind his back.

Ying picked up her fan and stuffed it up her sleeve, then she followed after him. "But what exactly will you be doing there? The others have been talking about war, about testing the air cannons. Is it true? Will it be dangerous?" she asked. When Ye-yang tilted his head sideways to look at her, a bemused glimmer in his gray eyes, she suddenly realized that she had once again stepped out of line. She bowed frantically. "I'm sorry, Beile-ye. I asked too many questions."

Probing into military secrets was a crime punishable by death—and she didn't yet want her head to roll.

To her surprise, a smile stretched across Ye-yang's face instead. The moonlight softened the angles of his face, and his eyes creased into the same shape as the crescent moon suspended in the darkened sky. Their eyes locked, and Ying's heart skipped a beat.

The boat was still sailing down the canal straits, though they had long left the glitzy Red Tower behind them and moved on to a quieter part of the city. A group of children gathered by the edge of the canal, setting small lotus-shaped lanterns afloat on the water's surface.

After what felt like a long moment frozen in time, Ye-yang finally pulled his gaze away, looking toward the bobbing lanterns instead.

"Do you do this too? Back in Huarin?" he asked.

"No. We have no rivers in Huarin and the sea surrounding the island is too choppy. Those lanterns would sink the moment they touch the water's surface," Ying said slowly, trying to collect her scattered thoughts.

Ye-yang called for Nergui, issuing some instructions to his attendant in a hushed voice. The latter scurried off, and moments later the boat shifted direction, coming alongside a small sampan belonging to a market seller peddling lanterns up and down the canal. Nergui ran back with two lanterns, handing them to his young master.

"Here in Fei, people like to set these lanterns afloat—for good luck. The current carries them down the canals and eventually sends them out into the open sea. They say that Abka Han will see the glow of the lanterns from the heavens and grant the wishes of the faithful," Ye-yang said, holding out one lantern to Ying.

Ying stared down at the lotus lantern sitting in her hands, its pale pink petals made from see-through gauze wrapped around a delicate wire frame. The candle flame flickered in the wind, bringing the slightest tinge of warmth to the otherwise frigid night air. If she had set one of these afloat back in Huarin, would Abka Han have protected her father from harm?

Ye-yang bent over the edge of the boat and gently set his lantern onto the water's surface. "I won't lie and say that Fu-li won't be dangerous," he suddenly said, "but it's not something I haven't seen before. At least with the Empire the enemy is always in the light. Those kinds of enemies are the easiest to deal with."

"Just because you survived once doesn't mean you'll be lucky a second time." Life was fragile—too fragile—and it could be stolen away far too easily.

Ying squatted beside him, clumsily dropping her lotus when

she had meant to set it gracefully upon the water's surface. It wobbled precariously, but thankfully survived her bungle and floated away alongside his. She puckered her lips into a pout, watching the lanterns drift away into darkness in unison like a pair of stars in the river.

A laugh escaped from Ye-yang's throat. He reached over and gave her a gentle pat on the head—the way an older brother would to a younger sibling. Ying bristled with irritation, and disappointment.

She couldn't deny the attraction she felt toward the reticent but quietly confident fourth beile, that had been quietly growing ever since that drunken rooftop night—or maybe ever since he first rescued her from the nine-tailed chimera on Muci. His stoic and sensible nature felt like an anchor for her in these times of uncertainty, a single lamp that lit the darkness that surrounded her. But she had enough common sense to know that it was impossible between them. She was worlds apart from someone like Ye-yang. He was a prince—and she an orphan from a washed-out clan.

One day he would marry a girl from a noble family—and even take a few concubines. Hell, he had just been at a brothel. The reminder was like a slap to her face.

Ye-yang's fingers touched her cheeks, brushing away a few stray strands of hair that had fallen across her face. She swiped at her fringe like a riled cat, turning to glare at him.

The young beile blinked back his surprise as he stared into her dark brown eyes. A pink tinge appeared on his cheeks and he swallowed, adjusting his fur-lined collar uncomfortably. It was strange, seeing him appear uneasy. Was it because of her? What *did* he actually think of her?

But she didn't have time to dwell on that, because Ye-yang suddenly dived toward her, pushing her down against the boat's wooden deck.

An arrow flew overhead, skimming the top of Ye-yang's head. Then several more followed, just over their bodies.

Ying lay on her back, her jaw hanging slack as she watched the arrows slice through the air. She clung to Ye-yang, who was pressed down above her, keeping his head just low enough to avoid the rain of arrows. His gaze hardened, piercing through the darkness in the direction of the assailants.

In the background, Nergui was yelling for reinforcements.

A series of heavy thuds struck the deck as several masked men leapt onto the boat.

Ye-yang grabbed Ying by the shoulder and hauled her back up to her feet, pushing her behind him as the men approached. They were surrounded, encircled by the enemy in front and trapped by the icy canal waters behind.

The assassins—there were at least nine or ten of them—raised their gleaming swords in the air, charging toward their marks. Ye-yang and Ying were outnumbered and there was nowhere to run.

Ying slid her fan out from her sleeve, grateful to have it at hand once again, its metal leaves snapping in a series of orderly clicks. She wrapped her fingers around its shaft, readying her thumb above the pivot.

Still keeping her shielded behind him, Ye-yang sprang into action. He grabbed the arm of the nearest man with lightning speed, slamming his fist into the man's neck. When he withdrew, Ying stared in shock at the blood that was dripping from his knuckles. A sharp, metal spike extended from the jade ring that Ye-yang always wore on his index finger. The assassin collapsed, dead.

Even though he was but one man, Ye-yang fended off the aggressive attacks of the enemy with stroke after methodical stroke, deflecting blows and evading swords with exacting precision. Blood completely stained his curled fist, but Ying knew that it didn't belong to him. It belonged to the victims of the ruthless silver blade that had been hidden within that innocuous ring. Ten men dwindled to just five.

A soft swoosh suddenly grazed the side of Ying's ear. An arrow appeared out of nowhere, lodging itself in Ye-yang's right shoulder blade. The beile, who had just dispatched another assassin and sent the helpless body flailing into the water, grimaced and took a quick glance at the offensive wooden shaft pierced through his back. He reached back and snapped it in half, leaving a short, splintered stump protruding, before continuing to engage the assailants.

In that moment, an assassin leapt at the opportunity to stab his sword at Ye-yang's back. Ying pointed her fan's blade in the attacker's direction, tapping rapidly on its pivot. Two bamboo darts shot out from their barrels and struck the chest of the man, just as the tip of his sword ripped the fabric of Ye-yang's robes. The assassin stumbled backward, glancing down at his chest and then ferociously at Ying.

The assassin turned his attention toward her, a murderous glint in his eyes. He flung a sharpened dart at her. Ying dodged right and quickly tapped her fan's pivot once more, but this time the man easily cut down her darts with a swing of his sword. The barrels were empty.

Out of the corner of her eye, Ying spotted a gas lamp swinging precariously from its hook, the tiny flame within swaying with the violent rocking of the boat. She grabbed it by hand, ignoring the searing heat that scalded her palm.

The man raised his sword, and she could see her own terrified reflection in the silver.

Ying quickly pulled out a small bronze plug from the base of the lamp and flung the entire lamp at her attacker as forcefully as she could.

Bang!

The lamp shattered in midair, exploding into a ball of flames.

Many of the lamps used by Antaran nobility were powered by a careful release of flammable kaen gas, kept in a small storage unit hidden at their bases. By pulling out the contraption that controlled the gas release, Ying triggered the small explosion.

The two assassins standing closest to her were flung off the deck by the force.

"Min!"

Ye-yang's face appeared in front of her, so close that the tips of their noses were almost touching. He flinched, gritting his teeth as beads of sweat started gathering above his brow. Flames licked the back of his dark robes and shards of broken glass had ripped through the fabric, carving themselves into his flesh. He had shielded her from the blast in the nick of time.

Behind them, a few of Ye-yang's guards had already boarded the boat and were busy dispatching the remaining few assassins.

"Ye-yang!" She clutched on to his shoulders, fear gripping her heart.

The beile's body swayed dangerously, his face gone deathly pale, then he collapsed atop her. Ying lost balance, struggling to keep her footing on deck while supporting Ye-yang at the same time. Before she could help it, they went toppling over the edge, falling into the dark, wintry waters of the canal and leaving the boat's flaming deck behind them.

The cold was biting at first, like a thousand tiny needles piercing through her skin, and then the numbness began. Starting with her fingers and toes, it quickly worked its way up her limbs and toward her core. It was reminiscent of the freezing, turbulent seawater around Huarin, which she had been forced to swim in many times when she was testing her flight apparatus.

Holding her breath, Ying wrapped her arms around the unconscious Ye-yang, kicking her legs desperately to keep them both from sinking into an icy grave. Through the rippling water's surface, she could still see the fire raging above.

Ying began to swim toward the nearest canal bank. Keeping one arm wrapped around Ye-yang's neck, she kept them carefully hidden beneath the surface of the water in case there were any enemy archers still lurking above, swimming as hard as she could toward the soft glow of light she could see in the distance. The lamps that the children had set afloat, drifting from the canal's edge toward the open sea. She was slowly but surely running out of air, and when she glanced back at Ye-yang's pale, serene expression, the thought that he could die flashed painfully through her mind.

It took almost all of Ying's energy to make it from the boat to the canal's edge, till she could see the children's lanterns floating directly above her head and their hazy faces peering down into the water. She broke through the surface gasping for breath, pulling Ye-yang up with her. With the help of some confused passersby, the two of them were dragged out of the water and onto dry land. Ying shivered uncontrollably as the frosty night winds chilled her bones.

"Ye-yang," she called, looking down at the young man whose head was resting on her thigh. "Wake up." She placed one trembling hand on his cheek, wishing that he would open his eyes and say something—anything.

Ye-yang's lips were a ghastly shade of white, his body quivering in her arms.

She adjusted her position slightly, and he emitted a low groan, brows furrowing tightly as if he was in great pain. His eyelids lifted, revealing a pair of tired eyes.

"Thank Abka Han!" Ying cried, tears streaming down her face.

On the canal, the flames on their boat had been swiftly extinguished by Ye-yang's men. The river had once again returned to calm, gently illuminated by the sprinkling of lotus-shaped lanterns floating on the surface. Ying had never been one to believe in praying to the heavens, but this time around she was grateful that she had—because Abka Han had granted her wish much sooner than she had expected.

CHAPTER 15

YING STEEPED IN THE HOT BATHWATER, FORCING herself to stay awake even though she was bone-weary. Steam filled the entire room, yet it still wasn't enough to dispel the cold from inside her. She sneezed three times in quick succession, rubbing her sore nose ruefully after that.

Ye-yang's guards had arrived shortly after they resurfaced, and they were both sent swiftly back to the fourth beile's manor, wrapped in several blankets. She was grateful for the cover of the thick wool layers, which she used to hide her drenched form and half her face, in case anyone realized Aihui Min looked suspiciously like a girl.

The beile was immediately attended to by physicians, his wounds having only been loosely bandaged for the journey back. As for Ying, the chief steward had offered to send a physician to assess her condition, but she rejected it, asking only for a warm bath and a dry set of clothes.

The memory of the assassin's murderous stare before he charged at her with his sword kept invading her mind, reminding her of how lucky she was to still be alive. Now that she had time to gather her thoughts, one question kept prodding about in her mind: Were those assassins after Ye-yang—or her?

Her fingers ran along the grooves of the jade pendant around her neck. Thankfully she had decided to leave her father's journal locked in the dormitory, else it would have been destroyed in the water. She had been worried about wandering all over the capital carrying something so important with her, in case the scarred assassin took the opportunity to attack again while she was outside guild walls, so she had locked it at the base of her trunk, buried beneath a thick pile of clothing and books. Since he had already ransacked her dormitory, she thought it unlikely that he would return to search it again.

She slid out of the water and stepped out of the wooden tub. After putting on the fresh set of clothes and braiding her hair in the usual men's style, pulled through a cloth band around the back of her head, she left the bathing quarters and headed over to Ye-yang's room.

It was the wee hours of the morning, but the fourth beile's manor was bustling with activity. Attendants rushed in and out of their master's quarters, entering with bronze basins of clean water but leaving with those same basins tainted with the reddish-black shade of blood.

"How is the fourth beile?" Ying asked one of the harried servants who had just exited the room. She stared down at the basin he was carrying, horrified by the bloodstained cloths that were hanging off the sides. The acute fear that she had felt while dragging Ye-yang through the freezing waters of the canal, the fear of possibly losing him so abruptly—just as she had lost her father—came flooding back.

The man shrugged his shoulders and rushed off.

Ying stepped across the threshold and entered the room. The pungent smell of medicinal herbs stung her nostrils, mixed with the slight metallic odor of blood. Her footsteps slowed. Qorchi and Nergui were standing in one corner with their heads bowed, conversing in low, hushed voices. When Nergui saw her standing by the doorway, he frowned.

"What are you doing here?" he demanded.

"How is he?" Ying repeated, craning her neck to get a glimpse of the inner chamber where Ye-yang was. "What did the physicians say? Are his injuries serious?"

"The beile is still unconscious," Qorchi replied sullenly. "The physicians say tonight is the critical period. If he tides it through, then it'll just be a matter of letting the wounds heal. If not, then . . ."

"You have no right to be asking these questions," Nergui said shrilly. He dismissed all the other servants, then marched over to her with his hands on his hips, narrow face flushed with anger. "I saw what happened on the boat. If it weren't for you, the beile wouldn't have suffered such severe injuries!" He spun around and faced Qorchi. "Why did you even let him in? You should have sent him right back to the guild and told the masters to give him fifty lashings!"

"He did save the beile from drowning," Qorchi muttered.

Nergui grabbed Ying by the arm and started dragging her out, but he had underestimated Ying's stubborn streak. She dropped to her knees, refusing to budge.

"Please, I know it's my fault. Let me make amends. Let me stay. I can keep watch tonight," she pleaded.

"Who do you think you are? You're just a stray that the beile brought home!" Nergui scolded, his face flushing purple with rage. "Perhaps the beile's charity has made you misunderstand your position in the hierarchy. This is Fei, not whatever shoddy backwater you came from. There is no place in the fourth beile's manor for a nobody like you—is that clear?"

Ying shifted her gaze to stare down at her fingers, and at the coarse cotton fabric of her sleeves. "I know," she said, though she made no attempt to stand up or leave. "I have no intentions of overstepping my boundaries. I only want to repay the fourth beile for the debt I owe him. Please." She kowtowed three times, her forehead rapping sharply against the lacquered floorboards.

"Let him stay," Qorchi interrupted, a hint of sympathy in his voice. "Before the beile lost consciousness, he did say that he wanted to speak to the boy, remember?"

"No one was asking you for your opinion," Nergui hissed.

He took another glance at Ying, then stormed out of the room in an angry huff.

Qorchi sighed, beckoning for Ying to stand. "What Nergui said was not wrong," he said. "The fourth beile's situation within the Aogiya High Command isn't as rosy as it may seem, as you may already have gathered after what happened tonight. He faces enemies on all fronts, and it is a precarious balancing act that he tries to keep up. He cannot afford to have any weaknesses, but—" Qorchi paused and stared at Ying for a moment, then he shook his head and let out another deep sigh. "I have looked after the beile since he was a child, and I know him well enough to see that he behaves *differently* around you. I'm not sure that's a good thing, to be honest." He waved her toward the inner chamber. "Get the servants to fetch me if the beile's condition takes a turn for the worse. The physician said we must try to keep his temperature down, else it could get critical." Lifting the hem of his robe, the steward stepped across the threshold and left.

Ying headed to the inner chamber, taking care not to interrupt the silence with her footsteps. All the windows of the room were tightly shut, keeping out the chilly draft, and bronze burners stood at each corner like stoic sentries watching over their master, basking the space in a comfortable warmth. The light gauze curtains hanging from the fourth beile's bed frame were drawn, and as she went closer she could make out the silhouette of the man lying perfectly still on the bed.

She lifted the curtain gingerly.

Ye-yang was on his chest, head tilted to the side and resting against a silk-covered pillow. A thick layer of white bandage was wrapped across his bare torso. The smell of herbs was overpowering, and she could only imagine the potency of the herbal paste that the physicians had applied to stem the bleeding and numb the pain.

Ying bit down hard on her lip as she looked down upon Ye-yang's ashen face. Even in his unconscious state he wore a frown between his brows, the tiny movements of his eyes beneath their lids betraying the deep unease that gripped him from within.

She placed a palm on his forehead, quickly pulling it back when she felt its heat.

Ying reached for the basin that had been left on the table by the attendants. She dipped a piece of cloth in the cold water and wrung it dry before placing it gently upon Ye-yang's brow. She spent much of the night repeating this over and over, diligently trying to keep his fever at bay, until eventually she could not help but succumb to her own exhaustion. She sank to the floor, head resting against the side of Ye-yang's bedframe.

But sleep was restless for her, her mind choosing to relive fractured fragments of the night's events—the masked assassins, the menacing gleam from the arrowheads and swords, the flames from the boat and the freezing dark waters of the canal,

Ye-yang lying in a pool of ever-flowing blood, like her father once had.

Ying jolted awake, dream and reality tangled in a frenzied mess inside her head. Someone squeezed her hand gently, reassuringly, bringing her back to the real world. A pair of concerned eyes were staring at her, their owner sitting up in his bed, robes secured around his waist. Ye-yang.

"You're awake!" she exclaimed, flinging her arms around his neck. Ye-yang cleared his throat awkwardly, and she quickly let go. She flushed, the relief at his regaining consciousness overshadowed by embarrassment at her own overreaction. "How do you feel? Does it still hurt? What am I talking about, of course it hurts, I should get the physician, or Qorchi, or—" She stood up to rush away, but Ye-yang tightened his grip on her hand, preventing her from going anywhere.

He shook his head. "There's no need. I'm fine," he said.

Ye-yang's face was still pallid, but his eyes had regained a semblance of their usual intensity and energy, and his lips curved upward in a tiny smile. He glanced briefly at his hand wrapped around hers, then he pulled her back down so she was sitting beside him.

This time, Ying didn't shy away from his touch, even as the slight coldness of his fingertips sent a small shudder through her. Life was too fragile, too short, for skirting around her own feelings. Even if she knew that moments like these were only fleeting, that there was no place for her here, as Nergui had said, she still wanted to hold on to each memory of him that she was fortunate enough to have.

"Thank you for what you did back there," he said softly. "You didn't have to save me. You should have just saved yourself. Withstanding that cold is not something that many would have been able to do."

"If it weren't for me, you wouldn't have fallen in in the first place. You didn't have to save me," Ying mumbled. Qorchi's words floated back to mind, about how Ye-yang treated her differently. If he hadn't shielded her from the blast, he would have come out of the attack unscathed. She was a liability to him. She looked up at his pale countenance, guilt turning cartwheels inside her.

Ye-yang removed the jade ring he always wore on his index finger, slipping it carefully onto hers. "You've seen me use this. The mechanism is here." He put pressure on an inconspicuous engraving of a serpent on the mottled jade surface, and a narrow silver blade slid out from within, its segments clicking rhythmically into place. "And if you want to retract it"—he rotated the ring a hundred and eighty degrees around, revealing another tiny engraving, this time of an eagle—"press this one. Got it?"

"Why are you giving this to me?" Ying asked, surprised—and touched—by his gift. She had never seen Ye-yang without the ring, so it had to be important to him. For him to be giving it to her—did it mean that she was even more important?

"I'll be away from the capital for some time. If you ever encounter any trouble, it won't hurt to have this with you." He looked away, then back at her pointedly. "For self-defense, not for picking fights with the other candidates."

"You're still going to Fu-li." Ying's expression darkened.

Ye-yang nodded. "Someone is hoping that I won't be able to show up," he said. "Can't let them have that victory."

"You think that the attack was from one of the other beiles?" Ying asked hesitantly.

Because what if it wasn't—what if those men were after me and my father's journal, and you were only in the wrong place at the wrong time?

"Erden probably had a hand in it, yes. Maybe Ye-han. I doubt Ye-lu would be foolish enough to attempt an assassination in the capital, but he'd be more than happy to get rid of one competitor. My father's favor has made me a threat to their ambitions, and putting me in charge of Fu-li has likely ruffled many feathers." Ye-yang paused, looking down at the jade ring that was now sitting on Ying's finger, and her hand that was still sitting in his.

"Why don't you just let the second beile go? Fu-li is the gate to the Empire. There'll be enemies on all sides. You could *die* out there."

"Ying, do you know what's worse than dying?" Ye-yang looked at her silently for a moment, then sighed. "It's when you lead a life worse than death. Without freedom, without choice, without dignity." His eyes glazed over, as if he were looking through her to someplace distant. "Ye-lin would probably have chosen death, had he been given a choice."

"That's bullshit. If you're dead, then it's all over. If you stay alive, at least you have a fighting chance. Dying is only an excuse to run away. Dying is for cowards. Aogiya Ye-yang, I didn't save your life just so you can throw it away," she warned. She had already come close to losing him once. She didn't want to go through that again.

Everyone treated death too carelessly, but to Ying, dying was the easy way out. An excuse to run away from responsibility. Her mother, her father, they had given up too easily. If only they had clung on to life a little harder, willed themselves to breathe a little longer, maybe everything would be different.

Ye-yang smiled when he heard his name leave her lips, a hint of color returning to his cheeks. "Of course, you're right," he said. "I don't plan on dying anytime soon, even though there are those who want me to." He looked down at their entwined fingers, gently stroking the back of her index finger with his. There was a wistfulness in his touch, as if he longed to hang on to this moment a little—just as she did. Eventually, he let go and got up from the bed slowly, walking toward the window.

Ying stared at the outline of his silhouette as he stood there looking out the window with his hands resting against his back, deep in thought. She wished that she could see the map in his mind. She wanted to know where he was headed—and if maybe, just maybe, there might be a place for her on this lonely journey he was on.

Someone snapped his fingers repeatedly in front of Ying's eyes. She swatted at the pesky fly, eyes still focused on the half-finished sketch she had been working on instead of listening to the dull lecture on kaen gas mining.

Six petals fanning out to form a concentric circle.

It was the day after Ye-yang and the bannermen had left for Fu-li. After leaving the beile's manor the morning after the assassination attempt, Ying hadn't seen him again. To take her mind off the worry that he might never return, she had thrown all her energy into developing her latest project—the Peony.

It was an idea inspired by the mesmerizing "Dance of a Thousand Flowers" she had seen at the Red Tower. A contraption—more specifically, a *weapon*—modeled after a blooming peony. As much as she detested the thought of spilled blood, she knew she needed something more to defend herself with, something that could sit hidden beneath the folds of her robes until the next time any danger appeared.

"Hello." Chang-en's beaming face appeared in front of her, messy strands of hair sticking out from his sloppily tied braids.

"Are you done doodling flowers? If you don't get your ass up, we're going to be late for our first Strategy class."

Ying snapped back to reality. She looked around the classroom in a daze. Everyone was gone save for Chang-en, who was squatting in front of her looking bemused. "Sorry," she said, hurriedly picking up her books.

The duo scurried toward the front gates to board the wagons that would take them to the venue for their first Strategy class—Wu Lin, the small patch of wood beyond the northeastern edge of the city that was perpetually shrouded in mist all year round. Unlike their other classes, where they had been broken into smaller groups, Strategy was to be taken as an entire cohort—all forty-one of them.

While they trundled along, the candidates buzzed enthusiastically among themselves about the mysterious Master Lianshu, who they were finally going to meet. They had already been in the guild for over two months, yet they had still not seen head nor tail of the elusive guild master. The longer this dragged on, the more ridiculous the rumors became. First, they said he had a petty feud with Gerel and thus refused to show up at any guild events out of spite; next they said he was a reclusive hermit who lived in a hidden underground cellar at a secret location within the guild compound; then he became a centenarian who was actually former Grand Master Aogiya, who had engineered the way to immortality.

It was absurd.

"Do you think he'll come flying down from the sky?"

"Or maybe he'll drill his way up from his hidden lair underground."

"Do you think he's really Grand Master Aogiya? Imagine that! I would die happy if I got to have just one lesson with him."

Chang-en snorted loudly. "Are you for real?" he snickered. "Your brains must be fried from too much studying. If Grand Master Aogiya was really alive, then old Quorin would never have gotten the chance to sit on that chair." He nudged Ying. "What do you reckon Lianshu's really like? I tried to ask my father about him, but he chased me out of the room in a huff."

"Let's just say there's a good reason why no one wants to—or can—talk about this . . . *person*," An-xi sniffled.

"You know something?" Chang-en asked, prodding An-xi with his elbow. The latter pulled a face and turned away, ending the conversation there.

The moment they passed through the city gates and out into the wilderness, the scenery drastically changed. Swirls of white mist curled around them, submerging them in a sea of fog. The thick foliage of the forest blocked out the rays of sunlight from above, plunging them into grim shadows that moved a little too ominously.

"Why are we here?" someone whispered, as if speaking loudly would awake whatever monsters lay in these woods.

That same question was probably echoing in the minds of every single candidate, including Ying. They observed the spooky surroundings warily, the prospect of the unknown striking fear into their hearts.

Their wagons finally came to a halt—in the middle of nowhere. A patch of forest that was identical to every other patch they had passed along the way, with wisps of cold mist like skeletal fingers that tickled their arms and legs.

"Excuse me," Chang-en called out to their cart driver, "do you know why we're here? Where's Master Lianshu?"

But he got no answer. Instead, once all the apprentice hopefuls had alighted, their surly drivers simply turned the wagons around and disappeared the way they came.

The last wheel had barely vanished from view when an arrow suddenly sliced through the air, almost taking Ye-kan's right ear off. It struck the trunk of a cedar tree with a thump.

"Who did that? Come out now!" the prince hollered, his face reddening with rage.

Ying's heart leapt up her throat, memories of the attacks she had faced immediately returning to her mind.

Is it him? Has he found me?

"Hey, wait, there's a note," Chang-en said. He was standing beside the arrow—the only one who was gutsy enough, or foolish enough, to do that—pointing at a small piece of parchment hanging off its shaft. He reached out and lifted it gingerly by one corner. "'Strategy Lesson One: Get back to the northeast city gate before the sun sets,'" he read. "It's signed by Master Lianshu!"

Ying slumped against a tree, relief washing over her. It wasn't another attack, it was merely part of their lesson. A most unorthodox start.

"Let me see that," Ye-kan said, marching over to the arrow and ripping it out of the bark. He read the message and scowled. Surprisingly, the boy didn't kick up a fuss like everyone expected him to. Instead, he flung the arrow and note onto the grass and stormed off. "What are you all waiting for?" he grumbled. "We have less than two incense sticks worth of time before nightfall."

"Haven't we been here before?" Chang-en mused, staring up at the nondescript foliage that surrounded them.

The candidates had split themselves into smaller groups to embark on this mission. Ying had ended up with Chang-en, An-xi, and Ye-kan. Their plan had been to take a straight path in the direction that the wagons had left in, assuming that the carts must have gone back to the city. Unfortunately, it seemed that they had been presumptuous.

They had been walking for a long time, yet were nowhere close to reaching their goal. Every stretch of forest looked the same. Through the gaps in the leaves, they could see the sunlight rapidly waning as time continued ticking toward their deadline.

"Hey, what are you kids doing here?" a boorish voice shouted.

"Arban?" Chang-en scratched his head, confused when he saw burly Arban leading his crew of four others toward them. "Did you change your mind and switch directions?"

"What are you talking about? I should be asking *you* that question. We've been walking in a straight line all this while."

Ying frowned.

When they parted ways, Arban's group had clearly chosen to go in the opposite direction from them, so how was it possible that they were meeting up if both groups insisted they had been going straight?

She raised her head and studied the rustling leaves, listening carefully for any sounds, any clues that might explain how they ended up in this situation.

"Min, what do you think—"

"Shh!" She pushed a finger against Chang-en's lips, shutting him up.

There in the background was a soft rush of water, like a river or a waterfall—or the opening of a sluice gate at the hour of dusk.

The water level near the northeast of the capital city was controlled by a large gate made of tarnished bronze. On rainy days, the gate would be lifted by thick, metal chains—like a rising guillotine—opening a gaping mouth in the city walls that would allow excess water to flow out of the canal and toward the open sea.

She pressed her ear against the damp ground, listening closely.

“Aihui Min, what are you doing?” Arban demanded.

“The mist in this forest is playing with our perception, giving us a wrong sense of direction. We think we’ve been walking in straight lines, but we’ve likely been going in circles instead,” Ying explained, straightening back up. She pointed to her left. “I think we should go this way. I can hear the sounds of water coming through the city’s sluice gates from that direction, so if we keep following it, we should emerge out of the forest eventually.”

“Why should we listen to you!” Arban shouted.

“You don’t have to if you don’t want to.”

A buzzing sound interrupted their argument, getting louder with each passing moment.

“What’s that?” An-xi asked, trembling. His dimunitive frame shrank as he wrapped his arms tightly around himself.

Right on cue, a dark cloud appeared between the trees, growing larger as it drew close. Bees. Each one the size of an eyeball, their golden bodies glinting dangerously each time they passed through a rare beam of fading sunlight.

“Run!” Chang-en screamed.

Bees? On Fei?

Bees were almost never seen on the Antaran isles because

of their wintry climate. The only time Ying had seen actual bees was in the greenhouse of a wealthy Kamar merchant, who managed to rear the fussy creatures using large, steam-driven boilers to keep them warm.

As the buzzing got louder and louder, all of them took off sprinting away from the rapidly advancing swarm, toward the direction Ying had pointed out.

"They're gaining on us," someone yelled.

"Abka Han save us, we're going to die!"

"Ah! My arm!" another exclaimed, clutching his upper arm after being stung by the barbed stinger.

Ying ran, but as time dragged, the strength in her legs faded away and her lack of stamina began to show. The other boys were pulling ahead, while the gap between her and the bees continued to shrink.

Ahead of her, Ye-kan suddenly stopped. He let out an exasperated groan, then turned and ran back toward her.

"What are you doing? Why—ah!"

Suddenly, Ying found herself hoisted onto Ye-kan's back, racing to catch up with the others.

"Put me down, I'll slow you down!" Ying protested.

"Don't worry, I'm keeping score of the number of life debts you owe me," the fourteenth prince replied between ragged breaths. Despite carrying Ying on his back, he still managed to keep pace with the rest.

Clinging on to his broad shoulders, it struck Ying for the first time that Ye-kan really wasn't a child anymore—and if they survived this, that she should probably stop treating him like one.

Thankfully, they didn't have much farther to go. Light was coming faster—the woods were thinning. A moment later, the group emerged from the frosty woods, and the river, sluice gate, and city walls appeared before their eyes. Everyone dashed for the water and leapt in.

Holding their breaths in the icy water, they kept a watchful eye on the surface, praying that the bees would go away. A large shadow passed overhead, then disappeared.

When they were certain that the bees were gone, Chang-en signaled to everyone to surface.

"Are they really g-g-gone?"

"It's so cold. I'm going to get hypothermia."

"I got stung by those things. Do you think they're poisonous?"

The bunch of them clambered onto the riverbank, collapsing with relief despite their shivering bodies and chattering teeth. Above them, the last vestiges of sunlight faded from the sky and day transitioned into night.

Their moment of respite was interrupted by slow clapping, and they turned to find a petite figure perched on a large rock, clad in the maroon robes of the guild.

"You?" Ying gasped, staring in disbelief.

CHAPTER 16

YING RECOGNIZED THE ECCENTRIC ARCHIVE KEEPER STRAIGHTAWAY, even though she was no longer hiding behind a gas mask and her frizzy hair had been pinned behind her head with two wooden chopsticks. This was not how she had expected them to meet again.

"It's Master Lianshu to you," the woman replied haughtily, tossing Ying a sideways glance. She surveyed the group of students, seemingly oblivious to the shock and incredulity written all over their faces. "Not bad, the few of you. Looks like you've accomplished your task within the time limit," she said. "Although I don't think you would have been able to do it without a push from my little friends."

She opened her right fist and a golden bee rose from her palm, hovering beside her like an obedient pet. Except it wasn't *really* a bee after all.

Now that they were studying it up close without the fear of being stung to death, they could see that the creature was entirely mechanical. An automaton with a round body crafted from bronze, suspended in the air by the rapid flapping of its thin, metallic wings. Ying had seen something similar—and more intricate—before.

It had been a mechanical butterfly with the most beautiful silver filigree wings, made by her father for Nian's twelfth birthday. A dancer for his dancer, their a-ma had said as he released the little automaton and let it twirl about in midair.

Still staring at the bee, Ying wondered if it had been created from the same design that Nian's butterfly had been.

Arban was the first one to snap out of the trance. "You sent those bees?" he exclaimed, jumping to his feet in a rage. "How dare you! What if one of us got hurt? You can't take responsibility for that!"

"Arban, shut up," An-xi hissed tersely from the side.

Master Lianshu was unfazed. She regarded the furious boy with a cool gaze and said, "I don't have to take responsibility for anything. All of you have already wagered your lives by entering the guild's apprenticeship trial. If you are incapable or unwilling to sacrifice yourselves for the High Command and the guild, then you should run back home now instead of wasting everyone's time."

The sharpness in her voice felt like a clean blade slicing through steel, and even the bearlike Arban, who was almost two heads taller than the guild master, seemed to wither under her scornful words. Everyone else cowered in fear. This woman carried an aura of authority and gravitas that was impossible to dismiss, with a keenness in her gray eyes that—

Ying took a double take.

Without the hazy glass distorting Lianshu's eyes, she could distinctly see those eyes were the shade of stormy skies. Like Ye-yang's. Like the High Commander's.

Lianshu . . . Aogiya Lianzhe . . . Aogiya Lianshu?

She leaned toward Ye-kan and whispered, "Do you know Master Lianshu?"

"You mean do I know my own aunt? Of course I do," Ye-kan muttered. "Look somewhere else and stop drawing attention to me." He had his head bowed, long strands of wet hair purposefully plastered over his face so that no one could actually see what he looked like.

Suddenly things began to make sense.

If Lianshu was an Aogiya, then it would explain why she had been allowed into the guild and even elevated to the position of guild master despite being a woman. She was the sister of the High Commander and the daughter of the guild's founder. If there was one thing that could overrule tradition—it was power.

The hope that had sprouted in Ying's heart at seeing a woman occupy a position of authority within the guild was mingled with the bitter realization of the double standards they faced. The Aogiya name alone unlocked every door for Lianshu that a girl from any other clan could never open.

Ying shot her hand up into the air. "Master Lianshu, I have a question," she said, cautiously depressing her voice, in case the guild master, as a fellow woman, saw through her secret.

A brief flicker of surprise crossed the guild master's eyes. "Yes?"

"At the start, we all thought we had been going in a straight line, but in actuality we were going in circles. Why's that so?"

Some of the other boys had suggested various supernatural reasons for the phenomenon they had experienced, but Ying didn't believe that. She believed in engineering—and this was Strategy class.

A smile quirked upon Lianshu's lips. "Ah, you noticed?" She hopped off the rock, then lifted the top fifth of it as if she were removing a hat off someone's head. Everyone quickly scrambled to their feet and moved forward to take a look, all of them flabbergasted to find that the rock was in fact hollow, its interior emptied out to house a complex set of pulleys and thick metal chains that descended down a dark pit burrowed deep into the earth.

Master Lianshu pulled two levers and the earth rumbled—the forest began to *move* before their eyes.

From their vantage point, they could see different sections of trees slide back and forth, seamlessly changing positions as if they sat on invisible wheels.

This is incredible, Ying thought. *There's an entire mechanical system buried underground controlling the movement of different plate fragments. We* were *walking in a straight line.*

It was the orientation of the forest that was changing without us realizing . . .

She turned her attention toward Master Lianshu's hands, which were deftly rotating a series of knobs on a simplified map of the forest, modeled out of shimmering tortoiseshell fragments.

"Not many people outside of the Engineers Guild and the High Command know that Wu Lin was artificially created as both a training ground for the bannermen of the Order and as a defensive barrier against any potential attacks from the eastern side of the isle. We call them 'mobile terrains.' This is your introduction to how engineering strategy and military strategy can come together to greatly enhance the capabilities of an army."

There was a fire burning in the guild master's eyes as she spoke, an infectious enthusiasm that stirred endless possibilities in Ying's mind.

One day, I'll be exactly like her, she thought.

"Okay, end of class. Get yourselves back to the guild now," Master Lianshu declared.

"How are we supposed to get back?" An-xi asked.

"Is that my problem?" The master turned and began striding away toward the city gates, leaving her shivering and exhausted charges to fend for themselves.

Ying quickly got up and chased after her.

"Master Lianshu," she panted, "there's something I want to ask you."

"What is it?" Lianshu snapped, not slowing down her pace.

"Can I please access the guild archives? I won't make a mess or look at anything that I shouldn't. I only want to take a look at my father's old books, that's all." Ying kept her head down, wary of facing Lianshu in such close proximity.

The master stopped, whirling around abruptly. Her eyebrows twitched to the agitated rhythm of those pulsating veins at her temples.

"You're the one who broke my booby trap system!" she said. "I already made it very clear, I will not have any opportunistic scoundrels trying to pull wool over my eyes and—"

"Look." Ying untied her clan pendant from her waistband, holding it out in front of Lianshu. It was a circular piece of pale green jade, with the characters "Aihui" carved by her father's own hand. "Every member of my family carries one of these. My name is Aihui Min, and my a-ma carved this for me when I was born."

Lianshu stared at the pendant for a moment, then she grabbed it from Ying, running her thumb along the grooves of the engravings. Her hands trembled. She looked up and shook Ying by the shoulders. "Where is he? Where's Shan-jin?"

"I told you before," Ying stammered, shaken by Lianshu's

violent reaction. "My father is dead. He died three months ago."

"He . . . what?"

Lianshu had been standing by the window for the longest time, and for a moment Ying wondered if the news she had brought had done enough damage to petrify the woman. A little like how monks were said to remain frozen in their lotus meditating positions when they attained enlightenment and their spirits moved on to the next realm. She was surprised that Lianshu didn't know about her father's death—but then again, the woman seemed to lead a reclusive existence.

She was sitting on the highest floor of the little pagoda that housed the guild archives, which she now knew to be the place where Lianshu had been hiding while everyone else invented tall tales about her skulking about in some rat-infested cellar. The room reminded her of her father's workshop—tools hanging from their hooks, neatly rolled-up scrolls sitting in piles, and shelves filled with stacks and stacks of books. She had been trying to catch a glimpse of Master Lianshu's brush writing, to see if it resembled that of the equations left on the back of her father's parchment, but she found no way of doing it without being too obvious.

Seeing that the master was still preoccupied with her own thoughts, Ying tried to inch a little farther right, trying to reach for a partially unrolled scroll lying on Lianshu's desk.

"We were supposed to climb the Kunrun peaks together, you know," Lianshu suddenly said.

Ying almost fell off her chair.

She bolted upright and retracted her outstretched hand, placing it stiffly upon her lap. To her relief, Lianshu hadn't turned around and noticed her suspicious behavior.

"There was a legend about an old hermit who lived up on the highest peak, who supposedly had a mystical book left by the gods. The book contained the greatest engineering secrets that could be known to humankind, and he who owned the book would wield power beyond comprehension." Lianshu laughed bitterly, shaking her head. She walked over to Ying and sat down across the circular table. "Shan-jin didn't believe that horseshit. I was the one who was fascinated with the myth and insisted that we make the trip one day. He didn't have the heart to turn me down."

"You must have been close."

"We were best friends. Shan-jin, me, and . . . never mind. It's all bygones now. Did your father not tell you anything about his time in the guild?"

"My father hardly spoke about his time in Fei or the guild. He didn't seem to like dredging up those memories."

Lianshu sighed deeply, emptying a cup of bland tea into her mouth. "If you want to look at your father's old works, they're on the second floor. You can take some of those books with you when you leave, but don't tell Gerel I let you, else he'll be nagging endlessly. Like a noisy cricket, that one." At the mention of the other master, Lianshu rolled her eyes emphatically.

"If you don't mind me asking, what exactly happened to my father here in the guild? Why did he choose to leave?" Ying asked, leaning forward. Lianshu was the first person she had met who seemed able to provide some of the answers that she was seeking.

Lianshu's fingers tightened around her ceramic teacup, shoulders visibly tensing. "There's no point in digging up the past," she said. "It's nothing. Some minor disagreements here and there. It would be disrespectful of me to tell you all these things when he explicitly wanted to keep it from you."

"But if you could just tell me—"

"No!" Lianshu shrieked. She pushed her chair back with a harsh screech and walked back to the open window. "I'm tired. Go downstairs and fetch the books you wanted and leave. They're on the third shelf from the left, shelved by clan name."

Alarmed by the sudden outburst, Ying got up and dashed for the door, turning back to take a final look at the guild master before she stepped out. Lianshu's back was hunched and her shoulders trembling. Was she crying? But why?

There were things that the guild master was keeping

from her, things about her father's past that could shed light upon his death—and she was determined to find out what they were.

~

Ever since Lianshu granted her permission to take the books out of the archives, Ying spent almost every night scouring the pages, trying to find clues hidden between the lines, anything that would take her one step closer to the truth behind her father's death. While everyone else was fast asleep and snoring, she would sneak out of the dormitory and sit outside by the little gourd-shaped pond in the courtyard, flipping through her father's old record books.

Tonight was no different. Her nose started stinging at the sight of her father's familiar handwriting.

Unlike the neat, narrow characters that she was used to seeing, her father's brushstrokes in his younger days seemed more carefree and buoyant. The brush danced across the page with vivacity, revealing a glimpse of the youth that Aihui Shan-jin used to be. In the margins of the pages, she also spotted several messy scribbles of jokes and nonsensical one-liners by someone else—presumably one of her father's close friends—that reminded her of what Chang-en kept doing in her books. She wondered if that person was Lianshu, but even if it was, the writing didn't match what was on her father's parchment or the letter sent to Wen, so it provided no answers as to the identities of those people.

It was difficult for her to imagine a youthful version of her father, going through life as a guild apprentice exactly the way she was now, yet these record books proved that such a time existed.

When her father had been happy here.

It would have been much easier if Lianshu would tell her everything she knew, but she wasn't going to harbor any expectations. Aogiya Lianshu was too much of a wild card, and she wasn't sure she could trust the woman either, not after she set a swarm of deadly bee automatons upon unsuspecting novices.

I'll need to work faster, she thought. Assassin attacks, guild master challenges, it was as if a lethal trap was waiting for her at every corner. If she didn't arm herself properly, her luck would run out eventually. With the new discovery of her father's association with Lianshu, she needed more time in the guild to investigate this new thread. If they had been best friends as Lianshu claimed, then it seemed strange that her father had never so much as mentioned Lianshu before.

In the earlier entries of her father's old notes, his work had been very conventional—improvements to existing vehicular engines and structures, adjustments to fertilizer composition, models of irrigation networks—the usual areas of engineering that apprentices were commonly put to work on. But as she progressed through the pages, she noticed a change. It started with tweaks to airship engines and sail structures, then ballonet and lift gas–related upgrades, then the pages were crammed with detailed sketches of old cannon models and gunpowder recipes.

Her father had been obsessively studying every single part of the airship before his spark of an idea for the air cannons came into being. Then his days in the guild were filled with nothing but.

This was when Ying hit a snag. In the final pages of her father's records, a hefty portion had been ripped out, leaving behind jagged edges where the pages should have been. Perplexed, Ying had flicked through the entire set of books again and again, but those missing pages were nowhere to be found.

If the trend in her father's research continued, then the missing pages likely contained more records of cannon development—much like what was in the secret journal he had asked her to burn. She pulled out that journal from between the folds of her robes and opened it, laying the books side by side.

He must have been on the brink of an important discovery, she mused to herself, the furrows across her forehead deepening as she considered everything she knew.

Her father's research might have treaded into risky territory, culminating in him leaving altogether. However, he hadn't given up on his work. Instead, he had carried on in secret back on Huarin—his journal was evidence of it. But some secrets couldn't be kept forever. Whoever it was who knew about her father's work in the guild had eventually extended their treacherous hand to Huarin, making another attempt to steal her father's knowledge.

Could it have been Gerel?

His inexplicable hatred for her father had transcended the decades. Perhaps jealousy was enough to drive a man to commit heinous crimes, beginning with theft and ending with murder.

Or could it have been one of the beiles or the noble clans?

The race for the High Commander's position was heating up, and different factions were constantly locking horns as they tussled to get their preferred candidate into the lead. Given the level of importance the High Commander had placed upon this military campaign against the Qirin empire, it was entirely possible that someone had thought of stealing her father's weapon designs so that they could claim credit for them.

She sighed, picking up a stray pebble and tossing it into the pond. "But where does the dragon symbol come into the picture?" she wondered out loud. She hadn't found any signs of dragons since arriving in the guild, and close to four months had already passed.

Unless the mastermind was a turncoat, selling the engineering secrets of the Antaran territories to the Empire?

"Why do you look so shocked?" Ye-kan's voice interrupted her train of thought.

Ying turned and saw the boy walking back toward the dormitory. She quickly stacked all the books together, slipping the one she had brought from Huarin right at the base. Ye-kan stopped beside her and peered down, arching one imperious brow.

"Well?" he demanded irritably. "What are you doing out here in the middle of the night? Haven't you learned your lesson about wandering around alone?"

Ying straightened herself up and smacked Ye-kan across the head. "Stop talking to me like that," she said. Ignoring the dismay written all over the boy's scrunched-up face, she pinched his right ear and gave it a good twist. "I'm older than you, so show some respect."

"I will not!" Ye-kan spat. "How many times must I tell you that I'm not a child! I'm also a prince of the nine isles—why can't you treat me the way you treat Ye-yang?"

Her mood lifted. Ying laughed, letting go of the boy's ear. "Where have you been? Looks like *you're* the one who's been wandering about after hours."

He scowled. "Getting a scolding," he said. "Turns out my aunt spotted me right from the beginning. She was only pretending not to so that it would keep me on edge. Today, she finally summoned me to the archives and gave me a good whipping with one of her sadistic machines. I swear that woman is unhinged!"

There was a fine line between being utterly brilliant and being completely delusional, and to Ying, Aogiya Lianshu was the former. Over the course of the few Strategy lessons they had received, she was awestruck by the wild feats of engineering the woman seemed to be capable of.

Ying's smile widened, and she reached over to ruffle Ye-kan's hair. She knew he hated it, which made her like doing it even more. "So what did she say? Is she going to tell the other masters? Have you sent home?" she asked.

The prince glared at her in annoyance, smoothing down his messed-up hair. "Thankfully not. She had a massive argument with my a-ma a few years back and hasn't spoken to him since, and she absolutely detests my e-niye, so she's not going to break precedent on my account. She only warned me not to give her any trouble, that's all," he grumbled. "I think she's *happy* that I'm here because she knows how much it'll tick off my e-niye when she finds out."

The Aogiya clan truly had some complex politics, Ying thought, and feuding siblings seemed to be a staple. She was immensely grateful that there had never been such problems in her own family, even if Wen occasionally grated on her nerves. How was he coping with his new position as clan chieftain? And what of Nian, who would no doubt need to serve as their brother's voice of reason when he went off on one of his moods?

"What's all that?" Ye-kan pointed at the stack of books sitting on the ground. He bent over and picked up the top one, flipping through it casually. He rubbed his fingers together, looking disgusted at the little dust bunnies that started to form.

"There's so much dust on these pages. Where did you dig these up from?"

"They're from the guild archives. Apparently Master Lianshu and my a-ma used to be on close terms." She was going to have to verify exactly how close that relationship was. Ying took the book from him, peeling away remnants of dust that still clung to the pages. "They're his work, from when he was an apprentice in the guild. Nothing special though, only the usual mundane things that junior apprentices work on."

Ye-kan squatted down by the edge of the pond and grabbed a fistful of grass from the gaps in the stone tiles, then he started plucking out one blade at a time, tossing them onto the water's surface. "You were really close to your father, huh? For you to come all this way, disguised like that"—he wrinkled up his nose—"just to accomplish what he didn't."

"Yeah, I was. We were inseparable. My little sister Nian—she's about your age—used to get jealous because A-ma and I spent so much time together tinkering in his workshop. But when I asked her to join in, she would get bored midway and scamper off to do other things instead."

"Must be nice to be able to spend that much time with your father," Ye-kan muttered.

"I'm sure the High Commander wants to spend more time with you too, just that he's too busy because, well, he *is* the leader of the Antaran territories," Ying offered. "I never knew boys cared about these things. My brothers never did. They'd rather spend their time riding horses and hunting pigeons."

Ye-kan puffed up his cheeks, sullenly yanking at the pathetic remains of grass. "Doesn't matter," he grumbled. "And stop looking at me like that! I don't need your sympathy."

"Of course not." She clutched her father's old books close to her chest, as if doing that would bring him back to her side once more.

If there was someone in need of sympathy, it was probably her.

Instead of heading back toward the dormitory, Ying turned and walked down the passageway leading to the workshops in the east wing. Ye-kan chased after her, bewildered.

"Aren't you going back to sleep?" he asked.

She shook her head. "I don't think I'll be able to sleep for a while, so I might as well not waste the time. I'm going to practice mixing that fertilizer formula that we were taught today." Or work on the Peony a little more. "Go back, you don't have to follow me."

~

But she didn't manage to shake the prince off her tail. Ye-kan insisted on tagging along, claiming that he wasn't sleepy despite his frequent yawns.

The duo wound their way down the dimly lit passageways. In the night, the guild felt even more forbidding and unwelcoming than it already did in the day, shadows flickering across its dusty gray floors and walls. The winds echoed down the narrow corridors, whistling a creepy tune.

"What's that?!" Ye-kan suddenly hissed, making Ying jump right out of her skin.

The boy was pointing toward one of the workshops at the far end of the long corridor that they were on, whose wooden latticed door was slowly swinging shut. Someone had just left the workshop, light footsteps tapping against the stone floor and receding into the distance.

"That looked like Master Gerel," the prince added, rubbing the back of his head thoughtfully. "But why's he here at this hour?"

"Same reason we are?" Ying offered, though she hardly meant it.

She wasn't certain it was Gerel—all she managed to catch a glimpse of was a corner of a dark robe that could have been maroon or black or any other shade in between. The workshop that had been vacated did belong to the guild master though.

Sensing the opportunity, Ying picked up the pace and walked quickly toward the workshop in question. She stopped in front of the doors, sucking in her breath as she stared at the crisscrossing latticework on the door panels. It wasn't locked. She reached out to push them open.

"Wait, what do you think you're doing? You can't just break into a guild master's workshop like that." Ye-kan caught up to her.

"If I don't say anything and you don't say anything, who's going to find out?" Ying replied. "Besides, it's not like I'm going to steal anything. I'll just take a quick look. You can stay outside if you want." She would rather not be doing this with Ye-kan around, but the opportunity was too good to be missed.

She stepped across the threshold and entered the workshop, standing still in the darkness while her vision acclimated. Unlike her father's workshop, or Lianshu's, Gerel's space was far neater and more orderly, almost like he had a compulsion for tidiness. The tabletops were spick-and-span, brushes hung from their racks in precise order of size, tools were kept in long wooden receptacles that sat in neat rows on the shelves—everything was in perfect harmony.

It did not, at first glance, look like the room of a traitor and spy.

But looks could be deceiving.

Ying moved quickly. She started with what looked to be Gerel's main workstation, where an ornate ink slab carved with motifs of cranes sat in one corner beside a small rack of brushes and a pile of neatly stacked books and scrolls. The creases on her forehead deepened as she flipped through the content, looking for a clue. Familiar brush writing, dragon symbols, mentions of her father's work—anything.

There was nothing out of the ordinary. Just typical

engineering books of the most boring nature, as was expected from a prude like Gerel.

"*What* are you doing?!" Ye-kan hissed from the doorway. "Get out of there now." His eyes darted back and forth anxiously.

Ying ignored him, moving on to a nearby shelf, where she spotted a few hefty stone jadeite seals. She lifted them one by one, turning them around to study the patterns carved on their undersides.

Nothing. None of it matched the seal that had been stamped onto the letter.

Incriminating things would be locked away, she thought, surveying the surroundings for any locked cupboards or drawers. There was only one, a low rosewood cabinet sitting by the windows on its curvaceous legs, with a large bronze padlock keeping its contents hidden away from prying eyes. Ying hurried over.

"Stop!" Ye-kan ran in and grabbed her by the arm before she could get her fingers on the lock. "Do you know how much trouble we could get into if anyone catches us here? We shouldn't even be in here!"

"Let go of me. I need a while more to—"

"What are the two of you doing in my workshop?!"

CHAPTER 17

YING AND YE-KAN WHIRLED AROUND, HORRIFIED TO find Master Gerel standing by the open doorway. The muscles on the right side of his face were twitching uncontrollably, his eyes almost bulging out of their bony sockets as he glared at them. Under the eerie illumination of the lamp in his hands, the scrawny guild master in his blood-red robes looked like a harbinger from hell.

"This is a misunderstanding," Ye-kan cried out, waving his hands about in the air in rampant denial. "It's not what it looks like!"

"Is that right?" Gerel walked into the workshop, setting the lamp down on the nearest surface with a loud clunk. The flame within flickered, casting ominous shadows against the walls. "Two apprentice candidates, skulking about a guild master's personal workshop in the middle of the night, trying to break into locked cabinets. Pray tell me, what am I misunderstanding?"

Ying gulped, her mind frazzled by the guild master's sudden appearance.

"We were on our way to the apprentice workshops to do some extra practice because we couldn't get to sleep, and we thought we saw someone sneaking out of your workshop so we came over to check," Ye-kan explained, his voice trembling. "We were only trying to make sure nothing was stolen, that's all."

Ying glanced sideways at her companion, grateful for his quick thinking. She remained silent, keeping her head bowed.

"Don't try to trick me with your cheap excuses!" Gerel bellowed, eyes flashing dangerously. "You think I don't know what you're here for? You're trying to steal the question for the second test!"

The both of them vehemently shook their heads, dropping to their knees.

"We weren't trying to do anything of that sort, Master Gerel," Ying said.

"And you think I'll believe that?"

"Master Gerel, think about it, why would the two of us do something like that?" Ye-kan said, looking up and holding the guild master's gaze. "Min is here under the fourth *beile*'s nomination, and I am representing the Bayara clan." He reached for his waistband and withdrew a circular white jade pendant, holding it out on the palm of his hands. "If we get caught attempting to cheat—which we undoubtedly will, given the astuteness of your good self and the other masters—we would have sullied our clan names and the beile's reputation. We have much more to lose by doing that than by failing the test altogether."

Ying turned to look at Ye-kan, awed by his cleverly worded explanation. The earlier fear and panic had vanished from his eyes, replaced by a degree of confidence that reminded her of Ye-yang and the other Aogiyas. Blood ran thicker than water, and in this moment Ye-kan's pedigree shone through.

The prince's words seemed to have some effect, as the anger on Gerel's face subsided. He solemnly studied the jade pendant that Ye-kan had shown him. The Bayara clan was one of the wealthiest clans on Fei, having built their riches off their monopoly of the salt trade. They also happened to be one of the guild's biggest sponsors.

An uneasy silence set in.

After a long, torturous moment, the guild master said, "Seeing as the padlock is still intact and the test scroll within remains untouched, I shall grant the two of you the benefit of the doubt. However, entering a guild master's workshop without prior permission is still a punishable offense." His thin lips curled upward in a cruel smile. "For that, you shall receive twenty strokes of the rod in front of all the other candidates, as a lesson to anyone else who might be thinking of taking a night gander."

"But the second test is in three days!" Ye-kan protested, his face reddening with indignation. "And you can't do that, because, because—"

"Because what?" Gerel snapped. "Don't test my patience.

This is already a lenient punishment. Unless you'd rather I expel you from the guild?"

Ye-kan pursed his lips together, the artery at his temple pulsating visibly. Then he deflated, shoulders sagging in resignation. Ying reached out and patted the back of his hand as a form of comfort, but the aggrieved boy immediately pulled it away.

After Gerel let them leave, the prince stormed back toward the dormitories in an incensed rage. Ying chased after him.

"Ye-kan, I'm sorry," she said, reaching out and catching hold of his shoulder.

The boy shrugged her hand off, whirling around to face her. "If you're sorry, then tell me, what were you doing rummaging around Gerel's workshop? What were you looking for? Did Ye-yang put you up to this?" he demanded.

Ying's expression dimmed at the mention of Ye-yang. She had heard nothing of the expedition to Fu-li since he left, and the silence left her apprehensive.

"No! It has nothing to do with him." She hesitated, chewing on her lower lip as she contemplated whether or not to let someone else in on the whole truth. She couldn't. Too much was at stake.

Ye-kan was too innocent and naive, and he didn't deserve to be involved in her schemes more than he had already been tonight. "Gerel was right, I wanted to cheat for the second test because I wasn't confident of clearing it on my own mettle," she lied. "You know how it went for the first test. If it hadn't been for the High Commander showing up unexpectedly, my name wouldn't have made it to the list."

"I see. So this is how it's going to be." Ye-kan's jaw tightened, his fists clenching by his sides. "I thought we were friends, Ying, but I guess I thought wrong." Swinging his sleeves, the fourteenth prince turned and marched off, disappearing down the long corridor.

Ying leaned her back against one of the stone pillars, letting the disappointment in those words, the hurt she saw in Ye-kan's eyes, steep in her heart and mind. But she couldn't have chosen otherwise. She couldn't tell him the truth, if only to protect him from being dragged into this treacherous whirlpool she was trying to navigate.

"I'm sorry," she whispered.

Three days later, the forty-one apprentice hopefuls were gathered at the Order's airship repair yard, lined up in neat rows while they awaited the arrival of the guild masters. Sweaty palms and chattering teeth formed a bizarre juxtaposition as the young men sought to assuage their own nervousness in the blustery cold.

It was an unusually cold day for Antaran summer, with flakes of snow drifting down from the gray skies above. "An inauspicious omen from Abka Han," someone said.

Ying stared blankly ahead, physically present but mentally on a separate plane of existence. The hetian jade pendant pressing against her chest provided a helpful dose of warmth, but at the same time, it reminded her of the heavy burden weighing down in her mind. The dull, throbbing pain at the back of her calves didn't help.

She had spent the past two days lying prone on the dormitory bed after enduring the twenty strokes of the rod that Gerel had meted out. It was a miracle the bones in her legs hadn't been broken. Still, it was better than having a beating dealt to her back, which would have required her to disrobe—making it impossible for her to keep her act up.

"Do you want to sit down? Conserve some energy for the test," Chang-en suggested helpfully from behind her.

Ying shook her head. She knew her face was ghastly pale, and the sensation of light-headedness struck her every now and then, threatening to make her pass out on the sandy ground, but she had to make it through today. She needed more time in the guild, more time to uncover the secrets harbored within its walls.

Out of the corner of her eye, she could see Ye-kan standing three rows away, looking similarly off-color. Ying had a newfound respect for him. There were many choices that would have made his life easier—telling Gerel the truth about their night escapade, revealing his Aogiya identity in exchange for pardon, returning to his comfortable life as a prince—but he did none of that. Instead, he had gritted his teeth silently while the heavy wooden rod landed over and over, glistening sweat gathered upon his brow as he suffered through the pain. And he must still be suffering now, the same way she was.

The guilt ate away inside her. It was her fault that Ye-kan had to put up with the shame.

A large carriage trundled through the imposing gates of the shipyard, the sound of its wheels grinding against the sand and the low whistle of its steam engine distracting Ying from her thoughts. The carriage's occupants alighted in a stream of maroon.

Gerel led the pack, as always, and walked up to the solemn lineup of apprentices-in-waiting. In his hand was a scroll, identical to the one that had carried the question for their first test. When he caught sight of Ying, ashen but present, he grimaced, then cleared his throat dramatically.

"We are gathered here for the second test in the guild's apprenticeship trial," he started. "After today, only half of you will remain."

An anxious buzz went around, panic and dread draining the color off the faces of the young men.

"The trial of the heart is a team challenge—because the guild does not build its achievements upon the backs of individuals alone. If you are accepted into the guild, you are expected to work well with your brethren, and to be humble and receptive toward the teachings of the masters."

"That's assuming the teachings are worth receiving," Chang-en whispered, a cheeky smirk on his face.

"If you are sharp of mind but weak of heart, then you will not be a right fit for the Engineers Guild, and your journey will end here," Gerel said as he undid the black string holding the scroll. "The task for today's test is"—he shifted his fingers, and the parchment unfurled, revealing a column of inky characters—"for each team to repair an unknown problem plaguing an assigned airship. Master Kyzo has ensured that every airship is different, which means that cheating will not be possible. You have three sticks of incense worth of time to complete this task."

A senior apprentice brought out three large sticks of incense, shoving them into the large bronze tripod filled with ash.

"Work together and employ what you have learned in Construction, Materials, and Design. The work that Master Kyzo and his fellow engineers do on a daily basis here at the Order's airship yard is one of the guild's key responsibilities, so all of you should take this seriously if you hope to join our ranks. For this test, your groups have been preassigned."

Gerel rattled off a list of names, to the groans and squeals of the test-takers. They had been grouped into fours or fives, with each group assigned a number that would correspond to an airship berth. Ying had been grouped with An-xi, both a blessing and a curse. Chang-en moved to join Ye-kan's line.

When he was done assigning groups, Gerel gestured to the senior apprentice, who promptly lit the first incense stick with a fire starter. A mad dash to the respective berths ensued, with some overzealous candidates resorting to pushing their competitors to waste a little time.

Ying dragged her feet toward her berth, stopping at the edge of the airship's inflated ballonet. The silver insignia of the cobra painted onto coal black now filled her with uncertainty instead of awe.

"Hurry up, Min!" An-xi hollered from the ship's deck. "You're wasting time!"

Tearing her gaze away from the snake, she clambered up the rope ladder and joined the others on deck.

Before they could start repairing anything, they needed to identify the fault. The boys flew into a frenzy, with the overbearing An-xi naturally assuming leadership and shouting out orders to the rest. While they were still scrambling all around the ship, there was an ominous groan and the entire hull began to rock.

Ying and the others immediately rushed to the bulwarks. She recognized that motion—it was a sign that the airship was about to lift off.

"What's going on?" someone cried.

The ropes tethering the airship to the ground had already been thrown off their pegs, leaving the ship free to ascend toward the skies. In the vicinity, all the other airships that carried the trial candidates had also been similarly released, each one slowly beginning to rise.

"Boys, I know Master Gerel said you have three sticks of incense, but if you ask me, that's a little generous," Master Kyzo chortled, his belly bouncing up and down with amusement as he surveyed the looks of shock and horror on the faces of the young candidates. "Now quit gawking and get to work. You don't have all day, y'know!"

There was a moment of stunned silence—then panic ensued.

"What are we going to do!"

"What if we don't manage to repair the fault in time? You don't think the ship will actually crash . . . Will it?"

"Well, hurry up then! You heard what Master Kyzo said. We don't have time!"

As the airship gained altitude, temperatures on deck plunged to frosty levels, but none of the candidates had a mind to care about how blue their lips were turning or how tiny ice crystals were forming upon their eyelashes. They scoured every inch of the ship, until—to their dismay—they found themselves squeezed into the tiny engine hold, staring at a smoking engine.

An engine malfunction was one of the worst possible faults that could blight an airship, because it was the singular most complex piece of machinery on board, responsible for keeping the ship's propellers spinning and the ballonet inflated. Wooden cogs and metal bolts and axles of all shapes and sizes surrounded a seemingly innocuous gas furnace, forming a complicated map that whirred and spun with impeccable precision.

The engine was the heart of the airship, and when the heart could not beat—the ship was as good as dead.

"Heavens save us," one of the boys muttered, pointing at a smoldering cog.

"Looks like a kaen gas explosion. It won't be long before the engine stops running altogether," An-xi said, looking equally devastated. "We're going to have to take it apart and fix in new parts from scratch—before we hit the ground."

"But where are we going to find new parts when we're airborne?"

The team of four exchanged distressed glances, the sizzling of the ruined engine sounding like the beating of funerary drums to their ears. *What is it like to die in an airship crash?* Ying wondered, then she quickly shoved the thought out of her head.

She had not come all this way to die.

"The parts of an engine are not uncommon. We might be able to find them in other parts of the ship," she said.

Engine study had been covered extensively while they were on repair and maintenance duty with Master Kyzo, and Ying had spent many sleepless nights studying airship plans. Unlike many of the other candidates, she never had the luxury of receiving tutelage in airship engineering—her family had not been wealthy enough to own one—so she had to put in double the effort to catch up.

Hopefully those lost hours of sleep would be of some use today.

"An-xi, there should be some pistons that we can use in the ship's boiler room, right?"

The petite boy stared at her in silence for a brief moment, then he frantically nodded. "Yes, yes," he replied, "the boiler pistons will be the same size as the ones we need for the engine."

Every airship had at least one large boiler, responsible for supplying hot steam to all the cabins for heating purposes through a series of bamboo pipes. Keeping warm was the least of their concerns now.

"And there'll be spare gears in the kitchen!" An-xi added with a flourish, his eyes lighting up. There was a small pulley system that allowed the ship's cooks to send food from the kitchen to the various cabins, but that could easily be dismantled.

They sprang into action, dashing to the respective areas of the ship to retrieve the parts they needed. By the time they regrouped, the engine was already spluttering to a stop. The propellers began to slow.

"We have to disassemble the engine and repair it with the replacement parts as quickly as we can," Ying said. "Once the engine stops, we'll only have less than half an incense worth of time before the gas in the ballonet runs out." When that happened, the ship would no longer be able to remain suspended, sending them plunging to their deaths.

No one moved. The other boys—including An-xi—were trembling from head to toe.

"Damn it," Ying swore, her brows knitting into a frown. As unsure as she was, she would have to take the gamble and do it herself. She reached for the first smoking cog and ripped it out.

An-xi let out a strangled cry. "Do you know what you're doing?" he squeaked.

"No, not really. Is that what you want to hear?" Ignoring the pain from the searing metal against her fingers, Ying disassembled the engine, leaving behind a gaping hole where the gears should have been. Charred remains of the old parts lay in a sorry pile by the side. "Tell me where the parts need to go," she said.

When An-xi didn't reply, Ying turned and grabbed him by the shoulders, shaking him hard. "Listen to me, Niohuru An-xi, I need you to tell me where each part should go. I've never touched an actual airship engine before—but you have. Your clan builds these damned things."

"A-a-according to the *Annals*, we'll first need to fix the pistons into position before we start assembling the inner gears, which need to connect to the axles leading out to the propellers,"

An-xi said. He held out a piston, pointing to the left corner of the engine's case. "There."

Ying did as she was told, fixing piston after piston, gear after gear. Soon, the rest of her team shook themselves out of their shocked state and moved to help, fishing for the correct parts or lending a hand to tighten screws and cogs.

"*Always start from the inside and work your way out. Big gears alternate with smaller ones—they're complementary. Support one another,*" Ying's father's voice echoed in her head from a distant memory.

She remembered sitting out on the grass in front of his workshop, blowing dandelions while her father tinkered with the broken ship engines that the village merchants brought over for fixing. She never understood why her father did all this labor for free, but he would patiently explain that payment didn't necessarily come in the form of coin. By helping the merchants fix their engines, he earned the chance to hone his craft, to become an even better engineer.

"*You see those fancy airships up in the skies?*" he once said, pointing at a fleet that had just floated by. "*They run on engines too. Remember, the principles are the same. Inside out, big and small, keep going until you complete the entire puzzle.*"

"*Big and small, just like you and me!*" the younger her had said, gleefully picking up two gears from her father's toolbox. "*I'm the little gear, and A-ma's the big gear.*"

"That's right, my precious lamb. Big and small, you've got to have both in order to make things work."

"I think we need a larger gear," she said to An-xi, pointing to the box of parts sitting near his feet. They had reached the final step, and their next move would decide whether or not they succeeded in passing the test—and staying alive.

"But the *Annals* said two small, followed by one large."

"Give me the big one," Ying repeated firmly.

An-xi hesitated for a moment, then he did as she said, passing over the largest gear in the box.

Droplets of sweat trickled down the sides of Ying's face as she carefully slotted it in. The gear clicked into place. Holding her breath, she signaled to one of the others to start the engine.

A loud hum filled the room as the machine roared to life.

All of them ran out of the engine hold and back onto the upper deck.

"The propellers are spinning again!" An-xi shouted with glee.

Ying looked up, watching as the black ballonet started to refill with kaen gas. The silver cobra straightened, rising like a malevolent creature from the depths, its slit-like eyes lording down upon them.

We did it, she thought, relief washing over her. *A-ma, can you see this? I did it.*

"Hey, look over there," her teammate called out, pointing

out from starboard side. "That other airship looks like it's in trouble."

There was another ship in the vicinity, with plumes of black smoke issuing from its portside sail—or where its sail should have been. Instead of having two bamboo-battened wings extending outward from the hull, the airship only had one outstretched, leaving it tilted heavily to one side. Left unresolved, the tension in the ropes tethering the ship's hull to its ballonet would eventually cause them to snap.

"Theirs must have been a fault with the sail's extension and retraction mechanism," An-xi remarked with a contemptuous smirk, his earlier anxiety nowhere to be seen. "Looks like someone's going to fail their trial."

"Fail? If they fail, they *die*," Ying retorted. "We have to do something."

"That's part of the risk involved in attempting the guild's apprenticeship trial. They all knew what they were signing up for, so whose fault is it if they die?" An-xi folded his arms across his skinny chest and sat down squarely on the deck. "It's not like we can do anything to help them anyway."

Ying could hear desperate shouts coming from the other airship—shouts belonging to Ye-kan. The young prince was often yelling at others in the guild, so she could recognize the shrill pitch of his voice anywhere.

That's Ye-kan and Chang-en's ship . . .

She glanced at her three teammates, but all of them were looking elsewhere, refusing to engage.

"Fine. If you won't do anything to help them, then I will," she declared. She marched over to the ship's steering apparatus and placed her hands on the large wooden wheel. With a deep breath, she spun the wheel to the right. Their ship veered sharply to one side, almost knocking all of them off their feet.

"What do you think you're doing?" An-xi shrieked. He ran over to her and tried to pry her fingers off the wheel. "Stop this! You'll get us all killed."

"If we stand by and watch our friends die, then maybe there's a special place in hell reserved for us too. Niohuru An-xi, is your heart really made from stone?"

The boy froze, then he looked past her shoulder at the other ship. Ying knew he could see them too, clinging to the masts and ropes as they made a last-ditch attempt to repair their faulty ship—before they were flung off the deck altogether and sent plummeting to the ground. Those weren't strangers. Those were people who they had lived with, laughed with, struggled with through the hardships of these trials. Those were their *friends*.

She felt his grip over her fingers loosen, then his arms fell back to his sides.

"We can buy them some time," she said.

"How?"

"I need your help. I'm going to bring our ship alongside

theirs. Once we're close enough, I'll give you the signal. Retract our starboard sail."

"What?" An-xi's eyes bulged. "But that'll throw our own ship off balance!" he exclaimed.

"Not if we get the timing right. When our sail is pulled back, we'll need to quickly lash the two ships together." That way, they would be forming one massive vehicle out of the two airships, with one sail from each helping the entire behemoth maintain stability.

When the realization dawned, An-xi ran toward the huge wooden levers on the starboard side of the deck, readying himself to pull in the sail. The other two boys scrambled to unwind mooring rope from the airship's iron bollards, positioning themselves by the bulwark.

Ying kept her eyes fixed upon the closing gap between their airship and the next, trying her best to steady her shaky hands on the steering wheel. The howling winds whipped across her cheeks, as if trying to warn her against the mindlessness of what she was doing. She held her breath and waited.

"Now!" she yelled.

An-xi leaned his entire weight onto the lever, and the loud, rhythmic clicking of the retracting sail could be heard amid the tangle of shouts from both the boys on the other ship and those on their own. Almost immediately, the airship rocked to the side, and the two hulls rammed violently against each other.

"Quick, tie the ships together!"

Abandoning the wheel, Ying rushed to help with the ropes. On the other ship, Ye-kan ran over to help her. Even as no words passed, the tacit understanding between them was perfectly clear. Over and under, over and under, they worked swiftly together until the final length of rope was used and the last knot secured. The wooden planks of the airship hulls creaked and yawned, like two giant beasts straining to free themselves from each other.

But the knots held.

"It worked?" Ying heard An-xi's voice echo from what felt like an infinite distance away, muffled by the buzzing in her ears from the adrenaline coursing through her veins.

Sliding down the deck to Ye-kan's side, Chang-en leaned against his ship's rail, exhausted but grinning from ear to ear. He wagged a finger at her and said, "Aihui Min, I honestly don't know if you're a genius or plain reckless, but whatever it is, I'm glad you're it."

CHAPTER 18

A LOUD GONG SOUNDED THRICE ACROSS THE entire airship yard, signaling the end of the second test. All the candidates shimmied down from their respective airships, some looking quite shaken and green in the face. They hurried and stumbled back to the gathering point, where the guild masters were already waiting.

Ying took her place in the line, her face still flushed from exertion. She raised her hand and wiped her leaky nose, trying not to think about the throbbing burns on her palms or the sores that had formed on her reddened fingers.

Everyone seemed to have landed safely, but did that mean that everyone had successfully passed the test? Chang-en's team had managed to repair their faulty sail mechanism after Ying and her crew helped them stabilize the ship. Technically they had managed to fulfill the task requirements.

"Enough chatter!" Master Gerel commanded, clapping his hands several times to get the candidates' attention. "The second test has come to an end. The guild masters will now convene to deliberate. After we have arrived at a conclusion, we will announce the names of the candidates who have qualified for the final test. Those of you who do not make it will have to leave the guild by tomorrow morning."

The master turned toward the airships and hollered a command, following which two senior airship engineers stepped off each ship.

"Were they on board with us all this while?" Ye-kan exclaimed.

"Of course," Chang-en replied. "Did you actually believe that the guild would let us die? *That* would have been the scandal of the year."

"Then why didn't they show up earlier? We almost died up there!"

Ying was equally astonished by this discovery. They had never been in danger of actual death throughout the trial. The senior engineers would have stepped in to rescue them if it looked like they were about to fail. To think she had put herself and her team through that harrowing experience, believing that she was a hero.

In the end, she was only a fool.

A hand landed on her shoulder and her head jolted up. To her surprise, it was An-xi standing behind her.

A lump of regret and guilt rose up her throat. "I'm sorry," she said.

But An-xi shook his head. "You didn't do anything wrong. You were absolutely right about one thing—that we can't just stand by and watch our friends die. For the record, I *don't* have a heart made of stone, despite what all of you might think. See that you remember that, Aihui Min."

A rare smile appeared on his weary face for the briefest of moments, then he turned and walked away.

The tension among the young hopefuls reached a peak when the guild masters finally returned from their deliberation. All eyes fell upon the roll of parchment in Gerel's hand.

"The guild masters have completed our evaluation. Twenty candidates have been identified to proceed to the final test." Gerel handed the parchment to a senior apprentice. "The decision is final, no appeals allowed. Those whose names are not on the board are to head back to clear your belongings immediately. The rest of you will resume lessons tomorrow."

With a wave of his hand he dismissed the assembly, and the masters turned to leave. The flock of young men sped toward the wooden board that had been set up by the side, where the senior apprentice was now plastering the list of fortunate names.

Ying trailed a distance behind the others, hesitant to unveil her fate. But she didn't have to do it for herself, because a shrill voice rang out the answer before the list came within her view.

"I made it!" An-xi was shouting, his usual smug arrogance returning to him.

"We did too," Chang-en said, slapping Ye-kan on the back.

The grouchy prince glowered, then turned and met Ying's gaze.

"You're in top place," Ye-kan mumbled, pointing at the first name on the list. It was the first thing he had said to her since their workshop break-in, and given how he had unconditionally trusted her judgment during the airship crisis, it seemed that their quarrel might finally be water under the bridge. The relief that the silent treatment was over struck Ying much more strongly than she had expected. Somewhere along the way, Ye-kan had become someone she valued in her life.

Ying slowly inched her way through the mass of jostling bodies until she could see the parchment for herself. Twenty names were written neatly in black ink—and this time, the name "Aihui Min" was not bringing up the rear, but sitting right at the top.

It was true. She was first. *But why?*

Shouts of protest had arisen from some of the other candidates, and the loudest voices came from Arban's group, who ranked beneath Ying's even though they had been the first ship to successfully mend their fault and land. Words like "favoritism" and "rigged" were being bandied around, and Arban's expression matched the shade of the airships' ballonets.

Ying spotted Master Kyzo lurking around chewing haw candy, observing the candidates' reactions with a bemused glint in his eyes. She ran over.

"Master Kyzo," she said. "Why am I in first place? Arban's

team finished faster than we did." If anything, she should have been penalized for being foolhardy and putting her teammates at risk.

"Let me ask you something first," Kyzo said, still chewing nonchalantly. "Why did you decide to help that other ship, even though your team had already completed your task? You could have left them to flounder, removed some of your competition."

"I . . . I couldn't. I thought they were going to die," she said, her voice dropping to a whisper. She could still feel the panic gripping her heart when she heard Ye-kan's voice screaming for help, when she saw the dark clouds of smoke billowing from the ship and the way its ballonet almost detached from the hull entirely.

Kyzo nodded, rubbing his chin with his free hand while his mechanical one rotated his candy stick.

"And that's why all the senior engineers and the guild masters unanimously voted for you to come in first place, even Gerel. This is the trial of the heart, child. The engineers on board were not merely there to swoop in to save your asses, they were also there to observe each one of you, how you worked together, how you worked for one another. Even though you didn't have to, and despite the initial protests from your own team members, you managed to rally them to your cause. If this had been an actual war, what you did would have saved an entire airship's worth of lives."

He patted her on the shoulder.

"By the way, you didn't follow the engine construction manual in the *Annals*, eh?"

Ying blinked, recalling how she had gone against An-xi's recommendation when slotting in the final gears.

"I like a maverick. Your engine was an even better version than the ones we have! It allowed for a marginally faster rotation of the axles connecting to the propellers, which meant that the airship could have an increased maximum speed. But you were lucky. Had the airship been allowed to operate for a longer period, it would overheat. Our existing propellers aren't built to withstand that level of rotation. I'll have to get my team to look into that," Kyzo explained. "You have the makings of a guild master, Aihui Min. Your father would have been very proud." Then he gave her a hard smack on the back, sending her lurching forward. "Now get your ass back to the guild and stop doubting our decision."

Taking another bite off his haw stick, Kyzo chuckled and went on his way, his merry laughter reverberating in the air.

Ying watched as the stout master trudged off, still trying to comprehend what she had been told.

The makings of a guild master?

She shifted her gaze toward her team's airship, now sitting ruefully at its berth. The dying cinder inside her was flickering to life once again, reignited by the words of promise that Kyzo had gifted her.

For the first time in her life, she understood the risks of becoming an engineer—as well as the potential. Being a member of the guild was not merely a shiny badge of honor, but an acceptance of the perils that came along with it. Beyond these trials, there would be no senior engineers waiting in the wings to rescue them if they failed. Beyond these trials, the threat of death would be real.

I have to become better.

She had to work hard enough to be worthy of the praise she had been given, of the trust that her friends had placed in her, and of the responsibility that came with being a full-fledged engineer. But could she do it? Did this life truly belong to her? Her father's death remained unsolved, assassins constantly lurking in the shadows—and there was still her family, no doubt expecting her to return to Huarin to lead the life everyone expected her to.

"The banners are back! The banners are back!" someone was shouting across the shipyard, distracting the candidates from their momentary distress.

"The banners are back?" Ying murmured. She stood on her tiptoes and glimpsed the engineer who had just run in through the gates of the shipyard, waving his hand excitedly in the air as he announced the news. A small crowd gathered around him, eager to hear the latest gossip in town.

The banners were back—and if the bannermen had returned

to the capital, that could only mean one thing. That Ye-yang was back too.

~

The streets of Fei thronged with excited citizens, eager to catch sight of the victorious bannermen and the beiles. In the span of an afternoon, the news of the banners' success had spread across the entire capital like wildfire. Defeating the Great Jade Empire, even in one small battle, was no mean feat.

The fourth beile and a handful of his bannermen had disguised themselves as merchants and infiltrated the city of Fu-li—one of the main sentries on the border of the Empire. While inside, they secretly bought over the services of many Empire soldiers, including some of the generals guarding the city. At the same time, they spread rumors within the marketplace, distracting the city's officials with promises of riches and gold so they paid little attention to the security of the city walls, allowing Erden and Ye-han's men to approach without anyone noticing. At the pivotal moment, in the depths of the night, Ye-yang and his men swarmed the Fu-li city gates from within the city, cutting down the enemy soldiers with ease and forcing the rest to swear fealty to the Cobra's Order. Had they been discovered any earlier, they would have been isolated behind enemy lines with no means of escape.

This was the first time the Antaran High Command had gone on the offensive against the Empire, and with that, the two sides would officially be at war.

Ying could not confess to understanding why the High Commander was so insistent on pursuing this military campaign. The Seven Grievances that the High Command had plastered on noticeboards all over the city had not convinced her of its necessity. Even if the Empire was exploiting the Antaran territories to some degree, was peace not a better option than provoking a sleeping giant and sending one's own sons to the battlefield? She was sitting by the window on the second floor of the Silver Spoon, peering at the street down below, at the crowd that was waiting eagerly for the victorious troops to parade by.

"One day I'm going to be marching with them," Chang-en proclaimed.

"You're an engineer. You're never going to be marching with the bannermen," An-xi said. "Why would you want to anyway unless you have a death wish? For every man that gets to the victory march, nine others die in an unmarked grave."

There were only three of them sitting in the private dining space that belonged to Chang-en's family. The food was as stellar as she remembered, but the room felt a lot emptier now that there were only the few of them remaining.

"I can still be an accompanying weapons engineer, even if I need to ride on a horse-drawn night soil wagon at the back of the contingent. Weaponry is the most prestigious division of the guild, why would you want to be posted anywhere else?"

"If you love weapons so much, then suit yourself." An-xi sniffed. "I prefer architecture and construction. Imagine being the one in charge of building the new palace! The kind of legacy you'll leave behind!"

Surviving the apprenticeship trial and entering the guild wasn't the end of the rat race. Once you were through the doors, apprentices fought tooth and nail for the right to join one of the many guild divisions, of which weapons engineering was by far the most highly sought after, if only because it received the most funding and recognition from the High Command. There were many other divisions that were equally important, which created and maintained structures that helped keep the nine isles running and the people fed and clothed, yet those were often considered secondary to Weaponry.

Ying guessed that her father must have belonged to Weaponry, but she was hesitant about following in those footsteps. There was much about war and weaponry that frightened and discomfited her. There were many other guild divisions that appealed more, like Transportation, which Master Kyzo belonged to, working on the airships and other vehicular designs, or maybe even the elusive Black Ops unit, which worked on cutting-edge innovations—though those sometimes blurred ethical lines, such as the grotesque chimeras.

But this might all be wishful thinking. She might not be able to remain in Fei long enough to be able to choose a guild division. Surviving the trial was one matter, surviving her father's killer was another.

While her two companions continued bickering about which divisions were superior, Ying stared out the window in a daze as she waited for the entourage to appear. She sat up when a sudden cacophony of cheering and hooting erupted down below.

The rows of bannermen had turned the corner. They were making their way down the far end of the street. The solemn pounding of horse hooves on the cobblestones resonated in the air, cutting through the cheers like lightning through the dense clouds. At the head of the pack, a lone figure rode atop his black steed, back stiff and proud like an obsidian god of war.

The weight lifted off Ying's shoulders. He was back, like he said he would be.

Ye-yang was the center of attention of today's military parade, the Plain White Banner colors flying ahead of the others. The other beiles rode a few steps behind, relegated to mere supporting characters in this display. Erden, in particular, seemed unable to disguise his displeasure at this new hierarchy, but he reluctantly held his position. Ye-yang's steely gaze was fixed on the path ahead, unwavering despite the deafening roar of the crowd.

"Looks like the fourth beile's star is rising," Chang-en said. "Maybe he'll become the heir apparent. The position has been vacant for a while now."

"It's not our place to discuss matters like succession," An-xi said tersely, eyeing the walls. "Such talk could be considered treason."

"As if anyone cares about what we say. If I was born an Aogiya, maybe I'd be at the head of that army."

"If you were an Aogiya, there'd be one more of them in the Juwan mines."

Leaning her chin on the windowsill, Ying watched as the contingent approached the Silver Spoon. Just as Ye-yang's black stallion passed by the entrance to the restaurant, he tilted his head upward. When their eyes met, the hardness in his gaze faltered momentarily, before the stony façade was raised once again. He turned back to face the road before him, continuing the march to the High Commander's manor.

After the bannermen and the exhilaration of the moment had passed, Ying and the others settled back down to finish the meal that had gone cold on the table. She picked absentmindedly at the rice in her bowl, as if her soul had left along with the contingent.

"I heard there'll be a huge victory banquet in a few days' time, after the other clansmen arrive in Fei. They'll be rewarded handsomely for throwing their weight behind this campaign," An-xi said. "There were some clans who dared use excuses to turn down the High Commander's request for backup. Bet they'll be pissing themselves now." He looked up at Ying, who hadn't heard a single word he said. "Min, your brother should be coming on behalf of your clan—isn't that right?"

"Huh?" Ying blinked, staring blankly at An-xi.

"Isn't your brother the new chieftain of the Aihui clan? I heard he threw in his lot with the Ula clan and pledged a good number of clansmen for the battle of Fu-li. He made a smart gamble."

"He did *what*?"

The other two launched into a heated discussion about Antaran clan politics, shooting casual barbs at one another whenever they had the chance, but Ying was too stunned by what An-xi had just divulged to pay any attention.

Wen was coming to Fei?

News of her brother's imminent arrival rattled Ying to the core. It had never occurred to her that anyone from her clan would ever make the journey to the capital. It was unheard of. Huarin was too far removed for the journey to be worthwhile—or perhaps that was something that her father had made them believe because he didn't want to associate with the capital. Evidently Wen had chosen a different path, and as the Aihui clan's new chieftain, he had already made decisions that went against everything their father had believed.

"What is he trying to play at?" Ying grumbled, slapping the surface of the bathwater. The steam that filled the room helped soothe her muscles but did nothing to ease the agitation in her mind.

Her brother had a chip on his shoulder, she knew that, but did he really have to go out of his way to prove a point?

Their clan had been dwindling in numbers for years, with many choosing to switch allegiances to wealthier, more progressive clans in hopes of securing a better future for themselves. When their father was alive, he had sent these clansmen on their way with his sincere blessings. "Everyone is entitled to choose their own path in life," he used to say. Wen disagreed. Letting them go was an affront to the clan's honor and only set the clan farther down the path to ruin.

Yet her brother had chosen to send so many of their own to Fu-li, knowing that it could be death they were facing. It was a reckless irony. Any casualties—and Ying was certain there would be many—would be an even more severe blow to the Huarin population. If Wen himself had come to any harm, the Aihui clan would be thrown into turmoil. None of their younger brothers were of age to assume command, and there were uncles and cousins from the extended family who would tear the clan apart like a pack of hungry wolves.

She sank down into the tub so that her head was submerged in the water, letting the heat from the geothermal springs slowly expel the frustration from her bones.

At least they won, she tried telling herself. At least Wen was safe. Not just safe—his gamble had paid off spectacularly. From what the others had said, the Aihui clan had played a pivotal role in the siege of Fu-li. They would likely be rewarded handsomely for it.

"He must be laughing himself to sleep," she gurgled underwater, words escaping in a string of fitful bubbles.

Wait a minute—that should be the least of her concerns. She shot out of the water, the murkiness that had been clouding her mind suddenly swept aside. The danger of Fu-li had passed, but the danger facing her was fast approaching. Her a-ge was coming to Fei. It would be disastrous if he found her here.

For however long her brother remained in the capital, she would have to tread on eggshells and make sure that she didn't accidentally appear before him. That was the easy part. What was challenging was making sure that no one breathed the name "Aihui Min" in front of Wen, else her cover would immediately be blown and she would be hauled back to Huarin having achieved nothing.

Her mind went off in tangents, sprouting idea after impossible idea to keep her brother at bay. Dragging herself out of the tub, she emptied out the used water and trudged over to the bamboo rack where she had hung her clothes.

Voices suddenly echoed from outside as heavy footsteps approached the bathing quarters. Shadows appeared through the rice paper of the latticed door panes. Ying yelped, grabbing her garments off the rack and diving behind the folding screen. Her long, wet hair was matted over her face, and the white cotton of her sloppily worn undergarment clung to her damp skin.

The door creaked open. She held her breath.

"The High Commander has set the celebratory banquet for three days' time," Nergui's ingratiating voice rang out. "Should we not be going back to the manor? I can get Tailor Wan to spin a few new robes for the occasion, befitting the biggest contributor to this spectacular victory."

"No, there's no need."

Ying itched to peep around the edge of the screen to catch a glimpse of the fourth beile, but she bit her lip and remained crouched. She couldn't go out now, not in this state of undress.

She hadn't expected Ye-yang to return straight to the Engineers Guild on the day of his arrival back in Fei. If she had known, she wouldn't have been possessed to take a bath at this hour.

"But, Beile-ye, the other clan chieftains will be attending the banquet, as will the noble families of Fei. There's word that the High Commander will be issuing the edict for your marriage. Surely a new set wouldn't hurt?"

Marriage edict?

Ying's fingers clutched on to the cotton fabric of her robes. Yes, of course Ye-yang should marry, sooner rather than later. She had noticed herself that the fourth beile's manor was uncharacteristically without a mistress, when most Antaran men would have at least one or two partners in their household by his age. Knowing that did nothing to lessen the bitter taste in her mouth.

Who would it be? Some daughter from one of the noble clans of Fei, princesses in all but name, or perhaps a girl from one of the bigger isles, from a rising clan whose support the High Command required.

She hated these unfamiliar pangs of jealousy that wormed their way inside her. She had tried many times to be more indifferent about things, to remind herself that her purpose in being here had nothing to do with Ye-yang—or who he would eventually marry—but she couldn't control those selfish emotions.

"If you really think a new set of clothes is necessary, Nergui, then by all means get it done. I trust you know my preferences. Why don't you ask the kitchen to prepare something for supper? It's been a tiring day."

"But who shall attend to you during your bath? I will get one of the guild attendants to fetch supper."

"No, you know my tastes better than them. Leave me, I don't need anyone here. Tell the attendants not to come in either. I want some time alone."

"Of course, Beile-ye," Nergui chirped.

Ying could almost see the delight oozing from every pore.

It was as if Nergui's existence was validated purely by Ye-yang's acknowledgment.

She heard Nergui's eager footsteps retreat out of the room, the door quietly clicking shut behind him. The air stilled, and the dense clouds of condensing steam hung thick.

Her legs were slowly numbing, blood vessels constricted by the awkward hunched position she had put herself in.

Please leave, she begged.

Thick silk robes fell onto the bamboo rack with a soft thud. A fresh stream of water rushed against the base of the tub. Footsteps, and then a soft splash.

He wasn't leaving.

Time slowed to a trickle, the steady drip of water droplets from the tips of her wet hair counting down the seconds that painfully ticked by. Ying shifted uncomfortably and curled into a fetal position on her side, twirling her long, inky strands of hair around her fingers to distract from the thousands of imaginary ants crawling up and down her legs.

How long does this bath need to take?

"I wouldn't think it's very comfortable to be hiding back there, but if you feel otherwise, then I stand corrected."

Ying's blood curdled in her veins, the hairs on the back of her neck bristling. She slowly inched herself toward the edge of the screen, like a caterpillar creeping along the ground.

Ye-yang had his back to her, his usually braided hair

cascading like a waterfall over the side of the wooden tub. His bare, lean arms were outstretched on both sides, resting comfortably along the rim of the tub.

"How did you even know I was here?" she asked. She sat herself up, but remained safely behind the screen so she wouldn't see anything.

"I could hear you breathing," Ye-yang replied. "And the droplets dripping from your hair when they hit the floorboards."

"But you couldn't have known it was me. What if it was an assassin?"

"A trained assassin wouldn't have been this careless." He pointed at the wet trail of footprints leading from the clothes rack to the wooden screen. "Neither would he have been using my bathtub." He shifted his hand back into a resting position. "It's been a while since I've had a proper bath. Since you're here, come over and give my back a scrub."

"What?" Ying spluttered at the thought. Blood rushed to her head, making her cheeks flame.

Ye-yang tilted his head in her direction. "Considering I sent Nergui and all the attendants away to help you hide your little intrusion, surely this is the least you could do?" he said.

"I can't! We're not— I mean, you and me, we're not exactly—"

"It's only a matter of time, Ying," Ye-yang replied softly.

The steam and quiet that filled the room coalesced around

her, and Ying could hear nothing in that moment but the sound of her own pounding heart. Ye-yang had spoken plainly, so plainly that he hadn't left her any space to hide.

"Please," he spoke again, breaking the silence, "I took an arrow to the arm and can't really reach."

An arrow to the arm? He's injured?

Ying stood up and stepped out from behind the screen. She turned hesitantly toward Ye-yang, but the first thing she saw was the ugly web of crisscrossing scar tissue that lined his back. She took a few steps forward. She could identify wounds from the exploding lamp shards that had struck him on the night of the assassination attempt, the newly formed tissue still reddened but otherwise healed. But there were even fresher lesions that lined his back—ruthless cuts that congealed into gnarled ridges on an already blighted landscape of older, darkened scars. The arrow to his arm wasn't the only injury he had come home with.

Her heart ached to look at it.

Clutching the small towel in her hand, she raised it to his back and then paused, acutely aware of the almost neglible distance between them. Ye-yang said it was only a matter of time—but till what, exactly? Surely he knew that they would eventually have to part. She was not meant to be in his world. His earlier conversation with Nergui had been a harsh reminder of that—that the mistress of his household would not be her.

Maybe this is the most I can do for you.

Squeezing the cloth between her fingers, she wrung the warm water over his back.

"What happened in Fu-li?" she asked quietly.

The victory parade she had seen in the morning had just been a glossy veneer, a façade to make people overlook the blood, sweat, and tears that had been spilled to justify that moment of glory. It was meant to make others forget about all the unlucky souls who would never be able to come home.

And even those who returned, like Ye-yang, would always bear the scars that reminded them of the atrocities they had witnessed—and committed.

"We caught the Empire by surprise, decimated their troops, and drove the stragglers out of the city. Their commanding generals perished and the city's governor fled. We seized over nine thousand horses, seven thousand sets of armor, and ten fully equipped airships. Some of the Empire's troops surrendered. They'll be drafted into the Eight Banners. For the first time, we now control one of the gateways to the Empire."

There was a detached manner in which Ye-yang was reciting the outcome of the Fu-li expedition. It made it seem as if he was reciting off a historian's record instead of recounting his own experience. As if the scars on his back weren't his at all.

Ying traced the angry, crooked line that seared down his back, her finger barely a hair's breadth away from his skin.

"Go ahead," he said. "It doesn't hurt. Not much anyway. I think the nerves on my back died a long time ago."

His careless tone wrenched at Ying's heart. She thought of herself, of her brothers, of all the young men she knew back in Huarin, and for the first time she felt she understood her father's decision to keep their clan withdrawn from the capital's politics.

"Is it worth it? This war we're fighting?" she asked. She gently scrubbed the unscathed areas of his skin with the cloth in her hand. As her fingertips brushed against his back, she tried to commit the touch to memory, knowing that this moment was unlikely to come again.

"Only if we win."

"But if we don't fight, then there's no winning or losing to be had. Isn't that a better option?"

Ye-yang turned to look at her, the corners of his lips tilting upward in a sad smile. He took her hand in his, rubbing his thumb over the ridges of her knuckles. "I wish I had your innocence, Ying," he said. "To be able to think the best of people, of this world that we live in."

"You mean my naivety."

Ying scowled. She knew that she had led a sheltered existence thanks to her father's careful protection, and that there were many complexities about the Antaran isles and the world at large that she hadn't yet recognized, but it didn't mean she knew nothing. Choosing peace was exactly that—a choice—despite knowing that it might put you at a disadvantage. That was what her a-ma had taught her. She tried to pull her hand away, but the prince held on tighter. He shook his head, a mirthful laugh escaping from his throat.

"No, that's not what I meant. I'm grateful for you being the way you are. You help . . . bring balance to my life. You remind me to constantly question why I'm doing the things I do, and whether or not there are better solutions to the ones we have chosen. When you're in a high position, such honesty is difficult to find."

She lifted her gaze and looked him in the eyes. "So have you found it? A better way to do whatever it is that the High Commander wants you to do? A solution that doesn't involve marching our people into war?"

Ye-yang set his lips in a line, looking thoughtful. After a short pause, he asked, "Do you know why the High Command uses the cobra as our emblem?"

Ying frowned, perplexed. "No," she admitted.

"Because the snake is the dragon's inferior. The dragon soars proudly in the sky, king of beasts, while the snake slithers on land, relegated to the shadows. The High Commander chose the cobra to represent the Antaran people, as a painful reminder of how the Empire and its emperor have lorded over the nine isles for centuries, forcing us to pay tribute in exchange for scraps of charity. We are not a weak people, but Abka Han has dealt us a weaker hand. We can be much more than what we are now, but we cannot remain bound to the nine isles."

There was a quiet determination in Ye-yang's voice, in the way his fists were clenched against the edge of the tub. Ying stared at the map of scars on his back, and through it she saw a reflection of his resolve. He agreed with the High Commander's actions, this war they were waging.

"But many will die," she said. Her a-ma had always been an advocate for peace, not war. He used to say that the world would be a better place for everyone if we could learn contentment, and use it to temper ambition. To him, the sacrifice of any man was one too many.

Perhaps that was why he left Fei. Left the guild.

But was he right to do that? What was the right thing to do? She didn't think she had the answer yet.

"If we don't fight, we are already dead. The nine isles are drying up, Ying. There is only so much that our barren land can provide." A pause. "If *I* don't fight, I might die sooner," he added.

Ye-yang returned her gaze, and in the misty gray Ying could see only pain and resignation—and it broke her heart. It made her yearn to protect him, to be that harbor from which he could hide from the storms—if only she could.

"It's okay, I'm used to it," he said kindly. "Let's not talk about these matters anymore. There's somewhere I want to show you later. Take it as a congratulatory present, for passing the second test."

"What is it?"

"Well, you'll just have to find out," Ye-yang replied with a mysterious wink.

CHAPTER 19

SINCE ARRIVING IN FEI, THIS WAS THE first time that Ying was truly Ying, not pretending to be someone else.

She had swapped out her gray guild robes for a pale blue silk dress with a white fur collar, intricate embroidery of peonies and chrysanthemums in silver thread adorning her sleeves and the entirety of her skirt. The material draped luxuriously around her lithe frame, far better than anything she owned back on Huarin. Ye-yang had prepared it for her, though he wouldn't say when. Her braids had been undone so her long hair could be left cascading down her back, adorned with a simple headdress of pearlescent beads.

A light white veil hung from her ears, shielding most of her face from view in case anyone recognized her.

Despite that, it was still liberating, not having to pretend to be someone else. Pretending to be a boy for a few days was fine, but to do so for months at the risk of being flogged when discovered was a torture.

They were winding their way down the bustling streets of the capital, squeezing through the crowds that thronged the night markets. The celebratory atmosphere from the bannermen's triumphant return still hung thick in the air, with high-spirited chatter and cheery faces all around. The effervescence was contagious. A wide smile stretched across Ying's face.

"Get out of the way!" a scratchy voice yelled, accompanied by the loud thumping of mechanical legs against the pavement.

Strong fingers wrapped themselves around her wrist, pulling her to the side. She lost her balance and wobbled, but instead of falling onto the rough pavement, she found her cheek pressing against Ye-yang's sturdy chest.

"Are you hurt?" Ye-yang asked.

Ying flexed her ankles, then shook her head. She was startled, but unharmed. She turned to look toward the culprit—a massive steam-driven carriage that had hurtled obnoxiously past on its spiderlike legs, oblivious to the many pedestrians that filled the street. She had been lucky. In its wake, many casualties were sprawled by the roadside, merchants wailing because their wares had been mercilessly knocked over by the reckless driver.

"There's no shortage of these pretentious young nobles around," Ye-yang said. "That carriage belonged to the Ula clan. They've been troublesome lately. They seem to think that with Ye-lin deposed, the next in line to take over the High Commander's mantle will be Number Fourteen, Lady Odval's son."

Ye-kan?

Ying didn't think he had that sort of ambition, but she also knew that it might not be up to him to decide. The competition for High Command was accompanied by strong undercurrents, involving many clans. The thought that Ye-yang and Ye-kan might stand in opposition one day dampened her mood.

"Come," Ye-yang said, taking her by the hand.

Her fingers instinctively stiffened at his touch, then she slowly let them close around his. It felt comfortable, like they were two ordinary young people in a blossoming relationship, without the walls placed between them by their respective identities and the burdens that came with that.

They continued walking along one of the main canals toward the outer fringes of the capital, leaving the lantern-lit streets and buzz of the night markets behind. Along the way, Ying saw several groups of children setting lotus lanterns afloat on the canal waters, and the memory of doing the same not so long ago lit a warm flicker in her heart.

"The city walls?" she murmured, looking up at the imposing gray brick looming ahead, forming a fortified barrier around the perimeter of Fei's riches.

Ye-yang merely smiled, leading the way up a flight of steps. The soldiers they passed by bowed and stepped aside, granting them free passage up to the top of the wall. Ying noticed a few of them peering curiously her way, and she was grateful for the cover provided by her veil.

"When I need some space to be alone, to clear my mind, I like to come up here," Ye-yang said. He walked up to a crenel of the stone battlement, looking out at the horizon beyond.

Ying peered down the long stretch of granite wall, reminiscent of the body of a dragon snaking quietly into the night, with beacons of flame lighting up the darkness at regular intervals. The smell of gunpowder wafted in the air, tickling her nose.

She walked up to Ye-yang's side, a gasp escaping from her lips when she saw the view before her.

"You can see the entire city from up here," she exclaimed, marveling at the intricate landscape of canals, bridges, and soaring pagodas that littered her field of view. Lit by incandescent lamps and lanterns that looked like a patchwork of dancing fireflies, the capital was shining in the dark. This was the Fei of her dreams, the city that she had imagined so many times in her mind.

Ye-yang nodded, then he turned to the parapet on the other side.

"Fei is quite magical at night," he said, "but I find that I like the view better on this side."

Ying followed, and the vibrant city lights were replaced by utter calm.

"It's the sea . . ."

"Yes. Unlike the city, the sea knows no bounds."

On the other side of the city wall, the ocean glistened

mysteriously under the moonlight. Ying closed her eyes, concentrating on the sound of the waves rushing against the shore. For a moment she thought she had been transported back to Huarin, standing atop the cliffs. She stretched her arms out on both sides, letting the sea breeze dance upon her fingertips.

"*A-ma, one day I'm going to jump right off this cliff and fly,*" she had once said.

"*You can do anything as long as you put your mind to it, my lamb.*"

She opened her eyes and the spell broke. She was back in Fei. The memory from her childhood faded back into the recesses of her mind.

Ye-yang placed his fur cloak upon her shoulders, saying, "You're still recovering from the trial . . . and your little night break-in. Don't catch a chill."

Ying turned to him in surprise. "How did you know?" she asked.

"Nergui."

"Of course. And did he report it as a crime so despicable and outrageous that I should be stripped of my position as your nominated candidate?"

"His exact words were: 'an undeserving fraud from some rural backwater who has to resort to cheating in order to stay in the guild,'" the beile replied, hints of a smile toying at the corners of his lips.

The muscles of Ying's cheeks twitched. "I wouldn't have expected any less from him," she said drily.

"Why were you in Gerel's workshop?" There was a curiosity in his tone, but no judgment.

"Do you think I was there to steal the trial question?"

Ye-yang shook his head. "Of course not. I trust you enough to know that you wouldn't do something like that. And I hope you trust *me* enough to tell me the truth."

Ying turned and held his gaze, those crystal-clear irises reflecting a sincerity that she had come to believe in.

Since coming to Fei, she had told no one about the real reason she was here, about her father's murder and her quest for justice. Every step she had taken had been fraught with difficulty and peril, and there were times when she was tempted to give up and run home, because she was afraid that she would lose her life here before achieving a single thing she had hoped to achieve.

It was exhausting, being alone. Carrying this burden on her own.

But Ye-yang understands, she thought. If there was one person who would understand what she was going through, it would be him. He was all alone too, struggling to survive among a pack of wolves, with no one to rely on except himself. And had he not been beside her every step of the way, since she embarked on this journey through uncharted waters?

He was the one who opened this door for her—and then held her hand through it all.

"You don't have to say anything if you—"

"I was looking for a clue," she admitted. "Something that could help me find my a-ma's murderer, or tell me why he was killed. I know that someone from the guild was involved, but I don't know how and I don't know who." The words rushed out of her like a river bursting its dam.

"Your father's death? What do you mean?" Ye-yang's gaze flickered, and his expression turned somber.

"Someone broke into his workshop to steal some of his work, but when he refused to surrender it, they killed him." Her voice choked up as the images of what happened that fateful day came flooding back to mind. She reached between the folds of her robes and took out the black jade pendant, holding it out on her palm.

Ye-yang picked it up, running his fingers along the grooves carved in the smooth stone. He frowned briefly, then relaxed as he continued studying the pendant.

"I snatched this from the man who murdered my father," Ying explained. "Do you recognize it?"

"No." He shook his head. "But do you have any suspicions about its owner? What makes you think someone from the Engineers Guild is involved?"

Ying bit down on her lower lip, the anger toward the

mastermind and his accomplices surging inside her once more. "Someone from the guild warned my brother against investigating A-ma's death. That person must know *something*. At first, I thought the Great Jade Empire could have been behind it—the dragon is their royal symbol, isn't it? And hetian jade comes from there. But I haven't found any other clues pointing in that direction." Was it because she hadn't been searching hard enough? Had she been too distracted by the guild's tests that she had left her father's grievance to flounder? "Actually, I haven't found much at all," she added miserably, thankful that she could hide her shame behind her veil.

"So that's why you were so interested in my weiqi set." Yeyang placed the jade pendant back on her palm, gently closing her fingers around it. "Keep this safe and don't show it to anyone. If the men who murdered your father know that you are searching for them, then you will also be in danger. If you want to protect your father's memory and what he has worked for, then the best you can do is to stay alive. Finish the guild's trial and do the work that your father couldn't."

Anger and helplessness swirled inside her as she listened. If only she was stronger, then she would have less to fear from these faceless enemies.

"I'll try to help you ask around and see if I can find anything helpful, but, Ying, take it from someone who's been through this before. There is no purpose in revenge, except to bring yourself more pain," he said quietly. He rested his hands upon the cold stone, pensive. After a long pause, he continued. "My e-niye passed on when I was twelve. Her dying wish was to return home to Yokre."

"Yokre . . . That's the exiled clan. The tenth isle . . ."

The Antaran people only ever spoke of the nine isles, but everyone knew that there was a tenth. Its name was never openly spoken since the establishment of the Aogiya High Command and unification of the nine isles, but stories of the feud between the incumbent High Commander and the chieftain of Yokre continued to spread across the grasslands. Yokre had once been the most powerful Antaran clan, and the only one who continued to resist Aogiya command, even till this day.

A bitter laugh escaped from Ye-yang's lips. "You cannot exile someone who never belonged in the first place," he said. "My uncle has few strengths, but stubbornness is one of them. Yokre refused to bow to the High Commander, choosing instead to look toward the Empire for support. Antaran swords cut down Antaran men, all because of the promise of power."

"What happened to your mother?"

"She was gravely ill. She begged the High Commander to let her return to her homeland one last time, but he said no. He forced her to make the cruel choice between her family and her son's future. As if rejecting a dying woman's wish wasn't enough, he chose to wage war against my uncle. If not for the devastation she suffered because of that, perhaps she would have survived."

Ying saw the way the beile's gaze hardened as he recounted his mother's tragic tale. There was anger in the way his fingers gripped the granite ledge. So many years had passed, yet the scars still remained.

"You wanted to seek revenge for her death?" she ventured hesitantly. "But he's your father. The closest blood relation you have."

"I did," Ye-yang admitted. "It took me many years before I learned how pointless it was. The dead cannot be brought back to life, Ying. Sometimes the best thing we can do for them is to let go and live better. My e-niye would have wanted that, and I'm sure your a-ma would feel the same."

"Easier said than done," Ying murmured. Ye-yang took years to overcome his grief, while her own wound was still raw and bleeding. The sea breeze sent a chill down her spine, and she pulled Ye-yang's cloak a little tighter around her shoulders.

"I will inherit the High Commander's mantle one day, Ying," Ye-yang suddenly said, a quiet determination in his words.

Ying was startled by his declaration. Everyone knew that the four beiles were contenders for the position, but for him to openly admit his ambition was dangerous—and showed how much he trusted her.

"I will become the next High Commander, a better one than he can ever be. One day, I'll even have the Empire beneath my feet. That is how I will do justice to my mother's name, and how I will properly lay her to rest." He turned to look at her, placing his hands on her shoulders. "If I want to conquer the world, will you stand by my side?"

A breath hitched in Ying's throat. It was such an alluring, grandiose proposal—yet it was also an impossibility. At best, she would only be able to serve him as an engineer, a subordinate. She could never be his partner or his equal. This version of them that could walk hand in hand among crowded streets and admire the endless seas together—was only a passing dream.

The selfish part of her didn't want him to become High Commander. She didn't want the gulf between them to widen until she could no longer reach him.

Yet she knew he would make a brilliant High Commander. She believed in that.

"Look! A meteor shower!" She pointed past his shoulder toward the sky, grateful for the distraction that allowed her to avoid answering a question she didn't yet know how to.

A glittering array of shooting stars was streaking across the inky black canvas.

"We have to make a wish." Ying clasped her hands together and closed her eyes.

When she opened them again, she turned and found

Ye-yang looking at her, his dimple deepening with the indulgent smile he wore.

"What did you wish for?" he asked.

"Don't you know that if you tell someone what your wish is, then it won't come true?" she scolded. "Why didn't you make a wish?"

"I don't believe in wishes. If I want something, then I'll make it come true myself."

"Oh really. So what is the wish that you're going to realize all by yourself, Beile-ye?" she teased, intentionally using his formal address to mock his arrogance.

He took a step toward her, until she could feel his warm breath tickling her forehead. The soft glow cast by the tranquil moon reflected a twinkle in his storm-gray eyes. Then he bent over, pressing his lips lightly against hers through the soft, barely there fabric of her veil.

"This," he murmured.

In that moment, Ying's mind was too astounded to think of anything but the warmth of his lips upon hers and the fingertips pressing against the small of her back—but if he had asked her again whether or not she would be willing to stay by his side—her heart might have said yes.

This would be the fifth—no, sixth—game of weiqi Ying had lost in a row. It was a record, considering she was one of the best weiqi players in the class. She hadn't even realized that the game was over, still flicking her white seed between her fingers.

The apprentice hopefuls had come to learn that Strategy class was as unpredictable as the master in charge of it. One lesson they would be dabbling in cutting-edge engineering technology and the next they would be forced to spend hours playing nothing but weiqi on the guild's front courtyard, in the freezing cold. "A master of strategy is a master of weiqi, and the cold clears the mind," Master Lianshu said, but they reckoned it was only an excuse for her to skive, because she would disappear for practically the whole lesson and reappear only to dismiss them and comment on how lacking their weiqi skills were.

"What's gotten into you?" Ye-kan asked, frowning as he swept all their seeds off the board. "Are you patronizing me?"

"No. You've been improving." She caught his skeptical look and added, "Really, since when have I given in to you, ever?"

The prince still looked unconvinced, though he let the matter slide. He slowly started sorting the seeds into their respective receptacles. "You're distracted though," he said. "Something happened last night. What was it?"

Ying blinked back her surprise. When she had returned to the guild after her night with Ye-yang, all the other boys in the room had already drifted off to sleep. She had assumed the same of Ye-kan, who had been curled up against the wall as usual. Apparently, she had been mistaken.

"Nothing happened," she fibbed, grabbing one of the bowls from his hand. She picked up a few white seeds, dropping them into the container absentmindedly. She had been trying, unsuccessfully, to push the memory of the kiss out of her mind, but Ye-kan's reminder shoved it back in once more.

She was almost annoyed with Ye-yang—even though deep down she wasn't unhappy about it.

Ye-kan flicked a seed at her. "You were with Ye-yang, weren't you?"

"How did you know?" Ying yelped.

"You obviously can't use the common baths, yet you come back with wet hair after everyone has gone to sleep. You can't be using Gerel's bathing quarters, can you?" Ye-kan narrowed his eyes, observing her suspiciously. "Does he *know*?"

Ying's shoulders sagged with relief. It was about the bath, not the rest of what transpired last night.

"No," she lied.

"Then what excuse did you give? Number Eight isn't that charitable, to let someone like you use his bath for no reason. If he doesn't know who you really are, then you must have something else that is of use to him."

"What does a kid like you know?" Ying reached over and slapped Ye-kan over the head. She was offended on Ye-yang's behalf. "Ye-yang only *appears* aloof and distant, but he's really not like that. Don't say such things about your brother."

"In case you've forgotten, one of my brothers wanted to do away with the rest of us. He's now rotting in the Juwan mines."

Ying pressed her lips together and thought long and hard, but she couldn't come up with a good retort. The Aogiya family was not like any other. In the Antaran territories, the Aogiyas were royalty and familial ties wore thin when power politics came into play.

"He's not like that," was all she mustered.

"Do you . . . like him?" Ye-kan asked, leaning forward across the weiqi board and tilting his face sideways so that he could see her reaction. He almost looked worried.

Ying slammed her container of seeds down onto the board and stood up. "This conversation is getting too ridiculous," she declared, turning to leave. The incense stick at the foot of the stairs had just fizzled out, which meant that Strategy class was over. This time, Master Lianshu hadn't even bothered to reappear for dismissal.

"You *like* him," Ye-kan repeated, scrambling to chase after her. They marched through the other pairs of weiqi players toward the stone steps. "Are you out of your mind? Of all the men there are out there, you had to fall for Number Eight?"

"I did not fall for him." The words didn't sound very convincing even to herself. "And I don't need you to tell me who I should or shouldn't like." Why was Ye-kan even so concerned about this? And who was he to sound upset if she did?

Ying marched up the long flight of stairs, eyes fixed directly ahead instead of looking at the fourteenth prince. She could hear Chang-en calling out to her from behind, but she wasn't in the mood.

Ye-kan was very persistent.

"Number Eight is exactly like the rest of them—the only thing he cares about is the High Commander's seat. You're just another piece on his weiqi board!" Ye-kan dropped his voice into a whisper. "He doesn't even know you're a girl, and what if he finds out? Do you think he'll marry you? Maybe he will—you and a whole cartload of other women, one from each major clan in the Eight Banners."

"That's enough!" Ying whirled around and glared at Ye-kan, eyes blazing with fury. "I already said, things aren't like that. And even if they are, it's still my decision to make, not yours. I don't care if you're a prince and you're used to people being at your beck and call. You're *nobody* to me." Ying stepped back, shaking her head. "Why do you even care so much about what I do and who I like? We're not related in any way, and we're not even friends."

The moment the words left her lips, she knew she had gone overboard. They had only just mended their relationship, and now things would be strained once more. Ye-kan gave her a frosty stare, and for a moment she thought she saw the shadow of a tempest inside them—reminiscent of the High Commander. Then he shoved past her so hard that she almost tripped and fell on the steps. She wobbled, quickly readjusting her center of gravity so she wouldn't end up with a broken neck.

"Ye-kan, I'm sorry," she called out. "I didn't mean it that way. I—"

Chang-en ran up the stairs to join her, looking up at Ye-kan's retreating silhouette. "What's with him?" he asked. "And didn't you hear me calling you?"

"It's nothing," Ying mumbled, continuing the upward trudge. She would have to try apologizing to Ye-kan again later, once he had some time to cool down. He would forgive her eventually, like Nian always did after she messed up.

"Quorin wants to see us four beile-sponsored candidates at his workshop," An-xi said, catching up with them.

"What about?"

Chang-en shrugged. "Don't know. Why don't we go find out?"

The trio made their way over to Quorin's workshop. Arban was already there, having dashed one step ahead, eager to maintain a good impression. Once they were all gathered, the aged grand master broke the seal of the envelope in his hand, severing the crimson ink cobra into two gruesome halves. He gingerly unfolded the letter within, as if it would disintegrate in his wrinkled fingers if he were not extra careful. He did a quick sweep of the four young men standing in front of him, clearing his throat.

"The High Commander has invited you to the victory banquet that will be held at the Qianlei Palace in two days' time," he said. "As such, the guild will grant you leave of absence from your evening classes, but you are to return immediately after the banquet."

"Us? We're invited to the banquet?" Chang-en's jaw hung wide open, extending his already long-drawn face into a comical oblong. "But why?"

"Insolent brat." The grand master picked up the mahogany ruyi that was sitting on his table, knocking Chang-en on the head with it. "Just because you have the backing of the first beile and the Tongiya clan doesn't mean you are in any position to question the High Commander's decisions. The four of you"—he looked toward the others—"are only attending at the behest of the beiles. All of them have made impressive contributions to the Antaran campaign, hence you should be immensely grateful to be basking in their glory. As potential apprentices of the Engineers Guild, I expect all of you to be on your best behavior during the banquet. Eat your food and don't create any unnecessary trouble, else I will not hesitate to strip you of your candidacy, regardless of your backing—is that clear?"

"Yes, Grand Master Quorin," they chorused.

The door to Quorin's workshop shut curtly behind them once they stepped out, with such decisive force that it stirred a small breeze to tickle the back of Ying's neck. She shivered, pulling her collar a little higher.

"Qianlei Palace—can you believe it? We get to attend the first banquet that'll ever be held in the palace!" Chang-en chirped. Beside him, An-xi was staring ahead, starry-eyed.

Ying remembered seeing the gold-topped roofs of the palace on her first day in Fei. It was still incomplete then. Over four months had already flown past since she arrived in the capital, and in two days she would have the good fortune of witnessing a monumental event—one that symbolized a new era in Antaran history.

For anyone else, this opportunity was certainly a blessing from Abka Han, but for her, this was a terrible predicament. It would be difficult enough avoiding Wen while they were both in the same city—but to be at the same banquet?

"Why are you wearing Ye-kan's silly hat?" An-xi asked when he saw Ying emerge from the guild compound.

She made her way toward the steam carriage that was parked outside the guild gates, where Chang-en and An-xi were waiting in their best attire. Arban had gone on ahead, not wanting to be stuck in their company.

Her two friends had sent word home immediately upon finding out about the banquet invitation, and their families had rushed to prepare new robes for them, eager to ensure that their clan names would not pale in comparison to any others. Ying had a new outfit too—a mandarin jacket the shade of azurite with silver cloud-patterned embroidery trellising along the sides, thrown on top of a simple yet elegant black long inner robe. It had come from the fourth beile's manor, reluctantly delivered by Nergui. He had shoved the entire bundle into her arms and then left with a loud grunt.

Unfortunately she could not enjoy the luxurious feel of the expensive silk against her skin, because she was itching too much from the pigmented dye that she had applied to her face, to create the appearance of blisters and pustules. When she came up to the others, she lifted the thin veil to reveal the fiery craters that lined her skin.

The duo recoiled in horror and disgust.

"What happened to you?" Chang-en exclaimed, waving his hand to get her to lower the veil.

"Allergic reaction," she mumbled.

The inspiration came from Ye-kan during the first guild test. The prince still wasn't speaking to her, but she figured she had been somewhat forgiven because she found the hat and a small tub of red cream lying on top of her trunk this morning. Ye-kan had a stinging tongue but a soft heart.

She had gone to Quorin earlier in the day to inform him of her little affliction, hoping to be granted leave of absence from the banquet. Unfortunately, he hadn't been in a charitable mood. He gave her a tongue-lashing for her carelessness, then sent her on her way. "*No one has the gall to turn down an invitation from the High Commander*" were his exact words.

"You too?" An-xi raised an eyebrow. "Maybe Ye-kan has some contagious disease that he spread to you because you sleep next to him." He took two steps back and slipped his hands into the sleeves of his sapphire-blue embroidered jacket, eyeing Ying suspiciously.

"Your imagination amazes me, Niohuru," Chang-en said. "In that case, maybe Min has passed the affliction to me too, since I sleep next to *him*." He inched closer to An-xi, just to ruffle the boy's feathers some more.

An-xi quickly scrambled up the carriage. "Come on, let's get going. We don't want to be late for such an important occasion," he said, shooting Chang-en a look of disgust.

Every bump along the road rattled Ying's nerves as the carriage rumbled its way down the streets toward the newly constructed palace of the Aogiya High Command. She lifted the curtains of the carriage and peeked anxiously toward their destination. The palace roofs had come into view—gracefully sloping eaves and gold-glazed tiles with emerald trim reflecting the rays of the setting sun with a blinding radiance. Today, guests would step foot into the majestic palace compound for the first time since its completion, the first of its kind for the Antarans. It was a sure symbol of greater things to come, a hint toward the ambitious future that the High Commander had planned—starting with the victory at Fu-li.

Ying adjusted the rim of the straw hat she was wearing, its thin veil providing little assurance to her insecurities. She prayed that it would be enough of a disguise for her as it had been for Ye-kan.

The carriage crossed a bridge and they arrived at the majestic white stone archway leading to the front courtyard of the Qianlei Palace. It came to a stop, and a palace attendant lifted the curtain to inform them that they were to complete the rest of the journey on foot. One by one they alighted, breathless at the grandeur that stood before them.

Qianlei Palace—the Palace of a Thousand Thunders—was unlike anything they had ever seen. The sprawling compound comprised numerous buildings that ran on either side of a central axis, lining an elongated courtyard that led the way to an imposing octagonal hall. This was the main hall of the palace—the Qinzheng Hall—with its thick crimson pillars and curved roof arches lined with glazed ridges, topped with the signature gold roof tiles that embellished every palace building. This was where the victory banquet was to be held.

The palace attendants led the banquet guests down the

expansive stone courtyard along a path lined with towering bronze statues of former Antaran heroes, lighting the way with small oval lanterns hanging from bamboo poles. Audible gasps and exclamations escaped the lips of the guests, as their eyes continued to absorb the breathtaking splendor of the palace grounds.

"I have no words for this," Chang-en declared as they stepped across the raised threshold and entered the Qinzheng Hall.

Ying's gaze swept across the intricately carved stone pillars and the impressive murals stretching along the roof beams and the ceiling, toward the calligraphy that hung on the walls and the red wooden lattice panels that lined the perimeter. Neat rows of low rosewood tables had been set up on the left and right of the hall, the silk-cushioned seats slowly filling up.

"Your seats are over here, my lords," the attendant who had been in charge of guiding them said, bowing politely before he took his leave.

An-xi took one glance at their assigned position and scowled. He sank down onto his seat, grumbling unintelligibly under his breath. As mere apprentice-designates of the guild, they had been relegated to the back row on the left of the hall, farthest from where the High Commander would be seated. From their vantage point, they could barely see anything from between the heads of the officials seated in front.

Ying heaved a sigh of relief at what they had been given and quickly slid into hers. She ran her fingers along the wooden floor, amazed at the warmth radiating from beneath.

"Steam pipes, running right beneath our feet," Chang-en explained. "Try this—it's top-grade." He reached over and pushed a porcelain cup toward Ying. An attendant had filled the cup with clear golden liquid with an intoxicating aroma. "Comes from the Empire, so you won't find any of it in a regular tavern or restaurant."

Ying raised the cup to her nose and gave it a sniff, then she took a hesitant sip. The sweetness took her by surprise, a burst of honey and fruit exploding inside her mouth, before it seared all the way down her throat and left a burning warmth in the pit of her stomach. She took another gulp, this time finishing every single drop that had been in the cup.

"Slow down. It's stronger than you think," Chang-en warned, chuckling when he saw her beckon for a refill.

Almost all the seats were filled now, save for a couple in the front row nearer the inner section of the hall. Most of the younger princes had arrived, easily identifiable from the identical silver embroidery of a coiled snake across their silk robes of varying colors. Ye-kan was nowhere to be seen, which could only mean that he had found some excuse to absent himself. Since he knew that Chang-en, An-xi, and Arban would be attending, he probably didn't want them finding out his true identity.

In between sips of her second cup of wine, Ying caught a glimpse of a familiar figure appearing at the entrance. She lowered her head immediately, the edge of her black veil sweeping across the rim of her wine cup.

Wen.

Ying sank a little lower in her seat. Wen looked like he had aged tremendously in the four months that she had been away, his deep-set eyes reflecting a conflicting mix of weariness and vigilance. Here, he was a fish out of water. She could sense the apprehension with every step he took, his eyes constantly darting back and forth, as if mistrustful of the other guests that filled the hall.

She felt a pang of sympathy for her brother. Like her, Wen had never ventured so far from Huarin before. In the short span of a few months, he had not only left their tiny isle and fought in a fierce battle on distant soil, he was also entering Fei for the first time. There was no shortage of condescending glances thrown his way from the stuck-up officials and nobles of the capital.

She watched Wen assume his position behind the chieftain of the Ula clan. An attendant came up to him to offer wine and he nodded stiffly in response, taking a big swig out of his cup.

A gong was struck and a hushed silence immediately fell upon the Qinzheng Hall.

The High Commander entered, and even from where she

was Ying could feel the repressive aura that rippled through the hall. He swept in like a hurricane, marching straight for his seat—a throne-like ebony chair the shade of night, whose backrest rose upward and curved into the carved head of a spitting cobra, polished several times over until its glossy veneer shone.

Behind him came his principal wife, Lady Odval—Ye-kan's mother—decked resplendently in shimmering turquoise silk and a dozen gold filigree pins in her hair, followed by the four beiles. She would be the only woman of the harem deemed worthy of a seat at tonight's banquet.

Ying's gaze drifted toward the young man who was picking up the rear, walking in a calm and unassuming manner, as if oblivious to the attention he was receiving. He was the hero of tonight's banquet, yet he seemed content to fade into the backdrop and be his brothers' shadow. As he walked toward his seat of honor, his gray eyes remained placid pools, still and tranquil. Her heart fluttered.

Aogiya Lianzhe stepped up the dais and turned to face the crowd. Everyone dropped to their knees in a respectful kowtow.

"May His Excellency live for a thousand years!"

CHAPTER 20

As the chorus of voices rang out across the octagonal hall, Ying thought she caught a hint of a crease appearing on the High Commander's forehead, but it was gone in the blink of an eye, replaced with a congenial smile.

"Rise," he said, his voice resonating with the richness of well-fermented wine. "It is indeed a joyous occasion, to be celebrating the victory of our men and the completion of the Qianlei Palace. We, the Eight Banners and the Antaran people, have gone where our forefathers never dared venture. Mark my words—this is only the beginning. The Antaran dynasty has only just arrived."

"What dynasty is it that you speak of, Your Excellency?" a shrill voice echoed from the entrance, sounding like fingernails scratching against yun-mu glass. A tall, lanky figure entered the hall flanked by two burly soldiers, strutting down the center aisle with the confidence of a proud peacock.

At one glance, Ying knew that the entrant was Qirin—not Antaran. His full head of hair was secured in a topknot and concealed under a black gauze hat, and his vermilion round-necked gown bore an embroidered crane that represented his rank in the Empire's royal court. She gripped her cup tightly to stop her fingers from trembling.

Qirin. The Empire.

And there at the left breast of the Qirin soldiers' clean white uniforms was a dragon stitched in gold thread—a symbol of their service to the Qirin emperor.

This was the first time Ying was seeing the dragon symbol in Fei. But was it the same dragon carved into the assassin's jade pendant? She craned her neck, but it was impossible to get a clearer look. Her hand instinctively moved toward her chest, where the black pendant remained hidden beneath her robes.

The man walked up to the raised dais, bowing half-heartedly to the High Commander. "Apologies for my tardiness, Your Excellency," he said. "I am Ambassador Huang, here at the behest of His Imperial Majesty of the Great Jade Empire, Emperor Ren-zu, Lord of *Ten* Thousand Years. I would have arrived earlier, except Fei's harbor was too shallow to accommodate our ship. We had to drop anchor farther offshore."

"Then it is I who should apologize for the *inadequacies* of our capital," the High Commander said, his steely gaze piercing the brazen envoy. "We were not expecting the Empire to send anyone, so we had not prepared a seat for you." He waved his hand and the attendants brought out a spare table and seat cushion, positioning it at the esteemed position to the right of the dais, ahead of even the beiles.

The Qirin ambassador took his seat, impervious to the undertones in the High Commander's words. "I have come to negotiate the terms of the truce on behalf of His Imperial Majesty," he said, saluting in the direction of the Empire with his fist in palm. "I believe you will find our terms quite generous."

"A truce?" The second beile scoffed. "Half your men threw down their arms and surrendered without a fight while the other half fled from Fu-li like a bunch of spineless cowards. It was a complete and utter defeat! I don't see what terms there are to speak of."

"How dare you!" The ambassador pointed a trembling finger at Erden, the color draining from his already pasty complexion. "You barbarians should be grateful that His Imperial Majesty would even—"

"Enough," the High Commander interjected. "Erden, do not be rude. Regardless of the reason, the ambassador is here as our guest and shall be treated with civility, as is the Antaran way." He glanced sideways at the skinny Qirin man, whose large nostrils were quivering with rage. "Ambassador, I invite you to join us for tonight's festivities, and we can leave the negotiations till morning." He clapped his hands twice, and a stream of attendants entered the hall carrying the first course of the banquet.

The tension in the air immediately dissipated.

"Qirin scum," An-xi muttered. "If not for their rich and fertile hinterlands, they would be nothing. Look at him, he wouldn't even last half a day on the nine isles."

"Let him have his moment," Chang-en said. "The Empire's days are numbered."

"It's not that simple. One victory at Fu-li means nothing. We caught them by surprise this time, but there won't be a second time. The emperor may be weak, but they have no shortage of loyal generals and clever tacticians, and their airship fleet . . ." An-xi tightened his grip around his wine cup. "I'm not sure our engineers are doing enough."

"You worry too much, Niohuru." Chang-en picked up a few sautéed bamboo shoots with his chopsticks, and shoved them into his mouth. "This is good. Very, very good."

"Stuff yourself to death," An-xi retorted, rolling his eyes.

Ying sat silently, listening to the exchange float back and forth. Her fingers rested on her chopsticks, and she stared down at the spread that had been laid out before her, but her mind wasn't able to focus on the delicacies. She knew little about the political tension between the Antarans and the Qirins, but she had seen enough in the preceding minutes to know that they were on the brink of a turbulent storm.

Midway through the banquet, the High Commander's chief steward called the guests to attention with the sounding of a small gong. When the noise in the hall toned down, he held out the scroll in his hands and slowly unfurled it, revealing the exquisite gold silk backing that encased the parchment.

Clearing his throat, he said, "By decree of His Excellency the High Commander, the Eight Banners have fought valiantly for the Antaran territories and deserve high praise for their achievements. For answering the call of the Seven Grievances that the Antaran territories have suffered at the hands of the Great Jade Empire"—the Qirin ambassador flinched—"the following rewards are to be bestowed."

The steward rattled off a long list of names. All the commanding generals of the different banners needed to be recognized, as did the chieftains of the various clans that volunteered men and resources toward this cause. Wen's name was called. He stood up and bowed respectfully to the High Commander, earning a mere nod in acknowledgment.

Was it worth it? Receiving fifty horses, twenty bolts of silk, and a trunk of silver taels in exchange for the blood that had been spilled by their clansmen? To Ying, the answer was an obvious no, but she wasn't the clan chieftain.

"To the first, second, and third beiles, for their leadership of their respective banners in supporting the advance on Fu-li, His Excellency grants fifty bolts of silk, five mu of land, and two hundred taels of gold. To the fourth beile, for offering the strategy and for overall command of the Eight Banners—one hundred bolts of silk, ten mu of land, a jade ruyi, and three hundred taels of gold."

The four beiles got to their feet and bowed to the High Commander, raising their voices in thanks.

Ying's eyes did a sweep across the hall as she chewed on her pickled black fungus. Several officials were whispering to one another, while several others looked pensive as they swirled the wine in their cups. With the victory at Fu-li, the currents within the Aogiya High Command would shift once again, as it had done when the former first beile was exiled. Ye-yang—the youngest of the four beiles—now wore the biggest target on his back.

"Your Excellency," a familiar voice called out, "may I present a gift to celebrate this joyous occasion?"

Wen was standing once again, waiting patiently for the High Commander to acknowledge his request. A low buzz went around as the guests debated the identity of this unfamiliar face.

Ying thought to fire a few darts at the pompous-looking men and women who were looking at her brother as they would a worm. They scorned his worn brocade robes, which bore none of the fancy embroidery favored by the people of Fei. As if clothes made a man. She knew it was Wen's best—he would have worn that same outfit proudly on the day he assumed clan leadership.

"Young Aihui Wen," the High Commander said, crow's feet appearing at the corners of his eyes as they crinkled into a smile, "I had been meaning to speak with you. My condolences on your father's passing. Your father and I . . . we go a long way back." He lowered his lids momentarily, and then those slate-gray irises regained their incisiveness. "Ula Temuu spoke highly of you the last time he was in the capital, and Temuu doesn't praise others often."

So the diplomatic visit by the Ula clan went well, Ying thought. Her muscles tensed as she waited, praying that neither Wen nor the High Commander would mention anything that could expose her presence here.

"What gift is it you speak of?"

"Your Excellency, it is only a dance—a small token of our appreciation toward your generosity. I fear it is too meager for as grand a stage as this."

"Nonsense." The High Commander turned to his steward, and moments later the palace musicians scurried in, readying their instruments. Brightly colored drums in varying shapes and sizes lined both sides of the hall, painted with the stylized images of the beasts that roamed the nine isles. "Come, let us show our Qirin guests what Antaran hospitality and grace looks like. The women of the grasslands are bold and spirited, quite unlike those that you have back home, Ambassador Huang."

The Qirin ambassador merely grunted.

A few dancers dressed in light satin and gauze outfits of snowy white entered the hall, balancing precariously on their qixie—embroidered shoes with high platforms resembling the hooves of a horse. Ying feared for their safety. Those shoes did not look like they were made for walking in, yet it seemed to be the trend among the well-groomed women of Fei.

"Nian?" she gasped, straightening her back.

Bringing up the rear was a petite figure dressed in fiery red, standing out from the others like a blossom amid the snow. On her head was a traditional Antaran headdress with cascading pearl beads that rustled like rain as she moved, catching the attention of everyone in the room.

"You know her?" Chang-en whispered.

"That's my younger sister. But I don't know what she's doing here."

"I would think that's quite obvious." An-xi snorted.

But it wasn't to Ying. She itched to push aside that cumbersome veil so that she could get a better look at the girl who had now taken her position in the center of the hall.

Nian's slender arms stretched out elegantly on both sides, fingers arched and poised as she waited for the musicians to begin. With the first beat of the drum, she flew into motion, spinning round and round on those unstable heels. The bells she wore on her wrists and ankles tinkled melodiously, melding seamlessly with the rhythm of the percussion.

Ying hadn't even known that her sister knew how to walk in those shoes, much less dance in them. While she had always scorned more traditional forms of Antaran entertainment like song and dance, Nian had reveled in them. Pride welled up inside her as she watched her little sister twirl and leap confidently across the floor, the other dancers only serving to accentuate her radiance. In the dimmed hall, Nian was a phoenix lighting up the night.

For a rare moment, Ying missed being able to live as a girl. Being able to wear those beaded headdresses that she loved, don colorful dresses with patterns of flowers and butterflies that her e-niye used to sew, and dancing around a lit bonfire on the Huarin grasslands with all the other girls.

The atmosphere in the Qinzheng Hall crystallized for what felt like an eternity, before the final stroke hit the sheepskin surface of the drum and the last reverberating baritone echoed from wall to varnished wall.

Nian leapt and two silk ribbons came flying out from her sleeves, to the astonished gasps of the audience, rippling dramatically like flames licking the air. She landed lightly on the wooden floor, soundlessly, elegantly, bringing a regretful close to the breathtaking performance.

The hall erupted in rapturous cheers and applause.

Wen beamed from ear to ear. Everyone had been enthralled and impressed by Nian's performance. Even the conceited Qirin ambassador had his eyebrows raised, as if questioning how such a dance was possible from the supposed "barbarians" of the Antaran isles.

Ying watched the faces of the many guests, all of whom had their eyes fixed upon the lithe figure of her sister. All except a pair of compelling gray eyes that were looking directly at her.

She choked on the mouthful of wine she had in her mouth, exploding in a fit of coughs and splutters.

What is wrong with him?!

Her cheeks were burning. She wasn't certain if it was from the alcohol or the embarrassment brought about by Ye-yang's unabashed stare. She had to bite her lip to stop herself from smiling.

The High Commander's pleased laughter resonated across the hall. "This is a true showcase of the talent of the grasslands!" he said, clapping his hands thrice. He glanced at Ambassador Huang. "What point is there in binding and restraining your women, if it means you don't get to witness such beauty?"

Ying scoffed at the hypocrisy. There were still plenty of barriers that existed against women in Antaran society, despite what the High Commander claimed—her inability to enter the Engineers Guild as a girl being one of them.

Aogiya Lianzhe turned his attention toward Wen. "It is a

magnificent gift you have brought tonight, young Aihui," he said. "Who might this beautiful young lady be?"

"This is my sister, Aihui Nian, Your Excellency."

"Ah, the Aihui clan is indeed blessed, to have such a promising new generation. Your father would be very proud. Your brother—"

Ying stopped breathing.

"A-ma, perhaps we should let the girl stand first," Ye-yang suddenly interrupted. "She's been kneeling for too long."

Aogiya Lianzhe laughed. "Does it pain you to watch a beauty suffer like this?" he joked. "Indeed, we should not torture the poor child any further." He beckoned toward the kneeling girl. "Come, child, stand and lift your head."

Ying slowly exhaled, relieved by her narrow escape.

Nian hesitantly did as she was told, tilting her bowed face toward the dais. Outwardly she showed no fear, but Ying caught the way her little fingers were twitching by her side—a small habit that betrayed her sister's nervousness.

The High Commander turned to Lady Odval, saying, "She would be a suitable match for Number Fourteen, don't you agree? They are about the same age. Maybe settling down will do him some good." He looked toward the princes, searching. "Where is that boy?"

Lady Odval's porcelain complexion and demure smile fractured ever so slightly. "He was feeling under the weather, so he asked to be excused. Fourteen is still a child. He couldn't possibly settle down ahead of his older brothers." Her gaze fell deliberately upon the fourth beile, who was calmly taking a bite out of a slice of abalone. "Number Eight, maybe? It's about time he had a woman to attend to his needs."

Chang-en let out a soft whistle as he listened in on the conversation taking place at the front of the hall. "Min, looks like your younger sister made a big impression," he said. "I can't wait to see the faces of all those arrogant girls in Fei when they have their dreams of becoming a prince consort dashed. The fourteenth prince is a great option—he's Lady Odval's son after all—but the fourth beile is just as good, especially considering his latest achievement. If she's lucky, she might even become principal wife of the next High Commander."

"Lady Odval won't ever let her precious son marry someone from the Aihui clan—no offense, Min," An-xi said. "She'll be eyeing one of the more powerful clans in the capital, probably her own Ula clan. Doesn't want her son's future to be hindered by a poor match, but she has no qualms about dragging someone else down. This is why you should never underestimate a woman, especially one that has the High Commander's ear."

None of what her friends were saying was getting through to Ying. Lady Odval's lilting, unassuming words echoed painfully around her ears, as if those glittering golden nail guards fixed upon the consort's fingers were clawing through her heart and mind.

"Number Eight?" The High Commander glanced at his son, arching a thick brow. He tapped a finger pensively against his wine cup for a moment, then said, "You have a point. We'll let Number Fourteen off the hook for a while longer. Number Eight, what say you? A beauty like Aihui Nian is more than suited to be the mistress of your household."

Ying's throat tightened, beads of sweat forming on her palms. She watched as Ye-yang stood up, bowing to the High Commander palm to fist.

She knew that the choice was not his to make—yet she hoped he would choose her still.

The beile hesitated for a moment, then he bowed and said, "As you decide, A-ma."

The chopsticks that Ying had been holding slipped from her trembling fingers.

"Good, good," the High Commander bellowed, pleased with his son's deference. "It is indeed a joyous day for the Aogiya clan, with yet another thing to rejoice about." He looked toward Wen. "Young Aihui, I'll do the honor of deciding upon this betrothal, then. After the shamans have identified an auspicious date, we shall welcome your sister into the Aogiya clan. I shall have the marriage edict drafted by the morning."

Wen came up to the front and prostrated on the floor beside Nian, who promptly followed suit. "The honor is ours, Your Excellency," he said, unable to disguise the jubilation in his voice.

Ying felt her chest constricting. The thumping within was so loud that she could barely register anything else that was happening around her. She watched as Wen returned to his seat and Nian slowly backed out of the hall, together with the other dancers, and then she sprang up to her feet, knocking over her cup in her haste.

"Where're you going?" Chang-en asked, peering up at her curiously.

"I . . . I just need to . . ." She spun on her heel and dashed toward the nearest open door.

Ying stumbled out of the hall, her eyes frantically searching for any sign of her sister's silhouette. She spotted a sliver of fieriness disappearing around a corner and gave chase. Dashing down the columned gallery, she finally glimpsed Nian walking toward one of the palace buildings with the other dancers. A palace attendant led the way with a lantern in hand, directing Nian to a private room to be changed before leading the others to a separate room.

Once they were out of sight, Ying slipped into the room and shut the doors, dropping the latch behind her. Her sister had shed her dance garments and was slipping on a pale pink gown with elegant peach blossoms trellising up the skirt.

Nian spun around, her sleek, angled eyes widening in shock when she saw Ying—in her elegant men's garb—standing by the entrance. She clutched on to the cross-folds of her outer garments and opened her mouth to scream, but Ying flew over and clamped a hand over her sister's mouth.

"Nian, it's me!" she hissed, flinging off her veiled hat with her free hand.

When she saw the flicker of recognition in Nian's eyes and the girl stopped the muffled protests, she let go.

"A-jie?" Nian exclaimed. "What are you doing here? You managed to get into the guild? But what in Abka Han's name happened to your face!"

Ying walked Nian over to the daybed and sat her down, clutching her sister's petite hands in her own. She wiped off the fake pustules from her face with her sleeve, staining the material with dirty streaks.

"It's a long story. I'll explain another time," she said. "Do you even realize what happened back there? You can't let A-ge do this to you! Pluck up the courage to stand up to him and say that you won't go through with this. You're not some pawn that can be traded like that for the sake of his ambition!"

"I don't understand what you're trying to say, A-jie."

"The marriage to the fourth beile. You don't even know him. How could you let yourself be betrothed to a man that you know nothing about? This is A-ge's idea, isn't it?"

A blush crept along Nian's neck, dusting her cheeks. She pursed her lips together, then said, "I'm not like you, A-jie. There aren't so many things that I want to do with my life. I'm happy enough to be married to a good man, to be loved and cared for, and to start a family of my own just like A-ma and E-niye did. The fourth beile seems like a promising young man, and he doesn't even have any other women. It's already much better than what I could ever get back on Huarin."

The blood ran icy cold in Ying's veins as she stared in disbelief at the tiny smile that was hanging on the corners of her sister's lips. Nian looked *happy*. She was happy with the outcome.

"You *want* to marry him?" she whispered.

"A-jie, why are you asking me things like these?" Nian chided, clipping Ying on the shoulder lightly. "How do you expect me to answer you?"

She didn't have to, because Ying already knew the answer from the sparkle in her eyes and the smile on her face. The air in the room seemed to thin, making it increasingly difficult for her to breathe.

Someone knocked at the door.

"Lady Aihui, have you finished changing? We should be heading back to the Qinzheng Hall now," the attendant said.

"A-jie, but you haven't told me what you're doing here? Entering the guild is already dangerous enough, but this is the

High Command! You could be executed if they find out about your charade," Nian asked in a hushed tone, clutching on to her sister's hand. "You should speak with A-ge. He'll help you. He's been so worried because you've been gone so long."

Ying blinked, trying desperately to calm the raging hurricane that was roaring in her mind. "No, not now. You don't have to worry about that, just help me keep this a secret. Don't tell A-ge you saw me here, understood?" She looked around the room, then got up to move toward the sandalwood screen that separated the outer from the inner quarters. "Go," she said to her sister, before disappearing behind the screen.

Squatting in the shadows, Ying listened as Nian's footsteps headed toward the double doors. The doors creaked open, then clapped shut, and the voices of Nian and the other girls slowly retreated into the distance till only a deafening silence remained.

Ying hugged her knees to her chest, rocking back and forth as she thought about Ye-yang agreeing to the marriage edict, about that bashful smile on Nian's face. This was how it was always going to be. She had seen it coming, hadn't she? Ye-yang was always going to have to marry another—except it was worse now, because that other girl was not some faceless princess, but her own sister. Could it have been her, if she had stayed in Huarin? After all, *she* was the older sister. Had this ending already been written in stone from the moment she boarded that ship and chose to come here?

The heavens had played a terrible joke on her, yet she only had herself to blame for all the decisions she made.

After a while, Ying stood back up and stepped out from behind the screen, heading out of the room. She took a deep breath of the chilly night air, letting the cold numb the ache in her heart.

Focus, Aihui Ying, she told herself. *You're not here to find a husband, you're here to seek justice, to become a great engineer, anything but that. Don't forget what you came here to do.*

Easier said than done.

CHAPTER 21

YING MEANDERED AIMLESSLY DOWN THE LONG GALLERIES of the Qianlei Palace, the fresh coat of lacquer from the crimson pillars tickling her nose. The itch to sneeze provided a welcome distraction to the wild thoughts running through her mind.

She stopped, looking around at her surroundings. Where was she?

She had emerged onto an expansive courtyard in front of an austere building with double eaves and a gracefully sloping roof, mythical stone creatures arranged in neat lines along the ridges of the roof corners. But Ying paid no attention to the intricate, majestic design of the building. Her gaze had been drawn directly to the fountain that was constructed in the center of the courtyard—a stone dragon with its jaw raised to the skies, spouting a torrent of water into the night.

A *dragon.*

Ying stepped forward gingerly, her eyes tracing the curvature of the beast's serpentine body, from its thrashing tail toward its savage jawline. The warmth of the hetian jade pressing against her chest seemed to grow into the flicker of a flame, searing against her skin.

Something growled.

A beast emerged from the shadows behind the fountain, eyes like the hollow pits of hell, baring its metallic teeth. A guard dog inched its way toward Ying, a menacing snarl still rumbling from its silver lips.

Another chimera.

Ying backed away slowly, her eyes still fixed upon the approaching creature.

It seemed to be guarding something, something important.

"Who's there?" a gruff voice barked through the darkness. A guard dressed in black brigandine armor stepped out from the building, hand resting threateningly on the hilt of his sword as he marched over. The mirror plate on his chest and metallic pauldrons reflected the moonlight, and as he approached, Ying noticed a suspicious black pendant suspended from a cord at his waist.

The hound snarled in reply, its rear arched and ready to pounce.

Then someone grabbed her by the wrist, and a pair of broad shoulders blocked her view of the advancing guard.

"Beile-ye," the guard greeted, bringing his fist across his chest in salute. He grabbed on to the hound's leash, stopping the creature from dashing forward.

"Go back to your station, nothing is the matter here," Yeyang said.

Ying craned her neck to get a better glimpse of the guard's pendant, but the man had already turned and headed back toward the building.

Ye-yang spun around and looked at her for a long moment, his expression unreadable, then he dragged her back down the long gallery. It wasn't until they left the stone fountain far behind that he finally slowed his pace and came to a stop. He let go of her hand.

"You're not supposed to be wandering around the palace on your own. If I had arrived a moment later, you would have been torn apart by that guard dog," he said, voice lowered as if he was afraid that someone would overhear.

"I don't need rescuing," Ying retorted. "I didn't ask for you to trouble yourself with saving me." Seeing Ye-yang made her simmering resentment boil over. That he appeared so calm and composed despite everything that had transpired in the banquet hall only infuriated her further.

"Why are you throwing a tantrum?"

"I'm *not*. I just don't think an insignificant person like myself is worth your time and energy, that's all, Beile-ye." Ying bobbed her head patronizingly, then swiveled on her heel to leave.

Ye-yang reached out and took hold of her hand, and the warmth of his fingers against her palm sent a shiver up her spine.

"Aihui Ying, I haven't given you permission to leave."

Ying felt a lump rise up her throat. She let the fourth beile spin her around like one of those stiff wooden dolls they sold in the markets.

"Look at me," he said.

She refused, tilting her head away. She didn't know what she would do if she looked at his face now, if she could do enough to stop the tears from spilling from her eyes.

"Ying," he said, pressing her hand against his chest, "you know what my circumstances are like. I couldn't reject the edict. Doing so in front of all those officials and the Qirin ambassador would have been a direct affront to the High Commander. Did you think about the consequences? Not just for me, but also for you. Remember what you're here for. Don't you want to prove that you deserve a place in the guild? We have committed treason by hiding your identity and sending you into the guild's trial. If you are exposed now, we will have achieved nothing!"

"I don't need the reminder," Ying replied stiffly. The anger inside her subsided as quickly as it had risen, leaving behind a bitter aftertaste of resignation. She had been upset, but not enough for it to cloud her reason. Ye-yang's words were true. A man like the High Commander would not have allowed his pride to be trampled upon at a setting like that, in front of so many pairs of watchful eyes. He had not asked Ye-yang a question—he had issued an order.

Even without the marriage edict, your paths do not belong together. If he chooses you, he will lose everything.

Qorchi's words suddenly floated back to mind. He had not been explicit, but she knew what the steward had implied. She had become Ye-yang's weakness, and her presence in his life, in his heart, would become his liability.

Whatever was between them, this irrational, unfathomable connection, had to end somewhere.

She took a deep breath, letting her own thoughts sediment inside her mind.

After a long silence, she said, "You are right, Beile-ye. I should not have forgotten what I came here for." She pressed her palms against his shoulders and pushed him away, still keeping her gaze directed at the floor. Tears were already misting up her eyes. "I am here for only two reasons, to seek my father's killer and to finish his work in the guild. That is all. We should never have gotten entangled in all this. Our paths were never meant to cross. Perhaps we should keep it that way."

Ye-yang's brows knitted together in a frown. "Do you mean that? Do I really mean nothing to you?" he questioned. "Give me some time, Ying. Trust me, I have my plans."

"I owe you a debt of gratitude for helping me get this far, Beile-ye, and I will do whatever is within my means to repay you for it."

The light in Ye-yang's eyes seemed to fade.

"And you will not bat an eyelid when I bow before Abka Han together with your sister and take her as my wife?" he challenged.

But she was done with this fight. What did he expect her to say? Did he expect her to say that she would wait for him indefinitely, when she had no inkling of those "plans" he claimed he had? She did not think she had it in her to sit quietly and wait for someone else to dictate her future. That was not who Aihui Ying was.

Ying dropped to her knees, prostrating against the cold stone floor. Her tears stained the slate a darker shade of gray. She prayed he wouldn't see.

"Nian is a good girl and she will run your household as best as she can," she said. "Please treat her well, Beile-ye."

Each word that left her lips was like an icy dagger stabbing at her heart, and she bit down hard on her lip so the metallic taste of blood would keep her mind sober.

Ye-yang flexed his fingers, repeatedly clenching and unclenching his fists. The creases across his forehead deepened, marring his usual composure.

"Fine," he said, "if that is what you want. Forget everything that happened. I apologize for my impulsiveness. It was ill-considered." He turned and walked away, curt footsteps clipping against the stone floor until they faded into the silence.

Ying was alone once again.

She lifted her head, staring vacantly at the empty corridor. The tears spilled from her eyes like a wretched waterfall, reminding her of how she had betrayed her own heart.

Even after the night winds had dried the streaks from her face and her reservoir of tears had been drained, the painful throbbing inside her chest remained. Ying didn't know how long she had been squatting along that gallery. Was the banquet already over?

She slowly dragged herself back to her feet, trudging one step at a time.

"This is for the best," she murmured. "You did what you had to do."

Her heart was still unconvinced.

She had wanted so much to run up to Ye-yang as he walked away from her, to cling to his arm and tell him that she didn't mean a single word she had said, that she didn't want him to marry anyone else—but she didn't. She couldn't. Just as he understood her circumstances and recognized what she was striving toward, she did likewise.

Ye-yang was in the eye of a treacherous political storm, with dozens of arrows pointing toward his back. One wrong step could destroy him entirely, as it had his older brother. As an Aogiya, there was no brotherhood to speak of, and it would always be ruler and subject before father and son. Ye-yang had his ambitions. She had seen the determination in his eyes when he had chosen to lead the march on Fu-li despite his injuries. He had carefully calculated each move like the shrewd weiqi player that he was, and he could win—she knew him well enough to know that.

She could not let herself become that pebble in his path, that obstacle that made all his efforts go to waste. If he defied his father's wishes, he would lose the succession battle.

And then there was Nian. Dear, sweet Nian, whom she would gladly have given the world to. How could she bear to break Nian's heart?

"Aihui Yi—Min!"

Ying turned to find Ye-kan walking toward her with large strides, a merry glimmer in his eyes. Unlike the drab gray robes she was used to seeing him in, the fourteenth prince was decked in a dignified outfit of forest-green silk with silver embroidery, much like the other beiles. She was surprised at how striking he appeared, the clothes fitting his broad shoulders and tall frame in a highly flattering manner. Behind him trailed two skinny attendants, scurrying along to keep up with the prince's footsteps.

She forced out a stiff smile. "Didn't expect to see you here," she said. "Almost mistook you for a grown man, with you dressed like that."

"I *am* a grown man!" Ye-kan retorted, thumping his chest confidently.

"You should not be speaking to the prince in this impudent manner!" one of the attendants hollered, his thin mustache quivering with displeasure. "You shall address the prince as—"

Ye-kan smacked the man on the head. "*I* haven't even said anything, so what makes *you* think you have the right to give a lecture!" he berated. "Get out of here. I don't need the two of you leeches sticking around."

"But, Your Highness, palace decorum dictates that—"

"Are you questioning my orders?" he raised his voice. "If you say one more word, I'll have you dragged out and given twenty strokes."

The attendants blanched, then they bowed hurriedly and scrambled away like two terrified ants.

"You didn't need to be so hard on them," Ying said. "They were only trying to do their job."

"That's nothing. One of the perks of having a terrible reputation," the prince said dismissively. "They need to know their place in the pecking order. So, what are you doing here? Shouldn't you be at the Qinzheng Hall with the others?"

"I needed some air," she fibbed. "Not angry with me anymore?"

Ye-kan shot her a dirty look, his lips twisting into a scowl. "I'm an exceptionally magnanimous person. I don't bear grudges against lesser beings."

The duo continued walking until they emerged through a

moon gate and entered what looked to be the palace gardens. The pebble-lined path was lit by candles that had been carefully placed in lanterns carved out of stone, gently illuminating the meticulously pruned blossom trees that sprinkled the garden. At the end of the path, a circular pavilion bordered a pond whose waters shimmered mysteriously under the moonlight.

"It's so tedious, isn't it? I hate those banquets. I skip nine out of ten of them, but my e-niye's called my bluff now," Ye-kan said. "Usually when I feign illness she lets me off the hook, but today she sent someone down to my manor to escort me here, insisting that recuperating in the palace would be better for me. It's a good thing I happened to be at the manor when her steward arrived and not at the guild, else my cover would have been blown!"

"Why don't you tell your mother that you want to enroll in the guild?"

Ye-kan shook his head vehemently. "She'll skin me alive if she finds out. She doesn't think engineering is a worthwhile pursuit. In her own words, 'princes are meant for bigger things,' and by bigger she means sitting on the High Commander's throne."

"Aren't you the least bit interested in it?"

"Should I be? If it's meant to be mine, it'll be mine. If it's not, then I'm not going to make my hair turn white over it. I've kept on fairly good terms with all my brothers for a reason—I'm not that naive, you know."

Ying smiled, impressed by the maturity that Ye-kan seemed to have when navigating his family's complex politics. "May you always be so enlightened," she mumbled.

She wondered if and when Ye-kan would be forced to grow up, to step out from under the shade of his mother's shadow and assume the burden of being an Aogiya, just like Ye-yang and the other princes had. She looked up at the full moon and prayed that the day would never come.

Then she remembered something.

"Ye-kan, do you know of a courtyard in the palace that has a fountain of a stone dragon?"

The prince tilted his head, blinking thoughtfully. He nodded, saying, "The courtyard in front of the Aogiya ancestral hall. How did you know? The ancestral hall and its surrounding courtyards are supposed to be out of bounds to anyone who doesn't belong to the clan. You could be flogged if anyone caught you there, that's if you don't meet the hellhounds first."

Ying shuddered at the reminder of the ferocious chimera and its gleaming teeth. One close encounter with the assassin's nine-tailed fox was enough for her—and she barely made it out of that one alive.

"But isn't the dragon a symbol of the emperor of the Great Jade Empire? I thought the Antarans weren't allowed to use it at all," Ying probed, grabbing on to Ye-kan's arm. There was something sitting uneasily at the back of her mind, shifting and lurching in the shadowy depths like a monster ready to pounce.

Ye-kan scoffed. "The Qirin emperor thinks he can impose his own superiority upon the nine isles, but who's ever going to know whether or not anyone else uses the dragon as a symbol? Besides, there's no reason for us to kowtow to the Empire. The armies of the nine isles are just as strong, if not stronger than theirs. If that weak and feeble emperor can declare himself a dragon, then my a-ma has every right to do the same. The High Command has been using the dragon insignia for a long time."

Ying dug inside the cross-folds of her robe and pulled out the jade pendant that was dangling off its cord. She held it out in front of Ye-kan's eyes. "Do you recognize this?" she asked, her words rolling into one another in a hasty jumble.

"Where did you even get this? You're not supposed to have it." The young prince frowned, prying the pendant out of her fingers. He held it up toward the moonlight, flipping it back and forth.

"What do you mean by that? You know what this is, don't you?"

"Of course. How many times do I need to tell you that I'm not some ignorant child! This pendant belongs to the High Commander's personal guard. They're the most highly skilled division of the Cobra's Order, but you'll be hard-pressed to find any one of them in plain sight. They all carry one of these. How did you get it?"

Ying's stomach did a backflip as the monster lurking at the back of her mind reared its ugly head. She stumbled backward, almost tripping over a stray pebble hiding amid the grass.

"What's wrong?" Ye-kan caught her by the arm before she fell.

Reaching out, Ying pressed her palm against the gnarled trunk of the willow tree that stood watch over the picturesque pond, trying desperately to stop her own knees from buckling.

Everything was wrong. Her mind was rapidly slotting the puzzle pieces together, but the story it was painting wasn't the one that she had expected. The dragon wasn't just a symbol of the Qirin emperor—it was also a symbol of the Aogiya High Command. All this while she had been looking toward distant shores in search of her father's murderer, when the culprit had been standing right before her all along.

"But why?" she murmured. "Why would he do that?"

None of it made any sense.

The High Commander, Aogiya Lianzhe, was the most powerful man in all the nine isles. He commanded an army that brought all the other clan chieftains to their knees. He was a legend and a hero—touted as the leader who would help the Antaran territories soar to greater heights, who would help them break free from the oppression of the Empire.

Why would a man of that stature resort to doing something like that? And in secret—rather than out in the open?

"What are you going on about?" Ye-kan waved his hand in front of her eyes. "You don't look so good."

She certainly didn't *feel* so good. The revelation had struck her like a bolt out of the blue. Maybe she was mistaken. Maybe the High Commander had nothing to do with any of this. Maybe he had been hoodwinked by some corrupt officials who had authorized the assassination without his knowing?

Ye-kan tossed the pendant up and down on the palm of his hand a few times, then handed it back to her. "He gave it to you, didn't he?" he asked, arching his eyebrows.

"Who?"

"Who else? Number Eight, of course. You're not going to be stealing these off one of the guards, so someone gave it to you. That person can only be my dear brother, the chief of the High Commander's personal guard."

"The . . . *what*?"

But he said he didn't recognize this pendant.

Ye-yang lied.

And if he could lie about this, then what else had he been lying to her about?

Bile rose up Ying's throat. She bent over and retched, vomiting into the pond.

Ye-kan stared at the contaminated water in shock, his face twisting in horror. Then he abruptly lifted her off her feet and marched back toward the garden's entrance.

"Put me down," she said, taken aback by the prince's sudden action.

"And then what? Let you collapse in the middle of the palace gardens and wait for the guards to find you?" Ye-kan adjusted her weight in his arms, huffing as he continued striding on. "You should take a look at your own reflection in a mirror. With a face that pale, you'll probably end up scaring the wits off one of my father's concubines and then there'll be shaman rites and incense sticks polluting the gardens for the next month."

"Where are you taking me?" she asked.

"Back to the guild. I'll send word to Chang-en and the others to let them know you've gone ahead," the prince said. "It's just as well. I should slip out of the palace before the banquet ends and my e-niye returns. She always has a mountain of grouses about my brothers and I don't want to hear her grumbling till dawn."

Seeing that he had no intention of setting her back down, Ying sighed, giving in to his stubbornness. Strangely enough, Ye-kan's presence helped soothe her. Wen and Nian were here in the palace, closer to her than they had been for the past four months, yet she felt like they were only getting farther away, their paths diverging. Ye-kan helped to fill that gap in her heart where her siblings should have been.

"You're quite strong for a kid," she said.

The prince rolled his eyes to the backs of their sockets. "I've said a dozen times. Stop. Calling. Me. A. Kid."

“If you call me a-jie, I’ll stop calling you a kid.”

“A-jie. Happy now?”

“Good boy.”

Ying obediently let Ye-kan help her into a carriage and set course for the guild, her mind rife with the latest revelations that had been forced upon her. She felt sick to the gut, but a physician would not solve anything. The only thing that could cure her discomfort was the truth—answers from someone who had asked her to place her trust in him on this same night.

And perhaps one who had been lying to her all along.

CHAPTER 22

YING LOOKED UP AT THE STROKES OF gold carved into the heavy wooden plaque of Ye-yang's manor, stone lions flanking her like silent sentries. The first time she had stood in front of these doors, she had been filled with excitement and anticipation for the adventure she was to embark on in this glamorous city. Now there was nothing left but dread.

It was the day after the banquet. She had lied about running an errand for Master Kyzo to sneak out of the guild, but she couldn't care less even if she was found out. She needed to know the truth. That was why she had come to Fei.

But it started pouring halfway there, heaven's idea of making a joke out of her misery.

The sun had barely risen. Raindrops pelted down from the sky, and her robes were adhering to her like a second skin, much like the day when she first met the beile. Perhaps it was for the better, so she could no longer tell whether the cold she felt was from the storm without or within.

She took a step forward and reached for the bronze knockers.

"Who is it at this hour?" an irate voice rang out from the other side.

Moments later, the doors creaked open and Qorchi's rotund face appeared, oil-paper umbrella in hand. He frowned when he saw her.

"What brings you here?"

"I need to speak to him. Now."

The lines on the steward's forehead deepened, but he stepped aside to let her in. "The beile has not yet returned from his morning meeting with the High Commander. We can get you a change of clothes first," he said while leading the way.

"No, there's no need. I'll just wait for him," Ying replied.

Qorchi took a quick glance at her disheveled appearance, then shrugged his shoulders. "If you say so. You can wait in the study."

They walked past the familiar bamboo grove and arrived at the two-story loft that housed Ye-yang's study. Qorchi pushed open the latticed doors and gestured at some wooden chairs on the ground floor.

"Wait down here," he said. "I'll send for some ginger tea." Clucking his tongue, he quickly disappeared through the curtain of rain.

Ignoring Qorchi's instruction, Ying made her way upstairs. The first floor of the loft was where Ye-yang received guests, but the second floor was where he worked. She didn't want to wait for him to give her an answer, she wanted it now.

The study was as she remembered, elegant and tidy, with a

half-finished game of weiqi still left on the board by the window. A memory of the round that she had played with Ye-yang in this very room floated to the forefront of her mind, leaving a pang in her heart.

She walked toward his desk, where a small pile of parchment scrolls sat beside a rack of hanging brushes, alongside the half-finished frame of a lamp that Ye-yang seemed to have been carving. An octagonal lamp, like the one her father had made for her mother.

Was it a gift meant for her?

Maybe this is a misunderstanding. I won't find anything here, just like how I didn't find anything in Gerel's workshop. I'm being paranoid. There has to be a good explanation for—

But then her gaze fell upon a sheet of parchment that was laid out on the table, held in place by the stone paperweights sitting upon their corners. An innocuous, partially written reply about the trade of rice—yet the handwriting left her reeling.

She recognized this.

Her mind reached back for a memory of a letter that she had seen stowed away in a locked cabinet in her brother's tent. A strangled cry escaped her lips.

It's the same. How could it be the same?

She reached for the red marble seal that rested beside the rack of brushes, fear pulsing through trembling fingers. Slowly, she lifted the heavy square block and turned it over. A creature bared its teeth at her, and the guild's motto stared back in mockery. She let go, and the seal tumbled to the ground with a loud crash.

"Ying?"

She looked up.

Ye-yang was standing at the top of the stairs, peering at her with a puzzled expression. "Is something wrong? Look at you, you're drenched to the bone. You need to take a warm bath and change out of those clothes or else you'll—"

"You wrote the letter?" Ying interrupted, holding up the flimsy parchment with her trembling fingers. "You were the one who sent that letter to my brother, warning him not to investigate A-ma's murder?"

On hindsight, she should have thought it suspicious that she never had the chance to glimpse Ye-yang's writing at all, even though she had lived in his manor for a short period of time. He must have been intentionally keeping it out of her sight as a precaution.

Ye-yang's gaze dimmed. He sighed. "Ying, please, I can explain everything," he said.

"Like how you never told me the jade pendant represents the High Commander's personal guard? Or that you—Aogiya Ye-yang—are the commander of the *bastards who killed my father*?" Ying was yelling, hyperventilating. The fear, uncertainty, and anguish bottled up inside her erupted like an avalanche the moment she set eyes upon him.

A tense silence filled the room.

Ye-yang stared at her quietly, and she turned away so she wouldn't have to see the pain and hurt reflecting in his gray eyes. How dare he, when he was the one who had taken a dagger to her heart?

"I was under orders," he said. "The High Commander's personal guard answer only to the High Commander. I am but an administrator appointed to oversee proceedings." *Excuses*, Ying thought. It was only too easy to divert blame. He strode toward her, his voice serious. "My father coveted Aihui Shan-jin's work and even tried to summon him back to the capital, back to the guild, but your father refused, so the guards were deployed. I feared that your brother would try to seek revenge and that doing so would bring harm upon your entire clan, so I sent him that letter. I only meant to help."

Ying closed her eyes, stumbling backward against the desk. She wished he had denied her accusations, told her she was mistaken about it all. But no, she was getting a full confession.

Another memory struck her, sending a chill down her spine.

"The first time we met on Muci, when I was running from the assassin—did you know who I was then?"

Ye-yang pursed his lips together, and his momentary hesitation told Ying that his reply would only be another stab at her heart. "My fleet docked at Muci to refuel on the way back from the Juwan mines. I had arranged to receive a report on the Aihui assignment then." An *assignment*. The cold-blooded murder of her dearest father—a mere assignment. "I did not expect for you to be there too, although I knew it the moment I picked up your clan pendant. It was never my intention to search for you, but . . . I did have a separate agenda when I realized who you were." He paused. "I only wanted to see if you had your father's journal, the one that the High Commander wanted."

Ying's laughter rang out, bitter and cold. She laughed at her own naivety and foolishness, at her willingness to believe in luck and destiny. It had all been one giant ruse from the beginning. She had walked straight into the wolf's den, thinking him her savior—and even imagining a rosy future where they might actually be together.

"So it was a trap right from the beginning," she said, the disappointment threatening to swallow her whole. "You offering to help me get into the guild, dissuading me from seeking revenge, and at the Red Tower . . ." At the Red Tower, when she thought she had seen Ye-yang speaking to someone who looked like her father's killer. She shook her head, scoffing at how gullible she was. "You knew all along, and I was foolish enough to think you were *helping* me."

"Things changed. That's not what it is now!" Ye-yang pleaded. He came closer, taking hold of her hand.

She yanked it away immediately, reviled by the mere thought of how he had deceived her. It hurt, the way her heart broke.

"Ying, please. It doesn't have to be this way. I admit that I made a mistake at the start, but that was before I got to know you! After that, I only tried to keep the truth from you in order to protect you. You are but one person, and it is the High Commander you are going against!" He placed his hands on her shoulders, willing her to listen.

Ying twisted away from him, taking a step back. His words, his touch—all of it felt like a mockery. "You're in no position to tell me what I should or shouldn't do or to claim that you did it for my sake, because you are an accomplice. You *knew* what I came for and you *knew* the answers. If you were truly repentant, you would have told me the truth from the start and let me make that decision for myself, instead of acting like you know better. You lied to me, Ye-yang, over and over. The only thing you care about protecting is your status and authority, just like the High Commander."

Ye-yang winced. "I'm not like him," he said quietly. "I just . . . I can't lose you to him, not like how I lost my e-niye." His usual confident, self-assured façade cracked, and his gray eyes revealed a vulnerability that Ying had never seen before.

But she could no longer trust what she saw.

She reached into the folds of her robes and pulled out the jade ring that he had once placed on her finger. She let its coolness rest on her skin one last time, then she set it down on the table, next to the octagonal lamp that felt like an insult to her father's memory.

"I don't know what to believe anymore, Ye-yang. I look at you and I don't know what's real and what's not," she said, steadying her voice. "I never want to see you again." She pushed past him and headed toward the stairs, but he reached out and grabbed hold of her wrist.

"Wait. The negotiations with the Qirin ambassador will fail, as they should. Tomorrow, his head will hang at the docks of Fei." Ye-yang's eyes burned, pleading for her to listen. "The Empire will not take this lying down. The High Commander has issued the order to strike first. We leave tomorrow at dawn," his voice echoed. "I will prove to you that everything I've said is real, I promise. If you still wish to seek revenge for your father's death, I will wield the sword on your behalf. Please just keep yourself safe and don't do anything rash while I'm gone."

Ying didn't answer. Blinking back her tears, she shrugged her arm free of his grip and bolted down the stairs, disappearing into the comforting cover of the pouring rain.

The next day, the fleet of the Cobra's Order left the shores of Fei when the first sliver of light cracked across the horizon. Loud, rhythmic drumming echoed down every street and canal, invigorating to some, ominous to others. Unlike the battle at Fu-li, which had been a quiet, secretive affair to avoid arousing the suspicion of Qirin spies that resided in Fei, today's departure was done with much pomp and fanfare.

The sun was blazing down from the heavens, as if yesterday's storm had never happened.

Ying was hanging off the side of an airship hull, suspended by a rope tied around her waist, slapping putty absentmindedly into holes in the wood. The pounding of the drums echoed in her ears, impossible to ignore. Then came the loud whir of propellers, deafening as they approached.

She looked up.

The cerulean sky was obscured by a shadow that resembled a storm cloud, and as it slowly drifted across the sun, it plunged the land into an eerie darkness. Black ballonets held up immense hulls, battened bamboo sails fully extended to their sides, undulating in frightening waves. The shabby old airship that Ying was patching up was nowhere close to the magnificence sailing overhead. Up there, that was the pride of the Cobra's Order, the finest airships of the Antaran isles, beginning on their long journey toward the Great Jade Empire.

He was on one of those airships.

She turned back toward her rotting wooden sideboard, poking at the putty with her fingers. The sun's rays shone down once again as the fleet's thunderous roars faded into peace and quiet once more. The next time she turned her gaze toward the skies, she could only see a small black haze retreating in the distance.

And he was gone.

As he should be.

"Do you think they'll be back before the final test?" Chang-en hollered from the airship's deck.

"Of course they will. The High Commander said he wanted to personally preside over the final test, so they *have* to be back before then," An-xi's voice wafted in the air, although Ying couldn't see him anywhere. He was probably hanging off the other side of the ship.

"As if anyone can predict how long this battle will last," Chang-en snorted in reply. "They might postpone the trial until the High Commander returns. Apparently the head of the Qirin ambassador has been hung at the docks. He was still alive and kicking at the banquet two nights ago. Can't imagine the Empire will be thrilled about that. What if the fighting goes on for a year?"

"Stop making baseless speculations!" An-xi snapped. "Do your work!"

Ying had almost forgotten about the High Commander presiding over the final test of the guild's trial. Her fingers tightened around the ball of white putty in her hand.

Aogiya Lianzhe—the man who was responsible for her father's death.

She was but a single person, wanting to go up against the most powerful man in the nine isles, and she knew how impossible that sounded. Ye-yang was not wrong about that. But he should never have underestimated her or tried to make that decision on her behalf. She was her father's daughter, and her father's courage ran in her blood, his ideas lived inside her mind.

I will finish what I came here to do, she silently vowed. Even without Ye-yang's help, or anyone's help for that matter, she would see things through till the end.

The final test would not merely be the gateway to upholding her father's reputation and name in the Engineers Guild, to achieving her own ambition of becoming a guild master.

It would also be an opportunity to see justice served.

Concentrating became exceedingly hard from then on.

Classes at the guild proceeded as normal, with no one speaking a word of the battle that was raging across the seas. The guild compound seemed quieter and more somber now that only twenty apprentice candidates were left. With the final test around the corner, tensions ran high, and no one seemed in the mood for idle chatter anymore. There were only three left in Ying's dormitory—Ye-kan, Chang-en, and herself. It was already one of the more crowded rooms. In An-xi's dormitory, he was the only one remaining.

It was just as well. Ying had no time to entertain small talk. She spent most of her free time working on her sketches and experimental designs in the guild workshops, making plans for what would happen once the fleet returned from battle and when she had the chance to face the High Commander once again.

The unfinished work that her father left behind had taken on a new life of its own now, with Ying's careful fanning of the dying embers. She had become intrigued—obsessed, even—with the potential that she saw in every line she drew and every equation she scribbled in charcoal. At the same time, she had been refining the prototypes of the Peony, which she had since renamed the flying guillotine.

After all, it was not a harmless, decorative flower. It was a weapon with a dozen curved blades that could take off a man's head. She had already gotten the basic blade retraction mechanisms to work, now all she had to do was figure out how to make the entire contraption a little slimmer, so that it could be concealed more easily.

Master Lianshu was repairing one of her bee automatons when Ying flung her latticed door open, almost tearing off the hinges. Her elbow slipped and the tweezer she had been holding jabbed into the bee's body, smashing the tiny gears inside.

"Master Lianshu, do you know if the guild keeps a store of ming-roen ore somewhere?"

The guild master stared at her ruined pet in despair, then ripped her magnifying goggles off her head and straightened her back with a loud crack. "Don't you know how to knock?" she shouted, flinging the goggles at Ying's head. "Look at what you made me do! One of these bees takes at least three days to build!" She looked around for something else to throw.

Ying ducked behind a shelf, staring warily at the cranky master through the gaps between piles of scrolls.

"I'm sorry, I'm sorry," she said, "you can hit me later, but can you answer my question please?"

Lianshu bristled, nostrils flaring like an angry horse. "Why are you looking for that? It's a controlled substance and you're not authorized."

"So the guild *does* have it!"

"Are you even listening to me? You. Are. Not. Authorized." Lianshu turned back toward her worktable, snorting in displeasure when she glanced at the bee's carcass. "If that's all you're here for, then you can leave." She walked to the circular rosewood table in the center of the room and sat down for a cup of tea.

"Is there any way I could get some? I need it for an experiment. Just a small bit. I promise I will be extra careful and I won't blow a hole through the guild." Ying ran over and sat down across from the master, leaning forward expectantly.

Lianshu's eyes narrowed into suspicious slits. She picked up a pair of chopsticks and jabbed at Ying's forehead with its tips. "Blow a hole through the guild? What sneaky plan have you got up your sleeve? Don't try that innocent look with me. I'm not so gullible," she said. "Unless you convince me of what you need it for, you can get out of my sight."

"I've been studying the composition of gunpowder that we use in cannons to see if I can make some modifications. One of the possibilities I'm exploring is adding a dash of ming-roen ore to the formula."

"The devil's ore is highly corrosive. It'll sooner eat a hole through the cannon itself." Lianshu frowned. "Silly idea. Now, get lost." She grabbed Ying by the arm and started hauling her toward the door.

"No, wait!" Ying said hurriedly, stretching out both arms to cling on to the doorframe to stop Lianshu from pushing her out. "I have a solution!"

"Spit it out."

"Instead of adding the ore to the gunpowder, we should add it to the cannonball itself. We can modify the structure of the cannonball so that there's a small interior cavity to inject a small quantity of the ore. When the cannonball is fired, the ore will eventually leak out from within as it corrodes through the iron shell, which would vastly increase its damage potential."

Lianshu let go of Ying, rubbing her chin thoughtfully. "Did you come up with that all by yourself?" she asked.

Ying nodded.

She had spent the longest time poring over her father's record books, including the contents of his secret journal, focusing her energy on the gunpowder formula and cannon designs. However, she had been struck by an epiphany while lying on a rooftop one night when a bird dropped an apricot pit on her head. Holding the apricot in her hand, she realized that there was a component to a cannon attack that her father had overlooked.

The cannonball.

The master wrinkled up her nose and hesitated, then she walked toward a shelf and picked up a book from the top of a pile. Holding it out, she blew the layer of dust off the surface, then threw it over to Ying.

"On your father's account, you can take a look at this," Lianshu said. "This is a translation of the original text. It comes from the Empire, but it might be of interest to you."

Ying peered down at the book in her hands, the characters "Huo Long Jing"—*Fire Dragon Manual*—emblazoned in bold Antaran strokes on the right of the cover. She flipped it open curiously, skimming through the pages.

Diagrams of cannons and projectiles of all shapes and sizes, fire arrows, and land and sea mines crammed the pages.

"This is . . ."

"A documentation of fire weapons that have been critical to any army's victory since they first appeared," Lianshu replied, her eyes glinting with fervor. "I've made some of my own notes inside, so that's a bonus for you. You won't find anything about devil's ore, because that's only found within the Antaran territories. You'll have to work that out yourself. We can have another discussion when you're done reading through it." The master snorted. "Trust Abka Han to gift us with a material that does nothing but destroy."

Ying continued poring over the book, mesmerized by the diverse range of work that had already been done by others, which she had barely begun to comprehend. Then her gaze locked upon a tiny row of words that had been scribbled next to one of the cannon sketches.

"It was you," she gasped, suddenly snapping her neck upward to stare at the woman who had resumed sipping her tea.

The handwriting in this book matched what was on the back of her father's parchment.

Master Lianshu is the one who A-ma was collaborating with.

She already had her suspicions, but this was proof that her conjecture was correct. Gerel couldn't have been the collaborator, given his bitter rivalry with her father, but Lianshu on the other hand, who claimed to be her father's best friend, was a far more likely candidate.

"Hmm? Are you quite all right, child?"

Ying studied the messy notes that the guild master had left behind on the manual once more, if only to verify that she had made no mistake. She took a few steps toward the woman, still reeling at her discovery.

"Master Lianshu, were you still in contact with my a-ma after he left the guild?"

Lianshu's fingers tightened around her ceramic teacup. "What do you mean by that?" the master asked, the stiff smile on her face betraying her unease.

"Might you have been working on something with him . . . fairly recently?"

An awkward laugh escaped from Lianshu's lips. She turned to look at Ying, shrugging her shoulders. "We exchange letters from time to time. Well, it was mostly me sending the letters and him ignoring them," she said, her eyebrows knitting in a frown. "Shan-jin could be a stubborn cow, you know? It was all for the sake of research and knowledge, so I really don't know why he was so reluctant to help. If he had been willing to work with me from the beginning, we might already have made a dozen breakthroughs that could change the face of Antaran engineering!"

There it was again, that zealous energy in the guild master's eyes that always appeared whenever she was too engrossed in describing some technology she was obsessed about. Aogiya Lianshu's one true love was engineering, Ying was almost certain of that, but did she realize what this passion of hers had cost her closest friend?

"So you've been trying to get my a-ma to work with you since he left the guild, but he only agreed twenty years later, is that right?"

Lianshu responded with a smug nod. "Couldn't resist

eventually. But his condition was that I wasn't allowed to share our research with anyone else, because of the damage it could cause, loss of lives, blah blah," she said, waving her hand dismissively. "I was on the verge of a breakthrough. Our design of the air cannon, the one your father built, has been stagnant for years. If my model succeeded, then it would increase the accuracy and damage radius of our cannons by at least threefold! Can you imagine that? Our cannons would far outstrip the Qirins'!"

Ying could not bring herself to feel a shred of enthusiasm about what Lianshu was saying. The realization washed upon her like a cold wave.

The cannon improvements that Lianshu and her father had been working on had immense potential to shift the tides in the military campaign against the Empire. If the High Commander had intercepted their correspondence and gotten wind of the developments, then it was entirely possible for him to opt to steal from Aihui Shan-jin had he not been able to get anything out of Lianshu. But why did he have to resort to killing her father? Was her father not worth more to him alive?

Aihui Shan-jin had returned to Huarin almost twenty years ago and lived a happy, contented life on his home isle, surrounded by a loving wife and adoring children. All of that had fallen apart because of Aogiya Lianshu's selfish thirst for knowledge and discovery, and her brother Lianzhe's hunger for power. If Lianshu hadn't reached out to her father, if her father had not agreed to help, then perhaps he would not be dead.

Lianshu was still rambling on about the sheer genius of her engineering designs, but Ying was no longer listening. She turned and ran out of the room, clutching the *Fire Dragon Manual* to her chest.

CHAPTER 23

THE REVELATION ABOUT HER FATHER'S DEATH LEFT Ying unmoored. She fluctuated between acceptance and denial, relief and anger, trapped within a turbulent storm of conflicting emotions.

So she flung herself into her research with an intensity and vehemence beyond anything she had ever done before, spending late nights sweating in the workshop in front of a blacksmith's forge. A sturdy pair of tongs and a worn anvil were her new best friends as she cycled through iterations of prototypes, hammering red-hot iron until it bent into the shape she desired—as if she could hammer away the truth she had yearned to find but now wished to forget.

In the center of a workshop table, sitting inside a sturdy bronze chest, was a small bamboo canister lined with layers of oiled leather. Silver liquid shimmered within, lightly teasing with its iridescence.

Devil's ore.

She'd found it on her workbench two days ago, and assumed it had come from Master Lianshu. As much as she loathed to accept anything from the woman who had indirectly caused her father's death, she needed the ore for her plans.

There were times where she would sit there staring at the silver pool, mesmerized by its beauty and terrified by its destructive power. Her father had never managed to complete his research on the air cannons, but now she was taking his research in a completely different direction—one that belonged to her alone.

What would he say if he saw this?

The guilt started creeping into her mind once more, like vines that pulled and tugged at her conscience. "*Burn it*," he had said. She hadn't listened. Maybe she should have, because then she would never have come to Fei and never have experienced the extent of betrayal and pain that she had been forced to go through.

After hours of melting and casting liquid metal to form crescent-shaped blades, Ying collapsed onto a chair and wiped the sweat off her brow. The hours spent in front of the intense flames of the forge were taking their toll on her, and exhaustion was written into every inch of her bones. Yet, she had never felt more alive.

Her flying guillotine was almost complete. The first weapon she had created entirely with her own effort.

If the design and construction of weaponry had been her father's area of interest, then it also ran in her blood. He had kept these out of her reach back on Huarin, peppering her mind with more tempered and harmless flights of fancy, but those had never managed to capture her imagination as much as the things she was dreaming of now.

Perhaps this was what it meant to be forging her own path.

The door creaked open and footsteps entered the workshop. Ying looked up to find Ye-kan standing by the doorway. He was peering around curiously.

"What are you doing here?"

"Is there any place I can't be?" he replied.

He walked farther in, eyeing the messy spread of papers and books laid out on the table.

"What's this?" he asked, picking up one of the sketches on the table.

It was an early design of her flying guillotine. The sketch was of a hat-like structure affixed to a long metal chain, with a series of curved blades surrounding the rim like the petals of a flower in bloom.

"You're supposed to fling it out"—she modeled the action dramatically with her right hand—"and it'll land on the enemy's head. Then when you pull back"—she yanked her hand toward her chest—"the blades swing inward and take the enemy's head with it."

Ye-kan stared at her, aghast. He blinked several times, then looked down at the sketch he was holding. He dropped it like a hot sweet potato.

"What's wrong with you?" he exclaimed. "That's so gory."

Ying took one look at his horrified expression and let out a bitter laugh. If he followed his older brothers out to the battlefield one day, perhaps he would not say the same thing. She hoped he never had to.

"I came to bring you this, by the way," the prince said, handing her a letter. "They delivered family letters today. Why do you even have one? I thought your family doesn't know you're here."

"They don't."

Only Nian knew she was in Fei, but she hadn't mentioned anything about the Engineers Guild. Ying stared down at the envelope, puzzled. She opened it and took out the sheet of paper inside.

She glanced at the sign-off and then quickly folded the paper shut, holding it out to the lit candle sitting in its bronze holder. The flame licked at the edge of the parchment, slowly consuming it until there was nothing left but a pile of soot on the tabletop.

"Why did you burn it?" Ye-kan asked.

"Nothing worth reading."

"Was it from Number Eight?" the prince continued probing, studying her face as if the answer would be written on it. "Did the two of you have a lovers' tiff?"

"Mind your words. The beile and I are not in that sort of a relationship," Ying replied curtly. She focused her attention back on the fiery forge, trying to push all thoughts of Ye-yang out of her mind.

Ye-kan arched a cynical brow. "Really?" he asked. "Then why do you look like you swallowed gunpowder?"

"Get out, Ye-kan, before I throw you out."

A smile tugged at the corners of Ye-kan's lips. He reached out and ruffled her hair—the way she always did to him. "I'll see myself out. Anyway, it's good if you've gained enlightenment and realized what a terrible choice Ye-yang would make. I'm glad my wise words weren't wasted after all." Beaming proudly, he turned and strode out of the workshop.

Ying stared at the small soot mound on the table, then blew it away until there was nothing left except a faint trail of gray, a reminder of what used to be.

The days continued to plod along, with time dragging its sorry heels whenever she had to sit through Gerel's dull History classes and speeding by when she was locked in the workshop perfecting her creations. The final assessment in the apprenticeship trial drew closer and closer, until there were only a few days left.

The remaining candidates were anxious about the upcoming test, but the uncertainty of the current situation unsettled them most. There was still no news of the High Commander's return from the Empire. News from the battlefront traveled back to Fei in drips and drabs, and no one really knew what was real and what was rumor.

It wasn't until three days before the appointed date of the final test that Master Gerel delivered an announcement to the class.

"Candidates, we have unfortunately been informed that the High Commander will not be able to return to the capital in time for the scheduled date of the final assessment. The guild masters have convened, and Grand Master Quorin has decided to postpone the test indefinitely until the High Commander's return."

Agitated murmurs started going around the room, burgeoning into loud, flustered exchanges after Gerel left.

"Why?" An-xi wailed repeatedly. "Why must they prolong my suffering?"

Chang-en walked over and patted him on the back. "At least it means more time for you to cram more into your brain."

"I don't need to cram any more! I already have the entire *Annals* memorized from back to front, *and* over a dozen other engineering manuals too. I can take the test today!"

"Does that mean we have to suffer through more lessons?" Chang-en asked, scratching his chin thoughtfully.

"If you don't want to take lessons, then why are you even in the guild, wasting valuable space," An-xi snapped, glaring at the other boy with venom dripping from his eyes.

Ying wasn't bothered about the delay of the test. In fact, she was happy with the news. A delay meant more time to perfect her plans, to ensure a higher chance of success.

From what little Chang-en and An-xi managed to dig out from their families, it seemed that the siege of the Empire was not progressing as smoothly as everyone had hoped. Every now and then, they would see supply airships lifting off and disappearing into the distance. Several returned with gaping holes in their hulls, broken sails, and bloodstains on their decks, their crew carted off to the infirmaries to be treated for injuries. She had already scrubbed several congealed pools of blood off wooden floorboards. Even though she tried not to think about it, each time she would still end up wondering whether any of it was his.

A series of footsteps rushing into the classroom pulled her out of her thoughts. She turned toward the doorway. To her surprise, the entrants were all women, dressed uniformly in pale pink silk robes, their hair neatly bound in a braided bun above their heads, held in place by simple bronze pins. They stood in two lines by the doorway, hands folded one over the other at the right side of their waists.

A shadow appeared at the door, a pair of heeled qixie clipping against the floorboards as a woman stepped slowly across the threshold.

"Lady Odval?" Chang-en murmured.

Ying instinctively turned to her left, where Ye-kan had been sitting. He was gone, but there was a cowering figure hiding behind one of the shelves at the back of the room.

"My Lady," An-xi was the first to greet, bobbing his head in a polite half-bow. It wasn't necessary for them to greet ladies of the harem, but as the High Commander's principal wife, Odval was the exception. She was the highest-ranking female member of the Aogiya family, and by extension, the highest-ranking woman in the nine isles.

The other young men promptly followed suit, even though some of them were still clueless about her identity.

The lady swept the room with her cold, distant gaze, and Ying withered like a grass flower in the presence of a peony. Odval was an incredibly attractive woman, age failing to tarnish a single inch of her porcelain skin and jet-black hair. On her head, her intricate dianzi was adorned with the brilliant blue of kingfisher feathers and the sparkle of gold filigree, adding to her regal aura.

She parted her rosebud lips, dabbed with rouge only sparingly at the bottom. "Come out," she said, her ethereal voice floating across the room. She should have sounded like a fairy descended from the heavens, but Ying felt as if someone were trailing a knifepoint across her neck.

Lady Odval stood there in her lilac splendor, arms folded across her chest with her long, gold nail guards impatiently tapping against the floral embroidery of her sleeves.

"You know I don't like to repeat myself."

A hunched figure stepped out from behind the shelves, head hung in shame.

"E-niye."

All eyes turned toward the back of the room, plenty of shocked expressions at the squeak that had just emerged from Ye-kan's mouth.

The lady reached out a hand and beckoned toward her son, the curved points of her fingernails proving an especially intimidating sight. Ying couldn't help admiring her. It was no wonder she had been able to climb up the ranks of Aogiya Lianzhe's harem and be so comfortable at the top. This woman was single-handedly responsible for the power and influence held by the Ula clan in today's political climate.

"You should have told me you were here," Lady Odval said, her plump lips curling into a smile that screamed danger. "I was searching all over for you. I almost sent the palace guards on a full search of the city. That would have been such an unnecessary disturbance, don't you agree, sweetheart?"

"Let's go back to the palace," Ye-kan mumbled, walking over and tugging at his mother's sleeve. Gone was his usual arrogance and cockiness, replaced by a timid quaking of his boots. Ignoring the stares of disbelief coming from his classmates, he turned and gave Ying a wistful grimace, then quickly disappeared out through the doorway.

Still smiling, Lady Odval looked around the room, her gaze pausing upon Ying momentarily. Then, she took the outstretched hand of her lady-in-waiting and left as gracefully as she had entered.

~

Ye-kan didn't return that night, or for the next few nights. Ying didn't expect him to, not after seeing the displeasure exuding from every beautiful inch of his mother. Even though everyone in Fei regarded the Engineers Guild in high esteem, Lady Odval looked upon them as vermin. Servants to the one true master—whom she undoubtedly believed would be her son in time to come.

With the High Commander away at battle, tensions in the capital were running high. It was no wonder the lady wanted to keep a close watch over her son, in case any of their political enemies tried to do away with him at this critical juncture.

The other boys gossiped about Ye-kan's identity for a few days, then the topic became stale and chatter died down, replaced by an even juicier piece of news that rocked the entire capital.

A rumor had started spreading that the High Commander had been gravely injured in the siege of the Empire. Some people were even speculating that he was already dead.

But the uncertainty that was hanging thick within the air of the Engineers Guild—and across the city of Fei—was resolved much sooner than anyone expected. Three days after the whispers first began, the High Commander returned to the capital. There was no victory march, no ostentatious display through the streets—just a steam carriage guarded tightly by a solemn entourage, swiftly making its way from the airship docks toward Qianlei Palace. A directive was issued from the palace and the rumors were quashed immediately.

Ying and the others were out on the front courtyard playing weiqi for Strategy when they saw a messenger come riding in through the heaving gates of the guild, dashing up the stone steps with a golden scroll in hand. Their lesson was abruptly cut short and they were summoned up to the main hall, where Grand Master Quorin and the other guild masters were already waiting.

When they had all formed their lines, Quorin held out the scroll in front of him and unfurled it, a dour expression on his craggy face.

"An edict has arrived from the palace," he said. "The High Commander has decreed that the final test of the guild's apprenticeship trial is to proceed *immediately*."

An instant uproar ensued, loud voices clamoring to express their shock and alarm. Master Gerel let out a sharp screech, silencing all of them.

"The final test—the trial of the soul—will take place over the span of three days. During this time, you are to draw upon everything you have learned from the masters to create an entirely new prototype from scratch. The theme for this test, provided by the High Commander himself, is: To kill a dragon."

Quorin flipped the scroll around so that the bold characters were visible to all of them.

To kill a dragon.

Ying's gaze drifted from the brushstrokes to a small anomaly at the bottom-left corner of the parchment. Slight speckles of red. It could have been an accidental spillage of ink from the High Commander's official seal—or blood.

Beside her, Chang-en let out a low whistle. "Weapons, that's a guild first," he murmured.

"What do you mean?" Ying asked.

"The final test is always a challenge of creation, but it's never gone into the realm of actual weaponry before. Weapons are something that only guild masters or senior apprentices get to work on."

"You will have free access to the apprentice workshops over these three days, and you may requisition any materials you require from the guild stores. At dawn on the fourth day, you are to submit sketches of your design and we will test each of your prototypes at the grassland beyond the eastern canal." Quorin handed the scroll to a senior apprentice, who proceeded to hang it from a wooden frame at the front of the hall. "This is your last chance to prove that you have what it takes to become a guild member. I expect all of you to put forward your strongest showing." Sweeping his hands behind his back, Quorin stepped off the platform and left the hall, with the other masters trailing behind him.

The candidates started to scatter, all anxious to begin their individual projects. The final test would mark the end of the trial, and no more than three apprentices would be accepted into the guild. An-xi was the first to dash off, disappearing before anyone even had the chance to ask him what he thought about all this.

"What do you make of the theme?" Chang-en asked.

"The Great Jade Empire," Ying replied. "The dragon represents the Empire."

But not for her.

For her, the dragon would be the High Commander himself.

CHAPTER 24

Compared to the rest, Ying had a relatively easier time for this assessment because she'd done half her work before the test had even begun.

She stared at the neat row of cannonballs sitting on the table, propped up by the ugly wooden stands that she had crudely whittled. Harried footsteps rushed back and forth around her as the others readied their prototypes for the final assessment. There was barely half a stick of incense left before they were to set off, and still there seemed to be a mountain of work to be done.

Ying's cannonball would be a fitting conclusion to her father's work at the guild, and the beginning of her own journey in engineering. A sheet of rice paper sat in front of her, bearing the sketches and design considerations behind her cannonballs, together with the small bamboo canister that hid the mingroen ore within—and something else, a thin, shapeless object wrapped within swaddles of cloth.

She still hadn't tested any of her prototypes. It was impossible to do that within the guild compound without melting the place to the ground. Not that it mattered, because she was confident that she could achieve her goal. It was a fortunate coincidence that the High Commander had picked the topic that he did, else she would have to find a different way to get her designs in front of him.

Taking a deep breath, she piled the cannonballs onto a sheet of cotton together with the canister of devil's ore and bundled them neatly. Slipping the other cloth-wrapped package beneath the cross-folds of her guild uniform, she ran out of the workshop to catch up with the others.

The wagons took them all the way to the outskirts of town, where the eastern canal ended and the cityscape transitioned into a sprawling grassland. The plot of land was blocked to unauthorized entry by a tall fence surrounding the perimeter, designated as a military training ground for the Eight Banners. Guards from the Order checked the carriages before letting them through, and the nineteen nervous candidates alighted, arms cradling their precious projects.

To Ying's surprise, a familiar figure was already waiting at the training ground, pacing up and down impatiently in his guild robes. When he saw her alight, his face lit up with a smile. He waved.

"What are you doing here?" Ying asked, walking over to the fourteenth prince. "Are you taking part in today's test?"

Ye-kan nodded excitedly. "I begged my e-niye for three whole days before she finally relented. But her condition is that

I have to return to the palace immediately after the test ends, because I'm supposed to wait on A-ma's bedside. Also, I'm not allowed to join the guild, even if I pass the trial," he said, pulling a face.

Ying frowned. "The High Commander . . . is he badly injured?"

Ye-kan grimaced, his expression turning solemn. "The palace physicians have tried their best, and they say he should recover with enough rest, but that's if he keeps his composure and doesn't let his emotions get out of hand." He lowered his voice. "A-ma's not in good shape. The campaign took a bad turn, and we've had to recall all our bannermen. The casualties are much more severe than we had anticipated." He paused, then added, "The beiles should be returning with the other men today or tomorrow."

He waited for a reaction from Ying, but she kept her expression neutral. As if Ye-yang's whereabouts didn't concern her.

In the background, Master Gerel began the roll call. Ying hurried to take her position, trying to empty her mind of everything she had just heard. What she needed to do now was focus on the task at hand—and what was to come.

A senior apprentice went around collecting their design sketches, disappearing with them.

"Good morning," Gerel greeted. "Without further ado, we

will proceed with today's evaluation. In the allocated time, you will test your prototypes and the guild masters will assess you based on the utility and impact of what you have produced. You may make use of any of the equipment provided at this training ground for your demonstration." He gestured toward a rack full of standard weaponry, including a cannon sitting stoically by the side. "Is that clear?"

A unified chorus of agreement rang out, and a gong was struck to signal that the final test had begun.

Then the ground began to vibrate—and the earth split apart.

The twenty candidates stared in shock as the ground before them divided like an opening trap door, revealing a yawning black hole that could have easily fit a small airship. Ying clutched her creation tightly against her chest, her heart thrumming with anticipation and anxiety as she waited for *it* to appear.

Some of the other boys began inching backward, while the rest were visibly trembling in their boots.

A thunderous roar rattled the air.

Someone screamed.

Then they saw it. A rush of gold sped out through the hole in the ground, its serpentine body undulating in powerful waves as it flew up toward the sky. Ying gasped, awestruck by the terrible beauty of the creature she was witnessing.

It was a dragon.

Unlike the chimeras, who were living, breathing animals that had been embellished with mechanical parts, this dragon was a complete automaton, with scales hammered from gold and teeth and talons that shone like polished steel.

It was hovering proudly above them, studying each and every candidate with the jerky motions of its smooth obsidian eyes, tethered within their bronze sockets.

"Abka Han save us," someone whispered, echoing the prayer that was running through almost everyone's minds.

When they heard that the theme for the final test was "to kill a dragon," none of them had expected that they would actually have to kill a literal dragon. How were they supposed to even land a scratch on a machine that seemed invincible?

An-xi was the first to spring into action. Gritting his teeth, the boy quickly unwrapped the linen from around his elongated bundle, revealing a set of cylindrical copper tubes that looked like the fireworks that the Antarans set off during festive occasions. He ran to an empty spot and squatted down, aiming his first cylinder toward the dragon's body. With shaky fingers, he struck a flint and lit the tip of the cord extending from the back of his tube, then he shoved the entire thing into the ground and stumbled several feet back, hands pressed against his ears.

There was a loud bang, and the entire cylinder went hurtling toward the towering beast that was still suspended in the air. In mid-flight, something silver shot out from An-xi's tube—like the sharpened tip of a spear—reflecting a blinding ray of light into Ying's eyes. She blinked, and in that instant the dragon's body lurched backward.

A silver rod was pierced into its upper torso, lodged between two scale plates.

"Yes! It worked!" the boy shrieked, his mousy braids bouncing as he jumped up and down in delight.

But though his invention had successfully found its target, it barely left a dent on the dragon's metallic hide. The next moment, the creature dipped its head downward.

"An-xi!" Chang-en threw himself forward and shoved the other boy to one side, just in the nick of time.

A ball of flames shot out from the dragon's gaping jaws. Ying thought she could see the kaen gas tube that had been built into its mouth. The ground where An-xi had been standing was charred to a crisp, and a sour, rancid smell was wafting in the air—the smell of burning kaen gas.

So that's what's keeping the dragon in flight, Ying thought, amazed at the ingenuity involved in the creation of the automaton. The snaking body of the creature was likely hollow, filled with pockets of gas that helped give it the lift it needed while also serving as fuel for the fiery weapon concealed within its mouth.

An-xi was sprawled on the ground, the blood drained from his sallow cheeks as he stared at the burnt patch of earth. He punched the dirt in frustration.

Taking An-xi's lead, the rest of the boys started to make their own moves. There was a flurry of movement as they unveiled their prototypes one by one, rushing to set things up so that they could be the first to bring the dragon down and succeed in this test.

Ying took a look around.

There were variations of crossbows, catapults, and multipronged spears, most of which were enhanced versions of existing weaponry. Ye-kan had built an automated missile launcher of sorts that rotated like a water wheel and could rapidly fire metal projectiles the size of someone's fist. Chang-en was holding one of the strangest inventions of the lot—a *pigeon* carved from wood.

"It's a hawk!" he scolded, when he caught the incredulous look in her eyes.

He lit a fuse at the base of the bird's tail, and to everyone's surprise, it took off soaring into the air. When it reached a certain height, a hatch popped open at its belly, firing a series of deadly arrows down toward the ground with remarkable force.

Only one of the arrows struck the dragon on the back, while the rest nearly impaled some of the other candidates. Chang-en shouted an apology, catching his mechanical hawk as it came gliding back down.

Ying didn't stop to watch him reload. Instead, she ran over to the silent cannon sitting by the side of the arena. Sucking in a breath, she carefully unwrapped what she had brought with her—orbs the shade of blackest night, gleaming as they reflected the sunbeams.

Alarmed shouts rang out as the dragon ejected another round of fiery breath, sending some of the boys leaping out of the way.

With shaky hands, Ying uncapped the bamboo canister and carefully wicked a small quantity of silver fluid into the tiny hole in her first cannonball. The piece of coarse twine disintegrated, disappearing together with the silvery tinge. Cannonball in hand, she shoved it down the barrel in one swift motion, then aimed the mouth of the cannon toward the levitating dragon.

It was a good thing her target was so large, and its movements somewhat stilted. It was likely also a prototype, same as their weapons. She spied Master Lianshu sitting by the sidelines, sucking on a stick of haw candy, her goldfish-like eyes glittering with pride as she gazed upon the monstrous automaton—and she could guess who created the beast.

Ying picked up a torch from the side of the weapons rack and set it alight, holding the flame toward the cannon's fuse. A spark. The woven cotton began to shorten rapidly, black smoke issuing as its fibers singed.

A loud explosion rang out as the pressure from the gunpowder sent the cannonball hurtling out of the sturdy barrel. Everyone clapped their hands to their ears, staring at the trajectory of the orb.

The cannonball struck the dragon on the left side of its torso, embedding itself into the creature's metal frame the same way An-xi's projectile had. Ying quickly followed with a second cannonball, this time striking the dragon directly in its left eye. Then a third, to its tail.

"Is that all, Aihui Min?" Master Gerel called out, not disguising the scorn in his tone. "Did you only bring ordinary cannonballs?"

"Look! Look!" someone suddenly shouted.

All eyes shifted toward the levitating automaton. The cannonballs that Ying fired had dislodged and fallen back down to the ground, leaving cavities in the dragon's body—holes that were *expanding*.

It was surreal, watching the fearsome dragon disintegrate before their eyes.

Everyone pressed their palms to their ears to block out the piercing screech that sounded like gear wheels malfunctioning. Then the dragon plunged down, crashing dramatically in a cloud of displaced dirt and grass.

Gerel pointed one trembling finger at the collapsed automaton that was still twisting and jerking its contorted frame. "What in Abka Han's name happened there? What sorcery is this!" he yelled. Lianshu had also scrambled to her feet, her expression a colorful blend of astonishment and awe.

"It worked," Ying mumbled, still in a daze. Exactly like she had hoped. The ore had seeped out through the tiny opening when it struck the dragon, then progressively ate away at whatever it touched, dissolving the creature from within.

If the cannonball had struck an army of men, they would have been reduced to a puddle of flesh and bone.

Before anyone could react, the thunderous clapping of hooves pounding the dirt approached. A man dressed in black brigandine armor rode into the training ground, accompanied by a nine-tailed fox.

"By order of the High Commander," he announced, "Aihui Min is summoned to the palace immediately." He glanced briefly at the damaged dragon lying in its pit, then surveyed the blank faces of the candidates. "Which one of you is Aihui Min?"

Ying raised one trembling hand, the other balled tightly into a fist by her side. Her gaze was fixed upon the gnarled scar that stretched across his left eye. It was him. Not hiding behind a mask this time, not lurking in the shadows, but standing before her in full uniform, with the insignia of the Cobra's Order pinned proudly at his right shoulder.

She had expected to be summoned. After all, she had intentionally baited the High Commander by imbuing hints of her father's work into the cannonball sketches she had submitted for the test. She just wished it weren't her father's murderer who would be escorting her there.

"What's the matter? Why is Aihui Min being sent for? The trial is not yet over," Ye-kan called out. He walked over to Ying's side, standing between her and the guard protectively.

Ying reached out and patted Ye-kan on the shoulder, signaling to him with a slight shake of the head. "It's all right," she said. She picked up her belongings and headed toward the guard. It was suffocating, having to approach the man who had killed her father and pretend that there was nothing wrong. Still, she kept her composure.

When she stood before him, she tilted her head upward and looked him straight in the eye. "I'm ready," she said.

The man grunted, jerking a thumb toward the carriage that was waiting by the gates. He showed no signs of recognizing her. She wondered if he would, had she been dressed as a girl instead of donning the guild's uniform, and what he would do if he did. Set his vicious fox on her again perhaps?

"Wait!" Ye-kan jogged over. "I'll come with you."

"Ye-kan, there's no need. You can stay here and listen to

guild masters' trial evaluation," Ying said, hurrying her steps.

"No," he said firmly, giving his father's guard a suspicious glare. "I'll come with you. The results are inconsequential to me anyway."

Realizing that the boy was not going to change his mind, Ying sighed, allowing him to clamber up into the carriage with her.

A pair of vermilion doors carved with the latticework motifs of curving serpents stood between her and the man who had single-handedly shattered her peaceful life. Ying glanced down at the obsidian pendant hanging off the broad belt of her escort. In broad daylight, she could clearly see the pattern carved into the stone, of the dragon soaring righteously toward the heavens.

An impostor. A snake who thinks he can fly.

The guard knocked on the door and announced her arrival.

"Send him in," a hoarse voice answered from within.

The doors were opened from the inside by an unsmiling attendant, who looked surprised to see the fourteenth prince also standing there.

"A-ma!" Ye-kan called out, stepping across the threshold and walking toward the inner chamber.

The High Commander sat reclining on his daybed, a familiar sheet of paper spread out on the table beside him. The room smelled overwhelmingly of sandalwood, coming from the incense burners sitting in the corners, but Ying could detect the repugnant odor of medicinal herbs that it was trying to suppress.

Ye-kan had been right when he said his father had not returned from the Qirin territories in good shape. It looked as if death was clawing at the doors she had just come through. Unlike the commanding, authoritative presence that she remembered, the High Commander's cheeks were sallow and ashen, his piercing gray eyes hazy and unfocused. Even the way he sat, with one elbow resting tired against the ebony armrest, made him appear frail and weak.

"Number Fourteen, what are you doing here?" the High Commander demanded, forehead wrinkling into a deep frown. "I did not summon you."

"E-niye said that I'm to wait by your side, in case you need anything. And since I was also participating in the guild's final test when you summoned Min for an audience, I thought I might as well come along," the prince replied.

"Your Excellency," Ying greeted, stepping out from behind Ye-kan. She had tried to convince him to leave, but he stubbornly refused. Now she could only hope that the High Commander would send him away. Ye-kan's presence could interfere with her plan, and she didn't want him to bear witness to what she might do.

She bowed stiffly, so that the slim package she had hidden beneath her robes wouldn't slip out with one careless move.

The High Commander's gaze shifted toward her, and he waved Ye-kan to the side. He studied her for a moment, then asked, "Aihui Min, this is your work?" He held out the parchment that was lying before him, pointing at the cannonball sketches that she had drawn for her test submission.

She nodded.

Aogiya Lianzhe's slate-gray irises seemed to regain a spark of vitality. His back straightened as he leaned forward, regarding her with interest. "This cannot have come from you alone. You have seen your father's work, am I right?" he probed, an urgency in his tone. "Is there more where this came from? Shan-jin's journal, do you have it?"

Ying inhaled sharply at the mention of her father's name. Her fingers clenched into fists, the fabric of her sleeves crumpling in her hands. Her father's journal was still safe within the guild, and the High Commander would never be able to lay his greedy hands on it, she would make sure of that.

"What journal? What's going on?" Ye-kan asked, confusion reflected in his eyes.

The High Commander picked up a stack of yellowed pages from his side and held them out. "The designs that you drew, they are completely aligned with Shan-jin's previous works. You must have seen them before," he said.

So he was the one who ripped out the pages from my father's old guild records.

She should have known.

"I don't know what you're talking about."

"Where is your father's journal? Tell me!" Aogiya Lianzhe bellowed, his patience wearing thin.

"Did you," Ying started, her voice dangerously quiet, slicing through the air like a sharpened blade, "send someone to kill my father? To *steal* his work?"

"Min, I don't understand," Ye-kan stammered, reaching out to place a hand on his friend's shoulder. "What are you talking about? What does any of this have to do with your father?"

Before the High Commander could answer, someone burst in through the doors, shouting at the top of her lungs. "Aogiya Lianzhe! What's the meaning of this? You sent your men to Huarin? *You* killed Shan-jin?"

It was Master Lianshu, her face flushed with rage as she marched forward and placed herself between Ying and the High Commander. Attendants and armed guards followed warily behind, though they did nothing to stop the woman from approaching. She was, after all, an Aogiya.

The High Commander's expression darkened, but he waved his hand to dismiss his men.

"Lianshu, it's been a long time since you willingly came to see me."

"For good reason," Lianshu snapped. "So? Is it true? Were

you responsible for Shan-jin's death? Were you trying to steal our cannon designs?"

Aogiya Lianzhe set his lips in a hard line, then he looked away and sighed. The harshness in the lines of his face suddenly dissipated, and for a moment Ying was almost deceived into thinking he was but a harmless old man, hovering between the gates of life and death. He looked past Lianshu's shoulder toward Ying.

"How did you know it was me, child?"

Ying retrieved the jade pendant from beneath the folds of her robes and threw it onto the floor in front of the High Commander. "I grabbed this off the man who murdered my father. This belongs to your personal guard, doesn't it? It belongs to him! I *saw* him do it!" She pointed an accusing finger at the scarred man, who was standing by the side of the room with one hand positioned warily upon his hilt.

The High Commander took one glance at the black jade, and the furrows across his forehead deepened. "How did you get this? It was Shan-jin's daughter who—" The realization dawned in his eyes. "You're not Aihui Min. You're Ying, Shan-jin's oldest girl." He threw his head back and laughed, as if he had just heard an amusing joke. Lianshu blanched, staring at Ying incredulously. "Bravo! You had us all fooled. To think you've been here all this while, parading about in the Engineers Guild, and yet no one suspected a thing. You have it, don't you? Your father's book."

"Even if I did, I would *never* give it to you," Ying spat.

Anger flashed like lightning in Aogiya Lianzhe's eyes. He was not accustomed to such open defiance. "I never intended to harm Shan-jin," he insisted. "I admit, I wanted the cannon designs and Lianshu refused to give it to me, forcing me to resort to other means. If he hadn't been so stubborn and resisted, then none of this would have happened. It was an accident."

Lianshu pointed an accusatory finger at her brother, the veins at her temples throbbing. "Shan-jin is *dead*, all because of your greed! If I had known this would happen, then I wouldn't have, I wouldn't have—" She spluttered, choking on her own words in her haste.

"I had no choice!" the High Commander shouted. "How many times did I try to convince him to help me? Convince you? Shan-jin was supposed to be my best friend! But he left and chose to lead that hermit life instead of supporting our cause. This isn't for my sake, it's for the sake of the Antaran territories, about each of the nine isles and every single person who lives on them. Shan-jin didn't just turn his back on me, he turned his back on all of us. I'm not the selfish one, Lianshu. You are. Shan-jin was."

"Don't try to push the blame to us. Your little war games have nothing to do with me. I made this clear to you years ago that I wanted no part in this," Lianshu retorted.

Ying closed her eyes, wishing she could drown out the cacophony that was ringing in her ears. Her father had been Aogiya Lianzhe's best friend? The scribbles she had discovered in her father's guild books, the playful jibes and exchanges—she finally knew who that mystery person was. There must have once been a time when her father and Aogiya Lianzhe had laughed and learned in those same workshops the way she, Chang-en, and Ye-kan had.

How could a friendship have disintegrated this way?

Accident or not, Aogiya Lianzhe had killed her father for the sake of his selfish goals. His best friend's blood was on his hands.

It was all excuses. From both of them. Lianshu was as guilty as her brother for what had happened. The righteous rage she was displaying now, the way she was acting like she was here to protect Ying—all of it was self-serving. To absolve herself of blame.

"Ying, are you all right?" Ye-kan whispered, placing a hand on her shoulder. "I'm so sorry, I didn't know any of this . . ."

She shook her head. "That's enough," she said.

"Aogiya Lianshu, why do you think you were able to become a guild master? Did you truly believe that it was because you were some engineering genius? That you were so fantastically brilliant that the guild willingly bent its admission rules for you?" the High Commander railed. "The only reason why you're wearing those robes is because you're an Aogiya. Yet you refuse to bear the responsibility of your clan name!"

"Enough!" Ying shouted, her voice ringing loud and clear across the entire room.

What had she been expecting? An apology? An explanation that it had all been a misunderstanding and that her father hadn't in fact been murdered by someone he considered a friend?

Her heart ached for her a-ma. For the way he had been betrayed so thoroughly by two people that he must have once trusted so dearly.

All eyes in the room settled upon her, waiting for what she had to say next.

"I would like to speak to the High Commander alone."

Lianshu frowned, and Ye-kan moved to grab hold of Ying's arm. The only one who looked pleased about her request was Aogiya Lianzhe.

"What are you trying to do?" the prince whispered.

"You heard the girl." The High Commander gestured with his index finger and his guards marched over. "Take the fourteenth prince and Lady Lianshu away," he commanded, and the surly men took hold of Ye-kan and Lianshu by the shoulders, dragging the duo toward the door.

"A-ma, what are you doing?" Ye-kan exclaimed. "Let me go! I'm not going anywhere. A-ma, don't do anything to Ying, please!"

"Aogiya Lianzhe, I swear, if you dare hurt the child in any way, I'll never forgive you!"

Within seconds, both of them were dragged out of the inner chamber and the doors were locked shut, leaving Ying with only the High Commander and his scar-faced confidant.

CHAPTER 25

WITH EVERYONE GONE, AN UNEASY SILENCE SET in, an eerie harbinger of what was to come. Aogiya Lianzhe was watching her, much like the first time around, like a cobra circling its prey. Ying willed her pounding heart to stay calm.

"Ying, you seem like a sensible child, far more sensible than my own sister. Hand over your father's journal. Someone like you has no use for it. Give it to me and I'll unleash its full potential, the way your father would have wanted. I'll use it to bring glory to the Antaran isles, to give our people a better life! You don't want to see the nine isles obliterated by the Empire, am I right?"

The feral shine in the High Commander's eyes brought fear and disgust into Ying's heart. Even now, he believed that he had done no wrong. He showed no remorse for her father's death, nor any signs of reining in his wild, blood-soaked ambitions.

This man dared call himself her father's best friend.

Ying's hand slipped between the cross-folds of her gray robes, reaching for the bundle she had hidden there. She hesitated.

"*Why did you make something like this, my little lamb?*" her father's voice echoed in her mind. She could hear his disappointment still.

She had been ten, catching grasshoppers with Wen and Nian out on the grassy patch near their family ger. Wen was much more adept than she was at the sport and being a show-off, so she had done something to turn the tables. She built a little grasshopper trap out of wood scraps and springs she borrowed from her father's workshop—a box that she hid in the tall grass, with a mechanism that would crush the legs of any hapless grasshopper who ventured into her trap. She had caught ten grasshoppers with it and she had been so proud, but when she brought her spoils to her father, he had looked at her with reproach.

"*Look at the grasshoppers, Ying. They will not survive long with their legs broken. Even if you release them, they are defenseless. The birds and the mice will have them for supper,*" he had said. "*Never use your gifts to harm others, my lamb. That is not what an engineer should ever do.*"

But, A-ma, you left Fei and the guild to avoid conflict and to stay true to your beliefs, yet they refused to let you go. Now they want to use your life's work to do the very thing you said we should never do.

She had to make a choice. Either surrender her father's work and allow the High Commander to use it to rain havoc upon the Qirins, or carry out her plan and deny Aogiya Lianzhe—but in doing so, stain her own two hands with blood.

"That's right. Give it to me, Ying." The High Commander

reached out his hand when he spotted the package she had pulled out. "For your contributions, I can overlook your little masquerade and grant you a place in the Engineers Guild."

She opened her eyes, resoluteness etched in those dark-brown irises. She did not need his charity. She did not need his hypocrisy. He had to pay for his crimes.

"No."

"No?"

The last signs of civility vanished from the High Commander's face as it twisted in rage. He snapped his fingers. "Take it from her," he ordered.

Ying's right arm was twisted in a viselike grip, preventing her from wrenching out her flying guillotine. The scar-faced man had appeared behind her. She could not let him disarm her, else all her efforts would be futile.

Her fan slid out into her free hand. Running on instinct, Ying flicked her wrist, and the metallic leaf unfolded. She swung at the guard, the sharp edge of her fan slicing through the man's dark sleeve and the skin beneath.

He let go, and she made a dash for the doors.

"Get hold of her!" the High Commander barked, spluttering from the exertion.

Ying turned and fired a few darts from her fan, one of them striking the guard in the shoulder. She tried to push the doors open, but they had been locked from the outside.

Gritting his teeth, the man yanked the dart out and threw it onto the floor. He raced forward and grabbed Ying by the shoulder, flinging her sideways. She crashed against one of the rosewood cabinets lining the wall, splintering the wood. The clothbound weapon that she had been holding went sliding across the floor.

The man walked slowly toward her, dragging the tip of his sword against the wooden floor. There was nothing but emptiness in his sunken eyes that filled Ying with dread. He was perhaps more of a machine than his nine-tailed chimera. She could taste blood in her mouth, bitter as gall. Was this how her father felt in his dying moments?

No.

This could not be her ending.

Spying a small bronze burner sitting on the floor by the cabinet, she lunged for it and shoved her hand inside, grabbing a handful of hot ash from burnt incense. The guard swung his sword. She hurled the gray powder toward his face and quickly rolled aside, narrowly escaping the descending blade. Using the cover from the ash cloud, Ying ran to pick up her fallen weapon.

She ripped the cloth away, revealing the menacing metallic contraption hiding underneath. In one hand she gripped a lead ring, and with the other she held a large bronze disc, a thin slice with a smaller circular hole carved in the middle, the right size to fit over a person's head. Interlocking silver links formed a long chain that joined the ring to the disc.

"What is that?" the High Commander demanded, noticing the silver glint. He straightened himself up on the daybed, squinting to get a better look. "Is it something else from Shan-jin's journals?" Even now, there was no disguising the greed in his voice.

"No, my father would never create something as bloodthirsty as this. I made this. I call it the flying guillotine," Ying replied, her voice emotionless, cold like the ice forming on the canals in the depths of winter.

I'm sorry, A-ma. I know you would not have wanted me to do this, but I must.

A man as unscrupulous as Aogiya Lianzhe did not deserve to rule over the Antaran isles.

She flung the bronze disc toward the High Commander with as much force as she could muster.

The High Commander reeled backward in shock, his eyes glued upon the rotating disc that was hurtling toward him. Ying had intended for the weapon to land over his head, but its trajectory was headed for his chest instead.

No matter, she had accounted for her own lack of skill in this respect.

She pulled on the ring in her hand, and two sets of curved blades flew out from their hiding place, sandwiched within the plane of the disc. One set jutted inward, and would have taken off the head of its unsuspecting victim, while the other jutted outward—a contingency she had worked in for a situation like this.

Like the petals of a peony in bloom.

The outer set of blades carved into Aogiya Lianzhe's chest. The High Commander cried out in anguish. Ying pulled at the ring again, and the disc clanged onto the ground, the dull golden sheen of its blades stained red.

Blood was spreading across the High Commander's chest, and the man was desperately clutching the table by his side, barely breathing.

I did it.

Time slowed. Cold sweat lined her palms.

She could hear death knocking at her own door.

Any moment now, the scarred man would recover from the ash stinging his eyes and put a sword through her back like he had intended.

But it didn't happen. Instead, the loud clanging of blades striking against each other rang in her ears, and she turned to witness a fierce battle between the High Commander's guard and . . . Ye-yang.

He's here.

Seeing Ye-yang brought on a wave of relief, her anger and disappointment at his betrayal temporarily forgotten. Maybe she *was* afraid of dying after all, and his appearance gave her hope that she might not need to bid farewell to this life yet. His hair was windswept, flecks of snow and dust clung on to the dark fabric of his riding clothes. Exhaustion lined his brow, but still he deftly fended off blow after blow.

"Number Eight, what are you doing?" the High Commander wheezed, blood trickling from the corners of his lips.

With a shout of fury, Ye-yang leapt into the air and twisted his body in a sideways roll, bringing the tip of his sword piercing toward the other man's back. The guard dropped to his knees, hands clutching at the blade that had emerged through the front of his chest. His body swayed, then collapsed, the last breath leaving his lips.

Ye-yang rushed over to Ying's side, wrapping an arm protectively around her. When she met his gaze, she saw nothing but concern there.

"I'm here. You're safe now," he said.

Then someone else entered the room.

"Your Excellency, is Number Fourteen here? He promised me he would return as soon as the guild's final trial was over, but there's still no sign of—" Lady Odval's saccharine voice trailed off, replaced with a high-pitched scream when she stepped into the inner chamber and saw the scene of disarray.

She rushed to the High Commander's side, gasping at the sight of the blood everywhere. But, as befitting her status and position in the household, she did not panic.

"Guards! Send for the physicians immediately!" she screamed, calling for the men who should have been stationed outside. Then she pointed one gold nail guard at Ying and Ye-yang. "And behead these two traitors at once!"

Seconds passed, but no guards came rushing in through the open doors.

"Guards!" Odval shouted once again, this time with a slight tremble in her voice.

Still, no one came.

Ye-yang guided Ying over to an empty chair and sat her down. Then, he turned back toward his father and the lady, his gaze switching immediately into cold steel. He walked over to the corpse of his father's guard and pulled his sword back out from the man's body.

"A-ma, Lady Odval, no one is coming. The palace guards don't answer to you anymore," he said quietly as he walked toward them.

"Number Eight, what is the meaning of this?" Odval's large eyes were livid with rage. "You're the one behind this? This is treason!"

"No, perhaps you are the one who's confused," Ye-yang replied, his voice clipped and detached. "A-ma was gravely wounded at Ningya—hundreds of our men bore witness to that. I see no difference in his current state. As for you, Lady Odval, given your oft-professed love for my father, I am sure you will be most willing to die alongside him, to keep him company on his journey to the next life."

A tremble went down Ying's spine when she heard Ye-yang's words. There was no hesitation, no apprehension—as if he had been working toward this moment all along.

"Excuse me?" Odval spluttered in disbelief. She had her back pressed against the daybed, her entire body shaking in fear. But there was no one to rescue her.

Ye-yang lifted his blade, slicing its tip swiftly across the woman's neck. A thin red line appeared across her porcelain skin, from which rivulets of blood began trickling downward. Her large, feline-like eyes remained open, indignant till the very end.

Ying bit her lip and looked away, unwilling to watch any further. The High Commander and his scarred subordinate owed her a debt of blood, but she had no grudge against Lady Odval. That was Ye-kan's mother. Yet she had stood by and let Ye-yang end Odval's life for his own agenda, an agenda that she seemed to have unwittingly become an accomplice to.

What have I done?

Had she helped to trigger a new blood feud? Was there no end to this cycle of bloodshed and vengeance?

"How long have you been planning for this, Number Eight?" Aogiya Lianzhe finally spoke, barely managing a whisper. He was valiantly clinging on to his final vestiges of life, but death already clouded his stormy eyes.

"Since the day my e-niye died of a broken heart because of your cruel ambitions. I will not be like you, A-ma. But go in peace, and rest assured that the nine isles are in good hands."

Ye-yang took one last look at his father, then he turned and picked Ying up in his arms, marching out of the High Commander's quarters without looking back. Behind them, Aogiya Lianzhe's bitter laughter rang out, and he uttered the last words that Ying would ever hear from him in this life.

"Out of all my sons, you are most like me, Ye-yang. Blood runs thicker than water. You will understand that one day."

Ye-yang took her back to his manor on horseback. They rode in silence the entire way.

His arms encircled her waist, and the warmth of his chest was pressing against her back, his shallow breaths tickling the side of her ear, yet Ying felt nothing but the cold of the darkest winter. She had rehearsed this several times before, what it would be like after she succeeded in seeking revenge, how she would react when she finally brought justice upon those who had taken her father from her.

Now that it had actually happened, she felt numb.

When they reached the fourth beile's manor, Ye-yang carried her all the way to his loft, ignoring the curious stares from the attendants along the way. He only set her down once they were behind closed doors.

Ye-yang reached out to pull her into his embrace, but Ying took a step back instead.

"Funny how we weren't even stopped by anyone on the way out of the palace, huh?" she said, directing her gaze toward the floor. The journey here had given her enough time to think things through.

So that was what Ye-yang had meant when he told his father and Lady Odval that the palace guards didn't answer to them anymore. Somehow, somewhen, Ye-yang had secretly and stealthily taken control of the entire palace—and possibly the entire capital.

He had everything within his calculations all along. He knew *what I was going to do, yet he let me do it anyway.*

Ying had told herself that she would remain indifferent, that she wouldn't show him how much the truth hurt, but when he cradled her cheeks in his palms and forced her to look into his face, the tears came trickling down. She burst into fitful sobs, laughing and crying at the same time, unable to reconcile the emotional impact of what she had done and what she had learned.

The High Commander was dead, and his blood was on her hands.

She was the one who killed him.

And Ye-yang, who had asked her to trust him, who had sworn to protect her, had *used* her like a weapon to cut down the obstacles standing in his way of absolute power. He could not bring himself to kill his own father—or he didn't want that blemish on his legacy—so he had her do it for him.

If he had mistimed his arrival by a single moment, she might have already paid for her actions with her life.

"It's over. Everything will be fine, Ying, I promise," Ye-yang said, wiping the tears gently from her cheeks. "Things will be better from now on. You can go back to the guild, fulfill your engineering dreams, do everything that your father would have wanted you to do. We've won."

She shook her head, a bitter smile hanging upon her lips. "No," she whispered. Did he honestly think that everything he had done could be wiped away just like that? There was no "we." Things would not be better. Perhaps they would never be. "I'm not staying. I'm going back home."

"But why?" Ye-yang blinked back his confusion. "If you're worried about what happened, there's no need for that. No one will ever find out what happened in the palace, I'll make sure of it."

"That's not it. I'm leaving, Ye-yang."

She finally understood why her father had chosen to leave, why he didn't like speaking about his time in Fei, and why his eyes were always filled with sorrow when he reminisced on those days. Fei was a place of broken dreams and false promises—for him, and now for her too. Here, it was too difficult to hold on to what mattered, to stay true to your beliefs and values.

This was why her father had told her to burn the book. Because he must have seen this coming. He was trying to save her from having her heart broken the way his had been.

A-ma, I was wrong.

"Ying, don't go," Ye-yang pleaded, catching hold of her hand as she turned to leave. He pulled her into his arms, burying his face against the crook of her neck. "Stay with me. I need you by my side. Please. I have no one else."

The raw emotion in his voice struck through to the inner reaches of Ying's heart, and in that moment he was once again the lonely, vulnerable young man that she had fallen for, trapped as a victim of his circumstances. She faltered, wanting to indulge in this for longer.

Then the High Commander's final words rang out in her mind.

"Out of all my sons, you are most like me, Ye-yang."

Maybe he was right.

To Ye-yang, there was never any need to choose between his ambitions and her. He believed that both could coexist in harmony. She didn't doubt that he cared about her, that she mattered to him the way he said she did, but at the same time, he had no qualms about using her as a stepping stone to achieve his ambitions. It was scarily similar to how Aogiya Lianzhe had treated his friendship with her father, and it chilled her to the bone.

When push came to shove, she didn't trust that he would choose her over everything else.

The fog in her mind cleared.

Ying slowly pushed him away. "I've already helped you once. Don't you think it's too much to ask me for more? Who might you want me to kill on your behalf next time?" she asked. "You said that if I wanted to seek revenge, that you would wield the sword on my behalf. But that was a lie. I was your sword, but you were never mine."

She knew that her words were cruel and cutting, but it was the truth. He had lied to her too many times, and her heart was too broken. Blinking back her tears, Ying walked out of the room—and he didn't come after her.

EPILOGUE

A CONDOR CIRCLED OVERHEAD, ITS CRIES DROWNED by the thunderous whirs of the airship contingent heading its way.

"By decree of the four beiles, the nine isles of the Antaran territories are to mourn the passing of His Excellency, the late High Commander, for a period of one hundred days from the last full moon," a dull voice droned across the skies, bearing the message of the new leaders of the High Command.

Ying sat perched at the edge of the cliff, watching as the black monstrosities passed her by, the repetitive words fading into the crash of waves down below. She took a deep breath, inhaling the fresh, earthy scent of the grasslands after the rain. The airships passed, and a clear patch of sky was returned to her.

She thought of the friendship between her father and Aogiya Lianzhe, ripped apart by their fundamental differences in goals and ideals. Perhaps now they could finally make peace with each other and rekindle the camaraderie that once was.

Sometimes she thought of Master Lianshu, and wondered if the woman felt any regret about what had transpired, or if she was still busy absolving herself of any responsibility.

In any case, Fei and the Engineers Guild no longer held

the same allure for her as they once had. The shining city was a distant memory now, a mirage of towering pagodas and soaring stone bridges, broad canals and narrow alleyways teeming with its uptight citizens. The imposing fortresslike walls of the guild, once a fervent dream that she had worshipped upon a pedestal, had been stripped of its glamour and mystery, leaving behind only the cold, heartless shell that it was.

Still beautiful, but frightening at the same time. She feared that the longer she stayed, the more her relationships with the people she cared about would begin to warp into forms she could no longer recognize, festering the way her father's had.

It was better this way. Leaving it a memory she could cherish and perhaps recall with a smile one day.

She plucked at the blades of damp grass by her sides, staring down at her village, and beyond at the massive ships docked some distance from the Huarin harbor. From her vantage point she could make out the spitting cobra figurehead at the bow of the flagship and the silver serpent painted across its battened sails, its hull painted the same shade of shadowy black as the airships that had just gone past. A vague echo of drumming and cheering drifted over from the mushroom-top gers as her clansmen celebrated the arrival of their distinguished guests.

A marriage ceremony would not be appropriate during the mourning period, but certain formalities still had to be completed out of respect for the wishes of the late High

Commander. The ships were here to deliver the dowry for Nian, as a promise from the Aogiya clan that they would honor their word.

Ying averted her gaze, staring out at the azure ocean instead. The pang in her heart was difficult to ignore, and to force herself to smile and bask in her sister's happiness was impossible. Each time she heard Nian speak of Ye-yang and of the beautiful life she thought she was going to lead, Ying felt the urge to withdraw, in case the cracks in her façade began to show and Nian found out about the secrets she was keeping about her relationship with the fourth beile.

So here she was—hiding.

The grass behind her rustled.

Ying turned. Her heart skipped a beat the moment she laid eyes on who it was, standing before her in his black-and-gold splendor, but then an icy wind blew past, reminding her of why he was here, and of what he had done.

"How have you been?" they both asked at the same time.

Ye-yang came closer, but stopped when he saw Ying move back. The light in his eyes faded.

"Fine, I suppose," she answered first. "Can't have been much, compared to what's been happening in Fei."

No one learned what truly happened in the High Commander's chambers that day. To the rest of the nine isles, the High Commander succumbed to the injuries suffered at

Ningya, and the Antaran High Command was in need of new leadership. Since Aogiya Lianzhe had not appointed a successor before he passed, it was decided that the four beiles would rule together as a council, surprisingly with Ye-yang—the youngest of the four—at its helm. As for Lady Odval, she would be buried alongside the former High Commander, after having given her life to continue serving him in the next. Her story of touching sacrifice had been told by storytellers all across the Antaran territories, bringing tears to the eyes of many a gullible soul.

Ying knew better. She had intentionally avoided Ye-kan until the day she set sail to return to Huarin, because she had nothing to offer him other than an apology. He had done nothing wrong, yet he had been collateral damage nonetheless. She didn't know if he'd ever find out the truth behind his mother's death, but she hoped he never would.

"We've decided to put a pause on the Qirin campaign, at least until the period of mourning is over. Ningya dealt us a heavy blow and our men need to recuperate."

"You mean it's not over?" Ying turned back to face the open sea, not wanting her expression to betray the upheavals taking place within.

Ye-yang shook his head ruefully. He hesitated for a moment, then walked up to stand beside her. "This war is not for the sake of my father's ambition alone. The future of the Antaran territories hinges on it," he explained.

His words echoed in Ying's ears, and it was as if she could see the ghost of the High Commander speaking through him.

"I know you're angry with me because of what happened that day. But I want you to know that I would never have allowed anyone to harm you," Ye-yang said. "I would have stepped in earlier if I thought you couldn't handle it yourself. Everything was under control."

"*Nothing* is under control, Ye-yang. You can make the best preparations and still something unexpected can happen. Don't make the same mistake that the High Commander made. He overestimated himself and underestimated everyone else. Look what came of it."

Reaching into the folds of his silk garment, Ye-yang retrieved an envelope and handed it to her. "This is your official acceptance letter into the Engineers Guild. The guild masters unanimously awarded you the top position after the final test. Even Gerel."

The name on the envelope was "Aihui Ying," not "Aihui Min." But had the guild really chosen to accept her as who she was? Or was it because of pressure from Ye-yang, forcing them to bend the rules the way they had done for Aogiya Lianshu?

Ying scoffed at her own skepticism. Clearly she had been cut so deep that she now viewed everything with doubt and cynicism.

She didn't even bother opening the envelope. Instead, she

held it out over the edge of the cliff and let go. Caught by a gust of wind, it somersaulted a few times in midair before drifting out toward the waves.

"My father left Fei because he had to make a choice between what he thought was right and what he knew was necessary—and he chose the former," she said. "That's what I'm going to choose too."

The war against the Empire might be critical for the Antaran isles, but Ye-yang would have to fight it without her. Her father had made the mistake of acceding to Lianshu, and that choice had ultimately set him on a path of tragedy. She would not do the same.

A pause.

"You still haven't forgiven me," Ye-yang said.

Ying shook her head. "There is nothing to forgive. There are some walls that we were never meant to cross, Ye-yang. We were a mistake from the very beginning." She turned toward him and smiled, but there was no joy. "Forget me," she said, "and live well."

"Wait." Ye-yang pulled out a small bundle that he had brought with him, carefully unwrapping the cloth to reveal an octagonal lamp. Each panel had been carved with scenes the same way her father used to.

From where she stood, Ying could see one panel with two figures clumsily whittled from the wood, setting lotus lanterns afloat upon the waters. He held the lantern out to her, and her heart ached to reach out and accept it, to return to a time when things were simpler and not marred by secrets and lies.

But she could not.

She stepped back, then turned and headed toward her horse.

"Ying," Ye-yang called out to her just as she mounted Ayanga, "remember when I said I don't believe in making wishes? If there's something I want, I'll get it myself. When I have the Empire in the palm of my hand and the Antaran territories see peace and prosperity once more, I'll come back for you, I swear. This isn't goodbye."

Wishes.

She had made a wish once.

I wished for both of us to get our heart's desire. If only I knew then that this is how it would end.

If she had a second chance, would she still have made that wish? Or made those decisions that would lead them here?

Blinking back the tears that were brimming in her eyes, Ying raised her arm into the air and waved. She could not turn back and look at him one more time, afraid that her resolve might not hold. Deep down, she knew that despite everything, she loved him still.

Tugging at the reins, she sent her horse galloping down the mountainside with her head held high.

Till we meet again, Ye-yang.

ACKNOWLEDGMENTS

Of Jade and Dragons is the first book of mine that's being traditionally published, that my friends and family—and all of you lovely readers—will actually be able to pick up in a bookstore. It has been such a surreal journey to have gotten this far. This book is a pandemic baby (it seems many people wrote books during lockdown, and I was one of them), and when I first wrote this book in 2020, I never imagined that we would ever get to this day.

First of all, thank you to my brilliant editors, Kelsey Murphy and Lowri Ribbons, for your boundless enthusiasm and for working with me on this book to make it shine. Thanks also to Naomi Colthurst, for having taken a chance on this book in the first place, and to my agents then and now, Anne Perry and Meg Davis, for being the best champions I could have ever asked for to embark on this publishing journey with. My gratitude also to the entire team at Viking Children's and Penguin Random House UK for your support in bringing this book to life, and to my cover illustrator and designers, the incredibly talented Kelly Chong, Lily Qian, and Ellice Lee, for giving me what must be the most beautiful cover that will ever grace the shelves (yes, I'm biased).

Next up, lots of love to the Chillichurls, the best crew of writer friends I could ever ask for! To Jenny Pang, Amy Leow, Saika Tsai, Cindy Chen, and Trisa Leung—love the bunch of you so much and I'm so grateful to have all of you on this journey with me. Thank you for being the first readers of all my manuscripts, for being the best cheerleaders, and for helping me to keep all my publishing secrets. I'm looking forward to the day when all our books fill the shelves!

The biggest turning point of this book's journey to being published was PitchWars, and I am so proud to have been part of the PitchWars Class of 2020. When I submitted it to PitchWars, I never thought that it would actually get picked up out of the thousands of submissions. My deepest thanks to my mentors, Kat Dunn and Daphne Tonge, for fishing this manuscript out of your slush pile and helping to polish it and make it sparkle! I don't think I would have made it this far without your generous guidance. This book would truly not be here without you! Thank you also to Xiran Jay Zhao and Meg Long, for your kind, encouraging words when you read my early draft of this book—I hope you will enjoy the final version! One of the best parts of being in PitchWars is the community, and I am so grateful for having been in the best PitchWars class ever. To everyone in the PitchWars Class of 2020: Thank you for being the loveliest, most supportive classmates a baby author could ask for. I am so thrilled to see so many of your books already on the shelves, and excited that this book will finally be able to join your ranks! Special shout-out to Tesia Tsai, for being one of the first people to read the ugly draft of this book and for liking it enough to make a beautiful aesthetic for it.

Pre-2020, I was pretty much clueless about publishing and how to go about getting a book sold. Without the generous sharing from some of the first writer friends I got to know online, I don't think I would have been able to make my publishing dream a reality. To that end, a big thank-you to Amery Wong, who was the first kind soul who reached out and added me to the Accidental Groupchat, which became my biggest source of information and support in navigating the publishing landscape in those early days.

Thank you to all the friends from the writing community who have been such fun, supportive, and encouraging companions to have along this journey: the SEAuthors—Wen-yi, Cath, Chiara, Cam, Sophie; the Path2Pub crew—Lucia, Mariana, Alex, Briana, Demri; Melody, Sher, Carrie, Elian, Lex, Hanna, Famke, Allie, and Samiha. Thank you also to the lovely folks who have helped me beta read this manuscript—LY Jimenez, Mia Liu, and Dorian Atgan—this story is better because of you.

Some of you may know that I cut my teeth on writing K-pop fanfiction on AFF many, many years ago, before transitioning to original fiction on Wattpad. Without the fantastic communities of readers and writers on both AFF and Wattpad and their never-ending encouragement, I would not have gained the confidence to continue writing till today. Thank you to my very first group of writing friends, the Kodawari gang from AFF—Jess, Tiff, and Mei—for your friendship and for being my entry point to the world of writing critique. I hope that all of you are doing well wherever you are and that you will get to see your name immortalized here the same way they are in Mei's high school yearbook! Shout-out also to the fantastic writers from AFF and Wattpad who have been such an inspiration to me: Korekrypta, Emilieee, kisoap, anashins, Kim Knights, and Meixia.

To my dearest family, thank you for your unconditional love and support, and for encouraging me to go ahead and pursue my dreams. This book is here because of you!

Last but not least, to all the readers who have picked up this book and were willing to give it a chance—my deepest thanks. I am so thrilled to have the opportunity to share this story with you, and I hope Ying and Ye-yang find a place in your heart the way they have in mine.